AF753146

It Ends with Us

Books by Colleen Hoover

SLAMMED SERIES

Slammed

Point of Retreat

This Girl

HOPELESS SERIES

Hopeless

Losing Hope

Finding Cinderella

All Your Perfects (stand-alone)

Finding Perfect

MAYBE SOMEDAY SERIES

Maybe Someday

Maybe Not

Maybe Now

IT ENDS WITH US SERIES

It Ends with Us

It Starts with Us

STAND-ALONES

Ugly Love

Confess

November 9

Without Merit

Too Late

Regretting You

Heart Bones

Layla

Verity

Reminders of Him

Also by Colleen Hoover and Tarryn Fisher

Never Never:

The Complete Series

It Ends with Us

Colleen Hoover

ATRIA PAPERBACK

NEW YORK LONDON TORONTO SYDNEY NEW DELHI

ATRIA
PAPERBACK

An Imprint of Simon & Schuster, LLC
1230 Avenue of the Americas
New York, NY 10020

This book is a work of fiction. Any references to historical events, real people, or real places are used fictitiously. Other names, characters, places, and events are products of the author's imagination, and any resemblance to actual events or places or persons living or dead is entirely coincidental.

Copyright © 2016 by Colleen Hoover

All rights reserved, including the right to reproduce this book or portions thereof in any form whatsoever. For information, address Atria Books Subsidiary Rights Department, 1230 Avenue of the Americas, New York, NY 10020.

First Atria Paperback edition August 2016

ATRIA PAPERBACK and colophon are trademarks of Simon & Schuster, LLC

The Simon & Schuster Speakers Bureau can bring authors to your live event. For more information or to book an event, contact the Simon & Schuster Speakers Bureau at 1-866-248-3049 or visit our website at www.simonspeakers.com.

Manufactured in the United States of America

85 87 89 90 88 86 84

Library of Congress Cataloging-in-Publication data is available.

ISBN 978-1-5011-1036-8
ISBN 978-1-5011-1037-5 (ebook)

For my father, who tried his very best not to be his worst.

And for my mother, who made sure we never saw him at his worst.

Part One

Chapter One

As I sit here with one foot on either side of the ledge, looking down from twelve stories above the streets of Boston, I can't help but think about suicide.

Not my *own*. I like my life enough to want to see it through.

I'm more focused on other people, and how they ultimately come to the decision to just end their own lives. *Do they ever regret it?* In the moment after letting go and the second before they make impact, there has to be a little bit of remorse in that brief free fall. Do they look at the ground as it rushes toward them and think, *"Well, crap. This was a bad idea."*

Somehow, I think not.

I think about death a lot. Particularly today, considering I just—twelve hours earlier—gave one of the most epic eulogies the people of Plethora, Maine, have ever witnessed. Okay, maybe it wasn't the most epic. It very well could be considered the most disastrous. I guess that would depend on whether you were asking my mother or me. *My mother, who probably won't speak to me for a solid year after today.*

Don't get me wrong; the eulogy I delivered wasn't profound enough to make history, like the one Brooke Shields delivered at Michael Jackson's funeral. Or the one delivered by Steve Jobs's sister. Or Pat Tillman's brother. But it was epic in its own way.

I was nervous at first. It was the funeral of the prodigious Andrew Bloom, after all. Adored mayor of my hometown of Plethora, Maine. Owner of the most successful real-estate agency within city limits. Husband of the highly adored Jenny Bloom, the most revered teaching assistant in all of Plethora. And father of Lily Bloom—that strange girl with the erratic red hair who once fell in love with a homeless guy and brought great shame upon her entire family.

That would be me. I'm Lily Bloom, and Andrew was my father.

As soon as I finished delivering his eulogy today, I caught a flight straight back to Boston and hijacked the first roof I could find. *Again, not because I'm suicidal.* I have no plans to scale off this roof. I just really needed fresh air and silence, and dammit if I can't get that from my third floor apartment with absolutely no rooftop access and a roommate who likes to hear herself sing.

I didn't account for how cold it would be up here, though. It's not unbearable, but it's not comfortable, either. At least I can see the stars. Dead fathers and exasperating roommates and questionable eulogies don't feel so awful when the night sky is clear enough to literally feel the grandeur of the universe.

I love it when the sky makes me feel insignificant.

I like tonight.

Well . . . let me rephrase this so that it more appropriately reflects my feelings in past tense.

I *liked* tonight.

But unfortunately for me, the door was just shoved open so hard, I expect the stairwell to spit a human out onto the rooftop. The door slams shut again and footsteps move swiftly across the deck. I don't even bother looking up. Whoever it is more than likely won't even notice me back here straddling the ledge to the left of the door. They came out here in such a hurry, it isn't my fault if they assume they're alone.

I sigh quietly, close my eyes and lean my head against the stucco wall behind me, cursing the universe for ripping this peaceful, introspective moment out from under me. The least the universe could do for me today is ensure that it's a woman and not a man. If I'm going to have company, I'd rather it be a female. I'm tough for my size and can probably hold my own in most cases, but I'm too comfortable right now to be on a rooftop alone with a strange man in the middle of the night. I might fear for my safety and feel the need to leave, and I really don't want to leave. As I said before . . . I'm comfortable.

I finally allow my eyes to make the journey to the silhouette leaning over the ledge. As luck would have it, he's definitely male. Even leaning over the rail, I can tell he's tall. Broad shoulders create a strong contrast to the fragile way he's holding his head in his hands. I can barely make out the heavy rise and fall of his back as he drags in deep breaths and forces them back out when he's done with them.

He appears to be on the verge of a breakdown. I contemplate speaking up to let him know he has company, or clearing my throat, but between thinking it and actually doing it, he spins around and kicks one of the patio chairs behind him.

I flinch as it screeches across the deck, but being as though he isn't even aware he has an audience, the guy doesn't stop with just one kick. He kicks the chair repeatedly, over and over. Rather than give way beneath the blunt force of his foot, all the chair does is scoot farther and farther away from him.

That chair must be made from marine-grade polymer.

I once watched my father back over an outdoor patio table made of marine-grade polymer, and it practically laughed at him. Dented his bumper, but didn't even put a scratch on the table.

This guy must realize he's no match for such a high-quality material, because he finally stops kicking the chair. He's now standing over it, his hands clenched in fists at his sides. To be honest, I'm a little envious. Here this guy is, taking his aggression out on patio furniture like a champ. He's obviously had a shitty day, as have I, but whereas I keep my aggression pent up until it manifests in the form of passive-aggressiveness, this guy actually has an outlet.

My outlet used to be gardening. Any time I was stressed, I'd just go out to the backyard and pull every single weed I could find. But since the day I moved to Boston two years ago, I haven't had a backyard. Or a patio. I don't even have weeds.

Maybe I need to invest in a marine-grade polymer patio chair.

I stare at the guy a moment longer, wondering if he's ever going to move. He's just standing there, staring down at the chair. His hands aren't in fists anymore. They're resting on his hips, and I notice for the first time how his shirt doesn't fit him very well around his biceps. It fits him everywhere else, but his arms are huge. He begins fishing around in his pockets until he finds what he's looking for and—in what I'm sure is probably an effort to release even more of his aggression—he lights up a joint.

I'm twenty-three, I've been through college and have done this very same recreational drug a time or two. I'm not going to judge this guy for feeling the need to toke up in private. But that's the thing—he's *not* in private. He just doesn't know that yet.

He takes in a long drag of his joint and starts to turn back toward the ledge. He notices me on the exhale. He stops walking the second our eyes meet. His expression holds no shock, nor does it hold amusement when he sees me. He's about ten feet away, but there's enough light from the stars that I can see his eyes as they slowly drag over my body without revealing a single thought. This guy holds his cards well. His gaze is narrow and his mouth is drawn tight, like a male version of the *Mona Lisa*.

"What's your name?" he asks.

I feel his voice in my stomach. That's not good. Voices should stop at the ears, but sometimes—not very often at all, actually—a voice will penetrate past my ears and reverberate straight down through my body. He has one of those voices. Deep, confident, and a little bit like butter.

When I don't answer him, he brings the joint back to his mouth and takes another hit.

"Lily," I finally say. *I hate my voice.* It sounds too weak to even reach his ears from here, much less reverberate inside *his* body.

He lifts his chin a little and nudges his head toward me. "Will you please get down from there, Lily?"

It isn't until he says this that I notice his posture. He's

standing straight up now, rigid even. Almost as if he's nervous I'm going to fall. *I'm not.* This ledge is at least a foot wide, and I'm mostly on the roof side. I could easily catch myself before I fell, not to mention I've got the wind in my favor.

I glance down at my legs and then back up at him. "No, thanks. I'm quite comfortable where I am."

He turns a little, like he can't look straight at me. "Please get down." It's more of a demand now, despite his use of the word *please*. "There are seven empty chairs up here."

"Almost six," I correct, reminding him that he just tried to murder one of them. He doesn't find the humor in my response. When I fail to follow his orders, he takes a couple of steps closer.

"You are a mere three inches from falling to your death. I've been around enough of that for one day." He motions for me to get down again. "You're making me nervous. Not to mention ruining my high."

I roll my eyes and swing my legs over. "Heaven forbid a joint go to waste." I hop down and wipe my hands across my jeans. "Better?" I say as I walk toward him.

He lets out a rush of air, as if seeing me on the ledge actually had him holding his breath. I pass him to head for the side of the roof with the better view, and as I do, I can't help but notice how unfortunately cute he is.

No. Cute is an insult.

This guy is *beautiful*. Well-manicured, smells like money, looks to be several years older than me. His eyes crinkle in the corners as they follow me, and his lips seem to frown, even when they aren't. When I reach the side of the building that overlooks the street, I lean forward and stare down at the cars below, trying not to appear impressed by him. I can tell by his haircut alone that he's the kind of man people are easily impressed by, and I refuse to feed into his ego. Not that he's done anything to make me think he even *has* one. But he is wearing a casual Burberry shirt, and I'm not sure I've ever been on the radar of someone who could casually afford one.

I hear footsteps approaching from behind, and then he leans against the railing next to me. Out of the corner of my eye, I watch as he takes another hit of his joint. When he's finished, he offers it to me, but I wave it off. The last thing I need is to be under the influence around this guy. His voice is a drug in itself. I kind of want to hear it again, so I throw a question in his direction.

"So what did that chair do to make you so angry?"

He looks at me. Like *really* looks at me. His eyes meet mine and he just stares, hard, like all my secrets are right there on my face. I've never seen eyes as dark as his. Maybe I have, but they seem darker when they're attached to such an intimidating presence. He doesn't answer my question, but my curiosity isn't easily put to rest. If he's going to force me down from a very peaceful, comfortable ledge, then I expect him to entertain me with answers to my nosy questions.

"Was it a woman?" I inquire. "Did she break your heart?"

He laughs a little with that question. "If only my issues were as trivial as matters of the heart." He leans into the wall so that he can face me. "What floor do you live on?" He licks his fingers and pinches the end of his joint, then puts it back in his pocket. "I've never noticed you before."

"That's because I don't live here." I point in the direction of my apartment. "See that insurance building?"

He squints as he looks in the direction I'm pointing. "Yeah."

"I live in the building next to it. It's too short to see from here. It's only three stories tall."

He's facing me again, resting his elbow on the ledge. "If you live over there, why are you here? Your boyfriend live here or something?"

His comment somehow makes me feel cheap. It was too easy—an amateurish pickup line. From the looks of this guy, I know he has better skills than that. It makes me think he saves the more difficult pickup lines for the women he deems worthy.

"You have a nice roof," I tell him.

He lifts an eyebrow, waiting for more of an explanation.

"I wanted fresh air. Somewhere to think. I pulled up Google Earth and found the closest apartment complex with a decent rooftop patio."

He regards me with a smile. "At least you're economical," he says. "That's a good quality to have."

At least?

I nod, because I *am* economical. And it *is* a good quality to have.

"Why did you need fresh air?" he asks.

Because I buried my father today and gave an epically disastrous eulogy and now I feel like I can't breathe.

I face forward again and slowly exhale. "Can we just not talk for a little while?"

He seems a bit relieved that I asked for silence. He leans

over the ledge and lets an arm dangle as he stares down at the street. He stays like this for a while, and I stare at him the entire time. He probably knows I'm staring, but he doesn't seem to care.

"A guy fell off this roof last month," he says.

I would be annoyed at his lack of respect for my request for silence, but I'm kind of intrigued.

"Was it an accident?"

He shrugs. "No one knows. It happened late in the evening. His wife said she was cooking dinner and he told her he was coming up here to take some pictures of the sunset. He was a photographer. They think he was leaning over the ledge to get a shot of the skyline, and he slipped."

I look over the ledge, wondering how someone could possibly put themselves in a situation where they could fall by accident. But then I remember I was just straddling the ledge on the other side of the roof a few minutes ago.

"When my sister told me what happened, the only thing I could think about was whether or not he got the shot. I was hoping his camera didn't fall with him, because that would have been a real waste, you know? To die because of your love of photography, but you didn't even get the final shot that cost you your life?"

His thought makes me laugh. Although I'm not sure I should have laughed at that. "Do you always say exactly what's on your mind?"

He shrugs. "Not to most people."

This makes me smile. I like that he doesn't even know me, but for whatever reason, I'm not considered *most people* to him.

He rests his back against the ledge and folds his arms over his chest. "Were you born here?"

I shake my head. "No. Moved here from Maine after I graduated college."

He scrunches up his nose, and it's kind of hot. Watching this guy—dressed in his Burberry shirt with his two-hundred-dollar haircut—making silly faces.

"So you're in Boston purgatory, huh? That's gotta suck."

"What do you mean?" I ask him.

The corner of his mouth curls up. "The tourists treat you like a local; the locals treat you like a tourist."

I laugh. "Wow. That's a very accurate description."

"I've been here two months. I'm not even in purgatory yet, so you're doing better than I am."

"What brought you to Boston?"

"My residency. And my sister lives here." He taps his foot and says, "Right beneath us, actually. Married a tech-savvy Bostonian and they bought the entire top floor."

I look down. "The *entire* top floor?"

He nods. "Lucky bastard works from home. Doesn't even have to change out of his pajamas and makes seven figures a year."

Lucky bastard, indeed.

"What kind of residency? Are you a doctor?"

He nods. "Neurosurgeon. Less than a year left of my residency and then it's official."

Stylish, well spoken, *and* smart. *And smokes pot.* If this were an SAT question, I would ask which one didn't belong. "Should doctors be smoking weed?"

He smirks. "Probably not. But if we didn't indulge on

occasion, there would be a lot more of us taking the leap over these ledges, I can promise you that." He's facing forward again with his chin resting on his arms. His eyes are closed now, like he's enjoying the wind against his face. He doesn't look as intimidating like this.

"You want to know something that only the locals know?"

"Of course," he says, bringing his attention back to me.

I point to the east. "See that building? The one with the green roof?"

He nods.

"There's a building behind it on Melcher. There's a house on top of the building. Like a legit house, built right on the rooftop. You can't see it from the street, and the building is so tall that not many people even know about it."

He looks impressed. "Really?"

I nod. "I saw it when I was searching Google Earth, so I looked it up. Apparently a permit was granted for the construction in 1982. How cool would that be? To live in a house on top of a building?"

"You'd get the whole roof to yourself," he says.

I hadn't thought of that. If I owned it I could plant gardens up there. I'd have an outlet.

"Who lives there?" he asks.

"No one really knows. It's one of the great mysteries of Boston."

He laughs and then looks at me inquisitively. "What's another great mystery of Boston?"

"Your name." As soon as I say it, I slap my hand against my forehead. It sounded so much like a cheesy pickup line; the only thing I can do is laugh at myself.

He smiles. "It's Ryle," he says. "Ryle Kincaid."

I sigh, sinking into myself. "That's a really great name."

"Why do you sound sad about it?"

"Because, I'd give anything for a great name."

"You don't like the name Lily?"

I tilt my head and cock an eyebrow. "My last name . . . is Bloom."

He's quiet. I can feel him trying to hold back his pity.

"I know. It's awful. It's the name of a two-year-old little girl, not a twenty-three-year-old woman."

"A two-year-old girl will have the same name no matter how old she gets. Names aren't something we eventually grow out of, Lily Bloom."

"Unfortunately for me," I say. "But what makes it even worse is that I absolutely love gardening. I love flowers. Plants. Growing things. It's my passion. It's always been my dream to open a florist shop, but I'm afraid if I did, people wouldn't think my desire was authentic. They would think I was trying to capitalize off my name and that being a florist isn't really my dream job."

"Maybe so," he says. "But what's that matter?"

"It doesn't, I suppose." I catch myself whispering, "*Lily Bloom's*" quietly. I can see him smiling a little bit. "It really is a great name for a florist. But I have a master's degree in business. I'd be downgrading, don't you think? I work for the biggest marketing firm in Boston."

"Owning your own business isn't downgrading," he says.

I raise an eyebrow. "Unless it flops."

He nods in agreement. "Unless it flops," he says. "So what's your middle name, Lily Bloom?"

I groan, which makes him perk up.

"You mean it gets worse?"

I drop my head in my hands and nod.

"Rose?"

I shake my head. "Worse."

"Violet?"

"I wish." I cringe and then mutter, "*Blossom.*"

There's a moment of silence. "Goddamn," he says softly.

"Yeah. Blossom is my mother's maiden name and my parents thought it was fate that their last names were synonyms. So of course when they had me, a flower was their first choice."

"Your parents must be real assholes."

One of them is. *Was.* "My father died this week."

He glances at me. "Nice try. I'm not falling for that."

"I'm serious. That's why I came up here tonight. I think I just needed a good cry."

He stares at me suspiciously for a moment to make sure I'm not pulling his leg. He doesn't apologize for the blunder. Instead, his eyes grow a little more curious, like his intrigue is actually authentic. "Were you close?"

That's a hard question. I rest my chin on my arms and look down at the street again. "I don't know," I say with a shrug. "As his daughter, I loved him. But as a human, I hated him."

I can feel him watching me for a moment, and then he says, "I like that. Your honesty."

He likes my honesty. I think I might be blushing.

We're both quiet again for a while, and then he says, "Do you ever wish people were more transparent?"

"How so?"

He picks at a piece of chipped stucco with his thumb until it breaks loose. He flicks it over the ledge. "I feel like everyone fakes who they really are, when deep down we're all equal amounts of screwed up. Some of us are just better at hiding it than others."

Either his high is setting in, or he's just very introspective. Either way, I'm okay with it. My favorite conversations are the ones with no real answers.

"I don't think being a little guarded is a negative thing," I say. "Naked truths aren't always pretty."

He stares at me for a moment. "*Naked truths*," he repeats. "I like that." He turns around and walks to the middle of the rooftop. He adjusts the back on one of the patio loungers behind me and lowers himself onto it. It's the kind you lie on, so he pulls his hands behind his head and looks up at the sky. I claim the one next to him and adjust it until I'm in the same position as him.

"Tell me a naked truth, Lily."

"Pertaining to what?"

He shrugs. "I don't know. Something you aren't proud of. Something that will make me feel a little less screwed up on the inside."

He's staring up at the sky, waiting on me to answer. My eyes follow the line of his jaw, the curve of his cheeks, the outline of his lips. His eyebrows are drawn together in contemplation. I don't understand why, but he seems to need conversation right now. I think about his question and try to find an honest answer. When I come up with one, I look away from him and back up to the sky.

"My father was abusive. Not to me—to my mother. He

would get so angry when they fought that sometimes he would hit her. When that happened, he would spend the next week or two making up for it. He would do things like buy her flowers or take us out to a nice dinner. Sometimes he would buy me stuff because he knew I hated it when they fought. When I was a kid, I found myself looking forward to the nights they would fight. Because I knew if he hit her, the two weeks that followed would be great." I pause. I'm not sure I've ever admitted that to myself. "Of course if I could, I would have made it to where he never touched her. But the abuse was inevitable with their marriage, and it became our norm. When I got older, I realized that not doing something about it made me just as guilty. I spent most of my life hating him for being such a bad person, but I'm not so sure I'm much better. Maybe we're both bad people."

Ryle looks over at me with a thoughtful expression. "Lily," he says pointedly. "There is no such thing as *bad people*. We're all just people who sometimes do bad things."

I open my mouth to respond, but his words strike me silent. *We're all just people who sometimes do bad things.* I guess that's true in a way. No one is exclusively bad, nor is anyone exclusively good. Some are just forced to work harder at suppressing the bad.

"Your turn," I tell him.

Based on his reaction, I think he might not want to play his own game. He sighs heavily and runs a hand through his hair. He opens his mouth to speak, but then clamps it shut again. He thinks for a bit, and then finally speaks. "I watched a little boy die tonight." His voice is despondent. "He was only five years old. He and his little brother found a gun in his parents' bedroom. The younger brother was holding it and it went off by accident."

My stomach flips. I think this may be a little too much truth for me.

"There was nothing that could be done by the time he made it to the operating table. Everyone around—nurses, other doctors—they all felt so sorry for the family. '*Those poor parents,*' they said. But when I had to walk into the waiting room and tell those parents that their child didn't make it, I didn't feel an ounce of sorrow for them. I wanted them to suffer. I wanted them to feel the weight of their ignorance for keeping a loaded gun within access of two innocent children. I wanted them to know that not only did they just lose a child, they just ruined the entire life of the one who accidentally pulled the trigger."

Jesus Christ. I wasn't prepared for something so heavy.

I can't even conceive how a family moves past that. "That poor boy's brother," I say. "I can't imagine what that's going to do to him—seeing something like that."

Ryle flicks something off the knee of his jeans. "It'll destroy him for life, that's what it'll do."

I turn on my side to face him, lifting my head up onto my hand. "Is it hard? Seeing things like that every day?"

He gives his head a slight shake. "It should be a lot harder, but the more I'm around death, the more it just becomes a part of life. I'm not sure how I feel about that." He makes eye contact with me again. "Give me another one," he says. "I feel like mine was a little more twisted than yours."

I disagree, but I tell him about the twisted thing I did a mere twelve hours ago.

"My mother asked me two days ago if I would deliver the eulogy at my father's funeral today. I told her I didn't feel comfortable—that I might be crying too hard to speak in front of a crowd—but that was a lie. I just didn't want to do it because I feel like eulogies should be delivered by those who respected the deceased. And I didn't much respect my father."

"Did you do it?"

I nod. "Yeah. This morning." I sit up and pull my legs beneath me as I face him. "You want to hear it?"

He smiles. "Absolutely."

I fold my hands in my lap and inhale a breath. "I had no idea what to say. About an hour before the funeral, I told my mother I didn't want to do it. She said it was simple and that my father would have wanted me to do it. She said all I had to do was walk up to the podium and say five great things about my father. So . . . that's exactly what I did."

Ryle lifts up onto his elbow, appearing even more interested. He can tell by the look on my face that it gets worse. "Oh, no, Lily. What did you do?"

"Here. Let me just reenact it for you." I stand up and walk around to the other side of my chair. I stand tall and act like I'm looking out over the same crowded room I was met with this morning. I clear my throat.

"Hello. My name is Lily Bloom, daughter of the late Andrew Bloom. Thank you all for joining us today as we mourn his loss. I wanted to take a moment to honor his life by sharing with you five great things about my father. The first thing . . ."

I look down at Ryle and shrug. "That's it."

He sits up. "What do you mean?"

I take a seat on my lounge chair and lie back down. "I stood up there for two solid minutes without saying another word. There wasn't one great thing I could say about that man—so I just stared silently at the crowd until my mother realized what I was doing and had my uncle remove me from the podium."

Ryle tilts his head. "Are you kidding me? You gave the anti-eulogy at your own father's funeral?"

I nod. "I'm not proud of it. I don't *think*. I mean, if I had my way, he would have been a much better person and I would have stood up there and talked for an hour."

Ryle lies back down. "Wow," he says, shaking his head. "You're kind of my hero. You just roasted a dead guy."

"That's tacky."

"Yeah, well. Naked truth hurts."

I laugh. "Your turn."

"I can't top that," he says.

"I'm sure you can come close."

"I'm not sure I can."

I roll my eyes. "Yes you can. Don't make me feel like the worst person out of the two of us. Tell me the most recent thought you've had that most people wouldn't say out loud."

He pulls his hands up behind his head and looks me straight in the eye. "I want to fuck you."

My mouth falls open. Then I clamp it shut again.

I think I might be speechless.

He shoots me a look of innocence. "You asked for the most recent thought, so I gave it to you. You're beautiful. I'm a guy. If you were into one-night stands, I would take you downstairs to my bedroom and I would fuck you."

I can't even look at him. His statement makes me feel a multitude of things all at once.

"Well, I'm not into one-night stands."

"I figured as much," he says. "Your turn."

He's so nonchalant; he acts as if he didn't just stun me into silence.

"I need a minute to regroup after that one," I say with a laugh. I try to think of something with a little shock value, but I can't get over the fact that he just said that. *Out loud.* Maybe because he's a neurosurgeon and I never pictured someone so educated throwing around the word *fuck* so casually.

I gather myself . . . somewhat . . . and then say, "Okay. Since we're on the subject . . . the first guy I ever had sex with was homeless."

He perks up and faces me. "Oh, I'm gonna need more of this story."

I stretch my arm out and rest my head on it. "I grew up in Maine. We lived in a fairly decent neighborhood, but the street behind our house wasn't in the best condition. Our backyard butted up to a condemned house adjacent to two abandoned lots. I became friends with a guy named Atlas who stayed in the condemned house. No one knew he was living there other than me. I used to take him food and clothes and stuff. Until my father found out."

"What'd he do?"

My jaw tightens. I don't know why I brought this up when I still force myself not to think about it on a daily basis.

"He beat him up." That's as naked as I want to get about that subject. "Your turn."

He regards me silently for a moment, as if he knows there's more to that story. But then he breaks eye contact. "The thought of marriage repulses me," he says. "I'm almost thirty years old and I have no desire for a wife. I *especially* don't want children. The only thing I want out of life is success. Lots of it. But if I admit that out loud to anyone, it makes me sound arrogant."

"Professional success? Or social status?"

He says, "Both. Anyone can have children. Anyone can get married. But not everyone can be a neurosurgeon. I get a lot of pride out of that. And I don't just want to be a great neurosurgeon. I want to be the best in my field."

"You're right. It does make you sound arrogant."

He smiles. "My mother fears I'm wasting my life away because all I do is work."

"You're a neurosurgeon and your mother is *disappointed* in you?" I laugh. "Good lord, that's insane. Are parents ever really happy with their children? Will they ever be good enough?"

He shakes his head. "My children wouldn't be. Not many people have the drive I do, so I'd only be setting them up for failure. That's why I'll never have any."

"I actually think that's respectable, Ryle. A lot of people refuse to admit they might be too selfish to have children."

He shakes his head. "Oh, I'm *way* too selfish to have children. And I'm definitely way too selfish to be in a relationship."

"So how do you avoid it? You just don't date?"

He cuts his eyes to me, and there's a slight grin affixed to his face. "When I have time, there are girls who satisfy those needs. I don't lack for anything in that department, if that's what you're asking. But love has never appealed to me. It's always been more of a burden than anything."

I wish I looked at love like that. It would make my life a hell of a lot easier. "I envy you. I have this idea that there's a perfect man out there for me. I tend to become jaded easily, because no one ever meets my standards. I feel like I'm on an infinite search for the Holy Grail."

"You should try my method," he says.

"Which is?"

"One-night stands." He raises an eyebrow, like it's an invitation.

I'm glad it's dark, because my face is on fire. "I could never sleep with someone if I didn't see it going anywhere." I say this out loud, but my words lack conviction when I say it to him.

He drags in a long, slow breath, and then rolls onto his back. "Not that kind of girl, huh?" He says this with a trace of disappointment in his voice.

I match his disappointment. I'm not sure I'd even want to turn him down if he made a move, but I might have just thwarted that possibility.

"If you wouldn't *sleep* with someone you just met . . ." His eyes meet mine again. "Exactly how far would you go?"

I don't have an answer for that. I roll onto my back because the way he's looking at me makes me want to rethink one-night stands. I'm not necessarily against them, I suppose. I've just never been propositioned for one by someone I would consider it with.

Until now. I *think*. Is he even propositioning me? I've always been terrible at flirting.

He reaches out and grabs the edge of my lounge chair. In one swift movement and with very minimal effort, he drags my chair closer to him until it bumps his.

My whole body stiffens. He's so close now, I can feel the warmth of his breath cutting through the cold air. If I were to look at him, his face would be mere inches from mine. I refuse to look at him, because he'd probably kiss me and I know absolutely nothing about this guy, other than a couple of naked truths. But that doesn't weigh on my conscience at all when he rests a heavy hand on my stomach.

"How far would you go, Lily?" His voice is decadent. Smooth. It travels straight to my toes.

"I don't know," I whisper.

His fingers begin to crawl toward the hem of my shirt. He begins to slowly inch it upward until a slither of my stomach is showing. "*Oh, Jesus,*" I whisper, feeling the warmth from his hand as he slides it up my stomach.

Against my better judgment, I face him again and the look in his eyes completely captivates me. He looks hopeful and hungry and completely confident. He sinks his teeth into his bottom lip as his hand begins to tease its way up my shirt. I know he can feel my heart thrashing around in my chest. Hell, he can probably *hear* it.

"Is this too far?" he asks.

I don't know where this side of me is coming from, but I shake my head and say, "Not even close."

With a grin, his fingers brush the underneath of my bra, lightly trickling over my skin that is now covered in chills.

As soon as my eyelids fall shut, the piercing of a ring rips through the air. His hand stiffens when we both realize it's a phone. *His* phone.

He drops his forehead to my shoulder. "Dammit."

I frown when his hand slips out from beneath my shirt. He fumbles in his pocket for his phone, standing up and walking several feet away from me to take the call.

"Dr. Kincaid," he says. He listens intently, his hand gripping the back of his neck. "What about Roberts? I'm not even supposed to be on call right now." More silence is followed with, "Yeah, give me ten minutes. On my way."

He ends the call and slides his phone back in his pocket. When he turns to face me, he looks a little disappointed. He points to the door that leads to the stairwell. "I have to . . ."

I nod. "It's fine."

He considers me for a moment, and then holds up a finger. "Don't move," he says, reaching for his phone again. He walks closer and holds it up as if he's about to snap a picture of me. I almost object, but I don't even know why. I'm fully clothed. It just doesn't feel that way for some reason.

He snaps a picture of me lying in the lounge chair, my arms relaxed above my head. I have no idea what he plans to do with that picture, but I like that he took it. I like that he had the urge to remember what I look like, even though he knows he'll never see me again.

He stares at the photo on his screen for a few seconds and smiles. I'm half-tempted to take a picture of him in return, but I'm not sure I want a reminder of someone I'll never see again. The thought of that is a little depressing.

"It was nice meeting you, Lily Bloom. I hope you defy the odds of most dreams and actually accomplish yours."

I smile, equally saddened and confused by this guy. I'm not sure that I've ever spent time with someone like him before—someone of a completely different lifestyle and tax bracket. I probably never will again. But I'm pleasantly surprised to see that we aren't all that different.

Misconception confirmed.

He looks down at his feet for a moment as he stands in somewhat of an unsure pose. It's as if he's suspended between the desire to say something else to me and the need to leave. He glances at me one last time—this time without so much of a poker face. I can see the disappointment in the set of his mouth before he turns and walks in the other direction. He opens the door and I can hear his footsteps fade as he rushes down the stairwell. I'm alone on the rooftop once again, but to my surprise, I'm a little saddened by that now.

Chapter Two

Lucy—*the roommate who loves to hear herself sing*—is rushing around the living room, gathering keys, shoes, a pair of sunglasses. I'm seated on the couch, opening up shoeboxes stuffed with some of my old things from when I lived at home. I grabbed them when I was home for my father's funeral this week.

"You work today?" Lucy asks.

"Nope. I have bereavement leave until Monday."

She stops in her tracks. "Monday?" She scoffs. "Lucky bitch."

"Yes, Lucy. I'm *so* lucky my father died." I say it sarcastically, of course, but I cringe when I realize it's not actually very sarcastic.

"You know what I mean," she mutters. She grabs her purse as she balances on one foot while sliding her shoe onto the other. "I'm not coming home tonight. Staying over at Alex's house." The door slams behind her.

We have a lot in common on the surface, but beyond wearing the same size clothes, being the same age, and both having four-letter names that start with an *L* and end with a *Y*, there's not much else there that makes us more than just roommates. I'm okay with that, though. Other than the incessant singing, she's pretty tolerable. She's clean and she's gone a lot. Two of the most important qualities in a roommate.

I'm pulling the lid off the top of one of the shoeboxes when my cell phone rings. I reach across the couch and grab it. When I see that it's my mother, I press my face into the couch and fake-cry into a throw pillow.

I bring the phone to my ear. "Hello?"

There's three seconds of silence, and then—"Hello, Lily."

I sigh and sit back up on the couch. "Hey, Mom." I'm really surprised she's speaking to me. It's only been one day since the funeral. That's 364 days sooner than I expected to hear from her.

"How are you?" I ask.

She sighs dramatically. "Fine," she says. "Your aunt and uncle went back to Nebraska this morning. It'll be my first night alone since . . ."

"You'll be fine, Mom," I say, trying to sound confident.

She's quiet for too long, and then she says, "Lily. I just want you to know that you shouldn't be embarrassed about what happened yesterday."

I pause. *I wasn't. Not even the slightest bit.*

"Everyone freezes up once in a while. I shouldn't have put that kind of pressure on you, knowing how hard the day was on you already. I should have just had your uncle do it."

I close my eyes. *Here she goes again.* Covering up what she doesn't want to see. Taking blame that isn't even hers to take. *Of course* she convinced herself that I froze up yesterday, and that's why I refused to speak. *Of course she did.* I have half a mind to tell her it wasn't a mistake. I didn't freeze up. I just had nothing great to say about the unremarkable man she chose to be my father.

But part of me does feel guilty for what I did—specifically

because it's not something I should have done in the presence of my mother—so I just accept what she's doing and go along with it.

"Thanks, Mom. Sorry I choked."

"It's fine, Lily. I need to go, I have to run to the insurance office. We have a meeting about your father's policies. Call me tomorrow, okay?"

"I will," I tell her. "Love you, Mom."

I end the call and toss the phone across the couch. I open the shoebox on my lap and pull out the contents. On the very top is a small wooden, hollow heart. I run my fingers over it and remember the night I was given this heart. As soon as the memory begins to sink in, I set it aside. Nostalgia is a funny thing.

I move a few old letters and newspaper clippings aside. Beneath all of it, I find what I was hoping was inside these boxes. And also sort of hoping *wasn't*.

My Ellen Diaries.

I run my hands over them. There are three of them in this box, but I'd say there are probably eight or nine total. I haven't read any of these since the last time I wrote in them.

I refused to admit that I kept a diary when I was younger because that was so cliché. Instead, I convinced myself that what I was doing was cool, because it wasn't technically a diary. I addressed each of my entries to Ellen DeGeneres, because I began watching her show the first day it aired in 2003 when I was just a little girl. I watched it every day after school and was convinced Ellen would love me if she got to know me. I wrote letters to her regularly until I turned sixteen, but I wrote them like one would write entries in a diary.

Of course I knew the last thing Ellen DeGeneres probably wanted was a random girl's journal entries. Luckily, I never actually sent any in. But I still liked addressing all the entries to her, so I continued to do that until I stopped writing in them altogether.

I open another shoebox and find more of them. I sort through them until I grab the one from when I was fifteen years old. I flip it open, searching for the day I met Atlas. There wasn't much that happened in my life worth writing about before he entered it, but somehow I filled six journals full before he ever came into the picture.

I swore I'd never read these again, but with the passing of my father, I've been thinking about my childhood a lot. Maybe if I read through these journals I'll somehow find a little strength for forgiveness. Although I fear I'm running the risk of building up even more resentment.

I lie back on the couch and I begin reading.

Dear Ellen,

Before I tell you what happened today, I have a really good idea for a new segment on your show. It's called, "Ellen at home."

I think lots of people would like to see you outside of work. I always wonder what you're like at your home when it's just you and Portia and the cameras aren't around. Maybe the producers can give her a camera and sometimes she can just sneak up on you and film you doing normal things, like watching TV or cooking or gardening. She could film you for a few seconds without you knowing and then she could scream, "Ellen at home!" *and scare you. It's only fair, since you love pranks.*

Okay, now that I told you that (I keep meaning to and have been forgetting) I'll tell you about my day yesterday. It was interesting. Probably my most interesting day to write about yet, if you don't count the day Abigail Ivory slapped Mr. Carson for looking at her cleavage.

You remember a while back when I told you about Mrs. Burleson who lived behind us? She died the night of that big snowstorm? My dad said she owed so much in taxes that her daughter wasn't able to take ownership of the house. Which is fine by her, I'm sure, because the house was starting to fall apart anyway. It probably would have been more of a burden than anything.

The house has been empty since Mrs. Burleson died, which has been about two years. I know it's been empty because my bedroom window looks out over the backyard, and there hasn't been a single soul that goes in or out of that house since I can remember.

Until last night.

I was in bed shuffling cards. I know that sounds weird, but it's just something I do. I don't even know how to play cards. But when my parents get into fights, shuffling cards just calms me down sometimes and gives me something to focus on.

Anyway, it was dark outside, so I noticed the light right away. It wasn't bright, but it was coming from that old house. It looked more like candlelight than anything, so I went to the back porch and found Dad's binoculars. I tried to see what was going on over there, but I couldn't see anything. It was way too dark. Then after a little while, the light went out.

This morning, when I was getting ready for school, I saw something moving behind that house. I crouched down at my bedroom window and saw someone sneaking out the back door. It was a guy and he had a backpack. He looked around like he was making sure no one saw him, and then he walked between our house and the neighbor's house and went and stood at the bus stop.

I'd never seen him before. It was the first time he rode my bus. He sat in the back and I sat in the middle, so I didn't talk to him. But when he got off the bus at school, I saw him walk into the school, so he must go there.

I have no idea why he was sleeping in that house. There's probably no electricity or running water. I thought maybe he did it as a dare, but today he got off the bus at the same stop as me. He walked down the street like he was going somewhere else, but I ran straight to my room and watched out the window. Sure enough, a few minutes later, I saw him sneaking back inside that empty house.

I don't know if I should say something to my mother. I hate to be nosy, because it's none of my business. But if that guy doesn't have anywhere to go, I feel like my mother would know how to help him since she works at a school.

I don't know. I might wait a couple days before I say something and see if he goes back home. He might just need a break from his parents. Same as I wish I could have sometimes.

That's all. I'll let you know what happens tomorrow.

—Lily

Dear Ellen,

I fast-forward through all your dancing when I watch your show. I used to watch the beginning when you danced through the audience, but I get a little bored with it now and would rather just hear you talk. I hope that doesn't make you mad.

Okay, so I found out who the guy is, and yes, he's still going over there. It's been two days now and I still haven't told anyone.

His name is Atlas Corrigan and he's a senior, but that's all I know. I asked Katie who he was when she sat next to me on the bus. She rolled her eyes and told me his name. But then she said, "I don't know anything else about him, but he smells." She scrunched up her nose like it grossed her out. I wanted to yell at her and tell her he can't help it, that he doesn't have any running water. But instead, I just looked back at him. I might have stared a little too much, because he caught me looking at him.

When I got home I went to the backyard to do some gardening. My radishes were ready to be pulled, so I was out there pulling them. The radishes are the only thing left in my garden. It's starting to get cold so there's not much else I can plant right now. I probably could have waited a few more days to pull them, but I was also outside because I was being nosy.

I noticed as I was pulling them that some were missing. It looked like they had just been dug up. I know I didn't pull them and my parents never mess with my garden.

That's when I thought about Atlas, and how it was more than likely him. I hadn't thought about how—if he doesn't have access to a shower—he probably doesn't have food, either.

I went inside my house and made a couple of sandwiches. I grabbed two sodas out of the fridge and a bag of chips. I put them in a lunch bag and I ran it over to the abandoned house and set it on the back porch by the door. I wasn't sure if he saw me, so I knocked real hard and then ran back to my house and went straight to my room. By the time I got to the window to see if he was going to come outside, the bag was already gone.

That's when I knew he'd been watching me. I'm kind of nervous now that he knows I know he's staying there. I don't know what I'll say to him if he tries to talk to me tomorrow.

—Lily

Dear Ellen,

I saw your interview with the presidential candidate Barack Obama today. Does that make you nervous? Interviewing people who could potentially run the country? I don't know a lot about politics, but I don't think I could be funny under that kind of pressure.

Man. So much has happened to both of us. You just interviewed someone who might be our next president and I'm feeding a homeless boy.

This morning when I got to the bus stop, Atlas was already there. It was just the two of us at first, and I'm not gonna lie, it was awkward. I could see the bus coming around the corner and I was wishing it would drive a little faster. Right when it pulled up, he took a step closer to me and, without looking up, he said, "Thank you."

The doors opened on the bus and he let me walk on first. I didn't say You're welcome *because I was kind of shocked by my reaction. His voice gave me chills, Ellen.*

Has a boy's voice ever done that to you?

Oh, wait. Sorry. Has a girl's *voice ever done that to you?*

He didn't sit by me or anything on the way there, but on the way back from school, he was the last one getting on. There weren't any empty seats, but I could tell by the way he scanned all the people on the bus that he wasn't looking for an empty seat. He was looking for me.

When his eyes met mine, I looked down at my lap real quick. I hate that I'm not very confident around guys. Maybe that's something I'll grow into when I finally turn sixteen.

He sat down next to me and dropped his backpack between his legs. That's when I noticed what Katie was talking about. He did kind of smell, but I didn't judge him for that.

He didn't say anything at first, but he was fidgeting with a hole in his jeans. It wasn't the kind of hole that was there to make jeans look stylish. I could tell it was there because it was a genuine hole, due to his pants being old. They actually looked a little too small for him, because his ankles were showing. But he was skinny enough that they fit him just fine everywhere else.

"Did you tell anyone?" he asked me.

I looked at him when he spoke, and he was looking right back at me like he was worried. It was the first time I had actually gotten a good look at him. His hair was dark brown, but I thought maybe if he washed it, it wouldn't be as dark as it looked right then. His eyes were bright, unlike the rest of him. Real blue eyes, like the kind you see on a Siberian husky. I shouldn't compare his eyes to a dog, but that's the first thing I thought when I saw them.

I shook my head and looked back out the window. I thought he might get up and find another seat at that point, since I said I didn't tell anyone, but he didn't. The bus made a few stops, and the fact that he was still sitting by me gave me a little courage, so I made my voice a whisper. "Why don't you live at home with your parents?"

He stared at me for a few seconds, like he was trying to decide if he wanted to trust me or not. Then he said, "Because they don't want me to."

That's when he got up. I thought I'd made him mad, but then I realized he got up because we were at our stop. I grabbed my stuff and followed him off the bus. He didn't try to hide where he was heading today like he usually does. Normally, he walks down the street and goes around the block so I don't see him cut through my backyard. But today he started to walk toward my yard with me.

When we got to where I would normally turn to go inside and he would keep walking, we both stopped. He kicked at the dirt with his foot and looked behind me at my house.

"What time do your parents get home?"

"Around five," I said. It was 3:45.

He nodded and looked like he was about to say something else, but he didn't. He just nodded again and started walking toward that house with no food or electricity or water.

Now, Ellen, I know what I did next was stupid, so you don't have to tell me. I called out his name, and when he stopped and turned around I said, "If you hurry, you can take a shower before they get home."

My heart was beating so fast, because I knew how much trouble I could get into if my parents came home and found a homeless guy in our shower. I'd probably very well die. But I just couldn't watch him walk back to his house without offering him something.

He looked down at the ground again, and I felt his embarrassment in my own stomach. He didn't even nod. He just followed me inside my house and never said a word.

The whole time he was in the shower, I was panicking. I kept looking out the window and checking for either of my parents' cars, even though I knew it would be a good hour before they got home. I was nervous one of the neighbors might have seen him come inside, but they didn't really know me well enough to think having a visitor would be abnormal.

I had given Atlas a change of clothes, and knew he not only needed to be out of the house when my parents got home, but he needed to be far away from our house. I'm sure my father would recognize his own clothes on some random teenager in the neighborhood.

In between looking out the window and checking the clock, I was filling up one of my old backpacks with stuff. Food that didn't need refrigerating, a couple of my father's T-shirts, a pair of jeans that were probably going to be two sizes too big for him, and a change of socks.

I was zipping up the backpack when he emerged from the hallway.

I was right. Even wet, I could tell his hair was lighter than it looked earlier. It made his eyes look even bluer.

He must have shaved while he was in there because he looked younger than he did before he got in the shower. I swallowed and looked back down at the backpack, because I was shocked at how different he looked. I was scared he might see my thoughts written across my face.

I looked out the window one more time and handed him the backpack. "You might want to go out the back door so no one sees you."

He took the backpack from me and stared at my face for a minute. "What's your name?" he said as he slung the pack over his shoulder.

"Lily."

He smiled. It was the first time he'd smiled at me and I had an awful, shallow thought in that moment. I wondered how someone with such a great smile could have such shitty parents. I immediately hated myself for thinking it, because of course parents should love their kids no matter how cute or ugly or skinny or fat or smart or stupid they are. But sometimes you can't control where your mind goes. You just have to train it not to go there anymore.

He held out his hand and said, "I'm Atlas."

"I know," I said, without shaking his hand. I don't know why I didn't shake his hand. It wasn't because I was scared to touch him.

I mean, I was scared to touch him. But not because I thought I was better than him. He just made me so nervous.

He put his hand down and nodded once, then said, "I guess I better go."

I stepped aside so he could walk around me. He pointed past the kitchen, silently asking if that was the way to the back door. I nodded and walked behind him as he made his way down the hall. When he reached the back door, I saw him pause for a second when he saw my bedroom.

I was suddenly embarrassed that he was seeing my bedroom. No one ever sees my bedroom, so I've never felt the need to give it a more mature look. I still have the same pink bedspread and curtains I've had since I was twelve. For the first time ever I felt like ripping down my poster of Adam Brody.

Atlas didn't seem to care how my room was decorated. He looked straight at my window—the one that looks out over the backyard—then he glanced back at me. Right before he walked out the back door he said, "Thank you for not being disparaging, Lily."

And then he was gone.

Of course I've heard the term disparaging *before, but it was weird hearing a teenage guy use it. What's even weirder is how everything about Atlas seems so contradictory. How does a guy who is obviously humble, well-mannered, and uses words like* disparaging *end up homeless? How does any teenager end up homeless?*

I need to find out, Ellen.

I'm going to find out what happened to him. You just wait and see.

—Lily

• • •

I'm about to open another entry when my phone rings. I crawl across the couch for it and I'm not the least bit surprised to see it's my mother again. Now that my father has passed and she's alone, she'll probably call me twice as much as she did before.

"Hello?"

"What do you think about my moving to Boston?" she blurts out.

I grab the throw pillow next to me and shove my face into it, muffling a scream. "Um. *Wow*," I say. "Really?"

She's quiet, and then, "It was just a thought. We can discuss it tomorrow. I'm almost to my meeting."

"Okay. Bye."

And just like that, I want to move out of Massachusetts. *She can't move here.* She doesn't know anyone here. She'd expect me to entertain her every day. I love my mother, don't get me wrong, but I moved to Boston to be on my own, and having her in the same city would make me feel less independent.

My father was diagnosed with cancer three years ago while I was still in college. If Ryle Kincaid were here right now, I'd tell him the naked truth that I was a little bit relieved when my father became too ill to physically hurt my mother. It completely changed the dynamic of their relationship and I no longer felt obligated to stay in Plethora to make sure she was okay.

Now that my father is gone and I never have to worry about my mother again, I was looking forward to spreading my wings, so to speak.

But now she's moving to Boston?

It feels like my wings were just clipped.

Where is a marine-grade polymer chair when I need one?!

I'm seriously stressing out and I have no idea what I'd do if my mother moves to Boston. I don't have a garden, or a yard, or a patio, or weeds.

I have to find another outlet.

I decide to clean. I place all of my old shoeboxes full of journals and notes in my bedroom closet. Then I organize my entire closet. My jewelry, my shoes, my clothes . . .

She cannot move to Boston.

Chapter Three

Six months later

"Oh."

That's all she says.

My mother turns and assesses the building, running a finger over the windowsill next to her. She picks up a layer of dust and wipes it between her fingers. "It's . . ."

"It needs a lot of work, I know," I interrupt. I point at the windows behind her. "But look at the storefront. It has potential."

She scrolls over the windows, nodding. There's this sound she makes in the back of her throat sometimes, where she agrees with a little hum but her lips remain tight. It means she doesn't *actually* agree. And she makes that sound. *Twice.*

I drop my arms in defeat. "You think this was stupid?"

She gives her head a slight shake. "That all depends on how it turns out, Lily," she says. The building used to house a restaurant and it's still full of old tables and chairs. My mother walks over to a nearby table and pulls out one of the chairs, taking a seat. "If things work out, and your floral shop is successful, then people will say it was a brave, bold, *smart* business decision. But if it fails and you lose your entire inheritance . . ."

"Then people will say it was a *stupid* business decision."

She shrugs. "That's just how it works. You majored in business, you know that." She glances around the room, slowly, as if she's seeing it the way it will look a month from now. "Just make sure it's brave and bold, Lily."

I smile. *I can accept that.* "I can't believe I bought it without asking you first," I say, taking a seat at the table.

"You're an adult. It's your right," she says, but I can hear a trace of disappointment. I think she feels even lonelier now that I need her less and less. It's been six months since my father died, and even though he wasn't good company, it has to be weird for her, being alone. She got a job at one of the elementary schools, so she did end up moving here. She chose a small suburb on the outskirts of Boston. She bought a cute two-bedroom house on a cul-de-sac, with a huge backyard. I dream of planting a garden there, but that would require daily care. My limit is once-a-week visits. Sometimes twice.

"What are you going to do with all this junk?" she asks.

She's right. There's so much junk. It'll take forever to clear this place out. "I have no idea. I guess I'll be busting my ass for a while before I can even think about decorating."

"When's your last day at the marketing firm?"

I smile. "Yesterday."

She releases a sigh, and then shakes her head. "Oh, Lily. I certainly hope this works out in your favor."

We both begin to stand when the front door opens. There are shelves in the way of the door, so I careen my head around them and see a woman walk in. Her eyes briefly scan the room until she sees me.

"Hi," she says with a wave. She's cute. She's dressed well,

but she's wearing white capris. A disaster waiting to happen in this dust bowl.

"Can I help you?"

She tucks her purse beneath her arm and walks toward me, holding out her hand. "I'm Allysa," she says. I shake her hand.

"Lily."

She tosses a thumb over her shoulder. "There's a help wanted sign out front?"

I look over her shoulder and raise an eyebrow. "There is?" *I didn't put up a help wanted sign.*

She nods, and then shrugs. "It looks old, though," she says. "It's probably been there a while. I was just out for a walk and saw the sign. Was curious, is all."

I like her almost immediately. Her voice is pleasant and her smile seems genuine.

My mother's hand falls down on my shoulder and she leans in and kisses me on the cheek. "I have to go," she says. "Open house tonight." I tell her goodbye and watch her walk outside, then turn my attention back to Allysa.

"I'm not really hiring yet," I say. I wave my hand around the room. "I'm opening up a floral shop, but it'll be a couple of months, at least." I should know better than to hold preconceived judgments, but she doesn't look like she'd be satisfied with a minimum wage job. Her purse probably cost more than this building.

Her eyes light up. "Really? I love flowers!" She spins around in a circle and says, "This place has a ton of potential. What color are you painting it?"

I cross my arm over my chest and grab my elbow. Rocking

back on my heels, I say, "I'm not sure. I just got the keys to the building an hour ago, so I haven't really come up with a design plan yet."

"Lily, right?"

I nod.

"I'm not going to pretend I have a degree in design, but it's my absolute favorite thing. If you need any help, I'd do it for free."

I tilt my head. "You'd work for free?"

She nods. "I don't really need a job, I just saw the sign and thought, '*What the heck*?' But I do get bored sometimes. I'd be happy to help you with whatever you need. Cleaning, decorating, picking out paint colors. I'm a Pinterest whore." Something behind me catches her eye and she points. "I could take that broken door and make it magnificent. *All* this stuff, really. There's a use for almost everything, you know."

I look around at the room, knowing full well I'm not going to be able to tackle this by myself. I probably can't even lift half this stuff alone. I'll eventually have to hire someone anyway. "I'm not going to let you work for free. But I could do $10 an hour if you're really serious."

She starts clapping, and if she weren't in heels, she might have jumped up and down. "When can I start?"

I glance down at her white capris. "Will tomorrow work? You'll probably want to show up in disposable clothes."

She waves me off and drops her Hermès bag on a dusty table next to her. "Nonsense," she says. "My husband is watching the Bruins play at a bar down the street. If it's okay, I'll just hang with you and get started right now."

• • •

Two hours later, I'm convinced I've met my new best friend. And she really is a Pinterest whore.

We write "Keep" and "Toss" on sticky notes, and slap them on everything in the room. She's a fellow believer in upcycling, so we come up with ideas for at least 75 percent of the stuff left in the building. The rest she says her husband can throw out when he has free time. Once we know what we're going to do with all the stuff, I grab a notebook and a pen and we sit at one of the tables to write down design ideas.

"Okay," she says, leaning back in her chair. I want to laugh, because her white capris are covered in dirt now, but she doesn't seem to care. "Do you have a goal for this place?" she asks, glancing around.

"I have *one*," I say. "Succeed."

She laughs. "I have no doubt you'll succeed. But you do need a vision."

I think about what my mother said. "*Just make sure it's brave and bold, Lily.*" I smile and sit up straighter in my chair. "Brave and bold," I say. "I want this place to be different. I want to take risks."

She narrows her eyes as she chews on the tip of the pen. "But you're just selling flowers," she says. "How can you be brave and bold with flowers?"

I look around the room and try to envision what I'm thinking. I'm not even sure what I'm thinking. I'm just getting itchy and restless, like I'm on the verge of a brilliant idea. "What are some words that come to mind when you think of flowers?" I ask her.

She shrugs. "I don't know. They're sweet, I guess? They're alive, so they make me think of life. And maybe the color pink. And spring."

"Sweet, life, pink, spring," I repeat. And then, "Allysa, you're brilliant!" I stand up and begin pacing the floor. "We'll take everything everyone loves about flowers, and we'll do the complete opposite!"

She makes a face to let me know she isn't following.

"Okay," I say. "What if, instead of showcasing the *sweet* side of flowers, we showcased the *villainous* side? Instead of pink accents, we use darker colors, like a deep purple or even black. And instead of just spring and life, we also celebrate winter and death."

Allysa's eyes are wide. "But . . . what if someone wants *pink* flowers, though?"

"Well, we'll still give them what they want, of course. But we'll also give them what they don't *know* they want."

She scratches her cheek. "So you're thinking *black* flowers?" She looks concerned, and I don't blame her. She's only seeing the darkest side of my vision. I take a seat at the table again and try to get her on board.

"Someone once told me that there is no such thing as bad people. We're all just people who sometimes do bad things. That stuck with me, because it's so true. We've all got a little bit of good and evil in us. I want to make that our theme. Instead of painting the walls a putrid sweet color, we paint them dark purple with black accents. And instead of only putting out the usual pastel displays of flowers in boring crystal vases that make people think of life, we go edgy. Brave and bold. We put out displays of darker flowers wrapped in things like leather or silver chains. And rather than put them in crystal vases, we'll stick them in black onyx or . . . I don't know . . . purple velvet vases lined with silver studs. The ideas are endless." I stand up again. "There are floral shops on every corner for people who love flowers. But what floral shop caters to all the people who *hate* flowers?"

Allysa shakes her head. "None of them," she whispers.

"Exactly. None of them."

We stare at each other for a moment, and then I can't take it another second. I'm bursting with excitement and I just start laughing like a giddy child. Allysa starts laughing, too, and she jumps up and hugs me. "Lily, it's so twisted, it's brilliant!"

"I know!" I'm full of renewed energy. "I need a desk so I can sit down and make a business plan! But my future office is full of old vegetable crates!"

She walks toward the back of the store. "Well, let's get them out of there and go buy you a desk!"

We squeeze into the office and begin moving crates out one by one and into a back room. I stand on the chair to make the piles taller so we'll have more room to move around.

"These are perfect for the window displays I have in mind." She hands me two more crates and walks away, and as I'm reaching on my tiptoes to stack them at the very top, the pile begins to tumble. I try to find something to grab hold of for balance, but the crates knock me off the chair. When I land on the floor, I can feel my foot bend in the wrong direction. It's followed by a rush of pain straight up my leg and down to my toes.

Allysa comes rushing back into the room and has to move

two of the crates from on top of me. "Lily!" she says. "Oh my God, are you okay?"

I pull myself up to a sitting position, but don't even try to put weight on my ankle. I shake my head. "My ankle."

She immediately removes my shoe and then pulls her phone out of her pocket. She begins dialing a number and then looks up at me. "I know this is a stupid question, but do you happen to have a refrigerator here with ice in it?"

I shake my head.

"I figured," she says. She puts the phone on speaker and sets it on the floor as she begins to roll up my pant leg. I wince, but not so much from the pain. I just can't believe I did something so stupid. If I broke it, I'm screwed. I just spent my entire inheritance on a building that I won't even be able to renovate for months.

"*Heeey*, Issa," a voice croons through her phone. "Where you at? The game's over."

Allysa picks up her phone and brings it closer to her mouth. "At work. Listen, I need . . ."

The guy cuts her off and says, "At *work*? Babe, you don't even have a job."

Allysa shakes her head and says, "Marshall, listen. It's an emergency. I think my boss broke her ankle. I need you to bring some ice to . . ."

He cuts her off with a laugh. "Your *boss*? Babe, you don't even have a job," he repeats.

Allysa rolls her eyes. "Marshall, are you drunk?"

"It's *onesie* day," he slurs into the phone. "You knew that when you dropped us off, Issa. Free beer until . . ."

She groans. "Put my brother on the phone."

"Fine, fine," Marshall mumbles. There's a rustling sound that comes from the phone, and then, "Yeah?"

Allysa spits out our location into the phone. "Get here right now. Please. And bring a bag of ice."

"Yes *ma'am,*" he says. The brother sounds like he may be a little drunk, too. There's laughter, and then one of the guys says, "*She's in a bad mood,*" and then the line goes dead.

Allysa puts her phone back in her pocket. "I'll go wait outside for them, they're just down the street. Will you be okay here?"

I nod and reach for the chair. "Maybe I should just try to walk on it."

Allysa pushes my shoulders back until I'm leaning against the wall again. "No, don't move. Wait until they get here, okay?"

I have no idea what two drunken guys are going to be able to do for me, but I nod. My new employee feels more like my boss right now and I'm kind of scared of her at the moment.

I wait in the back for about ten minutes when I finally hear the front door to the building open. "What in the *world*?" a man's voice says. "Why are you all alone in this creepy building?"

I hear Allysa say, "She's back here." She walks in, followed by a guy wearing a onesie. He's tall, a little bit on the thin side, but boyishly handsome with big, honest eyes and a head full of dark, messy, way-past-due-for-a-haircut hair. He's holding a bag of ice.

Did I mention he was wearing a onesie?

I'm talking a legit, full-grown man in a SpongeBob onesie.

"This is your husband?" I ask her, cocking an eyebrow.

Allysa rolls her eyes. "Unfortunately," she says, glancing back at him. Another guy (also in a onesie) walks in behind them, but my attention is on Allysa as she explains why they're wearing pajamas on a random Wednesday afternoon. "There's a bar down the street that gives out free beer to anyone who shows up in a onesie during a Bruins game." She makes her way over to me and motions for the guys to follow her. "She fell off the chair and hurt her ankle," she says to the other guy. He steps around Marshall and the first thing I notice are his arms.

Holy shit. I know those arms.

Those are the arms of a neurosurgeon.

Allysa is his sister? The sister that owns the entire top floor, with the husband who works in pajamas and brings in seven figures a year?

As soon as my eyes lock with Ryle's, his whole face morphs into a smile. I haven't seen him in—*God, how long ago was that*—six months? I can't say I haven't thought about him during the past six months, because I've thought about him quite a few times. But I never actually thought I'd see him again.

"Ryle, this is Lily. Lily, my brother, Ryle," she says, motioning toward him. "And that's my husband, Marshall."

Ryle walks over to me and kneels down. "Lily," he says, regarding me with a smile. "Nice to meet you."

It's obvious he remembers me—I can see it in his knowing smile. But like me, he's pretending this is the first time we've met. I'm not sure I'm in the mood to explain how we already know each other.

Ryle touches my ankle and inspects it. "Can you move it?"

I try to move it, but a sharp pain shoots all the way up my leg. I suck in air through my teeth and shake my head. "Not yet. It hurts."

Ryle motions to Marshall. "Find something to put the ice in."

Allysa follows Marshall out of the room. When they're both gone, Ryle looks at me and his mouth turns up into a grin. "I won't charge you for this, but only because I'm slightly inebriated," he says with a wink.

I tilt my head. "The first time I met you, you were high. Now you're drunk. I'm beginning to worry you aren't going to make a very qualified neurosurgeon."

He laughs. "It would appear that way," he says. "But I promise you, I rarely ever get high and this is my first day off in over a month, so I really needed a beer. Or five."

Marshall comes back with an old rag wrapped around some ice. He hands it to Ryle, who presses it against my ankle. "I'll need that first aid kit out of your trunk," Ryle says to Allysa. She nods and grabs Marshall's hand, pulling him out of the room again.

Ryle presses his palm against the bottom of my foot. "Push against my hand," he says.

I push down with my ankle. It hurts, but I'm able to move his hand. "Is it broken?"

He moves my foot from side to side, and then says, "I don't think so. Let's give it a couple of minutes and I'll see if you can put any weight on it."

I nod and watch as he adjusts himself across from me. He sits cross-legged and pulls my foot onto his lap. He looks around the room and then directs his attention back at me. "So what is this place?"

I smile a little too big. "Lily Bloom's. It'll be a floral shop in about two months' time."

I swear, his whole face lights up with pride. "No way," he says. "You did it? You're actually opening up your own business?"

I nod. "Yep. I figured I might as well try it while I'm still young enough to bounce back from failure."

One of his hands is holding the ice against my ankle, but the other one is wrapped around my bare foot. He's brushing his thumb back and forth, like it's no big deal that he's touching me. But his hand on my foot is way more noticeable than the pain in my ankle.

"I look ridiculous, huh?" he asks, staring down at his solid red onesie.

I shrug. "At least you went with a non-character choice. It gives it a bit more maturity than the SpongeBob option."

He laughs, and then his smile disappears as he leans his head into the door beside him. He stares at me appreciatively. "You're even prettier in the daytime."

Moments like these are why I absolutely hate having red hair and fair skin. The embarrassment doesn't only show up in my cheeks my whole face, arms, and neck grow flushed.

I rest my head against the wall behind me and stare at him just like he's staring at me. "You want to hear a naked truth?"

He nods.

"I've wanted to go back to your roof on more than one occasion since that night. But I was too scared you'd be there. You make me kind of nervous."

His fingers pause their strokes against my foot. "My turn?"

I nod.

His eyes narrow as his hand moves to the underneath of my foot. He slowly traces his fingers from the tops of my toes, down to my heel. "I still very much want to fuck you."

Someone gasps, and it isn't me.

Ryle and I both look at the doorway and Allysa is standing there, wide-eyed. Her mouth is open as she points down at Ryle. "Did you just . . ." She looks at me and says, "I am *so* sorry about him, Lily." And then she looks back at Ryle with venom in her eyes. "Did you just tell my boss you want to *fuck* her?"

Oh, dear.

Ryle pulls his bottom lip in and chews on it for a second. Marshall walks in behind Allysa and says, "What's going on?"

Allysa looks at Marshall and points at Ryle again. "He just told Lily he wants to *fuck* her!"

Marshall looks from Ryle to me. I don't know whether to laugh or crawl under the table and hide. "You did?" he says, looking back at Ryle.

Ryle shrugs. "It appears that way," he says.

Allysa puts her head in her hands, "Jesus Christ," she says, looking at me. "He's drunk. They're both drunk. Please don't judge me because my brother is an asshole."

I smile at her and wave it off. "It's fine, Allysa. Lots of people want to fuck me." I glance back at Ryle and he's still casually stroking my foot. "At least your brother speaks his mind. Not a lot of people have the courage to say what they're actually thinking."

Ryle winks at me and then carefully moves my ankle off his lap. "Let's see if you can put any weight on it," he says.

He and Marshall help me to my feet. Ryle points to a table a few feet away that's pushed up against a wall. "Let's try to make it to the table so I can wrap it."

His arm is secured around my waist, and he's gripping my arm tightly to make sure I don't fall. Marshall is more or less just standing next to me for support. I put a little weight on my ankle and it hurts, but it's not excruciating. I'm able to hop all the way to the table with a lot of assistance from Ryle. He helps me pull myself up until I'm seated on top of it, leaning against the wall with my leg stretched out in front of me.

"Well, the good news is that it isn't broken."

"What's the bad news?" I ask him.

He opens the first aid kit and says, "You'll need to stay off of it for a few days. Maybe even a week or more, depending on how it heals."

I close my eyes and lean my head against the wall behind me. "But I have so much to do," I whine.

He carefully begins to wrap my ankle. Allysa is standing behind him, watching him wrap it.

"I'm thirsty," Marshall says. "Anybody want something to drink? There's a CVS across the street."

"I'm good," Ryle says.

"I'll take a water," I say.

"Sprite," Allysa says.

Marshall grabs her hand. "You're coming with."

Allysa pulls her hand from his and crosses her arms over her chest. "I'm not going anywhere," she says. "My brother can't be trusted."

"Allysa, it's fine," I tell her. "He was making a joke."

She stares at me silently for a moment, and then says, "Okay. But you can't fire me if he pulls more stupid shit."

"I promise I won't fire you."

With that, she grabs Marshall's hand again and leaves the room. Ryle is still wrapping my foot when he says, "My sister works for you?"

"Yep. Hired her a couple of hours ago."

He reaches into the first aid kit and pulls out tape. "You do realize she's never had a job in her entire life?"

"She already warned me," I say. His jaw is tight and he doesn't look as relaxed as he did earlier. Then it hits me that he might think I hired her as a way to get closer to him. "I had no idea she was your sister until you walked in. I swear."

He glances at me, and then back down at my foot. "I wasn't suggesting you knew." He begins to tape over the ACE bandage.

"I know you weren't. I just didn't want you to think I was trying to trap you somehow. We want two different things from life, remember?"

He nods, and carefully sets my foot back on the table. "That is correct," he says. "I specialize in one-night stands and you're on the quest for your Holy Grail."

I laugh. "You have a good memory."

"I do," he says. A languid smile stretches across his mouth. "But you're also hard to forget."

Jesus. He *has* to stop saying things like that. I press my palms into the table and pull my leg down. "Naked truth coming."

He leans against the table next to me and says, "All ears."

I hold nothing back. "I'm very attracted to you," I say. "There's not much about you I don't like. And being as though you and I both want different things, if we're ever around each other again, I'd appreciate it if you could stop saying things that make me dizzy. It's not really fair to me."

He nods once, and then says, "My turn." He places his hand on the table next to me and leans in a little. "I'm very attracted to you, too. There's not much about *you* I don't like. But I kind of hope we're never around each other again, because I don't like how much I think about you. Which isn't all that much—but it's more than I'd like. So if you still aren't going to agree to a one-night stand, then I think it's best if we do what we can to avoid each other. Because it won't do either of us any favors."

I don't know how he ended up this close to me, but he's only about a foot away. His proximity makes it hard to pay attention to words that come out of his mouth. His gaze drops briefly to my mouth, but as soon as we hear the front door open, he's halfway across the room. By the time Allysa and Marshall make it to us, Ryle is busy restacking all the crates that fell. Allysa looks down at my ankle.

"What's the verdict?" she asks.

I push my bottom lip out. "Your doctor brother says I have to stay off of it for a few days."

She hands me my water. "Good thing you have me. I can work and do what I can to clean up while you rest."

I take a drink of the water and then wipe my mouth. "Allysa, I'm declaring you employee of the month."

She grins and then turns to Marshall. "Did you hear that? I'm the best employee she has!"

He puts his arm around her and kisses the top of her head. "I'm proud of you, Issa."

I like that he calls her *Issa*, which I'm assuming is short for Allysa. I think about my own name and if I'll ever find a guy who could shorten it into a sickeningly cute nickname. *Illy*.

Nope. Not the same.

"Do you need help getting home?" she asks.

I hop down and test my foot. "Maybe just to my car. It's my left foot, so I can probably drive just fine."

She walks over and puts her arm around me. "If you want to leave the keys with me, I'll lock up and come back tomorrow and start cleaning."

The three of them walk me to my car, but Ryle allows Allysa to do most of the work. He seems almost scared to touch me now for some reason. When I'm in the driver's seat, Allysa puts my purse and other things in the floorboard and sits in the passenger seat. She takes my phone out and begins programming her number into it.

Ryle leans into the window. "Make sure to keep ice on it as much as you can for the next few days. Baths help, too."

I nod. "Thanks for your help."

Allysa leans over and says, "Ryle? Maybe you should drive her home and take a cab back to the apartment, just to be safe."

Ryle looks down at me and then shakes his head. "I don't think that's a good idea," he says. "She'll be fine. I've had a few beers, probably shouldn't be driving."

"You could at least help her home," Allysa suggests.

Ryle shakes his head and then pats the roof of the car as he turns and walks away.

I'm still watching him when Allysa hands me back my phone and says, "Seriously. I'm really sorry about him. First he hits on you, then he's a selfish asshole." She climbs out of the car and closes the door, then leans through the window. "That's why he'll be single for the rest of his life." She points to my phone. "Text me when you get home. And call me if you need anything. I won't count favors as work-time."

"Thank you, Allysa."

She smiles. "No, thank *you*. I haven't been this excited about my life since that Paolo Nutini concert I went to last year." She waves goodbye and walks toward where Marshall and Ryle are standing.

They begin walking down the street and I watch them in my rearview mirror. As they turn the corner, I see Ryle glance over his shoulder and look back in my direction.

I close my eyes and exhale.

The two times I've spent with Ryle were on days I'd probably rather forget. My father's funeral and spraining my ankle. But somehow, him being present made them feel like less of the disasters they were.

I hate that he's Allysa's brother. I have a feeling this isn't the last time I'll be seeing him.

Chapter Four

It takes me half an hour to make it from my car to my apartment. I called Lucy twice to see if she could help me, but she didn't answer her phone. When I make it inside my apartment, I'm a little irritated to see her lying on the couch with the phone to her ear.

I slam our front door behind me and she glances up. "What happened to you?" she asks.

I use the wall for support as I hop toward the hallway. "Sprained my ankle."

When I make it to my bedroom door, she yells, "Sorry I didn't answer the phone! I'm talking to Alex! I was gonna call you back!"

"It's fine!" I holler back at her, and then slam my bedroom door shut. I go to the bathroom and find some old pain pills I had stuffed into a cabinet. I swallow two of them and then fall onto my bed and stare up at the ceiling.

I can't believe I'll be stuck in this apartment for an entire week. I grab my phone and text my mother.

Sprained my ankle. I'm fine, but can I send you a list of things to grab for me at the store?

I drop my phone onto my bed, and for the first time since she moved here, I'm thankful my mother lives fairly close to me. It actually hasn't been that bad. I think I like her more now that my father has passed away. I know it's because

I held a lot of resentment toward her for never leaving him. Even though a lot of that resentment has faded when it comes to my mother, I still have the same feelings when I think of my father.

It can't be good, still holding on to so much bitterness toward my father. But dammit, he was awful. To my mother, to me, to Atlas.

Atlas.

I've been so busy with my mother's move and secretly searching for a new building between work hours, I haven't had time to finish reading the journals I started reading all those months ago.

I hop pathetically to my closet, only tripping once. Luckily, I catch myself on my dresser. Once I have the journal in hand, I hop back to the bed and get comfortable.

I have nothing better to do for the next week now that I can't work. I might as well commiserate over my past while I'm forced to commiserate in the present.

Dear Ellen,

You hosting the Oscars was the greatest thing to happen to TV last year. I don't think I ever told you that. The vacuuming skit made me piss my pants.

Oh, and I recruited a new Ellen follower today in Atlas. Before you start judging me for allowing him inside my house again, let me explain how that came about.

After I let him take a shower here yesterday, I didn't see him again last night. But this morning, he sat by me on the bus again. He seemed a little happier than the day before, because he slid into the seat and actually smiled at me.

I'm not gonna lie, it was a little weird seeing him in my dad's clothes. But the pants fit him a lot better than I thought they were going to.

"Guess what?" he said. He leaned forward and unzipped his backpack.

"What?"

He pulled out a bag and handed it to me. "I found these in the garage. I tried to clean them up for you because they were covered in old dirt, but I can't do much without water."

I held the bag and stared at him suspiciously. It's the most I'd ever heard him say at once. I finally looked down at the bag and opened it. It looked like a bunch of old gardening tools.

"I saw you digging with that shovel the other day. I wasn't sure if you had any actual gardening tools, and no one was using these, so . . ."

"Thank you," I said. I was kind of in shock. I used to have a trowel, but the plastic broke off the handle and it started giving me blisters. I asked my mother for gardening tools for my birthday last year and when she bought me a full-sized shovel and a hoe, I didn't have the heart to tell her it's not what I needed.

Atlas cleared his throat and then, in a much quieter voice, he said, "I know it's not like a real gift. I didn't buy it or anything. But . . . I wanted to give you something. You know . . . for . . ."

He didn't finish his sentence, so I nodded and tied the bag back up. "Do you think you can hold them for me until after school? I don't have any room in my backpack."

He grabbed the bag from me and then brought his backpack up to his lap and put the bag inside of it. He wrapped his arms around his backpack. "How old are you?" he asked.

"Fifteen."

The look in his eyes made him seem a little bit sad about my age, but I don't know why.

"You're in tenth grade?"

I nodded, but honestly couldn't think of anything to say to him. I haven't really had much interaction with a lot of guys. Especially seniors. When I'm nervous, I kind of just clam up.

"I don't know how long I'll be staying at that place," he said, bringing his voice down again. "But if you ever need help with gardening or anything after school, it's not like I have much going on there. Being as though I have no electricity."

I laughed, and then wondered if I should have laughed at his self-deprecating comment.

We spent the rest of the bus ride talking about you, Ellen. When he made that comment about being bored, I asked him if he ever watched your show. He said he'd like to because he thinks you're funny, but a TV would require electricity. Another comment I wasn't sure if I should have laughed at.

I told him he could watch your show with me after school. I always record it on the DVR and watch it while I do my chores. I figured I could just keep the front door dead bolted, and if my parents got home early, I'd just have Atlas run out the back door.

I didn't see him again until the ride home today. He didn't sit by me this time because Katie got on the bus before him and sat next to me. I wanted to ask her to move, but then she'd think I had a crush on Atlas. Katie would have a field day with that one, so I just let her stay in my seat.

Atlas was at the front of the bus, so he got off before I did. He just kind of awkwardly stood there at the bus stop and waited for me to get off. When I did, he opened his backpack and handed me the bag of tools. He didn't say anything about my invitation to watch

TV from earlier this morning, so I just acted like it was a given.

"Come on," I told him. He followed me inside and I locked the dead bolt. "If my parents come home early, run out the back door and don't let them see you."

He nodded. "Don't worry. I will," he said, with kind of a laugh.

I asked him if he wanted anything to drink and he said sure. I made us a snack and brought our drinks to the living room. I sat down on the couch and he sat down in my dad's chair. I turned on your show and that's about all that happened. We didn't talk much, because I fast-forwarded through all the commercials. But I did notice he laughed at all the right times. I think good comedic timing is one of the most important things about a person's personality. Every time he laughed at your jokes, it made me feel better about sneaking him into my house. I don't know why. Maybe because if he's actually someone I could be friends with, it'd make me feel less guilty.

He left right after your show was over. I wanted to ask him if he needed to use our shower again, but that would have cut it real close to time for my parents getting home. The last thing I wanted was for him to have to run out of the shower and across my backyard naked.

Then again, that'd be kind of hilarious and awesome.

—Lily

Dear Ellen,

Come on, woman. Reruns? A full week of reruns? I get that you need time off, but let me make a suggestion. Instead of recording one show a day, you should record two. That way you'll get twice as much done in half the time, and we'd never have to sit through reruns.

I say "we" because I'm referring to Atlas and me. He's become my regular Ellen*-watching partner. I think he might love you as* *much as I do, but I'll never tell him I write to you on a daily basis. That might seem a little too fan-girl.*

He's been living in that house for two weeks now. He's taken a few more showers at my house and I give him food every time he visits. I even wash his clothes for him while he's here after school. He keeps apologizing to me, like he's a burden. But honestly, I love it. He keeps my mind off things and I actually look forward to spending time with him after school every day.

Dad got home late tonight, which means he went to the bar after work. Which means he's probably going to instigate a fight with my mother. Which means he'll probably do something stupid again.

I swear, sometimes I get so mad at her for staying with him. I know I'm only fifteen and probably don't understand all the reasons she chooses to stay, but I refuse to let her use me as her excuse. I don't care if she's too poor to leave him and we'd have to move into a crappy apartment and eat ramen noodles until I graduate. That would be better than this.

I can hear him yelling at her right now. Sometimes when he gets like this, I walk into the living room, hoping it'll calm him down. He doesn't like to hit her when I'm in the room. Maybe I should go try that.

—Lily

Dear Ellen,

If I had access to a gun or knife right now, I'd kill him.

As soon as I walked into the living room, I saw him push her down. They were standing in the kitchen and she'd grabbed his arm, trying to calm him down, and he backhanded her and knocked her straight to the floor. I'm pretty sure he was about to kick her, but he saw me walk into the living room and he stopped. He muttered something under his breath to her and then walked to their bedroom and slammed the door.

I rushed to the kitchen and tried to help her, but she never wants me to see her like this. She waved me away and said, "I'm fine, Lily. I'm fine, we just got into a stupid fight."

She was crying and I could already see the redness on her cheek from where he hit her. When I walked closer to her, wanting to make sure she was okay, she turned her back to me and gripped the counter. "I said I'm fine, Lily. Go back to your room."

I ran back down the hallway, but I didn't go back to my room. I ran straight out the back door and across the backyard. I was so mad at her for being short with me. I didn't even want to be in the same house as either of them, and even thought it was dark already, I went over to the house Atlas was staying in and I knocked on the door.

I could hear him moving inside, like he accidentally knocked something over. "It's me. Lily," I whispered. A few seconds later the back door opened and he looked behind me, then to the left and right of me. It wasn't until he looked at my face that he saw I was crying.

"You okay?" he asked, stepping outside. I used my shirt to wipe away my tears, and noticed he came outside instead of inviting me in. I sat down on the porch step and he sat down next to me.

"I'm fine," I said. "I'm just mad. Sometimes I cry when I get mad."

He reached over and tucked my hair behind my ear. I liked it when he did that and I suddenly wasn't nearly as mad anymore. Then he put his arm around me and pulled me to him so that my head was resting on his shoulder. I don't know how he calmed me down without even talking, but he did. Some people just have a calming presence about them and he's one of those people. Completely opposite of my father.

We sat like that for a while, until I saw my bedroom light turn on.

"You should go," he whispered. We could both see my mom standing in my bedroom looking for me. It wasn't until that moment that I realized what a perfect view he has of my bedroom.

As I walked back home, I tried to think about the entire time Atlas has been in that house. I tried to recall if I'd walked around after dark with the light on at night, because all I normally wear in my room at night is a T-shirt.

Here's what's crazy about that, Ellen: I was kind of hoping I had.

—Lily

I close the journal when the pain pills start to kick in. I'll read more tomorrow. *Maybe.* Reading about the things my dad used to do to my mom kind of puts me in a bad mood.

Reading about Atlas kind of puts me in a *sad* mood.

I try to fall asleep and think about Ryle, but the whole situation with him kind of makes me mad *and* sad.

Maybe I'll just think about Allysa, and how happy I am that she showed up today. I could use a friend—not to mention help—during these next few months. I have a feeling it's going to be more stressful than I bargained for.

Chapter Five

Ryle was correct. It only took a few days for my ankle to feel good enough that I could walk on it again. I waited a full week before attempting to leave my apartment, though. The last thing I need is to reinjure it.

Of course the first place I went was to my floral shop. Allysa was there when I arrived today, and to say I was shocked when I walked through the front doors is an understatement. It looked like a totally different building than the one I bought. There's still a ton of work that needs to be done, but she and Marshall had gotten rid of all the stuff we marked as trash. Everything else had been organized into piles. The windows had been washed, the floors had been mopped. She even had the area where I plan to put an office cleaned out.

I helped her for a few hours today, but she wouldn't let me do much that required walking at first, so I mostly drew out plans for the store. We picked out paint colors and set a goal date to open the store that's approximately fifty-four days from now. After she left, I spent the next few hours doing all the stuff she wouldn't let me do while she was there. It felt good to be back. But *Jesus Christ*, I'm tired.

Which is why I'm debating on whether or not to get up from the couch and answer the knock at my front door. Lucy is at Alex's again tonight and I just spoke to my mother five minutes ago on the phone, so I know it isn't either of them.

I walk to the door and check the peephole before opening it. I don't recognize him at first, because his head is down, but then he looks up and to the right and my heart freaks the hell out!

What is he doing here?

Ryle knocks again, and I try to brush my hair out of my face and smooth it down with my hands, but it's a lost cause. I worked my ass off today and I look like shit, so unless I have half an hour to take a shower, put on makeup, and throw on clothes before I open the door, he'll pretty much have to deal with me as is.

I open the door and his immediate reaction confuses me.

"Jesus Christ," he says, dropping his head against my door frame. He's panting like he's been working out, and that's when I notice that he doesn't look to be any more rested or clean than I am. He's got a couple of days' worth of stubble on his face—something I've never seen on him before—and his hair isn't styled like it usually is. It's a little erratic, like the look in his eye. "Do you have any idea how many doors I've knocked on to find you?"

I shake my head, because I don't. But now that he mentions it—*how in the hell does he know where I live?*

"Twenty-nine," he says. Then he holds up his hands and repeats the numbers with his fingers while he whispers, "*Two . . . nine.*"

I let my gaze drop down to his clothes. He's in scrubs, and I absolutely *hate* that he's in scrubs right now. *Holy hell. So* much better than the onesie and *way* better than the Burberry.

"Why did you knock on twenty-nine doors?" I ask with a tilt of my head.

"You never told me which apartment was yours," he says, matter-of-factly. "You said you lived in this building, but I couldn't remember if you even said which floor. And for the record, I almost started with the third floor. I would have been here an hour ago if I went with my gut instinct."

"Why *are* you here?"

He runs his hands down his face and then points over my shoulder. "Can I come in?"

I glance over my shoulder and then open the door farther. "I guess. If you tell me what you want."

He walks inside and I close the door behind us. He glances around, wearing his stupid hot scrubs, and puts his hands on his hips as he faces me. He looks a little disappointed, but I'm not sure if it's in me or himself.

"There's a really big naked truth coming, okay?" he says. "Brace yourself."

I fold my arms over my chest and watch as he inhales a breath, preparing to speak.

"These next couple of months are the most important months in my entire career. I have to be focused. I'm closing in on the end of my residency, and then I'll have to sit for my exams." He's pacing my living room, talking frantically with his hands. "But for the past week, I haven't been able to get you out of my head. I don't know why. At work, at home. All I can think about is how crazy it feels when I'm near you, and I need you to make it stop, Lily." He stops pacing and faces me. "*Please* make it stop. Just once—that's all it'll take. I swear."

My fingers are digging into the skin of my arms as I watch him. He's still panting a little, and his eyes are still frantic, but he's looking at me pleadingly.

"When is the last time you've had sleep?" I ask him.

He rolls his eyes like he's frustrated that I'm not getting it. "I just got off a forty-eight-hour shift," he says dismissively. "*Focus*, Lily."

I nod and replay his words in my head. If I didn't know better . . . I'd almost think he was . . .

I inhale a calming breath. "Ryle," I say carefully. "Did you seriously just knock on twenty-nine doors so you could tell me that the thought of me is making your life hell and I should have sex with you so that you'll never have to think of me again? Are you *kidding* me right now?"

He folds his lips together and, after about five seconds of thought, he slowly nods his head. "Well . . . yeah, but . . . it sounds way worse when you say it."

I release an exasperated laugh. "That's because it's ridiculous, Ryle."

He bites his bottom lip and looks around the room, like he suddenly wants to escape. I open the door and motion for him to walk out. He doesn't. His eyes fall to my foot. "Your ankle looks good," he says. "How does it feel?"

I roll my eyes. "Better. I was able to help Allysa at the store for the first time today."

He nods and then makes like he's walking toward the door to leave. But as soon as he reaches me, he spins toward me and slaps his palms against the door on either side of my head. I gasp at both his proximity and his persistence. "Please?" he says.

I shake my head, even though my body is starting to trade sides and beg my mind to cave to him.

"I'm really good at it, Lily," he says with a grin. "You'll barely even have to do any work."

I try not to laugh, but his determination is as endearing as it is annoying. "Goodnight, Ryle."

His head drops between his shoulders and he shakes it back and forth. He pushes off the door and stands up straight. He half-turns, heading for the hallway, but then suddenly drops to his knees in front of me. He wraps his arms around my waist. "Please, Lily," he says through self-deprecating laughter. "*Please* have sex with me." He's looking up at me with puppy dog eyes and a pathetic, hopeful grin. "I want you so, so bad and I swear, once you have sex with me you'll never hear from me again. I promise."

There's something about a neurosurgeon *literally* on his knees begging for sex that does me in. *That's pretty pathetic.*

"Get *up*," I say, pushing his arms away from me. "You're embarrassing yourself."

He slowly stands up, dragging his hands up the door on either side of me until he has me caged in between his arms. "Is that a yes?" His chest is barely touching mine and I hate how good it feels to be wanted this much. I should be turned off by it, but I can hardly breathe when I look at him. Especially when he has this suggestive smile on his face.

"I don't feel sexy right now, Ryle. I worked all day, I'm exhausted, I smell like sweat and probably taste like dust. If you give me a little while to shower first, I might feel sexy enough to have sex with you."

He's nodding feverishly before I'm even finished speaking. "Shower. Take all the time you need. I'll wait."

I push him away from me and close the front door. He follows me to the bedroom and I tell him to wait on the bed for me.

Luckily, I cleaned my bedroom last night. Normally I have clothes lying around everywhere, books piled up on my nightstand, shoes and bras that don't quite make it to my closet. But tonight it's clean. My bed is even made up, complete with the ugly, quilted throw pillows my grandmother passed down to every person in our family.

I make a quick glance around the room, just to make sure nothing embarrassing will catch his eye. He takes a seat on my bed and I watch as he scans the room. I stand in the doorway to my bathroom and try to give him one last out.

"You say this will make it stop, but I'm warning you right now, Ryle. I'm like a drug. If you have sex with me tonight, it's only going to make things worse for you. But once is all you're getting. I refuse to become one of the many girls you use to—how did you word it that night? *Satisfy* your *needs*?"

He leans back on his elbows. "You aren't that kind of girl, Lily. And I'm not the kind of guy who needs someone more than once. We have nothing to worry about."

I close the door behind me, wondering how in the hell this guy talked me into this.

It's the scrubs. The scrubs are my weakness. It has nothing to do with him.

I wonder if there's a way he could leave them on during the sex?

• • •

I've never taken more than half an hour to get ready, but it's almost an hour before I'm finished in the bathroom. I shaved more parts of me than was probably necessary, and then spent a good twenty minutes having a freak-out, and had to talk myself out of opening the door and telling him to leave. But now that my hair is dry and I'm cleaner than I've ever been, I think I might be able to do this. I can totally have a one-night stand. I'm twenty-three years old.

I open the door and he's still there on my bed. I'm a little disappointed to see that his scrub top is on the floor, but I don't see his pants, so he must still be wearing them. He's under the covers, though, so I can't tell.

I close the door behind me and wait for him to roll over and look at me, but he doesn't. I take a few steps closer, and that's when I notice he's snoring.

Not just a light—*oh I just fell asleep*—snore. It's a middle of REM sleep kind of snore.

"Ryle?" I whisper. He doesn't even budge when I shake him.

You've got to be kidding me.

I drop down onto the bed, not even caring if I wake him. I just spent an entire hour getting ready for him after busting my ass today, and this is how he treats this night?

I can't be mad at him, though, especially seeing how peaceful he looks. I can't imagine working a forty-eight-hour shift. Plus, my bed is really comfortable. It's so comfortable, it could make a person fall right back to sleep after a full night of rest. *I should have warned him about that.*

I check the time on my phone and it's almost 10:30 p.m. I put the phone on silent and then lie down next to him. His phone is on the pillow next to his head, so I grab it and swipe up the camera option. I hold his phone above us and make sure my cleavage looks good and pushed together. I snap a picture so he'll at least see what he missed out on.

I turn off the light and laugh to myself, because I'm falling asleep next to a half-naked man that I've never even kissed.

• • •

I can feel his fingers trailing up my arm before I even open my eyes. I force back a tired smile and pretend I'm still sleeping. His fingers trail over my shoulder and stop at my collarbone, just before they reach my neck. I have a small tattoo there that I got in college. It's a simple outline of a heart that's slightly open at the top. I can feel his fingers circle around the tattoo, and then he leans forward and presses his lips against it. I squeeze my eyes shut even tighter.

"Lily," he whispers, wrapping an arm around my waist. I moan a little, trying to wake up, and then roll onto my back so that I can look up at him. When I open my eyes, he's staring down at me. I can tell by the way the sunlight shines through my windows and across his face that it's not even seven a.m. yet.

"I am the most despicable man you've ever met. Am I right?"

I laugh, and nod a little. "Pretty damn close."

He smiles and then brushes my hair off my face. He leans forward and presses his lips to my forehead, and I hate that he just did that. Now *I'll* be the one plagued with sleepless nights, because I want to put this memory on repeat.

"I have to go," he says. "I'm really late. But one—I'm sorry. Two—I'll never do this again. This is the last you'll hear from me, I promise. And three—I'm *really* sorry. You have no idea."

I force a smile, but I want to frown because I absolutely hated his number two. I actually don't mind if he tries this again, but then I remind myself that we want two different things from life. And it's good that he fell asleep and we never even kissed, because if I would have had sex with him while he was wearing scrubs, I would have been the one showing up at his door on my knees, begging for more.

This is good. Rip the Band-Aid off and let him leave.

"Have a nice life, Ryle. I wish you all the success in the world."

He doesn't respond to my goodbye. He silently stares down at me with somewhat of a frown, and then says, "Yeah. You too, Lily."

Then he rolls away from me and stands up. I can't even look at him right now, so I roll onto my side so that my back is to him. I listen as he puts his shoes on and then reaches for his phone. There's a long pause before he moves again, and I know it's because he was staring at me. I squeeze my eyes shut until I hear the slam of the front door.

My face immediately grows warm, and I refuse to allow myself to mope. I force myself off the bed. I have work to do. I can't be upset that I'm not enough to make a guy want to remap all of his life goals.

Besides, I have my *own* life goals to worry about now. And I'm really excited about them. So much so, that I really don't have time for a guy in my life, anyway.

No time.

Nope.

Busy girl, here.

I am a brave and bold businesswoman with zero fucks to give for men in scrubs.

Chapter Six

It's been fifty-three days since Ryle walked out of my apartment that morning. Which means it's been fifty-three days since I've heard from him.

But that's okay, because for the last fifty-three days, I've been too busy to really give him much thought as I prepared for this moment.

"Ready?" Allysa says.

I nod, and she flips the sign to *Open* and we both hug and squeal like little kids.

We rush around the counter and wait for our first customer. It's a soft opening, so I haven't really done a marketing push yet, but we just want to make sure there aren't any kinks before our grand opening.

"It's really pretty in here," Allysa says, admiring our hard work. I look around us, bursting with pride. Of course I want to succeed, but at this point I'm not even sure if that matters. I had a dream and I busted my ass to make it come true. Whatever happens after today is just icing on the cake.

"It smells so good in here," I say. "I *love* this smell."

I don't know if we'll get any customers today, but we're both acting like this is the best thing that's ever happened to us, so I don't think that matters. Besides, Marshall will come in at some point today and my mother will come in after she gets off work. That's two customers for sure. That's plenty.

Allysa squeezes my arm when the front door begins to open. I suddenly grow a little panicked, because what if something goes wrong?

And then I do panic, because something just went wrong. *Terribly* wrong. My very first customer is none other than Ryle Kincaid.

He stops when the door closes behind him and he looks around in awe. "What?" he says, turning in a circle. "How in the . . . ?" He looks over at me and Allysa. "This is incredible. It doesn't even look like the same building!"

Okay, maybe I'm fine with him being the first customer.

It takes him a few minutes to actually make it to the counter because he can't stop touching things and looking at things. When he finally does reach us, Allysa runs around the counter and hugs him. "Isn't it beautiful?" she says. She waves her hand in my direction. "It was all her idea. All of it. I just helped with the dirty work."

Ryle laughs. "I find it hard to believe that your Pinterest skills didn't play a little part."

I nod. "She's being modest. Her skills were half of what brought this vision to life."

Ryle smiles at me and it might as well have been a knife to the chest, because *ouch*.

He slaps his hands on the counter and says, "Am I the first official customer?"

Allysa hands him one of our flyers. "You have to actually buy something to be considered a customer."

Ryle glances over the flyer and then sets it back down on

the counter. He walks to one of the displays and grabs a vase full of purple lilies. "I want these," he says, setting them on the counter.

I smile, wondering if he realizes he just picked lilies. *Kind of ironic.*

"Do you want us to deliver them somewhere?" Allysa says.

"You guys deliver?"

"Allysa and I don't," I reply. "We have a delivery driver on standby. We weren't sure if we'd actually need him today."

"Are you actually buying these for a girl?" Allysa asks. She's just prying into her brother's love life like a sister would naturally do, but I catch myself stepping closer to her so I can hear his answer better.

"I am," he says. His eyes meet mine and he adds, "I don't think about her very much, though. Hardly ever."

Allysa grabs a card and slides it to him. "Poor girl," she says. "You are such a dick." She taps her finger on the card. "Write your message to her on the front and the address you want them delivered to on the back."

I watch him as he bends over the card and writes on both sides. I know I don't have a right, but I'm brimming with jealousy.

"Are you bringing this girl to my birthday party Friday?" Allysa asks him.

I watch his reaction closely. He just shakes his head and without looking up he says, "No. Are you going, Lily?"

I can't tell by his voice alone if he's hoping I'll be there or hoping I won't. Considering the stress I seem to cause him, I'm guessing it's the latter.

"I haven't decided yet."

"She'll be there," Allysa says, answering for me. She looks at me and narrows her eyes. "You're coming to my party whether you like it or not. If you don't show up, I'll quit."

When Ryle is finished writing, he tucks the card into the envelope attached to the flowers. Allysa rings up his total and he pays in cash. He looks at me while he's counting out his money. "Lily, do you know that it's custom for a new business to frame the first dollar they make?"

I nod. *Of course* I know that. He *knows* I know that. He's just rubbing it in my face that his dollar will be the one framed on my wall for the life of this store. I almost encourage Allysa to give him a refund, but this is business. I have to leave my wounded pride out of it.

Once he has his receipt in hand, he taps his fist on the counter to get my attention. He dips his head a little and, with a genuine smile, he says, "Congratulations, Lily."

He turns and walks out of the store. As soon as the door closes behind him, Allysa is grabbing for the envelope. "Who in the hell is he sending flowers to?" she says as she pulls the card out. "Ryle doesn't *send* flowers."

She reads the front of the card out loud. "Make it stop."

Holy shit.

She stares at it for a moment, repeating the phrase. "*Make it stop?* What in the hell does that even *mean*?" she asks.

I can't take it another second. I grab the card from her and flip it over. She leans over and reads the back of it with me.

"He is such an idiot," she says with a laugh. "He wrote the address to our floral shop on the back." She takes the card out of my hands.

Wow.

Ryle just bought me flowers. Not just *any* flower. He bought me a bouquet of lilies.

Allysa picks up her phone. "I'll text him and tell him he screwed up." She shoots him a text and then laughs as she stares at the flowers. "How can a neurosurgeon be such an *idiot*?"

I can't stop grinning. I'm relieved she's staring at the flowers and not at me or she may put two and two together. "I'll keep them in my office until we figure out where he intended for them to go." I scoop up the vase and whisk away my flowers.

Chapter Seven

"Stop fidgeting," Devin says.

"I'm not fidgeting."

He loops his arm through mine as he walks me toward the elevator. "Yes, you are. And if you pull that top up over your cleavage one more time, it'll defeat the whole purpose of your little black dress." He grabs my top and yanks it back down, and then proceeds to reach inside to adjust my bra.

"Devin!" I slap his hand away and he laughs.

"Relax, Lily. I've touched way better boobs than yours and I'm still gay."

"Yeah, but I bet those boobs were attached to people you probably hang out with more than once every six months."

Devin laughs. "True, but that's half your fault. You're the one who left us high and dry to play with flowers."

Devin was one of my favorite people at the marketing firm I worked at, but we weren't close enough to where we actively became friends outside of work. He stopped by the floral shop this afternoon and Allysa took to him almost immediately. She begged him to come to the party with me and since I didn't really want to show up alone, I ended up begging him to come, too.

I smooth my hands over my hair and try to catch a glimpse of my reflection in the elevator walls.

"Why are you so nervous?" he asks.

"I'm not nervous. I just hate showing up to places where I don't know anyone."

Devin smirks knowingly and then says, "What's his name?"

I release a pent-up breath. *Am I that transparent?* "Ryle. He's a neurosurgeon. And he wants to have sex with me really, really bad."

"How do you know he wants to have sex with you?"

"Because he literally got down on his knees and said, '*Please, Lily. Please have sex with me.*'"

Devin raises an eyebrow. "He begged?"

I nod. "It wasn't as pathetic as it sounds. He's usually more composed."

The elevator dings and the doors begin to open. I can hear music pouring from down the hallway. Devin takes both of my hands in his and says, "So what's the plan? Do I need to make this guy jealous?"

"No," I say, shaking my head. "That wouldn't be right." But . . . Ryle does make it a point every time he sees me to tell me he hopes he never sees me again. "Maybe just a little?" I say, scrunching up my nose. "A smidge?"

Devin pops his jaw and says, "Consider it done." He puts his hand on my lower back as he walks me out of the elevator. There's only one visible door in the hallway, so we make our way over and ring the doorbell.

"Why is there only one door?" he says.

"She owns the whole top floor."

He chuckles. "And she works for *you*? Damn, your life just keeps getting more and more interesting."

The door begins to open, and I'm extremely relieved to

see Allysa standing in front of me. There's music and laughter pouring out of the apartment behind her. She's holding a champagne glass in one hand and a riding crop in the other. She sees me staring at the riding crop with a confused look on my face, so she tosses it over her shoulder and grabs my hand. "It's a long story," she says, laughing. "Come in, come in!"

She pulls me in and I squeeze Devin's hand and drag him behind me. She continues pulling us through a crowd of people until we reach the other side of the living room. "Hey!" she says, tugging on Marshall's arm. He turns around and smiles at me, then pulls me in for a hug. I glance behind him, and around us, but there's no sign of Ryle. *Maybe I got lucky and he got called in to work tonight.*

Marshall reaches out for Devin's hand and shakes it. "Hey, man! Good to meet you!"

Devin wraps an arm around my waist. "I'm Devin!" he yells over the music. "I'm Lily's sexual partner!"

I laugh and elbow him, then lean in to his ear. "That's Marshall. Wrong guy, but nice effort."

Allysa grabs my arm and starts to pull me away from Devin. Marshall begins speaking to him, and my hand is reaching out behind me as I'm being pulled in the opposite direction.

"You'll be fine!" Devin yells.

I follow Allysa into the kitchen, where she shoves a glass of champagne in my hand. "Drink," she says. "You deserve it!"

I take a sip of the champagne, but I can't even appreciate it now that I'm getting a look at her industrial-sized kitchen with two full stovetops and a fridge bigger than my apartment. "Holy shit," I whisper. "You actually *live* here?"

She giggles. "I know," she says. "And to think, I didn't even have to marry him for money. Marshall had seven bucks and drove a Ford Pinto when I fell in love with him."

"Doesn't he still drive a Ford Pinto?"

She sighs. "Yeah, but we have a lot of good memories in that car."

"Gross."

She wiggles her eyebrows. "So . . . Devin is cute."

"And probably more into Marshall than me."

"Ah, man," she says. "That's a bummer. I thought I was playing matchmaker when I invited him to the party tonight."

The kitchen door opens and Devin walks in. "Your husband is looking for you," he says to Allysa. She twirls her way out of the kitchen, giggling the whole time. "I really like her," Devin says.

"She's great, huh?"

He leans against the island and says, "So. I think I just met The Beggar."

My heart flutters down my chest. I think *The Neurosurgeon* has a better ring to it. I take another sip of my champagne. "How do you know it was him? Did he introduce himself?"

He shakes his head. "Nah, but he overheard Marshall introducing me to someone as '*Lily's date*.' I thought the look he gave me was going to set me on fire. That's why I came in here. I like you, but I'm not willing to die for you."

I laugh. "Don't worry, I'm sure that death glare he gave you was really his smile. They're superimposed most of the time."

The door swings open again and I immediately stiffen, but it's only a caterer. I sigh with relief. Devin says, "*Lily*," like my name is a disappointment.

"What?"

"You look like you're about to puke," he says, accusingly. "You really like him."

I roll my eyes. But then I let my shoulders drop and I fake cry. "I do, Devin. I do, I just don't *want* to."

He takes my glass of champagne and downs the remainder of it, then locks his arm in mine again. "Let's go mingle," he says, pulling me out of the kitchen against my will.

The room is even more crowded now. There have to be more than a hundred people here. I'm not even sure I know that many people.

We walk around and work the room. I stand back while Devin does most of the talking. He knows someone in common with every person he's met so far, and after about half an hour of following him around, I'm convinced he's made it a personal game to find someone in common with everyone here. The whole time I mingle with him, my attention is half on him and half on the room, searching for traces of Ryle. I don't see him anywhere and I begin to wonder if the guy Devin saw was even Ryle to begin with.

"Well, that's odd," a woman says. "What do you suppose it is?"

I look up and see that she's staring at a piece of art on the wall. It looks like a photograph blown up on canvas. I tilt my head to inspect it. The woman turns her nose up and says, "I don't know why anyone would bother turning that photograph into wall art. It's awful. It's so blurry, you can't even tell what it is." She walks away in a huff, and I'm relieved. I mean . . . it's a bit weird, but who am I to judge Allysa's taste?

"What do you think?"

His voice is low, deep, and *right* behind me. I close my eyes briefly and inhale a steadying breath before quietly exhaling, hoping he doesn't notice his voice has any effect on me whatsoever. "I like it. I'm not quite sure what it is, but it's interesting. Your sister has good taste."

He steps around me so that he's at my side, facing me. He takes a step closer until he's so close, he brushes my arm. "You brought a date?"

He's asking it like it's a casual question, but I know it isn't. When I fail to respond, he leans in until he's whispering in my ear. He repeats himself, but this time it isn't a question. "You brought a *date*."

I find the courage to look over at him and instantly wish I hadn't. He's in a black suit that makes the scrubs look like child's play. First I swallow the unexpected lump in my throat and then I say, "Is it a problem that I brought a date?" I look away from him and back at the photograph hanging on the wall. "I was trying to make things easier on you. You know. Just trying to *make it stop*."

He smirks and then downs the rest of his wine. "How *thoughtful* of you, Lily." He tosses his empty wineglass toward a trash can in the corner of the room. He makes the shot, but the glass shatters when it hits the bottom of the empty container. I glance around me, but no one saw what just happened. When I look back at Ryle, he's halfway down a hallway. He disappears into a room and I stand here, looking at the picture again.

That's when I see it.

The picture is blurred, so it was hard to make out at first. But I can recognize that hair from anywhere. That's *my* hair. It's hard to miss, along with the marine-grade polymer lounge chair I'm lying on. *This is the picture he took on the rooftop the first night we met.* He must have had it blown up and distorted so no one would notice what it was. I bring my hand to my neck, because my blood feels like it's bubbling. *It's really warm in here.*

Allysa appears at my side. "It's weird, huh?" she says, looking at the picture.

I scratch at my chest. "It's really hot in here," I say. "Don't you think?"

She glances around the room. "Is it? I hadn't noticed, but I'm a little drunk. I'll tell Marshall to turn on the air."

She disappears again, and the more I stare at the picture, the angrier I get. The man has a picture of me hanging in the apartment. He bought me flowers. He's giving me attitude because I brought a date to his sister's party. He's acting like there's actually something between us, and we've never even kissed!

It all hits me at once. The anger . . . the irritation . . . the half glass of champagne I had in the kitchen. I'm so mad, I can't even think straight. If the guy wants to have sex with me so bad . . . he shouldn't have fallen asleep! If he doesn't want me to swoon, he shouldn't buy me flowers! He shouldn't hang cryptic pictures of me where he lives!

All I want is fresh air. I need fresh air. Luckily, I know just where to find it.

Moments later, I burst through the door to the rooftop.

There are stragglers from the party up here. Three of them, seated on the patio furniture. I ignore them and walk to the ledge with the good view and lean over it. I suck in several deep breaths and try to calm myself down. I want to go downstairs and tell him to make up his damn mind, but I know I need to have a clear head before I do that.

The air is cold, and for some reason, I blame that on Ryle. Everything is his fault tonight. *All of it.* Wars, famine, gun violence—it all somehow links back to Ryle.

"Can we have a few minutes alone?"

I spin around, and Ryle is standing near the other guests. Immediately, all three of them nod and begin to stand up to give us privacy. I hold up my hands and say, "Wait," but none of them look at me. "It's not necessary. Really, you don't have to leave."

Ryle stands stoically with his hands in his pockets while one of the guests mutters, "It's fine, we don't mind." They begin to file back down the stairwell. I roll my eyes and spin back toward the ledge once I'm alone with him.

"Does everyone always do what you say?" I ask, irritated.

He doesn't respond. His footsteps are slow and deliberate as he closes in on me. My heart begins to beat like it's on a speed-date, and I start scratching at my chest again.

"Lily," he says from behind me.

I turn around and grip the ledge behind me with both hands. His eyes journey down to my cleavage. As soon as they do, I yank at the top of my dress so he can't see it, and then I grip the ledge again. He laughs and takes another step closer. We're almost touching now, and my brain is mush. It's pathetic. I'm pathetic.

"I feel like you have a lot to say," he says. "So I'd like to give you the opportunity to speak your naked truth."

"Hah!" I say with a laugh. "Are you sure about that?"

He nods, so I prepare to let him have it. I push against his chest and make my way around him so that he's the one leaning against the ledge now.

"I can't tell what you *want*, Ryle! And every time I get to the point where I start to not give a shit, you show up again out of the blue! You show up at my work, you show up at my apartment door, you show up at parties, you . . ."

"I live here," he says, excusing the last one. That pisses me off even more. I clench my fists.

"Ugh! You're driving me crazy! Do you want me or do you *not*?"

He stands up straight and takes a step toward me. "Oh, I want you, Lily. Make no mistake about that. I just don't *want* to want you."

My whole body sighs at that comment. Partly out of frustration and partly because everything he says makes me shiver and I hate that I allow him to make me feel like this.

I shake my head. "You don't get it, do you?" I say, softening my voice. I feel too defeated right now to keep yelling at him. "I like you, Ryle. And knowing that you only want me for one night makes me really, *really* sad. And maybe if this were a few months ago, we could have had sex and it would have been fine. You would have walked away and I could have easily moved on with my life. But it's not a few months ago. You waited too long, and too many pieces of me are invested in you now, so please. Stop flirting with me. Stop hanging pictures of me in your apartment. And stop sending me flowers. Because when you do those things, it doesn't feel *good*, Ryle. It actually kind of hurts."

I feel deflated and exhausted and I'm ready to leave. He regards me silently, and I respectfully give him time to make his rebuttal. But he doesn't. He just turns around, leans over the ledge, and stares down at the street like he didn't hear a single word I said.

I walk across the roof and open the door, half expecting him to call out my name or ask me not to leave. I get all the way back to the apartment before I finally lose all hope of that happening. I push through the crowd and make it through three different rooms before I spot Devin. When he sees the look on my face, he just nods and begins to make his way across the room toward me.

"Ready to go?" he asks, looping his arm through mine.

I nod. "Yes. *So* ready."

We find Allysa in the main living room. I tell her and Marshall goodnight, using the excuse that I'm just exhausted from opening week and I'd like to get some sleep before work tomorrow. Allysa gives me a hug and walks us to the front door.

"I'll be back on Monday," she says to me, kissing me on the cheek.

"Happy birthday," I say to her. Devin opens the door, but right before we step into the hallway, I hear someone yell my name.

I turn around and Ryle is pushing through the crowd on the other side of the room. "Lily, wait!" he yells, still trying to make his way over to me. My heart is erratic. He's walking quickly, stepping around people, growing more frustrated with every person in his way. He finally reaches a break in the crowd and makes eye contact with me again. He holds my gaze as he marches toward me. He doesn't slow down. Allysa has to step out of his way as he walks straight up to me. At first, I think he might kiss me, or at least give a rebuttal to everything I said to him upstairs. But instead, he does something I'm not at all prepared for. He scoops me up into his arms.

"Ryle!" I yell, gripping him around the neck, afraid he might drop me. "Put me down!" He has an arm wrapped under my legs and one under my back.

"I need to borrow Lily for the night," he says to Devin. "That okay?"

I look at Devin and shake my head, wide-eyed. Devin just smirks and says, "Be my guest."

Traitor!

Ryle starts to turn and walk back toward the living room. I look at Allysa as I pass her. Her eyes are wide with confusion. "I'm going to kill your brother!" I yell at her.

Everyone in the entire room is staring now. I'm so embarrassed, I just press my face against Ryle's chest as he walks me down the hallway and into his bedroom. Once the door is shut behind us, he slowly lowers my feet back to the floor. I immediately start to yell at him and try to push him out of the way of the bedroom door, but he spins me and shoves me against the door, grabbing both of my wrists. He presses them against the wall above my head and says, "Lily?"

He's looking at me so intently, I stop trying to fight him off of me and I hold my breath. His chest is pressing against mine, my back is pressed to the door. And then his mouth is on mine. Warm pressure against my lips.

Despite the strength behind them, his lips are like silk. I'm shocked at the moan that rushes through me, and even more shocked when I part my lips and want more. His tongue slides against mine and he releases my wrists to grab my face. His kiss grows deeper and I grasp at his hair, pulling him closer, feeling the kiss in my entire body.

Both of us become a medley of moans and gasps as the kiss brings us over the edge, our bodies wanting more than our mouths can deliver. I feel his hands as he reaches down and grabs my legs, lifting me up and hooking them around his waist.

My God, this man can kiss. It's as if he takes kissing as seriously as he takes his profession. He begins to pull me away from the door when I'm hit with the realization that yes, his mouth is capable of a lot. But what his mouth has failed to do is respond to everything I told him upstairs.

For all I know, I've just given in. I'm giving him what he wants: a one-night stand. And that's the last thing he deserves right now.

I pull my mouth from his and push on his shoulders. "Put me down."

He keeps walking toward his bed, so I say it again. "Ryle, put me down right now."

He stops walking and lowers me to the floor. I have to back away and face the other direction to gather my thoughts. Looking at him while I still feel his lips on mine is more than I can deal with right now.

I feel his arms go around my waist, and he rests his

head on my shoulder. "I'm sorry," he whispers. He turns me around and brings a hand up to my face and brushes his thumb across my cheek. "It's my turn now, okay?"

I don't respond to his touch. I keep my arms folded across my chest and wait to hear what he has to say before I allow myself to respond to his touch.

"I had that picture made the day after I took it," he says. "It's been in my apartment for months now, because you were the most beautiful thing I'd ever seen and I wanted to look at it every single day."

Oh.

"And that night I showed up at your door? I went searching for you because no one in the history of my life has ever crawled under my skin and refused to leave like you did. I didn't know how to handle it. And the reason I sent you flowers this week is because I am really, really proud of you for following your dream. But if I sent you flowers every time I've had the urge to send you flowers, you wouldn't even be able to fit inside your apartment. Because that's how much I think about you. And yes, Lily. You're right. I'm hurting you, but *I'm* hurting, too. And until tonight . . . I didn't know why."

I have no idea how I even possibly find the strength to speak after that. "Why are you hurting?"

He drops his forehead to mine and says, "Because. I have no idea what I'm doing. You make me want to be a different person, but what if I don't know how to be what you need? This is all new to me and I want to prove to you that I want you for so much more than just one night."

He looks so vulnerable right now. I want to believe the

genuine look in his eye, but he's been so adamant since the day that I met him that he wants the exact opposite of what I want. And it terrifies me that I'll give in to him and he'll walk away.

"How do I prove myself to you, Lily? Tell me and I'll do it."

I don't know. I barely know the guy. I know him enough to know that sex with him won't be enough for me, though. But how do I know sex won't be the only thing he wants?

My eyes instantly lock with his. "Don't have sex with me."

He stares at me for a moment, completely unreadable. But then he starts to nod his head like he's finally getting it. "Okay," he says, still nodding. "Okay. I will not have sex with you, Lily Bloom."

He walks around me to his bedroom door and he locks it. He flips off the light, leaving only a lamp on, and then takes off his shirt as he walks toward me.

"What are you doing?"

He tosses his shirt on a chair and then slips off his shoes. "We're going to sleep."

I glance at his bed. Then at him. "Right now?"

He nods and walks over to me. In one swift movement, he lifts my dress up and over my head, until I'm standing in the middle of his bedroom floor in my bra and panties. I cover myself, but he doesn't even look twice. He pulls me toward the bed and lifts the covers for me to crawl in. As he's walking over to his side of the bed he says, "It's not like we haven't slept together before without having sex. Piece of cake."

I laugh. He reaches his dresser and plugs his phone in to a charger. I take a moment to skim his bedroom. This certainly isn't the type of spare bedroom I'm used to. Three of my bedrooms could fit in here. There's a couch against the other wall, a chair facing a television and a full office off the bedroom that looks complete with a floor-to-ceiling library. I'm still trying to see everything around me when the lamp goes off.

"Your sister is *really rich,*" I say as I feel him pull the covers over both of us. "What the hell does she do with the ten bucks an hour I pay her? Wipe her ass with it?"

He laughs and grabs my hand, sliding his fingers through mine. "She probably doesn't even cash the checks," he says. "Have you ever checked?"

I haven't. Now I'm curious.

"Goodnight, Lily," he says.

I can't stop smiling, because this is kind of ridiculous. And so great.

"Goodnight, Ryle."

• • •

I think I might be lost.

Everything is so white and so clean, it's blinding. I shuffle through one of the living rooms and try to find my way to the kitchen. I have no idea where my dress ended up last night, so I pulled on one of Ryle's shirts. It falls past my knees, and I wonder if he has to buy shirts that are too big for him just so they'll fit his arms.

There are too many windows and way too much sun, so I'm forced to shield my eyes as I go in search of coffee.

I push through the kitchen doors and find a coffeemaker. *Thank you, Jesus.*

I set it to brew and then go in search for a mug when

the kitchen door opens behind me. I spin around and I'm relieved to see that Allysa isn't always a perfect concoction of makeup and jewelry. Her hair is in a messy topknot and mascara is smeared down her cheeks. She points at the coffeemaker. "I'm gonna need me some of that," she says. She pulls herself up on the island and then slouches forward.

"Can I ask you a question?" I say.

She barely has the energy to nod.

I wave my hand around the kitchen. "How did this happen? How in the hell did your entire house become spotless between the party last night and me waking up just now? Did you stay up and clean?"

She laughs. "We have people for that," she says.

"People?"

She nods. "Yep. There are people for *everything*," she says. "You'd be surprised. Think of something. Anything. We probably have people for it."

"Groceries?"

"People," she says.

"Christmas décor?"

She nods. "People for that, too."

"What about birthday gifts? Like for family members?"

She grins. "Yep. *People*. Everyone in my family receives a gift and a card for every occasion and I never have to lift a fingcr."

I shake my head. "Wow. How long have you been this rich?"

"Three years," she says. "Marshall sold a few apps he developed to Apple for a lot of money. Every six months, he creates updates and sells those, too."

The coffee transitions into a slow drip, so I grab a mug and fill it up. "You want anything in yours?" I ask. "Or do you have people for that?"

She laughs. "Yes. I have you, and I'd like sugar, please."

I stir some sugar into her cup and walk it over to her, then pour myself a cup. It grows quiet for a while as I mix in creamer, waiting for her to say something about me and Ryle. The conversation is inevitable.

"Can we just get the awkwardness out of the way?" she says.

I sigh, relieved. "Please. I hate this." I face her and take a sip of my coffee. She sets hers down beside her and then grips the countertop.

"How did that even *happen*?"

I shake my head, trying my best not to smile like I'm love-struck. I don't want her to think I'm weak, or a fool for giving in to him. "We met before I knew you."

She tilts her head. "Wait," she says. "Before we got to know each other *better* or before we knew each other at *all*?"

"At all," I say. "We had a moment one night, about six months before I met you."

"A moment?" she says. "As in . . . a one-night stand?"

"No," I say. "No, we never even kissed until last night. I don't know, I can't explain it. We just had this sort of flirtation thing going on for a really long time and it finally came to a head last night. That's all."

She picks up her coffee again and takes a slow drink from it. She stares down at the floor for a while and I can't help but notice she looks a little sad.

"Allysa? You're not mad at me, are you?"

She immediately shakes her head. "No, Lily. I just . . ." She sets down her coffee cup again. "I just know my brother. And I love him. I really do. But . . ."

"But what?"

Allysa and I both look in the direction of the voice. Ryle is standing in the doorway with his arms folded across his chest. He's wearing a pair of gray jogging pants that are barely hanging on to his hips. No shirt. *I'll be adding this outfit to all the other ones I've catalogued in my head.*

Ryle pushes off the door and makes his way into the kitchen. He walks over to me and takes my cup of coffee out of my hands. He leans in and kisses me on the forehead, then takes a drink as he leans against the counter.

"I didn't mean to interrupt," he says to Allysa. "By all means, continue your conversation."

Allysa rolls her eyes and says, "Stop."

He hands me back my cup of coffee and turns around to grab his own mug. He begins to pour from the pot. "It sounded to me like you were about to give Lily a warning. I'm just curious as to what you have to say."

Allysa hops off the counter and carries her mug to the sink. "She's my friend, Ryle. You don't have the best track record when it comes to relationships." She washes out the mug and then leans her hip into the sink, facing us. "As her *friend*, I have the right to give her my opinion when it comes to the guys she dates. That's what friends *do*."

I'm suddenly feeling uncomfortable as the tension grows thicker between the two of them. Ryle doesn't even take a drink of his coffee. He walks toward Allysa and pours it out in the sink. He's standing right in front of her, but she won't even look at him. "Well, as your *brother*, I would hope you had a little more faith in me than you do. That's what *siblings* do."

He walks out of the kitchen, shoving the door open. When he's gone, Allysa takes a deep breath. She shakes her head and pulls her hands up to her face. "Sorry about that," she says, forcing a smile. "I need to shower."

"You don't have people for that?"

She laughs as she exits the kitchen. I wash my mug in the sink and head back to Ryle's bedroom. When I open the door, he's sitting on the couch, scrolling through his phone. He doesn't look up at me when I walk in and for a second, I think he might be mad at me, too. But then he tosses his phone aside and leans back into the couch.

"Come here," he says.

He grabs my hand and pulls me down on top of him so that I'm straddling him. He brings my mouth to his and kisses me so hard, it makes me wonder if he's trying to prove his sister wrong.

Ryle pulls away from my mouth and slowly rakes his eyes down my body. "I like you in my clothes."

I smile. "Well I have to get to work, so unfortunately, I can't keep them on."

He brushes the hair from my face and says, "I have a really important surgery coming up that I need to prepare for. Which means I probably won't see you for a few days."

I try to hide my disappointment, but I have to get used to it if he really wants to try and make something work between us. He's already warned me that he works too much. "I'm busy, too. Grand opening is on Friday."

He says, “Oh, I’ll see you before Friday. Promise.”

I don’t hide my grin this time. “Okay.”

He kisses me again, this time for a solid minute. He starts to lower me to the couch, but then he shoves away from me and says. “Nope. I like you too much to make out with you.”

I lie down on the couch and watch him get dressed for work.

To my enjoyment, he puts on scrubs.

Chapter Eight

"We need to talk," Lucy says.

She's sitting on the couch, mascara streaked down her cheeks.

Oh, shit.

I drop my purse and rush over to her. As soon as I sit down next to her, she starts crying.

"What's wrong? Did Alex break up with you?"

She starts shaking her head and then I really start freaking out. *Please don't say cancer.* I grab her hand, and that's when I see it. "Lucy! You're engaged?"

She nods. "I'm sorry. I know we still have six months left on the lease, but he wants me to move in with him."

I stare at her for a minute. *Is that why she's crying? Because she wants out of her lease?* She reaches for a tissue and starts dabbing at her eyes. "I feel awful, Lily. You're going to be all alone. I'm moving and you won't have *anyone*."

What the . . .

"Lucy? Um . . . I'll be fine. I promise."

She looks up at me with hope in her expression. "Really?"

Why in the world does she have this impression of me? I nod again. "Yes. I'm not mad, I'm happy for you."

She throws her arms around me and hugs me. "Oh, thank you, Lily!" She starts giggling in between bouts of tears. When she releases me, she jumps up and says, "I have to go tell Alex!

He was so worried you wouldn't let me out of my lease!" She grabs her purse and shoes and disappears out the front door.

I lie back on the couch and stare up at the ceiling. *Did she just play me?*

I start laughing, because until this moment, I had no idea how much I've been waiting for this to happen. *The whole place to myself!*

What's even better, is when I do decide to have sex with Ryle, we can have it over here all the time and not have to worry about being quiet.

The last time I spoke to Ryle was when I left his apartment on Saturday. We agreed on a trial run. No commitments yet. Just a relationship feeler to see if it's something we both want. It's now Monday night and I'm a little disappointed I haven't heard from him. I gave him my phone number before we parted Saturday, but I don't really know texting etiquette, especially for *trial runs*.

Regardless, I'm not texting him first.

I decide to occupy my time with teenage angst and Ellen DeGeneres, instead. I'm not about to wait around to be beckoned by a guy I'm not even having sex with. But I don't know why I assume that reading about the *first* guy I had sex with will somehow get my mind off the guy I'm *not* having sex with.

Dear Ellen,

My great-grandfather's name is Ellis. My entire life, I thought that was a really cool name for such an old guy. After he died, I was reading the obituary. Would you believe that Ellis wasn't even his real name? His real name was Levi Sampson and I had no idea.

I asked my grandmother where the name Ellis came from. She said his initials were L.S. and everyone called him by his initials for so long, they just started sounding them out over the years.

Which is why they referred to him as Ellis.

I was looking at your name just now and it made me think of that. Ellen. Is that even your real name? You could be just like my great-grandfather and using your initials as a disguise.

L.N.

I'm onto you, "Ellen."

Speaking of names, do you think Atlas is a weird name? It is, isn't it?

Yesterday while I was watching your show with him, I asked him where he got his name from. He said he didn't know. Without even thinking, I told him he should ask his mother why she named him that. He just looked over at me for a second and said, "It's a little too late for that."

I don't know what he meant by that. I don't know if his mom died, or if she gave him up for adoption. We've been friends for a few weeks now and I still don't really know anything about him or why he doesn't have a place to live. I would just ask him, but I'm not sure if he really trusts me yet. He seems to have trust issues and I guess I can't blame him.

I'm worried about him. It started getting really cold this week and it's supposed to be even colder next week. If he doesn't have electricity, that means he doesn't have a heater. I hope he at least has blankets. Do you know how awful I would feel if he froze to death? Pretty freaking awful, Ellen.

I'll find some blankets this week and give them to him.

—Lily

Dear Ellen,

It's going to start snowing soon so I decided to harvest my garden today. I had already pulled the radishes so I just wanted to put some mulch and compost down, which wouldn't have taken me long, but Atlas insisted on helping.

He asked me a lot of questions about gardening and I liked that he seemed interested in my interests. I showed him how to lay the compost and mulch to cover the ground so that the snow wouldn't do too much damage. My garden is small compared to most gardens. Maybe ten feet by twelve feet. But it's all my dad will let me use of the backyard.

Atlas covered the whole thing while I sat cross-legged in the grass and watched him. I wasn't being lazy, he just took over and wanted to do it so I let him. I can tell he's a hard worker. I wonder if maybe keeping himself busy takes his mind off of things and that's why he always wants to help me so much.

When he was finished, he walked over and dropped down next to me on the grass.

"What made you want to grow things?" he asked.

I glanced over at him and he was sitting cross-legged, looking at me curiously. I realized in that moment that he's probably the best friend I've ever had, and we barely know anything about each other. I have friends at school, but they're never allowed to come over to my house for obvious reasons. My mother is always worried something might happen with my father and word might get out about his temper. I also never really get to go to other people's houses but I'm not sure why. Maybe my father doesn't want me staying over at friends' houses because I might witness how a good husband is supposed to treat his wife. He probably wants me to believe the way he treats my mother is normal.

Atlas is the first friend I've ever had that's ever been inside my house. He's also the first friend to know how much I like to garden. And now he's the first friend to ever ask me why I garden.

I reached down and pulled at a weed and started tearing it into little pieces while I thought about his question.

"When I was ten, my mother got me a subscription to a website called Seeds Anonymous," I said. "Every month I would get an unmarked package of seeds in the mail with instructions on how to plant them and care for them. I wouldn't know what I was growing until it came up out of the ground. Every day after school I'd run straight to the backyard to see the progress. It gave me something to look forward to. Growing things felt like a reward."

I could feel Atlas staring at me when he asked, "A reward for what?"

I shrugged. "For loving my plants the right way. Plants reward you based on the amount of love you show them. If you're cruel to them or neglect them, they give you nothing. But if you care for them and love them the right way, they reward you with gifts in the form of vegetables or fruits or flowers." I looked down at the weed I was tearing apart in my hands and there was barely an inch left of it. I wadded it up between my fingers and flicked it.

I didn't want to look over at Atlas because I could still feel him staring, so instead, I just stared out over my mulch-covered garden.

"We're just alike," he said.

My eyes flicked to his. "Me and you?"

He shook his head. "No. Plants and humans. Plants need to be loved the right way in order to survive. So do humans. We rely on our parents from birth to love us enough to keep us alive. And if our parents show us the right kind of love, we turn out as better humans overall. But if we're neglected . . ."

His voice grew quiet. Almost sad. He wiped his hands on his knees, trying to get some of the dirt off. "If we're neglected, we end up homeless and incapable of anything meaningful."

His words made my heart feel like the mulch he had just laid out. I didn't even know what to say to that. Does he really think that about himself?

He acted like he was about to get up, but before he did I said his name.

He sat back down in the grass. I pointed at the row of trees that lined the fence to the left of the yard. "You see that tree over there?" In the middle of the row of trees was an oak tree that stood taller than all the rest of the trees.

Atlas glanced over at it and dragged his eyes all the way up to the top of the tree.

"It grew on its own," I said. "Most plants do need a lot of care to survive. But some things, like trees, are strong enough to do it by just relying on themselves and nobody else."

I had no idea if he knew what I was trying to say without me coming out and saying it. But I just wanted him to know that I thought he was strong enough to survive whatever was going on in his life. I didn't know him well, but I could tell he was resilient. Way more than I would ever be if I were in his situation.

His eyes were glued to the tree. It was a long time before he even blinked. When he finally did, he just nodded a little and looked down at the grass. I thought with the way his mouth twitched that he was about to frown, but instead he actually smiled a little.

Seeing that smile made my heart feel like I had just startled it right out of a dead sleep.

"We're just alike," he said, repeating himself from earlier.

"Plants and humans?" I asked.

He shook his head. "No. Me and you."

I gasped, Ellen. I hope he didn't notice, but I definitely sucked in a rush of air. Because what the heck was I supposed to say to that?

I just sat there, really awkward and quiet until he stood up. He turned like he was about to walk home.

"Atlas, wait."

He glanced back down at me. I pointed at his hands and said, "You might want to take a quick shower before you go back. Compost is made from cow manure."

He lifted his hands and looked down at them and then he looked down at his compost-covered clothes.

"Cow manure? Seriously?"

I grinned and nodded. He laughed a little and then before I knew it, he was on the ground next to me, wiping his hands all over me. We were both laughing as he reached to the bag next to us and stuck his hand inside, then smeared it down my arms.

Ellen, I am confident that the next sentence I am about to write has never been written or spoken aloud before.

When he was wiping that cow shit on me, it was quite possibly the most turned-on I have ever been.

After a few minutes, we were both lying on the ground, breathing hard, still laughing. He finally stood up and pulled me to my feet, knowing he couldn't waste minutes if he wanted a shower before my parents came home.

Once he was in the shower, I washed my hands in the sink and just stood there, wondering what he meant earlier when he said we were just alike.

Was it a compliment? It sure felt like one. Was he saying that he thought I was strong, too? Because I certainly didn't feel strong most of the time. In that moment, just thinking about him made me feel weak. I wondered what I was going to do about the way I was starting to feel when I was around him.

I also wondered how long I can keep hiding him from my parents. And how long he'll be staying at that house. Winters in Maine are unbearably cold and he won't survive without a heater.

Or blankets.

I gathered myself and went in search of all the spare blankets I could find. I was going to give them to him when he got out of the shower, but it was already five and he left in a hurry.

I'll give them to him tomorrow.

—Lily

Dear Ellen,

Harry Connick Jr. is freaking hilarious. I'm not sure if you've ever had him on your show, because I hate to admit I've probably missed an episode or two since you've been on the air, but if you've never had him, you should. Actually, have you ever watched Late Night with Conan O'Brien? *He has this guy named Andy who sits on the couch for every episode. I wish Harry could sit on your couch for every episode. He just has the best one-liners, and the two of you together would be epic.*

I just want to say thank you. I know that you don't have a show on TV for the sole purpose of making me laugh, but sometimes it feels that way. Sometimes my life just makes me feel like I've lost the ability to laugh or smile, but then I turn on your show and no matter what mood I'm in when I turn on the TV, I always feel better by the time your show is over.

So yeah. Thanks for that.

I know you probably want an update on Atlas, and I'll give you one in a second. But first I need to tell you about what happened yesterday.

My mother is a teaching assistant over at Brimer Elementary. It's a bit of a drive and that's why she never gets home until around five o'clock. My dad works two miles from here, so he's always home right after five.

We have a garage, but only one car can fit in it because of all my dad's stuff. My dad keeps his car in the garage and my mom keeps her car in the driveway.

Well, yesterday my mom got home a little bit early. Atlas was still at the house and we were almost finished watching your show when I heard the garage door start to open. He ran out the back door and I rushed around the living room cleaning up our soda cans and snacks.

It had started snowing really hard around lunchtime yesterday and my mother had a lot of stuff to carry in, so she pulled up in the garage so she could bring it all in through the kitchen door. It was work stuff and a few groceries. I was helping her bring everything inside when my dad pulled up in the driveway. He started honking his horn because he was mad that my mom was parked in the garage. I guess he didn't want to have to get out of his car in the snow. That's the only thing I can think of that would make him want her to move her car right then and there, instead of just waiting until she was finished unloading it. Come to think of it, why does my father always get the garage? You would think a man wouldn't want the woman he loves to get the shittier parking spot.

Anyway, my mother got that real scared look in her eye when he started honking and she told me to take all her stuff to the table while she moved her car out.

I'm not sure what happened when she went back outside. I heard a crash, and then I heard her scream, so I ran to the garage thinking maybe she had slipped on ice.

Ellen . . . I don't even want to describe what happened next. I'm still a little shocked by the whole thing.

I opened the garage door and didn't see my mom. I just saw my dad behind the car doing something. I took a step closer and realized why I couldn't see my mom. He had her pushed down on the hood with his hands around her throat.

He was choking her, Ellen!

I might cry just thinking about it. He was yelling at her, staring down at her with so much hatred. Something about not having respect for how hard he works. I don't know why he was mad, really, because all I could hear was her silence while she struggled to breathe. The next few minutes are a blur, but I know I started screaming at him. I jumped on his back and I was hitting him on the side of his head.

Then I wasn't.

I don't really know what happened, but I'm guessing he threw me off of him. I just remembered one second I was on his back and the next second I was on the ground and my forehead hurt like you wouldn't believe. My mom was sitting next to me, holding my head and telling me she was sorry. I looked around for my dad, but he wasn't there. He'd gotten into his car and drove off after I hit my head.

My mom gave me a rag and told me to hold it to my head because it was bleeding and then she helped me to her car and drove me to the hospital. On the way there she only said one thing to me.

"When they ask you what happened, tell them you slipped on the ice."

When she said that, I just looked out my window and started crying. Because I thought for sure this was the final straw. That she would leave him now that he had hurt me. That was the moment I realized that she'd never leave him. I felt so defeated, but I was too scared to say anything to her about it.

I had to get nine stitches in my forehead. I'm still not sure what I hit my head on, but it doesn't really matter. The fact is, my father was the reason I was hurt and he didn't even stay and check on me. He just left us both there on the floor of the garage and left.

I got home really late last night and fell right to sleep because they had given me some kind of pain pill.

This morning when I walked to the bus, I tried not to look directly at Atlas so he wouldn't see my forehead. I had fixed my hair so that you couldn't really see it and he didn't notice right away. When we sat down next to each other on the bus, our hands touched when we were putting our stuff on the floor.

His hands were like ice, Ellen. Ice.

That's when I realized that I forgot to give him the blankets I had pulled out for him yesterday because my mother got home sooner than I expected. The incident in the garage sort of took over all my thoughts and I completely forgot about him. It had snowed and iced all night and he had been over there at that house in the dark all by himself. And now he was so cold, I didn't know how he was even functioning.

I grabbed both of his hands in mine and said, "Atlas. You're freezing."

He didn't say anything. I just started rubbing his hands in mine to warm them up. I laid my head on his shoulder and then I did the most embarrassing thing. I just started to cry. I don't cry very much, but I was still so upset by what happened yesterday and then I was feeling so guilty that I forgot to take him blankets and it all hit me right there on the ride to school. He didn't say anything. He just pulled his hands from mine so I'd stop rubbing them and then he laid his hands on top of mine. We just sat there like that the whole ride to school with our heads leaned together and his hands on top of mine.

I might have thought it was sweet if it wasn't so sad.

On the ride home from school is when he finally noticed my head.

Honestly, I had forgotten about it. No one at school even asked me about it and when he sat down next to me on the bus, I wasn't even trying to hide it with my hair. He looked right at me and said, "What happened to your head?"

I didn't know what to say to him. I just touched it with my fingers and then looked out the window. I've been trying to get him to trust me more in hopes he would tell me why he doesn't have a place to live, so I didn't want to lie to him. I just didn't want to tell him the truth, either.

When the bus started moving, he said, "Yesterday after I left your house, I heard something going on over there. I heard yelling. I heard you scream, and then I saw your father leave. I was going to come check on you to make sure everything was okay, but as I was walking over I saw you leaving in the car with your mother."

He must have heard the fight in the garage and saw her leaving to take me to get the stitches. I couldn't believe he came over to our house. Do you know what my dad would do to him if he saw him wearing his clothes? I got so worried for him because I don't think he knows what my father is capable of.

I looked at him and said, "Atlas, you can't do that! You can't come to my house when my parents are home!"

Atlas got real quiet and then said, "I heard you scream, Lily." He said it like me being in danger trumped anything else.

I felt bad because I know he was just trying to help, but that would have made things so much worse.

"I fell," I said to him. As soon as I said it, I felt bad for lying. And to be honest, he looked a little disappointed in me, because I think we both knew in that moment that it wasn't as simple as a fall.

Then he pulled up the sleeve of his shirt and held out his arm.

Ellen, my stomach dropped. It was so bad. All over his arm he had these small scars. Some of the scars looked just like someone had stuck a cigarette to his arm and held it there.

He twisted his arm around so I could see that it was on the other side, too. "I used to fall a lot, too, Lily." Then he pulled his shirtsleeve down and didn't say anything else.

For a second I wanted to tell him it wasn't like that—that my dad never hurts me and that he was just trying to get me off of him. But then I realized I'd be using the same excuses my mom uses.

I felt a little embarrassed that he knows what goes on at my house. I spent the whole rest of the bus ride looking out the window because I didn't know what to say to him.

When we got home, my mom's car was there. In the driveway, of course. Not the garage.

That meant Atlas couldn't come over and watch your show with me. I was gonna tell him I would bring him blankets later, but when he got off the bus he didn't even tell me bye. He just started walking down the street like he was mad.

It's dark now and I'm waiting on my parents to go to sleep. But in a little while I'm gonna take him some blankets.

—Lily

Dear Ellen,

I'm in way over my head.

Do you ever do things you know are wrong, but are somehow also right? I don't know how to put it in simpler terms than that.

I mean, I'm only fifteen and I certainly shouldn't have boys spending the night in my bedroom. But if a person knows someone needs a place to stay, isn't it that person's responsibility as a human to help them?

Last night after my parents went to sleep, I snuck out the back door to take Atlas those blankets. I took a flashlight with me because it was dark. It was still snowing really hard, so by the time I made it to that house, I was freezing. I beat on the back door and as soon as he opened it, I pushed past him to get out of the cold.

Only . . . I didn't get out of the cold. Somehow, it felt even colder inside that old house. I still had my flashlight on and I shined it around the living room and kitchen. There wasn't anything in there, Ellen!

No couch, no chair, no mattress. I handed the blankets off to him and kept looking around me. There was a big hole in the roof over the kitchen and wind and snow were just pouring in. When I shined my light around the living room, I saw his stuff in one of the corners. His backpack, plus the backpack I'd given him. There was a little pile of other stuff I'd given him, like some of my dad's clothes. And then there were two towels on the floor. One I guess he laid on and one he covered up with.

I put my hand over my mouth because I was so horrified. He'd been there living like that for weeks!

Atlas put his hand on my back and tried to walk me back out the door. "You shouldn't be over here, Lily," he said. "You could get in trouble."

That's when I grabbed his hand and said, "You shouldn't be here, either." I started to pull him out the front door with me, but he yanked his hand back. That's when I said, "You can sleep on my floor tonight. I'll keep my bedroom door locked. You can't sleep here, Atlas. It's too cold and you'll get pneumonia and die."

He looked like he didn't know what to do. I'm sure the thought of being caught in my bedroom was just as scary as getting pneumonia and dying. He looked back at his spot in the living room and then he just nodded his head once and said, "Okay."

So you tell me, Ellen. Was I wrong letting him sleep in my room last night? It doesn't feel wrong. It felt like the right thing to do. But I sure would get in a lot of trouble if we had been caught. He slept on the floor, so it's not like it was anything more than me just giving him somewhere warm to sleep.

I did learn a little more about him last night. After I snuck him in the back door and to my room, I locked my door and made a pallet for him on the floor next to my bed. I set the alarm for 6 a.m. and told him he'd have to get up and leave before my parents woke up, since sometimes my mom wakes me up in the mornings.

I crawled in my bed and scooted over to the edge of it so I could look down at him while we talked for a little while. I asked him how long he thought he might stay there and he said he didn't know. That's when I asked him how he ended up there. My lamp was still on, and we were whispering, but he got real quiet when I said that. He just stared up at me with his hands behind his head for a moment. Then he said, "I don't know my real dad. He never had anything to do with me. It's always just been me and my mom, but she got remarried about five years ago to a guy who never really liked me much. We fought a lot. When I turned eighteen a few months ago, we got in a big fight and he kicked me out of the house."

He took a deep breath like he didn't want to tell me any more. But then he started talking again. "I've been staying with a friend of mine and his family since then, but his dad got a transfer to Colorado and they moved. They couldn't take me with them, of course. His parents were just being nice by letting me stay with them and I knew that, so I told them I talked to my mom and that I was moving back home. The day they left, I didn't have anywhere to go. So I went back home and told my mom I'd like to move back in until I graduated. She wouldn't let me. Said it would upset my stepfather."

He turned his head and looked at the wall. "So I just wandered around for a few days until I saw that house. Figured I would just stay there until something better came along or until I graduated. I'm signed up to go to the Marines come May, so I'm just trying to hang on until then."

May is six months away, Ellen. Six.

I had tears in my eyes when he finished telling me all that. I asked him why he didn't just ask someone if they could help him. He said he tried, but it's harder for an adult than a kid, and he's already eighteen. He said someone gave him a number for some shelters who might help him. There were three shelters in a twenty-mile radius of our town, but two of them were for battered women. The other one was a homeless shelter, but they only had a few beds and it was too far away for him to walk there if he wanted to go to school every day. Plus, you have to wait in a long line to try and get a bed. He said he tried it once, but he feels safer in that old house than he did at the shelter.

Like the naïve girl I am when it comes to situations like his, I said, "But aren't there other options? Can't you just tell the school counselor what your mom did?"

He shook his head and said he's too old for foster care. He's eighteen, so his mother can't get in trouble for not allowing him to go back home. He said he called about getting food stamps last week, but he didn't have a ride or money to get to his appointment. Not to mention he doesn't have a car, so he can't very well find a job. He said he's been looking, though. After he leaves my house in the afternoons he goes and applies at places, but he doesn't have an address or a phone number to put down on the applications so that makes it harder for him.

I swear, Ellen, every question I threw at him, he had an answer for. It's like he's tried everything not to be stuck in the situation he's in, but there isn't enough help out there for people like him. I got so mad at his whole situation, I told him he was crazy for wanting to go into the military. I wasn't so much whispering when I said, "Why in the heck would you want to serve a country that has allowed you to end up in this kind of situation?"

You know what he said next, Ellen? His eyes grew sad and he said, "It's not this country's fault my mother doesn't give a shit about me." Then he reached up and turned off my lamp. "Goodnight, Lily," he said.

I didn't sleep much after that. I was too mad. I'm not even sure who I'm mad at. I just kept thinking about our country and the whole world and how screwed up it is that people don't do more for each other. I don't know when humans started only looking out for themselves. Maybe it's always been this way. It made me wonder how many people out there were just like Atlas. It made me wonder if there were other kids at our school who might be homeless.

I go to school every day and internally complain about it most of the time, but I've never once thought that school might be the only home some kids have. It's the only place Atlas can go and know he'll have food.

I'll never be able to respect rich people now, knowing they willingly choose to spend their money on materialistic things rather than using it to help other people.

No offense, Ellen. I know you're rich, but I guess I'm not referring to people like you. I've seen all the stuff you've done for others on your show and all the charities you support. But I know there are a lot of rich people out there who are selfish. Hell, there are even selfish poor people. And selfish middle-class people. Look at my parents. We aren't rich, but we certainly aren't too poor to help other people. Yet, I don't think my dad has ever done anything for a charity.

I remember one time we were walking into a grocery store and an old man was ringing a bell for the Salvation Army. I asked my dad if we could give him some money and he told me no, that he works hard for his money and he wasn't about to let me give it away. He said it isn't his fault that other people don't want to work. He spent the whole time we were in the grocery store telling me about how people take advantage of the government and until the government stops helping those people by giving them handouts, the problem won't ever go away.

Ellen, I believed him. That was three years ago and all this time I thought homeless people were homeless because they were lazy or drug addicts or just didn't want to work like other people. But now I know that's not true. Sure, some of what he said was true to an extent, but he was using the worst-case scenarios. Not everyone is homeless because they choose to be. They're homeless because there isn't enough help to go around.

And people like my father are the problem. Instead of helping others, people use the worst-case scenarios to excuse their own selfishness and greed.

I'll never be like that. I swear to you, when I grow up, I'm going to do everything I can to help other people. I'll be like you, Ellen. Just probably not as rich.

—Lily

Chapter Nine

I drop the journal on my chest. I'm surprised to feel tears running down my cheeks. Every time I pick up this journal I think I'll be fine—that it all happened so long ago and I won't still feel what I felt back then.

I'm such a sap. It gives me this longing to hug so many people from my past. Especially my mother because for the past year, I haven't really thought about everything she had to go through before my father died. I know it probably still hurts her.

I grab my phone to call her and look at the screen. There are four missed texts from Ryle. My heart immediately skips. *I can't believe I had it on silent!* Then I roll my eyes, annoyed with myself, because I should *not* be this excited.

Ryle: Are you asleep?

Ryle: I guess so.

Ryle: Lily . . .

Ryle. : (

The sad face was sent ten minutes ago. I hit Reply and type, "Nope. Not asleep." About ten seconds later, I get another text.

Ryle: Good. I'm walking up your stairs right now. Be there in twenty seconds.

I grin and jump out of bed. I go to the bathroom and check my face. *Good enough.* I run to the front door and open it as soon as Ryle makes it up the stairwell. He practically drags himself up the top step, and then stops to rest when he finally reaches my door. He looks so tired. His eyes are red and there are dark circles under them. His arms slip around my waist and he pulls me to him, burying his face in my neck.

"You smell so good," he says.

I pull him inside the apartment. "Are you hungry? I can make you something to eat."

He shakes his head as he wrestles out of his jacket, so I skip the kitchen and head for the bedroom. He follows me, and then throws his jacket over the back of the chair. He kicks off his shoes and pushes them against the wall.

He's wearing scrubs.

"You look exhausted," I say.

He smiles and puts his hands on my hips. "I am. I just assisted in an eighteen-hour surgery." He bends down and kisses the heart tattoo on my collarbone.

No wonder he's exhausted. "How is that even possible?" I say. "Eighteen *hours*?"

He nods and then walks me to the side of the bed where he pulls me down next to him. We adjust ourselves until we're facing each other, sharing a pillow. "Yeah, but it was amazing. Groundbreaking. They'll write about it in medical journals, and I got to be there, so I'm not complaining. I'm just really tired."

I lean in and give him a peck on the mouth. He brings his hand to the side of my head and pulls back. "I know you're probably ready to have hot, sweaty sex, but I don't have the energy tonight. I'm sorry. But I've missed you and for some reason I sleep better when I sleep next to you. Is it okay that I'm here?"

I smile. "It's more than okay."

He leans in and kisses my forehead. He grabs my hand and then holds it between us on the pillow. His eyes close, but I keep mine open and stare at him. He has the type of face that people shy away from, because you could get lost in it. And to think, I get to look at this face all the time. I don't have to be modest and look away, because he's mine.

Maybe.

This is a trial run. I have to remember that.

After a minute, he releases my hand and begins to flex his fingers. I look down at his hand and wonder what that must be like . . . to have to stand for so long and use your fine motor skills for eighteen hours straight. I can't think of much else that would match that level of exhaustion.

I slide out of the bed and retrieve some lotion out of my bathroom. I go back to the bed and sit cross-legged next to him. I squirt some lotion on my hand and then pull his arm to my lap. He opens his eyes and looks up at me.

"What are you doing?" he mumbles.

"Shh. Go back to sleep," I say. I press my thumbs into the palm of his hand and rotate them upward and then out. His eyes fall shut and he groans into the pillow. I continue massaging his hand for about five minutes before switching to his other hand. He keeps his eyes closed the whole time. When I'm finished with his hands, I roll him onto his stomach and straddle his back. He assists me in pulling off his shirt, but his arms are like noodles.

I massage his shoulders and his neck and his back and his arms. When I'm finished, I roll off of him and lie down beside him.

I'm running my fingers through his hair and massaging his scalp when he opens his eyes. "Lily?" he whispers, looking at me sincerely. "You just might be the best thing that's ever happened to me."

Those words wrap around me like a warm blanket. I don't know what to say in response. He lifts a hand and gently cups my cheek, and I feel his stare deep in my stomach. Slowly, he leans forward and presses his lips to mine. I expect a peck, but he doesn't pull back. The tip of his tongue slides across my lips, parting them softly. His mouth is so warm, I moan as his kiss grows deeper.

He rolls me onto my back and then drags his hand down my body, straight to my hip. He moves closer, sliding his hand down my thigh. He pushes against me and a surge of heat shoots inside me. I grab a fistful of his hair and whisper against his mouth. "I think we've waited long enough. I would very much like for you to fuck me now."

He practically growls with a renewed sense of energy and begins to pull my shirt off. It becomes an interlude of hands and moans and tongues and sweat. I feel like this is the first time I've ever been touched by a man. The few who came before him were all boys—nervous hands and timid mouths. But Ryle is all confidence. He knows exactly where to touch me and exactly how to kiss me.

The only time he's not giving my body his undivided attention is when he reaches to the floor and fishes a condom out of his wallet. Once he's back under the covers and the condom is in place, he doesn't even hesitate. He takes me brazenly in one swift thrust and I gasp into his mouth, every muscle in me tensing.

His mouth is fierce and needy, kissing me everywhere he can reach. I grow so dizzy, I can do nothing but succumb to him. He's unapologetic in the way he fucks me. His hand comes between my headboard and the top of my head as he pushes harder and harder, the bed crashing against the wall with every push.

My fingernails dig into the skin of his back as he buries his face against my neck.

"Ryle," I whisper.

"Oh, *God*," I say.

"Ryle!" I scream.

And then I bite down on his shoulder to muffle every sound that comes after it. My whole body feels it—from my head to my toes and back up again.

I'm afraid I might literally pass out for a moment, so I tighten my legs around him and he tenses. "*Jesus*, Lily." His body ripples with tremors, and he shoves against me one last time. He groans, stilling himself on top of me. His body jerks with his release and my head falls back against the pillow.

It's a full minute before either of us is able to move. And even then, we choose not to. He presses his face into the pillow and lets out a deep sigh. "I can't . . ." He pulls back and looks down at me. His eyes are full of something . . . I don't know what. He presses his lips to mine and then says, "You were so right."

"About what?"

He slowly pulls out of me, coming down on his forearms. "You warned me. You said one time with you wouldn't be enough. You said you were like a drug. But you failed to tell me you were the most addictive kind."

Chapter Ten

"Can I ask you a personal question?"

Allysa nods as she perfects a bouquet of flowers about to go out for delivery. We're three days away from our grand opening, and it just keeps getting busier by the day.

"What is it?" Allysa asks, facing me. She leans into the counter and starts picking at her fingernails.

"You don't have to answer it if you don't want to," I warn.

"Well I can't answer it if you don't ask it."

That's a good point. "Do you and Marshall donate to charity?"

Confusion crosses her face and she says, "Yeah. Why?"

I shrug. "I was just curious. I wouldn't judge you or anything. I've just been thinking lately about how I might like to start a charity."

"What kind of charity?" she asks. "We donate to a few different ones now that we have money, but my favorite is this one we got involved with last year. They build schools in other countries. We've funded three new constructions in the past year alone."

I knew I liked her for a reason.

"I don't have that kind of money, obviously, but I'd like to do *something.* I just don't know what yet."

"Let's get through this grand opening first and then you can start thinking about philanthropy. One dream at a time,

Lily." She walks around the counter and grabs the trash can. I watch as she pulls the full bag out of it and ties it in a knot. It makes me wonder why—if she has people for everything—she would even want a job where she had to take out the trash and get her hands dirty.

"Why do you work here?" I ask her.

She glances up at me and smiles. "Because I like you," she says. But then I notice the smile completely leave her eyes right before she turns and walks toward the back to throw out the trash. When she comes back, I'm still watching her curiously. I say it again.

"Allysa? Why do you work here?"

She stops what she's doing and takes in a slow breath like maybe she's contemplating being honest with me. She walks back to the counter and leans against it, crossing her feet at her ankles.

"Because," she says, looking down at her feet. "I can't get pregnant. We've been trying for two years but nothing has worked. I was tired of sitting at home crying all the time, so I decided I should find something to keep my mind busy." She stands up straight and wipes her hands across her jeans. "And you, Lily Bloom, are keeping me *very* busy." She turns and starts messing with the same bouquet of flowers again. She's been perfecting them for half an hour. She picks up a card and stuffs it in the flowers, and then turns around and hands me the vase. "These are for you, by the way."

It's obvious Allysa wants to change the subject, so I take the flowers from her. "What do you mean?"

She rolls her eyes and waves me off to my office. "It's on the card. Go read it."

I can tell by her annoyed reaction that they're from Ryle. I grin and run to my office. I take a seat at my desk and pull out the card.

Lily,

I'm having serious withdrawals.

—Ryle

I smile and put the card back in the envelope. I grab my phone and snap a picture of me holding the flowers with my tongue sticking out. I text it to Ryle.

Me: I tried to warn you.

He immediately starts texting me back. I watch anxiously as the dots on my phone move back and forth.

Ryle: I need my next fix. I'll be finished here in about thirty minutes. Can I take you to dinner?

Me: Can't. Mom wants me to try a new restaurant with her tonight. She's an obnoxious foodie. : (

Ryle: I like food. I eat food. Where are you taking her?

Me: A place called Bib's on Marketson.

Ryle: Is there room for one more?

I stare at his text for a moment. *He wants to meet my mother?* We aren't even officially dating. I mean . . . I don't *care* if he meets my mother. She would love him. But he went from not wanting anything to do with relationships, to possibly agreeing to test-drive one, to meeting the parents, all within five days? *Good God.* I really *am* a drug.

Me: Sure. Meet us there in half an hour.

I walk out of my office and straight up to Allysa. I hold my phone in front of her face. "He wants to meet my mother."

"Who?"

"Ryle."

"My brother?" she says, looking as shocked as I feel.

I nod. "Your brother. *My mother.*"

She grabs my phone and looks at the texts. "Huh. That's so weird."

I take my phone from her hands. "Thanks for the vote of confidence."

She laughs and says, "You know what I mean. It's Ryle we're talking about here. He's never, in the history of being Ryle Kincaid, met a girl's parents."

Of course hearing her say that makes me smile, but then I wonder if maybe he's doing this just to please me. If maybe he's doing things he doesn't really want to do just because he knows I want a relationship.

And then I smile even bigger, because isn't that what it's all about? Sacrificing for the person you like so that you can see them happy?

"Your brother must *really* like me," I say teasingly. I look back up at Allysa, expecting her to laugh, but there's a solemn look on her face.

She nods and says, "Yeah. I'm afraid he does." She grabs her purse from beneath the counter and says, "I'm gonna head out now. Let me know how it goes, okay?" She moves past me and I watch her as she makes her way out the door, and then I just stare at the door for a long time.

It bothers me that she doesn't seem excited about the prospect of me dating Ryle. It makes me wonder if that has more to do with her feelings toward me or her feelings toward him.

• • •

Twenty minutes later, I flip the sign to closed. *Just a few more days.* I lock the door and walk to my car, but stop short when I see someone leaning against it. It takes me a moment to recognize him. He's facing the other direction, talking on his cell phone.

I thought he was meeting me at the restaurant, but okay.

The horn beeps on my car when I hit the Unlock button, and Ryle spins around. He grins when he sees me. "Yes, I agree," he says into the phone. He wraps an arm around my shoulder and pulls me against him, pressing a kiss to the top of my head. "We'll talk about it tomorrow," he says. "Something really important just came up."

He hangs up the phone and slides it into his pocket, then he kisses me. It's not a hello kiss. It's an I've-been-thinking-about-you-nonstop kiss. He wraps both arms around me and spins me until I'm backed up against my car, where he continues to kiss me until I start to feel dizzy again. When he pulls back, he's looking down at me appreciatively.

"You know which part of you drives me the craziest?" He brings his fingers to my mouth and traces my smile. "These," he says. "Your lips. I love how they're as red as your hair and you don't even have to wear lipstick."

I grin and kiss his fingers. "I better watch you around my mom, then, because everyone says we have the same mouth."

He pauses his fingers against my lips and he stops smiling. "Lily. Just . . . *no*."

I laugh and open my door. "Are we taking separate cars?"

He pulls the door open for me the rest of the way and says, "I took an Uber here from work. We'll ride together."

• • •

My mother is already seated at a table when we arrive. Her back is to the door as I lead the way.

I'm instantly impressed by the restaurant. My eyes are drawn to the warm, neutral colors painted on the walls and the almost full-sized tree in the middle of the restaurant. It looks like it's growing straight out of the floor, almost as if the entire restaurant was designed around the tree. Ryle follows closely behind me with his hand on my lower back. Once we reach the table, I begin to pull off my jacket. "Hey, Mom."

She looks up from her phone and says, "Oh, hey, honey." She drops her phone in her purse and waves her hand around the restaurant. "I already love it. Look at the lighting," she says, pointing up. "The fixtures look like something you'd grow in one of your gardens." That's when she notices Ryle, who is standing patiently next to me as I slide into the booth. My mother smiles at him and says, "We'll take two waters for now, please."

My eyes dart to Ryle and then back to my mother. "*Mom*. He's with me. He's not the waiter."

She looks up at Ryle again with confusion. He just smiles and reaches out his hand. "Honest mistake, ma'am. I'm Ryle Kincaid."

She returns the handshake, looking back and forth between us. He releases her hand and slides into the booth. She looks a little flustered when she finally says, "Jenny Bloom.

Nice to meet you." She places her attention back on me and raises an eyebrow. "A friend of yours, Lily?"

I can't believe I'm not better prepared for this moment. What in the heck do I introduce him as? My trial run? I can't say *boyfriend,* but I can't very well say *friend. Prospect* seems a little dated.

Ryle notices my pause, so he puts his hand on my knee and squeezes reassuringly. "My sister works for Lily," he says. "Have you met her? Allysa?"

My mother leans forward in her booth and says, "Oh! Yes! Of course. You two look so much alike now that you mention it," she says. "It's the eyes, I think. And the mouth."

He nods. "We both favor our mother."

My mother smiles at me. "People always say they think Lily favors me."

"Yes," he says. "Identical mouths. Uncanny." Ryle squeezes my knee under the table again while I try and suppress my laughter. "Ladies, if you'll excuse me, I need to head to the gentlemen's room." He leans in and kisses me on the side of the head before standing. "If the waiter comes, I'll just take water."

My mother's eyes follow Ryle as he walks away, and then she slowly turns back to me. She points at me and then to his empty seat. "How come I haven't heard about this guy?"

I smile a little. "Things are kind of . . . it's not really . . ." I have no idea how to explain our situation to my mother. "He works a lot, so we haven't really spent that much time together. At all. This is actually the first time we've been to dinner together."

My mother raises an eyebrow. "Really?" she says, leaning back in her seat. "He sure doesn't treat it like that. I mean—

he seems comfortably affectionate with you. Not normal behavior with someone you've just met."

"We didn't just meet," I say. "It's been almost a year since the first time I met him. And we've spent time together, just not on a date. He works a lot."

"Where does he work?"

"Massachusetts General Hospital."

My mother leans forward and her eyes practically bulge from her head. "Lily!" she hisses. "He's a *doctor*?"

I nod, suppressing my grin. "A neurosurgeon."

"Can I get you ladies something to drink?" a waiter asks.

"Yeah," I say. "We'll take three . . ."

And then I clamp my mouth shut.

I stare at the waiter and the waiter stares back at me. My heart is in my throat. I can't remember how to speak.

"Lily?" my mother says. She flicks her hand toward the waiter. "He's waiting for your drink order."

I shake my head and begin to stutter. "I'll . . . um . . ."

"Three waters," my mother says, interrupting my fumbled words. The waiter snaps out of his trance long enough to tap his pencil on his pad of paper.

"Three waters," he says. "Got it." He turns and walks away, but I watch as he glances back at me before pushing through the doors to the kitchen.

My mother leans forward and says, "What in the world is wrong with you?"

I point over my shoulder. "The waiter," I say, shaking my head. "He looked exactly like . . ."

I'm about to say, "*Atlas Corrigan*," when Ryle walks up and slides back into the seat.

He glances back and forth between us. "What'd I miss?"

I swallow hard, shaking my head. *Surely that wasn't really Atlas.* But those eyes—his mouth. I know it's been years since I saw him, but I'll never forget what he looked like. It *had* to be him. I know it was and I know he recognized me, too, because the second our eyes met . . . it looked like he'd seen a ghost.

"Lily?" Ryle says, squeezing my hand. "You okay?"

I nod and force a smile, then clear my throat. "Yep. We were just talking about you," I say, glancing back at my mother. "Ryle assisted in an eighteen-hour surgery this week."

My mother leans forward with interest. Ryle begins to tell her all about the surgery. Our water arrives, but it's a different waiter this time. He asks if we've had a chance to go over the menu and then tells us the chef's specials. The three of us order our food and I'm doing everything I can to focus, but my attention is all over the restaurant looking for Atlas. *I need to regroup.* After a few minutes, I lean over to Ryle. "I need to run to the restroom."

He stands up to let me out and my eyes are scanning the face of every waiter as I make my way across the room. I push through the door to the hallway that leads to the restrooms. As soon as I'm alone, my back meets the wall of the hallway. I lean forward and release a huge breath. I decide to take a moment and regain my composure before heading back out there. I bring my hands up to my forehead and close my eyes.

For nine years I've wondered what happened to him. *Years.*

"Lily?"

I glance up and suck in a breath. He's standing at the end of the hallway like a ghost straight out of the past. My eyes travel to his feet to make sure he's not suspended in the air.

He isn't. He's real, and he's standing right in front of me.

I stay pressed against the wall, not sure what to say to him. "Atlas?"

As soon as I say his name, he blows out a quick breath of relief and then takes three huge steps forward. I catch myself doing the same. We meet in the middle and throw our arms around each other. "Holy shit," he says, holding me in a tight embrace.

I nod. "Yeah. Holy shit."

He puts his hands on my shoulders and takes a step back to look at me. "You haven't changed at all."

I cover my mouth with my hand, still in shock, and give him the once-over. His face looks the same, but he's no longer the scrawny teenager I remember. "I can't say the same for you."

He looks down at himself and laughs. "Yeah," he says. "Eight years in the military will do that to ya."

We're both in shock, so nothing is said right after that. We just keep shaking our heads in disbelief. He laughs and then I laugh. Finally, he releases my shoulders and folds his arms over his chest. "What brings you to Boston?" he asks.

He says it so casually, and I'm thankful for that. Maybe he doesn't remember our conversation all those years ago about Boston, which would save me a lot of embarrassment.

"I live here," I say, forcing my answer to sound as casual as his question. "I own a flower shop over on Park Plaza."

He smiles knowingly, like it doesn't at all surprise him. I glance toward the door, knowing I should get back out there. He notices and then takes another step back. He holds my gaze for a moment and it gets really quiet. Way too quiet. There's so much to say but neither of us even knows where to start. The smile leaves his eyes for a moment and then he motions toward the door. "You should probably get back to your company," he says. "I'll look you up sometime. You said Park Plaza, right?"

I nod.

He nods.

The door swings open and a woman walks in holding a toddler. She moves between us, which puts even more distance between us. I take a step toward the door, but he remains in the same spot. Before I walk out, I turn back to him and smile. "It was really good to see you, Atlas."

He smiles a little, but it doesn't touch his eyes. "Yeah. You too, Lily."

• • •

I'm mostly quiet for the rest of the meal. I'm not sure Ryle or my mother even notice, though, because she's having no issue firing question after question at him. He takes it like a champ. He's very charming with my mother in all the right ways.

Unexpectedly running into Atlas tonight put such a wrinkle in my emotions, but by the end of dinner, Ryle has smoothed them back out again.

My mother takes her napkin and wipes her mouth, then points at me. "New favorite restaurant," she says. "Incredible."

Ryle nods. "I agree. I need to bring Allysa here. She loves trying new restaurants."

The food really is good, but the last thing I need is for either of these two to want to come back here. "It was okay," I say.

He pays for our meals, of course, and then insists we walk my mother to her car. I can already tell she'll be calling me about him tonight, simply by the prideful look on her face.

Once she's gone, Ryle walks me to my car.

"I requested an Uber so you wouldn't have to go out of your way to take me home. We have approximately . . ." He looks down at his phone. "One and a half minutes to make out."

I laugh. He wraps his arms around me and kisses my neck first, and then my cheek. "I would invite myself over, but I have an early surgery tomorrow and I'm sure my patient would appreciate it if I didn't spend the majority of the night inside you."

I kiss him back, both disappointed and relieved he's not coming over. "I have a grand opening in a few days. I should probably sleep, too."

"When's your next day off?" he says.

"Never. When's yours?"

"Never."

I shake my head. "We're doomed. There's just too much drive and success between the two of us."

"That means the honeymoon phase will last until we're eighty," he says. "I'll come to your grand opening Friday and then the four of us will go out and celebrate." A car pulls up beside us and he wraps his hand in my hair and kisses me goodbye. "Your mother is wonderful, by the way. Thank you for letting me come to dinner."

He backs away and climbs inside the car. I watch as it pulls out of the parking lot.

I have a really good feeling about that man.

I smile and turn toward my car, but throw a hand up to my chest and gasp when I see him.

Atlas is standing at the rear of my car.

"Sorry. Wasn't trying to scare you."

I blow out a breath. "Well, you did." I lean against the car and Atlas stays where he is, three feet away from me. He looks out at the street. "So? Who's the lucky guy?"

"He's . . ." My voice falters. This is all so weird. My chest is still constricted and my stomach is flipping, and I can't tell if it's leftover nerves from kissing Ryle or if it's the presence of Atlas. "His name is Ryle. We met about a year ago."

I instantly regret saying we met that long ago. It makes it sound like Ryle and I have been dating that long and we aren't even officially dating. "What about you? Married? Have a girlfriend?"

I'm not sure if I'm asking to extend the conversation he started, or if I'm genuinely curious.

"I do, actually. Her name is Cassie. We've been together almost a year now."

Heartburn. I think I have heartburn. *A year*? I place my hand on my chest and nod. "That's good. You seem happy."

Does he seem happy? I have no idea.

"Yeah. Well . . . I'm really glad I got to see you, Lily." He turns around to walk away, but then spins and faces me again, his hands shoved in his back pockets. "I will say . . . I kind of wish this could have happened a year ago."

I wince at his words, trying not to let them penetrate. He turns and walks back toward the restaurant.

I fumble with my keys and hit the button to unlock the car. I slide in and pull the door shut, gripping the steering wheel. For whatever reason, a huge tear falls down my cheek. A huge, pathetic, what-the-hell-is-this-wetness tear. I swipe at it and push the button to start my car.

I didn't expect to feel this much hurt after seeing him.

But it's good. This happened for a reason. My heart needed closure so I can give it to Ryle, but maybe I couldn't do that until this happened.

This is good.

Yes, I'm crying.

But it'll feel better. This is just human nature, healing an old wound to prepare for a fresh new layer.

That's all.

Chapter Eleven

I curl up in my bed and stare at it.

I'm almost finished with it. There aren't very many more entries.

I pick up the journal and place it on the pillow beside me.

"I'm not going to read you," I whisper.

Although, if I read what's left, I'll be finished. Having seen Atlas tonight and knowing he has a girlfriend and a job and more than likely a home is enough closure I need on that chapter. And if I just finish the damn journal, I can put it back in the shoebox and never have to open it again.

I finally pick it up and roll onto my back. "Ellen DeGeneres, you are *such* a bitch."

Dear Ellen,

"Just keep swimming."

Recognize that quote, Ellen? It's what Dory says to Marlin in Finding Nemo.

"Just keep swimming, swimming, swimming."

I'm not a huge fan of cartoons, but I'll give you props for that one. I like cartoons that can make you laugh, but also make you feel something. After today, I think that's my favorite cartoon. Because I've been feeling like drowning lately, and sometimes people need a reminder that they just need to keep swimming.

Atlas got sick. Like really sick.

He's been crawling through my window and sleeping on the floor for a few nights in a row now, but last night, I knew something was wrong as soon as I looked at him. It was a Sunday, so I hadn't seen him since the night before, but he looked awful. His eyes were bloodshot, his skin was pale, and even though it was cold, his hair was sweaty. I didn't even ask if he was feeling okay, I already knew he wasn't. I put my hand on his forehead and he was so hot, I almost yelled for my mother.

He said, "I'll be fine, Lily," and then he started to make his pallet on the floor. I told him to wait there and then I went to the kitchen and poured him a glass of water. I found some medicine in the cabinet. It was flu medicine and I wasn't even sure if that's what was wrong with him, but I made him take some anyway.

He laid there on the floor, curled up into a ball, when, about half an hour later he said, "Lily? I think I'm gonna need a trash can."

I jumped up and grabbed the trash can from under my desk and knelt down in front of him. As soon as I set it down, he hunched over it and started throwing up.

God, I felt bad for him. Being so sick and not having a bathroom or a bed or a house or a mother. All he had was me and I didn't even know what to do for him.

When he was finished, I made him drink some water and then I told him to get on the bed. He refused, but I wasn't having it. I put the trash can on the floor next to the bed and made him move to the bed.

He was so hot and shaking so bad I was just scared to leave him on the floor. I laid down next to him and every hour for the next six hours he continued getting sick. I kept having to take the trash can to the bathroom to empty it out. I'm not gonna lie, it was gross. The grossest night I've ever had, but what else could I do? He needed me to help him and I was all he had.

When it came time for him to leave my room this morning, I told him to go back to his house and I'd be over to check on him before school. I'm surprised he even had the energy to crawl out of my window. I left the trash can next to my bed and waited for my mom to come wake me up. When she did, she saw the trash can and immediately held her hand to my forehead. "Lily, are you okay?"

I groaned and shook my head. "No. I was up all night sick. I think it's over now, but I haven't slept."

She picked up the trash can and told me to stay in bed, that she'd call the school and let them know I wasn't coming. After she left for work, I went and got Atlas and told him he could stay with me at the house all day. He was still getting sick, so I let him use my room to sleep. I'd check on him every half hour or so and finally around lunch he stopped throwing up. He went and took a shower and then I made him some soup.

He was too tired to even eat it. I got a blanket and we both sat down on the couch and covered up together. I don't know when I started feeling comfortable enough to snuggle up to him, but it just felt right. A few minutes later, he leaned over a little and pressed his lips against my collarbone, right between my shoulder and my neck. It was a quick kiss and I don't think he meant for it to be romantic. It was more like a thank-you gesture, without using actual words. But it made me feel all kinds of things. It's been a few hours now and I keep touching that spot with my fingers because I can still feel it.

I know it was probably the worst day of his life, Ellen. But it was one of my favorites.

I feel really bad about that.

We watched Finding Nemo *and when that part came up where Marlin was looking for Nemo and he was feeling really defeated, Dory said to him, "When life gets you down do you wanna know what you've gotta do? . . . Just keep swimming. Just keep swimming. Just keep swimming, swimming, swimming."*

Atlas grabbed my hand when Dory said that. He didn't hold it like a boyfriend holds his girlfriend's hand. He squeezed it, like he was saying that was us. He was Marlin and I was Dory, and I was helping him swim.

"Just keep swimming," I whispered to him.

—Lily

Dear Ellen,

I'm scared. So scared.

I like him a lot. He's all I think about when we're together and I feel worried sick about him when we're not. My life is beginning to revolve around him and that's not good, I know. But I can't help it and I don't know what to do about it, and now he might leave.

He left after we finished watching Finding Nemo *yesterday and then when my parents went to bed, he crawled in my window last night. He had slept in my bed the night before because he was sick, and I know I shouldn't have done it, but I put his blankets in the washing machine right before I went to bed. He asked where his pallet was and I told him he'd have to sleep on the bed again because I wanted to wash his blankets and make sure they were clean so he wouldn't get sick again.*

For a minute, it looked like he was going to go back out the window. But then he shut it and took off his shoes and crawled in the bed with me.

He wasn't sick anymore, but when he laid down I thought maybe

I had gotten sick because my stomach felt queasy. But I wasn't sick. I just always feel queasy when he's that close to me.

We were facing each other on the bed when he said, "When do you turn sixteen?"

"Two more months," I whispered. We just kept staring at each other, and my heart was beating faster and faster. "When do you turn nineteen?" I asked, just trying to make conversation so he couldn't hear how hard I was breathing.

"Not until October," he said.

I nodded. I wondered why he was curious about my age and it made me wonder what he thought about fifteen-year-olds. Did he look at me like I was just a little kid? Like a little sister? I was almost sixteen, and two and a half years apart in age isn't that bad. Maybe when two people are fifteen and eighteen, it might seem a little too far apart. But once I turn sixteen, I bet no one would even think twice about a two-and-a-half-year age difference.

"I need to tell you something," he said.

I held my breath, not knowing what he was going to say.

"I got in touch with my uncle today. My mom and I used to live with him in Boston. He told me once he gets back from his work trip I can stay with him."

I should have been so happy for him in that moment. I should have smiled and told him congratulations. But I felt all of the immaturity of my age when I closed my eyes and felt sorry for myself.

"Are you going?" I asked.

He shrugged. "I don't know. I wanted to talk to you about it first."

He was so close to me on the bed, I could feel the warmth of his breath. I also noticed he smelled like mint, and it made me wonder if he uses bottled water to brush his teeth before he comes over here. I always send him home every day with lots of water.

I brought my hand up to the pillow and started pulling at a feather sticking out of it. When I got it all the way out, I twisted it between my fingers. "I don't know what to say, Atlas. I'm happy you have a place to stay. But what about school?"

"I could finish down there," he said.

I nodded. It sounded like he already made up his mind. "When are you leaving?"

I wondered how far away Boston is. It's probably a few hours, but that's a whole world away when you don't own a car.

"I don't know for sure that I am."

I dropped the feather back onto the pillow and brought my hand to my side. "What's stopping you? Your uncle is offering you a place to stay. That's good, right?"

He tightened his lips together and nodded. Then he picked up the feather I'd been playing with and he started twisting it between his fingers. He laid it back down on the pillow and then he did something I wasn't expecting. He moved his fingers to my lips and he touched them.

God, Ellen. I thought I was gonna die right then and there. It was the most I'd ever felt inside my body at one time. He kept his fingers there for a few seconds, and he said, "Thank you, Lily. For everything." He moved his fingers up and through my hair, and then he leaned forward and planted a kiss on my forehead. I was breathing so hard, I had to open my mouth to catch more air. I could see his chest moving just as hard as mine was. He looked down at me and I watched as his eyes went right to my mouth. "Have you ever been kissed, Lily?"

I shook my head no and tilted my face up to his because I needed him to change that right then and there or I wasn't gonna be able to breathe.

Then—almost as if I were made of eggshells—he lowered his

mouth to mine and just rested it there. I didn't know what to do next, but I didn't care. I didn't care if we just stayed like that all night and never even moved our mouths, it was everything.

His lips closed over mine and I could kind of feel his hand shaking. I did what he was doing and started to move my lips like he was. I felt the tip of his tongue brush across my lips once and I thought my eyes were about to roll back in my head. He did it again, and then a third time, so I finally did it, too. When our tongues touched for the first time, I kind of smiled a little, because I'd thought about my first kiss a lot. Where it would be, who it would be with. Never in a million years did I imagine it would feel like this.

He pushed me on my back and pressed his hand against my cheek and kept kissing me. It just got better and better as I grew more comfortable. My favorite moment was when he pulled back for a second and looked down at me, then came back even harder.

I don't know how long we kissed. A long time. So long, my mouth started to hurt and my eyes couldn't stay open. When we fell asleep, I'm pretty sure his mouth was still touching mine.

We didn't talk about Boston again.

I still don't know if he's leaving.

—Lily

• • •

Dear Ellen,

I need to apologize to you.

It's been a week since I've written to you and a week since I've watched your show. Don't worry, I still record it so you'll get the ratings, but every day we get off the bus, Atlas takes a quick shower and then we make out.

Every day.

It's awesome.

I don't know what it is about him, but I feel so comfortable with him. He's so sweet and thoughtful. He never does anything I don't feel comfortable with, but so far he hasn't tried anything I don't feel comfortable with.

I'm not sure how much I should divulge here, since you and I have never met in person. But let me just say that if he's ever wondered what my boobs feel like . . .

Now he knows.

I can't for the life of me figure out how people function from day to day when they like someone this much. If it were up to me, we would kiss all day and all night and do nothing in between except maybe talk a little. He tells funny stories. I love it when he's in a talkative mood because it doesn't happen very often, but he uses his hands a lot. He smiles a lot, too, and I love his smile even more than I love his kiss. And sometimes I just tell him to shut up and stop smiling or kissing or talking so I can stare at him. I like looking at his eyes. They're so blue that he could be standing across a room and a person could tell how blue his eyes were. The only thing I don't like about kissing him sometimes is when he closes his eyes.

And no. We still haven't talked about Boston.

—Lily

Dear Ellen,

Yesterday afternoon when we were riding the bus, Atlas kissed me. It wasn't anything new to us because we had kissed a lot by this point, but it's the first time he ever did it in public. When we're together everything else just seems to fade away, so I don't think he even thought about other people noticing. But Katie noticed. She was sitting in the seat behind us and I heard her say, "Gross," as soon as he leaned over and kissed me.

She was talking to the girl next to her when she said, "I can't believe Lily lets him touch her. He wears the same clothes almost every day."

Ellen, I was so mad. I also felt awful for Atlas. He pulled away from me and I could tell what she said bothered him. I started to turn around to yell at her for judging someone she doesn't even know, but he grabbed my hand and shook his head no.

"Don't, Lily," he said.

So I didn't.

But for the rest of the bus ride, I was so angry. I was angry that Katie would say something so ignorant just to hurt someone she thought was beneath her. I was also hurt that Atlas appeared to be used to comments like that.

I didn't want him to think I was embarrassed that anyone saw him kiss me. I know Atlas better than any of them do, and I know what a good person he is, no matter what his clothes look like or that he used to smell before he started using my shower.

I leaned over and kissed him on the cheek and then rested my head on his shoulder.

"You know what?" I said to him.

He slid his fingers through mine and squeezed my hand. "What?"

"You're my favorite person."

I felt him laugh a little and it made me smile.

"Out of how many people?" he asked.

"All of them."

He kissed the top of my head and said, "You're my favorite person, too, Lily. By a long shot."

When the bus came to a stop on my street, he didn't let go of my hand when we started to walk off. He was in front of me in the aisle and I was walking behind him, so he didn't see it when I turned around and flipped off Katie.

I probably shouldn't have done it, but the look on her face made it worth it.

When we got to my house, he took the house key out of my hand and unlocked my front door. It was weird, seeing how comfortable he is at my house now. He walked in and locked the door behind us. That's when we noticed the electricity in the house wasn't working. I looked out the window and saw a utility truck down the street working on the power lines, so that meant we couldn't watch your show. I wasn't too upset because it meant we would probably just make out for an hour and a half.

"Does your oven run off gas or electricity?" he asked.

"Gas," I said, a little confused that he was asking about our oven.

He kicked off his shoes (which were really just a pair of my father's old shoes) and he started walking toward the kitchen. "I'm going to make you something," he said.

"You know how to cook?"

He opened the refrigerator and started moving things around. "Yep. I probably love to cook as much as you love to grow things." He took a few things out of the refrigerator and preheated the oven. I leaned against the counter and watched him. He wasn't even looking at a recipe. He was just pouring things into bowls and mixing them without even using a measuring cup.

I had never seen my father lift a finger in the kitchen. I'm pretty sure he wouldn't even know how to preheat our oven. I kind of thought most men were like that, but watching Atlas work his way around my kitchen proved me wrong.

"What are you making?" I asked him. I pushed my hands on the island and hoisted myself onto it.

"Cookies," he said. He walked the bowl over to me and stuck a spoon in the mixture. He brought the spoon up to my mouth and I tasted it. One of my weaknesses is cookie dough, and this was the best I'd ever tasted.

"Oh, wow," I said, licking my lips.

He set the bowl down beside me and then leaned in and kissed me. Cookie dough and Atlas's mouth mixed together is like heaven, in case you're wondering. I made a noise deep in my throat that let him know how much I liked the combination, and it made him laugh. But he didn't stop kissing me. He just laughed through the kiss and it completely melted my heart. A happy Atlas was near mind-blowing. It made me want to uncover every single thing about this world that he likes and give it all to him.

When he was kissing me, I wondered if I loved him. I've never had a boyfriend before and have nothing to compare my feelings to. In fact, I've never really wanted a boyfriend or a relationship until Atlas. I'm not growing up in a household with a great example of how a man should treat someone he loves, so I've always held on to an unhealthy amount of distrust when it comes to relationships and other people.

There have been times I've wondered if I could ever allow myself to trust a guy. For the most part, I hate men because the only example I have is my father. But spending all this time with Atlas is changing me. Not in a huge way, I don't think. I still distrust most people. But Atlas is changing me enough to believe that maybe he's an exception to the norm.

He stopped kissing me and picked up the bowl again. He walked it over to the opposite counter and started spooning dough onto two cookie sheets.

"You want to know a trick to cooking with a gas oven?" he asked.

I'm not sure I really ever cared about cooking before, but he somehow made me want to know everything he knew. It might have been how happy he looked when he talked about it.

"Gas ovens have hot spots," he said as he opened the oven door and put the cookie sheets inside. "You have to be sure and rotate the pans so they'll cook evenly." He closed the door and pulled the oven mitt off his hand. He tossed it on the counter. "A pizza stone helps, too. If you just keep it in the oven, even when you aren't baking pizza, it helps eliminate the hot spots."

He walked over to me and placed his hands on either side of me. The electricity kicked on right as he was pulling down the collar of my shirt. He kissed the spot on my shoulder he always loves kissing and slowly slid his hands up my back. I swear, sometimes when he's not even here I can still feel his lips on my collarbone.

He was about to kiss me on the mouth when we heard a car pull into the driveway and the garage door start to open. I jumped off the island, looking around the kitchen frantically. His hands went up to my cheeks and he made me look at him.

"Keep an eye on the cookies. They'll be finished in about twenty minutes." He pressed his lips to mine and then released me, rushing to the living room to grab his backpack. He made it out the back door right when I heard the engine to my father's car shut off.

I started gathering all the ingredients together when my father walked into the kitchen from the garage. He looked around and then saw the light on in the oven.

"Are you cooking?" he asked.

I nodded because my heart was beating so fast, I was scared he'd hear the trembling in my voice if I responded out loud. I scrubbed for a moment at a spot on the counter that was perfectly clean. I cleared my throat and said, "Cookies. I'm baking cookies."

He set his briefcase down on the kitchen table and then walked to the refrigerator and pulled out a beer.

"The electricity has been out," I said. "I was bored so I decided to bake while I waited for it to come back on."

My father sat down at the table and spent the next ten minutes asking me questions about school and if I'd thought about going to college. Occasionally when it was just the two of us, I saw glimpses of a how a normal relationship with a father could be. Sitting at the kitchen table with him discussing colleges and career choices and high school. As much as I hated him most of the time, I still longed for more of these moments with him. If he could just always be the guy he was capable of being in these moments, things would be so much different. For all of us.

I rotated the cookies like Atlas had said to do and when they were finished, I pulled them out of the oven. I took one off the cookie sheet and handed it to my father. I hated that I was being nice to him. It almost felt like I was wasting one of Atlas's cookies.

"Wow," my father said. "These are great, Lily."

I forced a thank-you, even though I didn't make them. I couldn't very well tell him that, though.

"They're for school so you can only have one," I lied. I waited until the rest of them cooled and then I put them in a Tupperware container and took them to my room. I didn't even want to try one without Atlas, so I waited until later last night when he came over.

"You should have tried one when they were hot," he said. "That's when they're the best."

"I didn't want to eat them without you," I said. We sat on the bed with our backs against the wall and proceeded to eat half the

bowl of cookies. I told him they were delicious, but failed to tell him they were by far the greatest cookies I'd ever eaten. I didn't want to inflate his ego. I kind of liked how humble he was.

I tried to grab at another one, but he pulled the bowl away and put the lid back on it. "If you eat too many you'll make yourself sick and you won't like my cookies anymore."

I laughed. "Impossible."

He took a drink of water and then stood up, facing the bed. "I made you something," he said, reaching into his pocket.

"More cookies?" I asked.

He smiled and shook his head, then held out a fist. I lifted my hand and he dropped something hard in the palm of my hand. It was a small, flat outline of a heart, about two inches long, carved out of wood.

I rubbed my thumb over it, trying not to smile too big. It wasn't an anatomically correct heart, but it also didn't look like the hand-drawn hearts. It was uneven and hollow in the middle.

"You made this?" I asked, looking up at him.

He nodded. "I carved it with an old whittling knife I found at the house."

The ends of the heart weren't connected. They just curved in a little, leaving a little space at the top of the heart. I didn't even know what to say. I felt him sit back down on the bed but I couldn't stop looking at it long enough to even thank him.

"I carved it out of a branch," he said, whispering. "From the oak tree in your backyard."

I swear, Ellen. I never thought I could love something so much. Or maybe what I was feeling wasn't for the gift, but for him. I closed my fist around the heart and then leaned over and kissed him so hard, he fell back onto the bed. I threw my leg over him and straddled him and he grabbed my waist and grinned against my mouth.

"I'm gonna carve you a damn house out of that oak tree if this is the reward I get," he whispered.

I laughed. "You have to stop being so perfect," I told him. "You're already my favorite person but now you're making it really unfair to all the other humans because no one will ever be able to catch up to you."

He brought his hand to the back of my head and rolled me until I was on my back and he was the one on top. "Then my plan is working," he said, right before kissing me again.

I held on to the heart while we kissed, wanting to believe it was a gift for no reason at all. But part of me was scared it was a gift to remember him by when he leaves for Boston.

I didn't want to remember him. If I had to remember him, it would mean he wasn't a part of my life anymore.

I don't want him to move to Boston, Ellen. I know that's selfish of me because he can't keep living in that house. I don't know what I'm more afraid might happen. Watching him leave or selfishly begging him not to go.

I know we need to talk about it. I'll ask him about Boston tonight when he comes over. I just didn't want to ask him last night because it was a really perfect day.

—Lily

Dear Ellen,

Just keep swimming. Just keep swimming.

He's moving to Boston.

I don't really feel like talking about it.

—Lily

Dear Ellen,

This is going to be a big one for my mother to hide.

My father is usually pretty cognizant of hitting her where it won't leave a visible bruise. The last thing he probably wants is for people in the town to know what he does to her. I've seen him kick her a few times, choke her, hit her on the back and the stomach, pull her hair. The few times he's hit her on the face, it's always just been a slap, so the marks wouldn't stay for long.

But never have I seen him do what he did last night.

It was really late when they got home. It was a weekend, so he and my mom went to some community function. My father has a real estate company and he's also the town mayor, so they have to do things in the public a lot like go to charity dinners. Which is ironic, since my father hates charities. But I guess he has to save face.

Atlas was already in my room when they got home. I could hear them fighting as soon as they walked through the front door. A lot of the conversation was muffled, but for the most part, it sounded like my father was accusing her of flirting with some man.

Now I know my mother, Ellen. She would never do something like that. If anything, a guy probably looked at her and it made my father jealous. My mother is really beautiful.

I heard him call her a whore and then I heard the first blow. I started to climb out of my bed but Atlas pulled me back and told me not to go in there, that I might get hurt. I told him it actually helps sometimes. That when I go in there, my father backs off.

Atlas tried to talk me out of it, but finally I got up and went out into the living room.

Ellen.

I just . . .

He was on top of her.

They were on the couch and he had his hand around her throat, but his other hand was pulling up her dress. She was trying to fight him off and I just stood there, frozen. She kept begging him to get off her and then he hit her right across the face and told her to shut up. I'll never forget his words when he said, "You want attention? I'll give you some fucking attention." And that's when she got real still and stopped fighting him. I heard her crying, and then she said, "Please be quiet. Lily is here."

She said, "Please be quiet."

Please be quiet while you rape me, dear.

Ellen, I didn't know one human was capable of feeling so much hate inside one heart. And I'm not even talking about my father. I'm talking about me.

I walked straight to the kitchen and I opened a drawer. I grabbed the biggest knife I could find and . . . I don't know how to explain it. It was like I wasn't even in my own body. I could see myself walking across the kitchen with the knife in my hand, and I knew I wasn't going to use it. I just wanted something bigger than myself that could scare him away from her. But right before I made it out of the kitchen, two arms went around my waist and picked me up from behind. I dropped the knife, and my father didn't hear it but my mother did. We locked eyes as Atlas carried me back to my bedroom. When we were back inside my room, I just started hitting him in the chest, trying to get back out there to her. I was crying and doing everything I could to get him out of my way, but he wouldn't move.

He just wrapped his arms around me and said, "Lily, calm down." He kept saying it over and over, and he held me there for a long time until I accepted that he wasn't gonna let me go back out there. He wasn't gonna let me have that knife.

He walked over to the bed and grabbed his jacket and started putting on his shoes. "We'll go next door," he said. "We'll call the police."

The police.

My mother had warned me not to call the police in the past. She said it could jeopardize my father's career. But in all honesty, I didn't care at that point. I didn't care that he was the mayor or that everyone who loved him didn't know the awful side of him. The only thing I cared about was helping my mother, so I pulled on my jacket and went to the closet for a pair of shoes. When I stepped out of my closet, Atlas was staring at my bedroom door.

It was opening.

My mother stepped inside and quickly shut it, locking it behind her. I'll never forget what she looked like. She had blood coming down from her lip. Her eye was already starting to swell, and she had a clump of hair just resting on her shoulder. She looked at Atlas and then me.

I didn't even take a moment to feel scared that she caught me in my room with a boy. I didn't care about that. I was just worried about her. I walked over to her and grabbed her hands and walked her to my bed. I brushed the hair off her shoulder and then from her forehead.

"He's gonna go call the police, Mom. Okay?"

Her eyes grew real wide and she started shaking her head. "No," she said. She looked over at Atlas and said, "You can't. No."

He was already at the window about to leave, so he stopped and looked at me.

"He's drunk, Lily," she said. "He heard your door shut, so he went to our bedroom. He stopped. If you call the police, it'll just make it worse, believe me. Just let him sleep it off, it'll be better tomorrow."

I shook my head and could feel the tears stinging my eyes. "Mom, he was trying to rape you!"

She ducked her head and winced when I said that. She shook her head again and said, "It's not like that, Lily. We're married, and sometimes marriage is just . . . you're too young to understand it."

It got really quiet for a minute, and then I said. "I hope to hell I never do."

That's when she started to cry. She just held her head in her hands and she started to sob and all I could do was wrap my arms around her and cry with her. I'd never seen her this upset. Or this hurt. Or this scared. It broke my heart, Ellen.

It broke me.

When she was finished crying, I looked around the room and Atlas had left. We went to the kitchen and I helped her clean up her lip and her eye. She never did say anything about him being there. Not one thing. I waited for her to tell me I was grounded, but she never did. I realized that maybe she didn't acknowledge it because that's what she does. Things that hurt her just get swept under the rug, never to be brought up again.

—Lily

Dear Ellen,

I think I'm ready to talk about Boston now.

He left today.

I've shuffled my deck of cards so many times, my hands hurt. I'm scared if I don't get out how I feel on paper, I'll go crazy holding it all in.

Our last night didn't go over so well. We kissed a lot at first, but we were both too sad to really care about it. For the second time in two days, he told me he changed his mind and that he wasn't leaving. He didn't want to leave me alone in this house. But I've lived with these parents for almost sixteen years. It was silly of him to turn down a home in favor of being homeless, just because of me. We both knew that, but it still hurt.

I tried to not be so sad about it, so when we were lying there, I asked him to tell me about Boston. I told him maybe one day when I got out of school, I could go there.

He got this look in his eye when he started talking about it. A look I'd never seen. Sort of like he was talking about heaven. He told me about how everyone has the greatest accents there. Instead of car, they say cah. He must not realize that he sometimes says his r's like that, too. He said he lived there from the ages of nine until he was fourteen, so I guess maybe he picked up a little bit of the accent.

He told me about how his uncle lives in an apartment building with the coolest rooftop deck.

"A lot of apartments have them," he said. "Some even have pools."

Plethora, Maine, probably didn't even have a building that was tall enough for a rooftop deck. I wondered what it would feel like to be that high up. I asked him if he ever went up there and he said yes. That when he was younger, sometimes he would go to the roof and just sit up there and think while he looked out over the city.

He told me about the food. I already knew he liked to cook but I had no idea how much passion he had for it. I guess because he doesn't have a stove or a kitchen, so other than the cookies he baked me, he's never really talked about cooking before.

He told me about the harbor and how, before his mother remarried, she used to take him fishing out there. "I mean, Boston isn't any different from any other big city, I guess," he said. "There's not a lot that makes it stand out. It's just . . . I don't know. There's a vibe. A really good energy. When people say they live in Boston, they're proud of it. I miss that sometimes."

I ran my fingers through his hair and said, "Well, you make it sound like the best place in the world. Like everything is better in Boston."

He looked at me and his eyes were sad when he said. "Everything is almost better in Boston. Except the girls. Boston doesn't have you."

That made me blush. He kissed me real sweet and then I said to him, "Boston doesn't have me yet. Someday I'll move there and I'll find you."

He made me promise. Said if I moved to Boston, everything really would be better there and it would be the best city in the world.

We kissed some more. And did other things that I won't bore you with. Although, that's not to say they were boring.

They were not.

But then this morning I had to tell him goodbye. And he held me and kissed me so much, I thought I might die if he let go.

But I didn't die. Because he let go and here I am. Still living. Still breathing.

Just barely.

—Lily

I flip to the next page, but then slam the book shut. There's only one more entry and I don't know that I really feel like reading it right now. Or ever. I put the journal back in my closet, knowing that my chapter with Atlas is over. He's happy now.

I'm happy now.

Time can definitely heal all wounds.

Or at least most of them.

I turn off my lamp and then pick up my phone to plug it in. I have two missed text messages from Ryle and one from my mother.

Ryle: Hey. Naked Truth commencing in 3 . . . 2 . . .

Ryle: I was worried that being in a relationship would add to my responsibilities. That's why I've avoided them my whole life. I already have enough on my plate, and seeing the stress my parents' marriage seemed to cause them, and the failed marriages of some of my friends, I wanted no part in something like that. But after tonight, I realized that maybe a lot of people are just doing it wrong. Because what's happening between us doesn't feel like a responsibility. It feels like a reward. And I'll fall asleep wondering what I did to deserve it.

I pull my phone to my chest and smile. Then I screen-shot the text because I'm keeping it forever. I open up the third text message.

Mom: A doctor, Lily? AND your own business? I want to be you when I grow up.

I screen-shot that one, too.

Chapter Twelve

"What are you doing to those poor flowers?" Allysa asks from behind me.

I clamp another silver washer closed and slide it down the stem. "Steampunk."

We both stand back and admire the bouquet. At least . . . I *hope* she's looking at it with admiration. It turned out better than I thought it would. I used florist dip dye to turn some white roses a deep purple. Then I decorated the stems with different steampunk elements, like tiny metal washers and gears, and even super-glued a small clock to the brown leather strap that's holding the bouquet together.

"*Steampunk?*"

"It's a trend. Kind of a subgenre of fiction, but it's catching on in other areas. Art. Music." I turn around and smile, holding up the bouquet. "And now . . . *flowers*."

Allysa takes the flowers from me and holds them up in front of her. "They're so . . . weird. I love them so much." She hugs them. "Can I have them?"

I pull them away from her. "No, they're our grand opening display. Not for sale." I take the flowers from her and grab the vase I made yesterday. I found a pair of old button-up women's boots at a flea market last week. They reminded me of the steampunk style, and the boots are actually where I got the idea for the flowers. I washed the boots last week, dried them, and then super-glued pieces of metal to them. Once I brushed them with Mod Podge, I was able to line the inside with a vase to hold water for the flowers.

"Allysa?" I place the flowers on the center display table. "I'm pretty sure this is exactly what I was supposed to do with my life."

"Steampunk?" she asks.

I laugh and spin around. "Create!" I say. And then I flip the sign to open, fifteen minutes early.

We both spend the day busier than we thought we'd be. Between phone orders, Internet orders, and walk-ins, neither of us even has time to take a lunch break.

"You need more employees," Allysa says as she passes me, holding two bouquets of flowers. That is at one o'clock.

"You need more employees," she says to me at two o'clock, holding the phone to her ear and writing down an order while ringing someone up at the register.

Marshall stops by after three o'clock and asks how it's going. Allysa says, "She needs more employees."

I help a woman take a bouquet to her car at four o'clock, and as I'm walking back inside, Allysa is walking out, holding another bouquet. "You need more employees," she says, exasperated.

At six o'clock, she locks the door and flips the sign. She falls against the door and slides to the floor, looking up at me.

"I know," I tell her. "I need more employees."

She just nods.

And then we laugh. I walk over to where she's seated and I sit next to her. We lean our heads together and look at the store. The steampunk flowers are front and center, and although I refused to sell this particular bouquet, we had eight preorders for more of them.

"I'm proud of you, Lily," she says.

I smile. "I couldn't have done it without you, Issa."

We sit there for several minutes, enjoying the rest we're finally giving our feet. This was honestly one of the best days I've ever had, but I can't help but feel a nagging sadness that Ryle never stopped by. He also never texted.

"Have you heard from your brother today?" I ask.

She shakes her head. "No, but I'm sure he's just busy."

I nod. I know he's busy.

We both look up when someone knocks on the door. I smile when I see him cupping his hands around his eyes with his face pressed to the window. He finally looks down and sees us sitting on the floor.

"Speak of the devil," Allysa says.

I jump up and unlock the door to let him in. As soon as I open it, he's pushing his way inside. "I missed it? I did. I missed it." He hugs me. "I'm sorry, I tried to get here as soon as I could."

I hug him back and say, "It's fine. You're here. It was perfect." I'm giddy with excitement that he made it at all.

"*You're* perfect," he says, kissing me.

Allysa brushes past us. "*You're* perfect," she mimics. "Hey Ryle, guess what?"

Ryle releases me. "What?"

Allysa grabs the trash can and drops it on the counter. "Lily needs to hire more employees."

I laugh at her constant repetition. Ryle squeezes my hand and says, "Sounds like business was good."

I shrug. "I can't complain. I mean . . . I'm no *brain* surgeon, but I'm pretty good at what I do."

Ryle laughs. "You guys need any help cleaning up?"

Allysa and I put him to work, helping us clean up after the big day. We get everything finished and prepped for tomorrow, and then Marshall arrives just as we're finishing up. He's carrying a bag when he walks inside and drops it on the counter. He begins to pull out huge lumps of some kind of material and tosses them at each of us. I catch mine and unfold it.

It's a onesie.

With kittens all over it.

"Bruins game. Free beer. Suit up, team!"

Allysa groans and says, "Marshall, you made six million dollars this year. Do we *really* need free beer?"

He shoves a finger against her lips, pushing them in opposite directions. "Shh! Don't speak like a rich girl, Issa. Blasphemy."

She laughs and Marshall grabs the onesie out of her hand. He unzips it and helps her into it. Once we're all suited up, we lock the door and head to the bar.

I've never in my life seen so many men in onesies. Allysa and I are the only women wearing them, but I kind of like that. It's loud. So loud, and each time the Bruins make a good play, Allysa and I have to cover our ears from the screams. After about half an hour, a booth on the top floor opens up and we all run upstairs to claim it.

"Much better," Allysa says as we slide in. It's much quieter up here, although still loud compared to normal standards.

A waitress comes over to take our drink order. I order red wine, and as soon as I do, Marshall practically jumps out of his seat. "Wine?" he yells. "You're in a onesie! You don't get free wine with a onesie!"

He tells the waitress to bring me a beer, instead. Ryle tells her to bring me wine. Allysa wants water, and this upsets Marshall even more. He tells the waitress to bring four bottles of beer and then Ryle says, "Two beers, red wine, and a water." The waitress is very confused by the time she leaves our table.

Marshall throws his arm around Allysa and kisses her. "How am I supposed to try and knock you up tonight if you aren't a little wasted?"

The look on Allysa's face changes, and I feel instantly bad for her. I know Marshall only said that in fun, but it has to bother her. She was just telling me a few days ago how depressed she is that she can't get pregnant.

"I can't have beer, Marshall."

"Then drink wine, at least. You like me more when you're tipsy." He laughs at himself, but Allysa doesn't.

"I can't have wine, either. I can't have *any* alcohol, actually."

Marshall stops laughing.

My heart does a flip-flop.

Marshall turns in the booth and grabs her shoulders, making her face him straight-on. "Allysa?"

She just starts nodding and I don't know who starts crying first. Me or Marshall or Allysa. "I'm gonna be a dad?" he yells.

She's still nodding, and I'm just bawling like an idiot. Marshall jumps up in the booth and yells, "I'm gonna be a dad!"

I can't even explain what this moment is like. A grown man in a onesie, standing up in a booth at a bar, yelling to whoever will listen that he's gonna be a dad. He pulls her up and they're both standing in the booth now. He kisses her and it's the sweetest thing I've ever seen.

Until I look at Ryle and catch him chewing on his bottom lip like he's trying to blink back a potential tear. He glances at me and sees me staring, so he looks away. "Shut up," he says. "She's my sister."

I smile and lean over and kiss him on the cheek. "Congratulations, Uncle Ryle."

Once the parents-to-be stop making out in the booth, Ryle and I both stand up and congratulate them. Allysa said she's been feeling sick for a while, but just took a test this morning before our grand opening. She was going to wait and tell Marshall tonight when they got home, but she couldn't hold it in for another second.

Our drinks come and we order food. Once the waitress walks away, I look at Marshall. "How did you two meet?"

He says, "Allysa tells the story better than I do."

Allysa perks up and leans forward. "I hated him," she says. "He was Ryle's best friend and he was always at the house. I thought he was so annoying. He had just moved to Ohio from Boston and he had that Boston accent. He thought it made him so cool but I just wanted to slap him every time he spoke."

"She's *so* sweet," Marshall says, sarcastically.

"You were an idiot," Allysa replies, rolling her eyes. "Anyway, one day Ryle and I had a few friends over. Nothing big, but our parents were out of town, so of course we had a little get-together."

"There were thirty people there," Ryle says. "It was a party."

"Okay, a party," Allysa says. "I walked into the kitchen and Marshall was standing there pressed up against some floozy."

"She wasn't a floozy," he says. "She was a nice girl. Tasted like Cheetos, but . . ."

Allysa glares at him so he shuts up. She turns back to me. "I lost it," she says. "I started yelling at him to take his whores to his own house. The girl was literally so terrified of me, she ran for the door and didn't come back."

"Cock blocker," Marshall says.

Allysa punches him in the shoulder. "Anyway. After I cock blocked him, I ran to my room, embarrassed that I did that. It was out of pure jealousy, and I didn't even realize I liked him that way until I saw his hands on some other girl's ass. I threw myself on my bed and started crying. A few minutes later, he walked into my room and asked me if I was okay. I rolled over and yelled, 'I *like* you, you stupid fuck-face!'"

"And the rest is history . . ." Marshall says.

I laugh. "Awe. Stupid fuck-face. How sweet."

Ryle holds up a finger and says, "You're leaving out the best part."

Allysa shrugs. "Oh yeah. So Marshall walked over to me, pulled me off the bed, kissed me with the same mouth he was just kissing the floozy with, and we made out for half an hour. Ryle walked in on us and started screaming at Marshall. Then Marshall pushed Ryle out of my bedroom, locked the door, and made out with me for another hour."

Ryle is shaking his head. "Betrayed by my best friend."

Marshall pulls Allysa to him. "I like her, you stupid fuck-face."

I laugh, but Ryle turns to me with a serious look on his

face. "I didn't speak to him for an entire month, I was so mad. I eventually got over it. We were eighteen, she was seventeen. Wasn't much I could do in the way of keeping them apart."

"Wow," I say. "I sometimes forget how close in age you two are."

Allysa smiles and says, "Three kids in three years. I feel so sorry for my parents."

The table grows quiet. I see an apologetic look pass from Allysa to Ryle.

"Three?" I ask. "You have another sibling?"

Ryle straightens up and takes a sip of his beer. He sets it back down on the table and says, "We had an older brother. He passed away when we were kids."

Such a great night, ruined by a simple question. Luckily, Marshall redirects the conversation like a pro.

I spend the rest of the evening listening to stories about them growing up. I'm not sure I've ever laughed as hard as I have tonight.

When the game is over, we all walk back to the shop to retrieve our cars. Ryle said he caught an Uber over earlier, so he'll just ride with me. Before Allysa and Marshall leave, I tell her to hold on. I run inside the store and grab the steampunk flowers and run them back to their car. Her face lights up when I hand them to her.

"I'm happy you're pregnant but that's not why I'm giving you these flowers. I just want you to have them. Because you're my best friend."

Allysa squeezes me and whispers in my ear. "I hope he marries you someday. We'll be even better sisters."

She climbs inside the car and they leave, and I just stand

there watching them because I don't know that I've ever had a friend like her in my whole life. Maybe it's the wine. I don't know, but I love today. Everything about it. I especially love how Ryle looks, leaning against my car, watching me.

"You're really beautiful when you're happy."

Ugh! This day! Perfect!

• • •

We're making our way up the stairs to my apartment when Ryle grabs my waist and pushes me against the wall. He just starts kissing me, right there in the stairwell.

"Impatient," I mutter.

He laughs and cups my ass with both of his hands. "Nope. It's this onesie. You really should consider making this your business attire." He kisses me again and doesn't stop kissing me until someone passes us, heading down the stairs.

The guy mumbles, "Nice onesies," as he squeezes past us. "Did the Bruins win?"

Ryle nods. "Three to one," he responds, without looking up at the guy.

"Nice," the guy says.

Once he's gone, I step away from Ryle. "What is this onesie thing? Does every male in Boston know about this?"

He laughs and says, "Free beer, Lily. It's free beer." He pulls me up the stairs, and when we walk in the door, Lucy is standing at the kitchen table taping up a box of her stuff. There's another box she hasn't taped up yet and I could swear I see a bowl that I bought at HomeGoods sticking out of the top. She said she'd have all her stuff out by next week, but I have a feeling she'll conveniently have some of *my* stuff out, too.

"Who are you?" she asks, looking Ryle up and down.

"Ryle Kincaid. I'm Lily's boyfriend."

Lily's boyfriend.

Did you hear that?

Boyfriend.

It's the first time he's confirmed it, and he said it so confidently. "My boyfriend, huh?" I walk into the kitchen and grab a bottle of wine and two wineglasses.

Ryle comes up behind me as I'm pouring the wine and snakes his arms around my waist. "Yep. Your boyfriend."

I hand him a glass of wine and say, "So I'm a girlfriend?"

He holds up his glass and clinks it against mine. "To the end of trial runs and the beginning of sure things."

We're both smiling as we take a drink of our wine.

Lucy stacks the boxes together and walks toward the front door. "Looks like I got out right in time," she says.

The door closes behind her and Ryle raises an eyebrow. "I don't think your roommate likes me very much."

"You'd be surprised. I didn't think she liked me, either, but yesterday she asked me to be a bridesmaid in her wedding. I think she's just hoping for free flowers, though. She's very opportunistic."

Ryle laughs and leans against the refrigerator. His eyes fall to a magnet that says "*Boston*" on it. He pulls it off the refrigerator and raises an eyebrow. "You'll never get out of Boston purgatory if you keep souvenirs of Boston on your fridge like a tourist."

I laugh and grab the magnet, slapping it back on the fridge. I like that he remembers so much about the first night we met. "It was a gift. It only counts as touristy if I bought it myself."

He steps over to me and takes my glass of wine from my hands. He sets both of our glasses on the countertop, and then leans in and gives me a deep, passionate, drunken kiss. I can taste the tart fruitiness of the wine on his tongue and I like it. His hands go to the zipper on my onesie. "Let's get you out of these clothes."

He pulls me toward the bedroom, kissing me while we both struggle out of our clothes. By the time we make it to my bedroom, I'm down to my bra and panties.

He shoves me against the door, and I gasp at the unexpectedness of it.

"Don't move," he says. He presses his lips to my chest, then begins to kiss me slowly as he makes his way down my body.

Oh, Lord. Can this day seriously get any better?

I run my hands through his hair, but he grabs my wrists and presses them against the door. He climbs back up my body, squeezing my wrists tightly. He raises an eyebrow in warning. "I said . . . don't move."

I try not to smile, but it's hard to disguise. He drags his mouth back down my body. He slowly lowers my panties to my ankles, but he told me not to move, so I don't kick them off.

His mouth slides up my thigh until . . .

Yeah.

Best.

Day.

Ever.

Chapter Thirteen

Ryle: Are you at home or still at work?

Me: Work. Should be done in about an hour.

Ryle: Can I come see you?

Me: You know how people say there is no such thing as a stupid question? They're wrong. That was a stupid question.

Ryle: :)

Half an hour later, he's knocking at the front door of the floral shop. I closed the shop almost three hours ago, but I'm still here, trying to get caught up on the chaos that was the first month. The store is still too new to get an accurate projection of how well or how bad it's doing. Some days are great and some are so slow I send Allysa home. But overall, I'm happy with how it's gone so far.

And happy with how things are going with Ryle.

I unlock the door to let him in. He's in light blue scrubs again, and he still has a stethoscope around his neck. Fresh from work. Very nice touch. I swear, every time I see him straight off a shift, I have to hide the stupid grin on my face. I give him a quick kiss and then turn back toward my office. "I have a few things to finish up and then we can go back to my place."

He follows me into my office and closes the door. "You got a couch?" he asks, looking around my office.

I've spent some of this week putting the finishing touches

on it. I bought a couple of lamps so I don't have to turn on the overpowering fluorescent lights. The lamps give the room a soft glow. I also bought a few plants to keep here permanently. It's no garden, but it's as close as it gets. It's come a long way since this room was being used as storage for vegetable crates.

Ryle walks over to the couch and falls down onto it, face-first. "Take your time," he mumbles into the pillow. "I'll just nap until you're finished."

I sometimes worry about how hard he pushes himself with work, but I don't say anything. I've been sitting in my office going on twelve hours now, so I don't have much room to talk when it comes to being too ambitious.

I spend the next fifteen or so minutes finalizing orders. When I'm finished, I close my laptop and look over at Ryle.

I thought he'd be asleep, but instead he's on his side with his head propped up on his hand. He's been watching me this whole time, and seeing the smile on his face makes me blush. I push my chair back and stand up.

"Lily, I think I like you too much," he says as I make my way over to him.

I scrunch up my nose as he sits up on the couch and pulls me onto his lap. "Too much? That doesn't sound like a compliment."

"That's because I don't know if it is," he says. He adjusts my legs on either side of him and then wraps his arms around my waist. "This is my first real relationship. I don't know if I'm supposed to like you this much yet. I don't want to scare you away."

I laugh. "Like that could ever happen. You work way too much to smother me."

He rubs his hands up my back. "Does it bother you that I work too much?"

I shake my head. "No. I worry about you sometimes because I don't want you to burn yourself out. But I don't mind that I have to share you with your passion. I actually really like how ambitious you are. It's kind of sexy. It might even be my favorite thing about you."

"You know what I like the most about you?"

"I already know this answer," I say, smiling. "My mouth."

He leans his head back against the couch. "Oh yeah. That does come first. But do you know what my second favorite thing about you is?"

I shake my head.

"You don't put pressure on me to be something I'm incapable of being. You accept me exactly how I am."

I smile. "Well, in all fairness, you're a little different from when I first met you. You aren't so anti-girlfriend anymore."

"That's because you make it easy," he says, sliding a hand inside the back of my shirt. "It's easy being with you. I can still have the career I've always wanted, but you make it ten times better with the way you support me. When I'm with you, I feel like I get to have my cake and eat it, too."

Now both of his hands are beneath my shirt, pressed against my back. He pulls me toward him and kisses me. I grin against his mouth and whisper, "Is it the best cake you've ever tasted?"

One of his hands moves to the back of my bra and he unfastens it with ease. "I'm pretty sure, but maybe I need another taste of it to be positive." He pulls my shirt and bra over my head. I begin to push myself off of him so I can pull off my jeans, but he pulls me back onto his lap. He grabs his stethoscope and puts it in his ears, then presses the diaphragm against my chest, right over my heart.

"What's got your heart so worked up, Lily?"

I shrug innocently. "It might have a little to do with you, Dr. Kincaid."

He drops the end of the stethoscope and then lifts me off of him, pushing me back onto the couch. He spreads my legs and kneels down on the couch between them, placing the stethoscope against my chest again. He uses his other hand to hold himself up as he continues listening to my heart.

"I'd say you're at about ninety beats per minute," he says.

"Is that good or bad?"

He grins and lowers himself on top of me. "I'll be satisfied when it reaches one forty."

Yeah. If it reaches 140, I'm thinking I'll be satisfied, too.

He lowers his mouth to my chest and my eyes fall shut when I feel his tongue slide across my breast. He takes me in his mouth, keeping the stethoscope pressed against my chest the entire time. "You're at about one hundred now," he says. He wraps the stethoscope around his neck again and then pulls back, unbuttoning my jeans. Once he slides them off of me, he turns me over until I'm on my stomach, my arms draped over the arm of the couch.

"Get on your knees," he says.

I do what he says and before I'm even adjusted, I feel the cold metal of the stethoscope meet my chest again, this time with his arm snaked around me from behind. I remain still as he listens to my heartbeat. His other hand slowly begins to find its way between my legs and then inside my panties and then inside of me. I grip the couch but try to keep the noises to a minimum while he listens to my heart.

"One hundred and ten," he says, still unsatisfied.

He pulls my hips back to meet him and then I can feel him freeing himself from his scrubs. He grips my hip with one hand while shoving my panties aside with the other. Then he pushes forward until he's all the way inside of me.

I'm grasping the couch with two desperate fists when he pauses to listen to my heart again. "Lily," he says with mock disappointment. "One twenty. Not quite where I want you."

The stethoscope disappears again and his arm curls around my waist. His hand slides down my stomach and settles between my legs. I can no longer keep up with his rhythm. I can barely even stay on my knees. He's somehow holding me up with one hand and destroying me in the best possible way with his other hand. Right when I start to tremble, he pulls me upright until my back meets his chest. He's still inside me, but now he's focused on my heart again as he moves his stethoscope around to the front of my chest.

I let out a moan and he presses his lips to my ear. "Shh. No noises."

I have no idea how I make it through the next thirty seconds without making another sound. One of his arms is wrapped around me with the stethoscope pressed to my chest. His other arm is tight against my stomach as his hand continues its magic between my legs. He's still somehow deep inside me and I'm trying to move against him, but he's rock solid as the tremors begin to rush through me. My legs are shaking and my hands are at my sides, gripping the tops of his thighs as it takes every ounce of my strength not to scream out his name.

I'm still shaking when he lifts my hand and places the diaphragm against my wrist. After several seconds, he pulls the stethoscope away and tosses it to the floor. "One fifty," he says with satisfaction. He pulls out of me and flips me onto my back and then his mouth is on mine and he's inside me again.

My body is too weak to move and I can't even open my eyes and watch him. He thrusts against me several times and then holds still, groaning into my mouth. He drops on top of me, tense, yet shaking.

He kisses my neck and then his lips meet the tattoo of the heart on my collarbone. He finally settles against my neck and sighs.

"Have I already mentioned tonight how much I like you?" he asks.

I laugh. "Once or twice."

"Consider this the third time," he says. "I like you. Everything about you, Lily. Being inside of you. Being outside of you. Being near you. I like it all."

I smile, loving how his words feel against my skin. Inside my heart. I open my mouth to tell him I like him, too, but my voice is cut off by the sound of his phone.

He groans against my neck and then pulls out of me and reaches for his phone. He pulls his scrubs back into place and laughs as he looks at his caller ID.

"It's my mother," he says, leaning over and kissing the top of my knee that's resting against the back of the couch. He tosses the phone aside and then stands and walks over to my desk, grabbing a box of tissues.

This is always awkward, having to clean up after sex. But I can't say it's ever been this awkward before, knowing his mother is on the other end of that ring.

Once all my clothes are back in place, he pulls me against him on the couch and I lie down on top of him, resting my head on his chest.

It's after ten now and I'm so comfortable I debate just sleeping here for the night. Ryle's phone makes another noise, alerting him to a new voice mail. The thought of seeing him interact with his mother makes me smile. Allysa talks about their parents some, but I've never really talked to Ryle about them before.

"Do you get along with your parents?"

His arm is stroking mine gently. "Yeah, I do. They're good people. We hit a rough patch when I was a teenager, but we worked through it. I talk to my mother almost daily now."

I fold my arms over his chest and rest my chin on them, looking up at him. "Will you tell me more about your mother? Allysa told me they moved to England a few years ago. And that they were in Australia on vacation, but that was like a month ago."

He laughs. "My mother? Well . . . my mother is very overbearing. Very judgmental, especially of the people she loves the most. She's never missed a single church service. And I have never heard her refer to my father as anything other than Dr. Kincaid."

Despite the warnings, he smiles the whole time he talks about her.

"Your father is a doctor, too?"

He nods. "Psychiatrist. He chose a field that also allowed him to have a normal life. Smart man."

"Do they ever visit you in Boston?"

"Not really. My mother hates flying, so Allysa and I fly to England a couple of times a year. She does want to meet you, though, so you might be going with us on the next trip."

I grin. "You've told your mother about me?"

"Of course," he says. "This is kind of a monumental thing, you know. Me having a girlfriend. She calls me every day to make sure I haven't screwed it up somehow."

I laugh, which makes him reach for his phone. "You think I'm kidding? I guarantee she somehow brought you up in the voice mail she just left." He presses a few keys and then begins to play the voice mail.

"Hey, sweetheart! It's your mom. Haven't spoken to you since yesterday. Miss you. Give Lily a hug for me. You do still see her, right? Allysa says you can't stop talking about her. She is still your girlfriend, right? Okay. Gretchen's here, we're having high tea. Love you. Kiss kiss."

I press my face against his chest and laugh. "We've only been dating a few months. How much do you talk about me?"

He pulls my hand up between us and kisses it. "Too much, Lily. Way too much."

I smile. "I can't wait to meet them. Not only did they raise an incredible daughter, but they made you. That's pretty impressive."

His arms tighten around me and he kisses the top of my head.

"What was your brother's name?" I ask him.

I can feel a slight stiffness in him after I ask that. I regret bringing it up, but it's too late to take it back.

"Emerson."

I can tell by his voice that it's not something he wants to talk about right now. Instead of pressing it further, I lift my head and scoot forward, pressing my mouth to his.

I should know better. Kisses can't seem to stop at just kisses when it comes to me and Ryle. In a matter of minutes, he's inside of me again, but this time it's everything the other time wasn't.

This time we make love.

Chapter Fourteen

My phone rings. I pick it up to see who it is and I'm a little taken aback. It's the first time Ryle has ever called me. We always just text. How odd to have a boyfriend for over three months that I've never once spoken to on the phone.

"Hello?"

"Hey, girlfriend," he says.

I smile cheesily at the sound of his voice. "Hey, boyfriend."

"Guess what?"

"What?"

"I'm taking the day off tomorrow. Your floral shop doesn't open until one o'clock on Sundays. I'm on my way to your apartment with two bottles of wine. You want to have a sleepover with your boyfriend and have drunken sex all night and sleep until noon?"

It's really embarrassing what his words do to me. I smile and say, "Guess what?"

"What?"

"I'm cooking you dinner. And I'm wearing an apron."

"Oh yeah?" he says.

"*Just* an apron." And then I hang up.

A few seconds later, I get a text message.

Ryle: Pic, please.

Me: Get over here and you can take the picture yourself.

I'm almost finished preparing the casserole mixture when the door opens. I pour it into the glass pan and don't turn around when I hear him walk into the kitchen. When I said I was just wearing an apron, I meant it. I'm not even wearing panties.

I can hear him suck in a rush of air when I reach over to the oven and stick the casserole inside. I might reach a little too far for show when I do it. When I close the oven, I don't face him. I grab a rag and start wiping down the oven, making sure to sway my hips as much as possible. I squeal when I feel a piercing sting on my right butt cheek. I spin around and Ryle is grinning, holding two bottles of wine.

"Did you just *bite* me?"

He gives me an innocent look. "Don't tempt the scorpion if you don't want to get stung." He eyes me up and down while he opens one of the bottles. He holds it up before he pours us a glass and says, "It's vintage."

"*Vintage*," I say with mock impression. "What's the special occasion?"

He hands me a glass and says, "I'm going to be an uncle. I have a smoking hot girlfriend. And I get to perform a very rare, possibly once-in-a-lifetime craniopagus separation on Monday."

"A cranio-*what*?"

He finishes off his glass of wine and pours himself another one. "Craniopagus separation. Conjoined twins," he says. He points to a spot on the top of his head and taps it. "Attached right here. We've been studying them since they were born. It's a very rare surgery. *Very* rare."

For the first time, I think I'm genuinely turned on by

him as a doctor. I mean, I admire his drive. I admire his dedication. But seeing how excited he is about what he's doing for a living is seriously sexy.

"How long do you think it'll take?" I ask.

He shrugs. "Not sure. They're young, so being under general anesthesia for too long is a concern." He holds up his right hand and wiggles his fingers. "But this is a very special hand that has been through almost half a million dollars' worth of specialty education. I have a lot of faith in this hand."

I walk over to him and press my lips to his palm. "I'm a little fond of this hand, too."

He slides the hand down to my neck and then spins me so that I'm flush against the counter. I gasp, because I wasn't expecting that.

He pushes himself against me from behind and slowly slides his hand down the side of my body. I press my palms into the granite and close my eyes, already feeling the rush of the wine.

"This hand," he whispers, "is the steadiest hand in all of Boston."

He pushes on the back of my neck, bending me further over the counter. His hand meets the inside of my knee and he glides it upward. Slowly. *Jesus.*

He pushes my legs apart, and then his fingers are inside me. I moan and try to find something to hold on to. I grip the faucet, just as he begins to work magic.

And then, just like a magician, his hand disappears.

I hear him walking out of the kitchen. I watch as he passes the front of the counter. He winks at me, downs the rest of his glass of wine and says, "I'm gonna take a quick shower."

What a tease.

"You asshole!" I yell after him.

"I'm not an asshole!" he yells from my bedroom. "I'm a highly trained neurosurgeon!"

I laugh and pour myself another glass of wine.

I'll show him who the tease really is.

• • •

I'm on my third glass of wine when he walks out of my bedroom.

I'm on the phone with my mother, so I watch him from the couch as he makes his way to the kitchen and pours himself another glass.

That is some seriously good wine.

"What are you doing tonight?" my mother asks.

I have her on speakerphone. Ryle is leaning against a wall, watching me talk to her. "Not much. Helping Ryle study."

"That sounds . . . not very interesting," she says.

Ryle winks at me.

"It's actually very interesting," I say to her. "I help him study a lot. Mostly reviewing fine-motor control of the hands. In fact, we'll probably be up all night studying."

The three glasses of wine has made me frisky. I can't believe I'm flirting with him while I'm on the phone with my mother. *Gross.*

"I gotta go," I tell her. "We're taking Allysa and Marshall out to dinner tomorrow night, so I'll call you on Monday."

"Oh, where are you taking them?"

I roll my eyes. The woman can't take a hint. "I don't know. Ryle, where are we taking them?"

"That place we went to that one time with your mom," he says. "Bib's? I made reservations for six o'clock."

My heart feels like it slinks down my chest. My mother says, "Oh, good choice."

"Yeah. If you like stale bread. Bye, Mom." I hang up and look at Ryle. "I don't want to go back there. I didn't like it. Let's try something new."

I fail to tell him why I *really* don't want to go back there. But how do you tell your brand-new boyfriend that you're trying to avoid your first love?

Ryle pushes off the wall. "You'll be fine," he says. "Allysa's excited to eat there, I told her all about it."

Maybe I'll get lucky and Atlas won't be working.

"Speaking of food," Ryle says. "I'm starving."

The casserole!

"Oh shit!" I say, laughing.

Ryle rushes to the kitchen and I stand up and follow him in there. I walk in just as he pulls the oven door open and waves away the smoke. *Ruined.*

I get dizzy all of a sudden from standing up too fast after having three glasses of wine. I grab the counter beside him to steady myself, just as he reaches in to pull the burnt casserole out.

"Ryle! You need a . . ."

"Shit!" he yells.

"Pot holder."

The casserole falls from his hand and lands on the floor,

shattering everywhere. I lift up my feet to avoid broken glass and mushroom chicken splatter. I start laughing as soon as I realize he didn't even think to use a pot holder.

Must be the wine. *This is some seriously strong wine.*

He slams the oven shut and moves to the faucet, shoving his hand under the cold water, muttering curse words. I'm trying to suppress my laughter, but the wine and the ridiculousness of the last few seconds are making it hard. I look at the floor—at the mess we're about to have to clean up—and the laughter bursts from me. I'm still laughing as I lean over to get a look at Ryle's hand. I hope he didn't hurt it too bad.

I'm instantly not laughing anymore. I'm on the floor, my hand pressed against the corner of my eye.

In a matter of one second, Ryle's arm came out of nowhere and slammed against me, knocking me backward. There was enough force behind it to knock me off balance. When I lost my footing, I hit my face on one of the cabinet door handles as I came down.

Pain shoots through the corner of my eye, right near my temple.

And then I feel the weight.

Heaviness follows and it presses down on every part of me. So much gravity, pushing down on my emotions. Everything shatters.

My tears, my heart, my laughter, my *soul*. Shattered like broken glass, raining down around me.

I wrap my arms over my head and try to wish away the last ten seconds.

"Goddammit, Lily," I hear him say. "It's not funny. This hand is my fucking career."

I don't look up at him. His voice doesn't penetrate through my body this time. It feels like it's stabbing me now, the sharpness of each of his words coming at me like swords. Then I feel him next to me, his *goddamn hand* on my back.

Rubbing.

"Lily," he says. "Oh, God. *Lily*." He tries to pull my arms from my head, but I refuse to budge. I start shaking my head, wanting the last fifteen seconds to go away. *Fifteen seconds*. That's all it takes to completely change everything about a person.

Fifteen seconds that we'll never get back.

He pulls me against him and starts kissing the top of my head. "I'm so sorry. I just . . . I burned my hand. I panicked. You were laughing and . . . I'm so sorry, it all happened so fast. I didn't mean to push you, Lily, I'm sorry."

I don't hear Ryle's voice this time. All I hear is my father's voice.

"I'm sorry, Jenny. It was an accident. I'm so sorry."

"I'm sorry, Lily. It was an accident. I'm so sorry."

I just want him away from me. I use every ounce of strength I have in both my hands and legs and I force him *the fuck* away from me.

He falls backward, onto his hands. His eyes are full of genuine sorrow, but then they're full of something else.

Worry? Panic?

He slowly pulls up his right hand and it's covered in blood. Blood is trickling out of his palm, down his wrist. I look at the floor—at the shattered pieces of glass from the casserole dish. *His hand*. I just pushed him onto glass.

He turns around and pulls himself up. He sticks his

hand under the stream of water and starts rinsing away the blood. I stand up, just as he pulls a sliver of glass out of his palm and tosses it on the counter.

I'm full of so much anger, but somehow, concern for his hand still finds its way out. I grab a towel and shove it into his fist. There's so much blood.

It's his right hand.

His surgery Monday.

I try to help stop the bleeding, but I'm shaking too bad. "Ryle, your hand."

He pulls the hand away and, with his good hand, he lifts my chin. "*Fuck* the hand, Lily. I don't care about my hand. Are you okay?" He's looking back and forth between my eyes frantically as he assesses the cut on my face.

My shoulders begin to shake and huge, hurt-filled tears spill down my cheeks. "No." I'm a little in shock, and I know he can hear my heart breaking with just that one word, because I can feel it in every part of me. "Oh my God. You *pushed* me, Ryle. You . . ." The realization of what has just happened hurts worse than the actual action.

Ryle wraps his arm around my neck and desperately holds me against him. "I'm so sorry, Lily. *God*, I'm so sorry." He buries his face against my hair, squeezing me with every emotion inside of him. "Please don't hate me. *Please*."

His voice slowly starts to become Ryle's voice again, and I feel it in my stomach, in my toes. His entire career depends on his hand, so it has to say something that he's not even worried about it. *Right?* I'm so confused.

There's too much happening. The smoke, the wine, the

broken glass, the food splattered everywhere, the blood, the anger, the apologies, *it's too much.*

"I'm so sorry," he says again. I pull back and his eyes are red and I've never seen him look so sad. "I panicked. I didn't mean to push you away, I just panicked. All I could think about was the surgery Monday and my hand and . . . I'm so sorry." He presses his mouth to mine and breathes me in.

He's not like my father. He can't be. He's nothing like that uncaring bastard.

We're both upset and kissing and confused and sad. I've never felt anything like this moment—so ugly and painful. But somehow the only thing that eases the hurt just caused by this man *is* this man. My tears are soothed by his sorrow, my emotions soothed with his mouth against mine, his hand gripping me like he never wants to let go.

I feel his arms go around my waist and he picks me up, carefully stepping through the mess we've made. I can't tell if I'm more disappointed in him or myself. Him for losing his temper in the first place or me for somehow finding comfort in his apology.

He carries me and kisses me all the way to my bedroom. He's still kissing me when he lowers me to the bed and whispers, "I'm sorry, Lily." He moves his lips to the spot on my eye that hit the cabinet, and he kisses me there. "I'm so sorry."

His mouth is on mine again, hot and wet, and I don't even know what's happening to me. I'm hurting so much on the inside, yet my body craves his apology in the form of his mouth and hands on me. I want to lash out at him and react like I always wish my mother would have reacted when my father hurt her, but deep down I want to believe that it really was an accident. Ryle isn't like my father. *He's nothing like him.*

I need to feel his sorrow. His regret. I get both of these things in the way he kisses me. I spread my legs for him and his sorrow comes in another form. Slow, apologetic thrusts inside of me. Every time he enters me, he whispers another apology. And by some miracle, every time he pulls out of me, my anger leaves with him.

• • •

He's kissing my shoulder. My cheek. My eye. He's still on top of me, touching me gently. I've never been touched like this . . . with such tenderness. I try to forget what happened in the kitchen, but it's everything right now.

He pushed me away from him.

Ryle pushed me.

For fifteen seconds, I saw a side of him that *wasn't* him. That wasn't *me.* I laughed at him when I should have been concerned. He shoved me when he should have never touched me. I pushed him away and caused him to cut his hand.

It was awful. The whole thing, the entire fifteen seconds it lasted, was absolutely awful. I never want to think about it again.

He still has the rag balled up in his hand and it's soaked with blood. I push against his chest.

"I'll be right back," I tell him. He kisses me one more time and rolls off of me. I walk to the bathroom and close the door. I look in the mirror and gasp.

Blood. In my hair, on my cheeks, on my body. It's all his

blood. I grab a rag and try to wash some off, and then I look under the sink for the first aid kit. I have no idea how bad his hand is. First he burned it, then he sliced it open. Not even an hour after he was just telling me how important this surgery was to him.

No more wine. We're never allowed vintage wine again.

I grab the box from under the sink and open the bedroom door. He's walking back into the bedroom from the kitchen with a small bag of ice. He holds it up, "For your eye," he says.

I hold up the first aid kit. "For your hand."

We both smile and then sit back down on the bed. He leans against the headboard while I pull his hand to my lap. The whole time I'm dressing his wound, he's holding the bag of ice against my eye.

I squeeze some antiseptic cream onto my finger and dab it against the burns on his fingers. They don't look as bad as I thought they might be, so that's a relief. "Can you prevent it from blistering?" I ask him.

He shakes his head. "Not if it's second-degree."

I want to ask him if he can still perform the surgery if his fingers have blisters on them come Monday, but I don't bring it up. I'm sure that's on the forefront of his mind right now.

"Do you want me to put some on your cut?"

He nods. The bleeding has stopped. I'm sure if he needed stitches, he'd get some, but I think it'll be fine. I pull the ACE bandage out of the first aid kit and begin wrapping his hand.

"Lily," he whispers. I look up at him. His head is resting against the headboard, and it looks like he wants to cry. "I feel terrible," he says. "If I could take it back . . ."

"I know," I say, cutting him off. "I know, Ryle. It was

terrible. You pushed me. You made me question everything I thought I knew about you. But I know you feel bad about it. We can't take it back. I don't want to bring it up again." I secure the bandage around his hand and then look him in the eye. "But Ryle? If anything like that ever happens again . . . I'll know that this time wasn't just an accident. And I'll leave you without a second thought."

He stares at me for a long time, his eyebrows drawn apart in regret. He leans forward and presses his lips against mine. "It won't happen again, Lily. I swear. I'm not like him. I know that's what you're thinking, but I swear to you . . ."

I shake my head, wanting him to stop. I can't take the pain in his voice. "I know you're nothing like my father," I say. "Just . . . please don't ever make me doubt you again. Please."

He brushes hair from my forehead. "You're the most important part of my life, Lily. I want to be what brings you happiness. Not what causes you to hurt." He kisses me and then stands up and leans over me, pressing the ice to my face. "Hold this here for about ten more minutes. It'll prevent it from swelling."

I replace his hand with mine. "Where are you going?"

He kisses me on the forehead and says, "To clean up my mess."

He spends the next twenty minutes cleaning the kitchen. I can hear glass being tossed into the trash can, wine being poured out in the sink. I go to the bathroom and take a quick shower to get his blood off of me and then I change the sheets on my bed. When he finally has the kitchen cleaned up, he comes to the bedroom with a glass. He hands it to me. "It's soda," he says, "The caffeine will help."

I take a drink of it and feel it fizz down my throat. It's actually the perfect thing. I take another drink and set it on my nightstand. "What's it help with? The hangover?"

Ryle slides into bed and pulls the covers over us. He shakes his head. "No, I don't think soda actually helps anything. My mom just used to give me a soda after I'd had a bad day and it always made me feel a little better."

I smile. "Well, it worked."

He brushes his hand down my cheek and I can see in his eyes and in the way he touches me that he deserves at least one chance at forgiveness. I feel if I don't find a way to forgive him, I'll somewhat be placing blame on him for the resentment I still hold for my father. *He's not like my father.*

Ryle loves me. He's never come out and said it before, but I know he does. And I love him. What happened in the kitchen tonight is something I'm confident won't happen again. Not after seeing how upset he is that he hurt me.

All humans make mistakes. What determines a person's character aren't the mistakes we make. It's how we take those mistakes and turn them into lessons rather than excuses.

Ryle's eyes somehow grow even more sincere and he leans over and kisses my hand. He settles his head into the pillow and we just lie there, staring at each other, sharing this unspoken energy that fills all the holes the night has left in us.

After a few minutes, he squeezes my hand. "Lily," he says, brushing his thumb over mine. "I'm in love with you."

I feel his words in every part of me. And when I whisper, "*I love you, too,*" it's the most naked truth I've ever spoken to him.

Chapter Fifteen

I arrive at the restaurant fifteen minutes late. Right when I was about to close tonight I had a customer come in to order flowers for a funeral. I couldn't turn them away because . . . sadly . . . funerals are the best business for florists.

Ryle waves me over to the table and I walk straight to them, doing my best not to look around. I don't want to see Atlas. I tried twice to get them to change the restaurant location, but Allysa was hell-bent on eating here after Ryle told her how good it was.

I slide into the booth and Ryle leans over and kisses me on the cheek. "Hey, girlfriend."

Allysa groans. "God, you guys are so cute, it's sickening." I smile at her, and her eyes immediately go to the corner of my eye. It doesn't look as bad as I thought it might today, which is probably due to Ryle forcing me to keep ice on it. "Oh my God," Allysa says. "Ryle told me what happened but I didn't think it was that bad."

I glance at Ryle, wondering what he told her. *The truth?* He smiles and says, "Olive oil was everywhere. When she slipped, it was so graceful you'd think she was a ballerina."

A lie.

Fair enough. I would have done the same thing.

"It was pretty pathetic," I say with a laugh.

Somehow, we get through dinner without a hitch. No

sign of Atlas, no thoughts of last night, and Ryle and I both avoid the wine. After we're finished with our food, our waiter approaches the table. "Care for dessert?" he asks.

I shake my head, but Allysa perks up. "What do you have?"

Marshall looks just as interested. "We're eating for two, so we'll take anything chocolate," he says.

The waiter nods, and when he walks away, Allysa looks at Marshall. "This baby is the size of a bedbug right now. You better not encourage bad habits for the next several months."

The waiter returns with a dessert cart. "The chef gives all expectant mothers dessert on the house," he says. "Congratulations."

"He does?" Allysa says, perking up.

"Guess that's why it's called Bib's," Marshall says. "Chef likes the babies."

We all look at the cart. "Oh, God," I say, looking at the options.

"This is my new favorite restaurant," Allysa says.

We pick out three desserts for the table. The four of us spend the time waiting for it to be served discussing baby names.

"No," Allysa says to Marshall. "We're not naming this baby after a state."

"But I love Nebraska," he whines. "Idaho?"

Allysa drops her head in her hands. "This is going to be the demise of our marriage."

"Demise," Marshall says. "That's actually a good name."

Marshall's murder is thwarted by the arrival of dessert. Our waiter places a piece of chocolate cake in front of Allysa, and steps aside to make room for the waiter behind him who is holding the other two desserts. The waiter motions toward the guy placing our desserts down and says, "The chef would like to extend his congratulations."

"How was the meal?" the chef asks, looking at Allysa and Marshall.

By the time his eyes make it to mine, my anxiety is seeping from me. Atlas locks eyes with me, and without thinking, I blurt out, "You're the *chef*?"

The waiter leans around Atlas and says. "The chef. The owner. Sometimes waiter, sometimes dishwasher. He gives a new meaning to hands-on."

The next five seconds go unnoticed by everyone at our table, but they play out in slow motion to me.

Atlas's eyes fall to the cut on my eye.

The bandage wrapped around Ryle's hand.

Back to my eye.

"We love your restaurant," Allysa says. "You have an incredible place here."

Atlas doesn't look at her. I see the roll of his throat as he swallows. His jaw hardens and he says nothing as he walks away.

Shit.

The waiter tries to cover for Atlas's hasty retreat by smiling and showing way too many teeth. "Enjoy your dessert," he says, scuffling off to the kitchen.

"Bummer," Allysa says. "We find a new favorite restaurant and the chef is an asshole."

Ryle laughs. "Yeah, but the assholes are the best ones. Gordon Ramsay?"

"Good point," Marshall says.

I put my hand on Ryle's arm. "Bathroom," I tell him.

He nods as I scoot out of the booth, and Marshall says, "What about Wolfgang Puck? You think he's an asshole?"

I walk across the restaurant, head down, fast paced. As soon as I get into the familiar hallway, I keep going. I push open the door to the women's restroom and then turn around and lock it.

Shit. Shit, shit, shit.

The look in his eye. The anger in his jaw.

I'm relieved he walked away, but I'm half-convinced he's probably going to be waiting outside the restaurant when we leave, ready to kick Ryle's ass.

I breathe in my nose, out my mouth, wash my hands, repeat the breathing. Once I'm more calm, I dry my hands on a towel.

I'll just go back out there and tell Ryle I'm not feeling well. We'll leave and we'll never come back. They all think the chef is an asshole, so that can be my excuse.

I unlock the door, but I don't pull it open. It starts pushing open from the other side, so I step back. Atlas steps inside the bathroom with me and locks the door. His back rests against the door as he stares at me, focused on the cut near my eye.

"What happened?" he asks.

I shake my head. "Nothing."

His eyes are narrow, still ice blue but somehow burning with fire. "You're lying, Lily."

I muster enough of a smile to get me by. "It was an accident."

Atlas laughs, but then his face falls flat. "Leave him."

Leave him?

Jesus, he thinks this is something else entirely. I take a step forward and shake my head. "He's not like that, Atlas. It wasn't like that. Ryle is a good person."

He tilts his head and leans it forward a little bit. "Funny. You sound just like your mother."

His words sting. I immediately try to reach around him for the door, but he grabs my wrist. "*Leave* him, Lily."

I yank my hand away. I turn my back to him and inhale a deep breath. I release it slowly as I face him again. "If it's any comparison at all, I'm more scared of you right now than I've *ever* been of him."

My words make Atlas pause for a moment. His nod starts out slowly, and then gets more prominent as he steps away from the door. "I certainly didn't mean to make you feel uncomfortable." He motions toward the door. "Just trying to repay the concern you've always shown me."

I stare at him for a moment, unsure how to take his words. He's still raging on the inside, I can see it. But on the outside, he's calm—collected. Allowing me to leave. I reach forward and unlock the door, then pull it open.

I gasp when my eyes meet Ryle's. I quickly glance over my shoulder to see Atlas filing out of the bathroom with me.

Ryle's eyes fill with confusion as he looks from me to Atlas. "What the *fuck*, Lily?"

"Ryle." My voice shakes. *God, this looks so much worse than it is.*

Atlas steps around me and turns toward the doors to the kitchen, as if Ryle doesn't even exist to him. Ryle's eyes are glued to Atlas's back. *Keep walking, Atlas.*

Right when Atlas reaches the kitchen doors, he pauses.

No, no, no. Keep walking.

In what becomes one of the most dreadful moments I can imagine, he spins around and strides toward Ryle, grabbing him by the collar of his shirt. Almost as soon as it happens, Ryle forces Atlas back and slams him against the opposite wall. Atlas lunges for Ryle again, this time shoving his forearm against Ryle's throat, pinning him against the wall.

"You touch her again and I'll cut your fucking hand off and shove it down your throat, you worthless piece of shit!"

"Atlas, stop!" I yell.

Atlas releases Ryle forcefully, taking a huge step back. Ryle is breathing heavily, staring at Atlas long and hard. Then his focus moves directly to me. "*Atlas?*" He says his name with familiarity.

Why is Ryle saying Atlas's name like that? Like he's heard me say it before? I've never told him about Atlas.

Wait.

I did.

That first night on the roof. It was one of my naked truths.

Ryle lets out a disbelieving laugh and points at Atlas, but he's still looking at me. "*This* is Atlas? The homeless boy you *pity*-fucked?"

Oh, God.

The hallway instantly becomes a blur of fists and elbows and my screams for them to stop. Two waiters push through the door behind me and shove past me, separating them just as quickly as it started.

They're pushed apart against opposite walls, staring

each other down, breathing heavily. I can't even look at either of them.

I can't look at Atlas. Not after what Ryle just said to him. I also can't look at Ryle because he's probably thinking the absolute worst possible thing right now.

"Out!" Atlas yells, pointing at the door, but looking at Ryle. "Get the hell out of my restaurant!"

I meet Ryle's eyes as he begins to walk past me, scared of what I'll see in them. But there isn't any anger there.

Only hurt.

Lots of hurt.

He pauses as if he's about to say something to me. But his face just twists into disappointment and he walks back out into the restaurant.

I finally glance up at Atlas and can see disappointment all across his face. Before I can explain away Ryle's words to him, he turns and walks away, pushing through the kitchen doors.

I immediately turn and run after Ryle. He grabs his jacket from the booth and walks toward the exit without even looking at Allysa and Marshall.

Allysa looks up at me and holds her hands up in question. I shake my head, grab my purse and say, "It's a long story. We'll talk tomorrow."

I follow Ryle outside and he's walking toward the parking lot. I run to catch up to him and he just stops and punches at the air.

"I didn't bring my fucking *car!*" he yells, frustrated.

I pull my keys out of my purse and he walks up to me and snatches them from my hand. Again, I follow him, this time to my car.

I don't know what to do. I don't know if he even wants to speak to me right now. He just saw me locked in a bathroom with a guy I used to be in love with. Then, out of nowhere, that guy attacks him.

God, this is so bad.

When we reach my car, he heads straight for the driver's side door. He points to the passenger side and says, "Get in, Lily."

He doesn't speak to me the entire time we're driving. I say his name once, but he just shakes his head like he's not ready to hear my explanation yet. When we pull into my parking garage, he gets out of the car as soon as he turns it off, like he can't get away from me fast enough.

He's pacing the length of the car when I get out. "It wasn't what it looked like, Ryle. I swear."

He stops pacing, and when he looks at me, my heart doubles over. There's so much pain in his eyes right now, and it's not even necessary. It was all due to a stupid misunderstanding.

"I didn't want this, Lily," he says. "I didn't want a relationship! I didn't want this stress in my life!"

As much as he's hurting because of what he thinks he saw, his words still piss me off. "Well, then *leave*!"

"What?"

I throw my hands up. "I don't want to be your burden, Ryle! I'm so sorry my presence in your life is so *unbearable*!"

He takes a step forward. "Lily, that's not at all what I'm saying." He throws his hands up in frustration and then walks past me. He leans against my car and folds his arms over his chest. There's a long stretch of silence while I wait for what he has to say. His head is down, but he lifts it slightly, looking up at me.

"Naked truths, Lily. That's all I want from you right now. Can you please give me that?"

I nod.

"Did you know he worked there?"

I purse my lips together and wrap my arm over my chest, grabbing at my elbow. "Yes. That's why I didn't want to go back, Ryle. I didn't want to run into him."

My answer seems to release a little of his tension. He runs a hand down his face. "Did you tell him what happened last night? Did you tell him about our fight?"

I take a step forward and shake my head adamantly. "No. He assumed. He saw my eye and your hand and he just assumed."

He blows out a laden breath and leans his head back, looking up at the roof. It looks like it's almost too painful for him to even ask the next question.

"Why were you alone with him in the bathroom?"

I take another step forward. "He followed me in there. I know nothing about him now, Ryle. I didn't even know he owned that restaurant, I thought he was just a waiter. He's not a part of my life anymore, I swear. He just . . ." I fold my arms together and drop my voice. "We both grew up in abusive households. He saw my face and your hand and . . . he was just worried for me. That's all it was."

Ryle brings his hands up and covers his mouth. I can hear the air rushing through his fingers as he releases his breath. He stands up straight, allowing himself a moment to soak in all I've just said.

"My turn," he says.

He pushes off the car and takes the three steps toward me that previously separated us. He puts both hands on my cheeks and looks me dead in the eyes. "If you don't want to be with me . . . please tell me right now, Lily. Because when I saw you with him . . . that *hurt.* I never want to feel that again. And if it hurts this much now, I'm terrified to think of what it could do to me a year from now."

I can feel the tears begin to stream down my cheeks. I place my hands on top of his and shake my head. "I don't want anyone else, Ryle. I only want you."

He forces the saddest smile I've ever seen on a human. He pulls me to him and holds me there. I wrap my arms around him as tight as I can as he presses his lips to the side of my head.

"I love you, Lily. *God,* I love you."

I squeeze him tight, pressing a kiss to his shoulder. "I love you, too."

I close my eyes and wish I could wash away the entire last two days.

Atlas is wrong about Ryle.

I just wish *Atlas* knew he was wrong.

Chapter Sixteen

"I mean . . . I'm not trying to be selfish, but you didn't taste the dessert, Lily." Allysa groans. "Oh, it was *sooo* good."

"We're never going back there," I say to her.

She stomps her foot like a little kid. "But . . ."

"Nope. We have to respect your brother's feelings."

She folds her arms over her chest. "I know, I know. Why did you have to be a hormonal teenager and fall in love with the best chef in Boston?"

"He wasn't a chef when I knew him."

"Whatever," she says. She walks out of my office and closes the door.

My phone buzzes with an incoming text.

Ryle: 5 hours down. About 5 more to go. So far so good. Hand is great.

I sigh, relieved. I wasn't sure if he'd be able to do the surgery today, but knowing how much he was looking forward to it makes me happy for him.

Me: Steadiest hands in all of Boston.

I open my laptop and check my email. The first thing I see is an inquiry from the *Boston Globe*. I open it and it's from a journalist interested in running an article about the store. I grin like an idiot and start emailing her back when Allysa knocks on the door. She opens it and sticks her head in.

"Hey," she says.

"Hey," I say back.

She taps her fingers on the doorframe. "Remember a few minutes ago when you told me I could never go back to Bib's because it's unfair to Ryle that the boy you loved when you were a teenager is the owner?"

I fall back against my chair. "What do you want, Allysa?"

She scrunches up her nose and says, "If it isn't fair that we can't go back there because of the owner, how is it fair that the owner gets to come here?"

What?

I close my laptop and stand up. "Why would you say that? Is he here?"

She nods and slips inside my office, closing the door behind her. "He is. He asked for you. And I know you're with my brother and I'm with child, but can we please just take a moment to silently admire the perfection that is that man?"

She smiles dreamily and I roll my eyes.

"Allysa."

"Those *eyes*, though." She opens the door and walks out. I follow behind her and catch sight of Atlas. "She's right here," Allysa says. "Would you like me to take your coat?"

We don't take coats.

Atlas glances up when I walk out of my office. His eyes cut to Allysa and he shakes his head. "No, thank you. I won't be long."

Allysa leans forward over the counter, dropping her chin on her hands. "Stay as long as you like. In fact, are you looking for an extra job? Lily needs to hire more people and we're looking for someone who can lift really heavy things. Requires a lot of flexibility. Bending over."

I narrow my eyes at Allysa and mouth, *"Enough."*

She shrugs innocently. I hold my door open for Atlas, but avoid looking directly at him as he passes me. I feel a world of guilt for what happened last night, but also a world of anger for what happened last night.

I walk around my desk and drop into my seat, prepared for an argument. But when I look up at him, I clamp my mouth shut.

He's smiling. He waves his hand around in a circle as he takes a seat across from me. "This is incredible, Lily."

I pause. "Thank you."

He continues smiling at me, like he's proud of me. Then he places a bag between us on the desk and pushes it toward me. "A gift," he says. "You can open it later."

Why is he buying me gifts? He has a girlfriend. I have a boyfriend. Our past has already caused enough problems in my present. I certainly don't need gifts to exacerbate that.

"Why are you buying me gifts, Atlas?"

He leans back in his seat and crosses his arms over his chest. "I bought it three years ago. I've been holding on to it in case I ever ran into you."

Considerate Atlas. He hasn't changed. Dammit.

I pick up the gift and set it on the floor behind my desk. I try to release some of the tension I'm feeling, but it's really hard when everything about him makes me so tense.

"I came here to apologize to you," he says.

I wave off his apology, letting him know it isn't necessary. "It's fine. It was a misunderstanding. Ryle is fine."

He laughs under his breath. "That's not what I'm apologizing for," he says. "I'd never apologize for defending you."

"You weren't defending me," I say. "There was nothing to defend."

He tilts his head, giving me the same look that he gave me last night. The one that lets me know how disappointed in me he is. It stings deep in my gut.

I clear my throat. "Why are you apologizing, then?"

He's quiet for a moment. Contemplative. "I wanted to apologize for saying that you sounded like your mother. That was hurtful. And I'm sorry."

I don't know why I always feel like crying when I'm around him. When I think about him. When I read about him. It's like my emotions are still tethered to him somehow and I can't figure out how to cut the strings.

His eyes drop to my desk. He reaches forward and grabs three things. A pen. A sticky note. My phone.

He writes something down on the sticky note and then proceeds to pull my phone apart. He slips the case off and puts the sticky note between the case and the phone, then slides the cover back over it. He pushes my phone back across the desk. I look down at it and then up at him. He stands up and tosses the pen on my desk.

"It's my cell phone number. Keep it hidden there in case you ever need it."

I wince at the gesture. The *unnecessary* gesture. "I won't need it."

"I hope not." He walks to the door and reaches for the doorknob. And I know this is my only chance to get out what I have to say before he's out of my life forever.

"Atlas, wait."

I stand up so fast, my chair scoots across the room and bumps against the wall. He half turns and faces me.

"What Ryle said to you last night? I never . . ." I bring a nervous hand up to my neck. I can feel my heart beating in my throat. "I *never* said that to him. He was hurt and upset and he misconstrued my words from a long time ago."

The corner of Atlas's mouth twitches, and I'm not sure if he's trying not to smile or trying not to frown. He faces me straight on. "Believe me, Lily. I know that wasn't a *pity* fuck. I was there."

He walks out the door, and his words knock me straight back into my seat.

Only . . . my seat is no longer there. It's still on the other side of my office and I'm now on the floor.

Allysa rushes in and I'm lying on my back behind my desk. "Lily?" She runs around the desk and stands over me. "Are you okay?"

I hold up a thumb. "Fine. Just missed my chair."

She reaches out her hand and helps me to my feet. "What was that all about?"

I glance at the door as I retrieve my chair. I take a seat and look down at my phone. "Nothing. He was just apologizing."

Allysa sighs longingly and looks back at the door. "So does that mean he doesn't want the job?"

I've got to hand it to her. Even in the midst of emotional turmoil, she can make me laugh. "Get back to work before I dock your pay."

She laughs and makes to leave. I tap my pen against my desk and then say, "Allysa. Wait."

"I know," she says, cutting me off. "Ryle doesn't need to know about that visit. You don't have to tell me."

I smile. "Thank you."

She closes the door.

I reach down and pick up the bag with my three-year-old gift inside of it. I pull it out and can easily tell it's a book, wrapped in tissue paper. I tear the tissue paper away and fall against the back of my chair.

There's a picture of Ellen DeGeneres on the front. The title is *Seriously . . . I'm Kidding*. I laugh and then open the book, gasping quietly when I see it's autographed. I run my fingers over the words of the inscription.

Lily,

Atlas says just keep swimming.

—Ellen DeGeneres

I run my finger over her signature. Then I drop the book on my desk, press my forehead against it, and fake cry against the cover.

Chapter Seventeen

It's after seven before I get home. Ryle called an hour ago and said he wouldn't be coming over tonight. The confusher-cackle (whatever that big word he used was) separation was a success, but he's staying at the hospital overnight to make sure there aren't complications.

I walk in the door to my quiet apartment. I change into my quiet pajamas. I eat a quiet sandwich. And then I lie down in my quiet bedroom and open my quiet new book, hoping it can quiet my emotions.

Sure enough, three hours and the majority of a book later, all the emotions from the last several days begin to seep out of me. I place a bookmark on the page where I stopped reading and I close it.

I stare at the book for a long time. I think about Ryle. I think about Atlas. I think about how sometimes, no matter how convinced you are that your life will turn out a certain way, all that certainty can be washed away with a simple change in tide.

I take the book Atlas bought me and put it in the closet with all my journals. Then I pick up the one that's filled with memories of him. And I know it's finally time to read the last entry I wrote. Then I can close the book for good.

Dear Ellen,

Most of the time I'm thankful you don't know I exist and that I've never really mailed you any of these things I write to you.

But sometimes, especially tonight, I wish you did. I just need someone to talk to about everything I'm feeling. It's been six months since I've seen Atlas and I honestly don't know where he is or how he's doing. So much has happened since the last letter I wrote to you, when Atlas moved to Boston. I thought it was the last time I'd see him for a while, but it wasn't.

I saw him again after he left, several weeks later. It was my sixteenth birthday and when he showed up, it became the absolute best day of my life.

And then the absolute worst.

It had been exactly forty-two days since Atlas left for Boston. I counted every day like it would help somehow. I was so depressed, Ellen. I still am. People say that teenagers don't know how to love like an adult. Part of me believes that, but I'm not an adult and so I have nothing to compare it to. But I do believe it's probably different. I'm sure there's more substance in the love between two adults than there is between two teenagers. There's probably more maturity, more respect, more responsibility. But no matter how different the substance of a love might be at different ages in a person's life, I know that love still has to weigh the same. You feel that weight on your shoulders and in your stomach and on your heart no matter how old you are. And my feelings for Atlas are very heavy. Every night I cry myself to sleep and I whisper, "Just keep swimming." But it gets really hard to swim when you feel like you're anchored in the water.

Now that I think about it, I've probably been experiencing the stages of grief in a sense. Denial, anger, bargaining, depression, and acceptance. I was deep in the depression stage the night of my sixteenth birthday. My mother had tried to make the day a good one. She bought me gardening supplies, made my favorite cake, and the two of us went to dinner together. But by the time I had crawled into bed that night, I couldn't shake the sadness.

I was crying when I heard the tap on my window. At first, I thought it had started raining. But then I heard his voice. I jumped up and ran to the window, my heart in hysterics. He was standing there in the dark, smiling at me. I raised the window and helped him inside and he took me in his arms and held me there for so long while I cried.

He smelled so good. I could tell when I hugged him that he'd put on some much-needed weight in just the six weeks since I'd last seen him. He pulled back and wiped the tears off my cheeks. "Why are you crying, Lily?"

I was embarrassed that I was crying. I cried a lot that month—probably more than any other month of my life. It was probably just the hormones of being a teenage girl, mixed with the stress of how my father treated my mother, and then having to say goodbye to Atlas.

I grabbed a shirt from the floor and dried my eyes, then we sat down on the bed. He pulled me against his chest and leaned against my headboard.

"What are you doing here?" I asked him.

"It's your birthday," he said. "And you're still my favorite person. And I've missed you."

It was probably no later than ten o'clock when he got there, but we talked so much, I remember it was after midnight the next time I looked at the clock. I can't even remember what all we talked about, but I do remember how I felt. He seemed so happy and there was a light in his eyes that I'd never seen there before. Like he'd finally found his home.

He said he wanted to tell me something and his voice grew serious. He readjusted me so that I was straddling his lap, because he wanted me to look him in the eyes when he told me. I was thinking maybe he was about to tell me he had a girlfriend or that he was leaving even sooner for the military. But what he said next shocked me.

He said the first night he went to that old house, he wasn't there because he needed a place to stay.

He went there to kill himself.

My hands went up to my mouth because I had no idea things had gotten that bad for him. So bad that he didn't even want to live anymore.

"I hope you never know what it's like to feel that lonely, Lily," he said.

He went on to tell me that the first night he was at that house, he was sitting in the living room floor with a razor blade to his wrist. Right when he was about to use it, my bedroom light went on. "You were standing there like an angel, backlit by the light of heaven," he said. "I couldn't take my eyes off you."

He watched me walk around my bedroom for a while. Watched me lie on the bed and write in my journal. And he put down the razor blade because he said it'd been a month since life had given him any sort of feeling at all, and looking at me gave him a little bit of feeling. Enough to not be numb enough to end things that night.

Then a day or two later is when I took him the food and set it on his back porch. I guess you already know the rest of that story.

"You saved my life, Lily," he said to me. "And you weren't even trying."

He leaned forward and kissed that spot between my shoulder and my neck that he always kisses. I liked that he did it again. I don't like much about my body, but that spot on my collarbone has become my favorite part of me.

He took my hands in his and told me he was leaving sooner than he planned for the military, but that he couldn't leave without telling me thank you. He told me he'd be gone for four years and that the last thing he wanted for me was to be a sixteen-year-old girl not living my life because of a boyfriend I never got to see or hear from.

The next thing he said made his blue eyes tear up until they looked clear. He said, "Lily. Life is a funny thing. We only get so many years to live it, so we have to do everything we can to make sure those years are as full as they can be. We shouldn't waste time on things that might happen someday, or maybe even never."

I knew what he was saying. That he was leaving for the military and he didn't want me to hold on to him while he was gone. He wasn't really breaking up with me because we weren't ever really together. We'd just been two people who helped each other when we needed it and got our hearts fused together along the way.

It was hard, being let go by someone who had never really grabbed hold of me completely in the first place. In all the time we've spent together, I think we both sort of knew this wasn't a forever thing. I'm not sure why, because I could easily love him that way. I think maybe under normal circumstances, if we were together like typical teenagers and he had an average life with a home, we could be that kind of couple. The kind who comes together so easily and never experiences a life where cruelty sometimes intercepts.

I didn't even try to get him to change his mind that night. I feel like we have the kind of connection that even the fires of hell couldn't sever. I feel like he could go spend his time in the military and I'll spend my years being a teenager and then it will all fall back into place when the timing is right.

"I'm going to make a promise to you," he said. "When my life is good enough for you to be a part of it, I'll come find you. But I don't want you to wait around for me, because that might never happen."

I didn't like that promise, because it meant one of two things.

Either he thought he might never make it out of the military alive, or he didn't think his life would ever be good enough for me.

His life was already good enough for me, but I nodded my head and forced a smile. "If you don't come back for me, I'll come for you. And it won't be pretty, Atlas Corrigan."

He laughed at my threat. "Well, it won't be too hard to find me. You know exactly where I'll be."

I smiled. "Where everything is better."

He smiled back. "In Boston."

And then he kissed me.

Ellen, I know you're an adult and know all about what comes next, but I still don't feel comfortable telling you what happened over those next couple of hours. Let's just say we both kissed a lot. We both laughed a lot. We both loved a lot. We both breathed a lot. A lot. And we both had to cover our mouths and be as quiet and still as we could so we wouldn't get caught.

When we were finished, he held me against him, skin to skin, hand to heart. He kissed me and looked straight in my eyes.

"I love you, Lily. Everything you are. I love you."

I know those words get thrown around a lot, especially by teenagers. A lot of times prematurely and without much merit. But when he said them to me, I knew he wasn't saying it like he was in love with me. It wasn't that kind of "I love you."

Imagine all the people you meet in your life. There are so many. They come in like waves, trickling in and out with the tide. Some waves are much bigger and make more of an impact than others. Sometimes the waves bring with them things from deep in the bottom of the sea and they leave those things tossed onto the shore. Imprints against the grains of sand that prove the waves had once been there, long after the tide recedes.

That was what Atlas was telling me when he said "I love you." He was letting me know that I was the biggest wave he'd ever come across. And I brought so much with me that my impressions would always be there, even when the tide rolled out.

After he said he loved me, he told me he had a birthday present for me. He pulled out a small brown bag. "It isn't much, but it's all I could afford."

I opened the bag and pulled out the best present I'd ever received. It was a magnet that said "Boston" on the top. At the bottom in tiny letters, it said "Where everything is better." I told him I would keep it forever, and every time I look at it I'll think of him.

When I started out this letter, I said my sixteenth birthday was one of the best days of my life. Because up until that second, it was.

It was the next few minutes that weren't.

Before Atlas had shown up that night, I wasn't expecting him, so I didn't think to lock my bedroom door. My father heard me in there talking to someone, and when he threw open my door and saw Atlas in bed with me, he was angrier than I'd ever seen him. And Atlas was at a disadvantage by not being prepared for what came next.

I'll never forget that moment for as long as I live. Being completely helpless as my father came down on him with a baseball bat. The sound of bones snapping was the only thing piercing through my screams.

I still don't know who called the police. I'm sure it was my mother, but it's been six months and we still haven't talked about that night. By the time the police got to my bedroom and pulled my father off of him, I didn't even recognize Atlas, he was covered in so much blood.

I was hysterical.

Hysterical.

Not only did they have to take Atlas away in an ambulance, they also had to call an ambulance for me because I couldn't breathe. It was the first and only panic attack I've ever had.

No one would tell me where he was or if he was even okay. My father wasn't even arrested for what he'd done. Word got out that Atlas had been staying in that old house and that he had been homeless. My father became revered for his heroic act—saving his little girl from the homeless boy who manipulated her into having sex with him.

My father said I'd shamed our whole family by giving the town something to gossip about. And let me tell you, they still gossip about it. I heard Katie on the bus today telling someone she tried to warn me about Atlas. She said she knew he was bad news from the moment she laid eyes on him. Which is crap. If Atlas had been on the bus with me, I probably would have kept my mouth shut and been mature about it like he tried to teach me to be. Instead, I was so angry, I turned around and told Katie she could go to hell. I told her Atlas was a better human than she'd ever be and if I ever heard her say one more bad thing about him, she'd regret it.

She just rolled her eyes and said, "Jesus, Lily. Did he brainwash you? He was a dirty, thieving homeless kid who was probably on drugs. He used you for food and sex and now you're defending him?"

She's lucky the bus stopped at my house right then. I grabbed my backpack and walked off the bus, then went inside and cried in my room for three hours straight. Now my head hurts, but I knew the only thing that would make me feel better is if I finally got it all out on paper. I've been avoiding writing this letter for six months now.

No offense, Ellen, but my head still hurts. So does my heart. Maybe even more right now than it did yesterday. This letter didn't help one damn bit.

I think I'm going to take a break from writing to you for a while. Writing to you reminds me of him, and it all hurts too much. Until he comes back for me, I'm just going to keep pretending to be okay. I'll keep pretending to swim, when really all I'm doing is floating. Barely keeping my head above water.

—Lily

I flip to the next page, but it's blank. That was the last time I ever wrote to Ellen.

I also never heard from Atlas again, and a huge part of me never blamed him. He almost died at the hands of my father. There's not much room for forgiveness there.

I knew he survived and that he was okay, because my curiosity has sometimes gotten the best of me over the years and I'd find what I could about him online. There wasn't much, though. Enough to let me know he'd survived and that he was in the military.

I still never got him out of my head, though. Time made things better, but sometimes I would see something that would remind me of him and it would put me in a funk. It wasn't until I was in college for a couple of years and dating someone else that I realized maybe Atlas wasn't supposed to be my whole life. Maybe he was only supposed to be a part of it.

Maybe love isn't something that comes full circle. It just ebbs and flows, in and out, just like the people in our lives.

On a particularly lonely night in college, I went alone to a tattoo studio and had a heart put in the spot where he used to kiss me. It's a tiny heart, about the size of a thumbprint, and it looks just like the heart he carved for me out of the oak tree. It's not fully closed at the top and I wonder if Atlas carved the heart like that on purpose. Because that's how my heart feels every time I think about him. It just feels like there's a little hole in it, letting out all the air.

After college I ended up moving to Boston, not necessarily because I was hoping to find him, but because I had to see for myself if Boston really was better. Plethora held nothing for me anyway, and I wanted to get as far away from my father as I could. Even though he was sick and could no longer hurt my mother, he still somehow made me want to escape the entire state of Maine, so that's exactly what I did.

Seeing Atlas in his restaurant for the first time filled me with so many emotions, I didn't know how to process them. I was glad to see that he was okay. I was happy that he looked healthy. But I would be lying if I said I wasn't a little bit heartbroken that he never tried to find me like he promised.

I love him. I still do and I always will. He was a huge wave that left a lot of imprints on my life, and I'll feel the weight of that love until I die. I've accepted that.

But things are different now. After today when he walked out of my office, I thought long and hard about us. I think our lives are where they're supposed to be. I have Ryle. Atlas has his girlfriend. We both have the careers we'd always hoped for. Just because we didn't end up on the same wave, doesn't mean we aren't still a part of the same ocean.

Things with Ryle are still fairly new, but I feel that same depth with him that I used to feel with Atlas. He loves me just like Atlas did. And I know if Atlas had a chance to get to know him, he would be able to see that and he'd be happy for me.

Sometimes an unexpected wave comes along, sucks you up and refuses to spit you back out. Ryle is my unexpected tidal wave, and right now I'm skimming the beautiful surface.

Part Two

Chapter Eighteen

"Oh, God. I think I might throw up."

Ryle puts his thumb under my chin and tilts my face up to his. He grins at me. "You'll be fine. Stop freaking out."

I shake my hands out and bounce up and down inside the elevator. "I can't help it," I say. "Everything you and Allysa have told me about your mother makes me so nervous." My eyes widen and I bring my hands up to my mouth. "Oh, God, Ryle. What if she asks me questions about *Jesus*? I don't go to church. I mean, I read the Bible when I was younger, but I don't know answers to any Bible trivia questions."

He's really laughing now. He pulls me to him and kisses the side of my head. "She won't talk about Jesus. She already loves you, based on what I've told her. All you have to do is be you, Lily."

I start nodding. "Be me. Okay. I think I can pretend to be me for one evening. Right?"

The doors open and he walks me out of the elevator, toward Allysa's apartment. It's funny watching him knock, but I guess he technically doesn't live here anymore. Over the last few months, he just sort of slowly began staying with me. All of his clothes are at my apartment. His toiletries. Last week he even hung that ridiculous blurry photograph of me up in our bedroom, and it really felt official after that.

"Does she know we live together?" I ask him. "Is she okay

with that? I mean, we aren't married. She goes to church every Sunday. Oh, no, Ryle! What if your mother thinks I'm a blasphemous whore?"

Ryle nudges his head toward the apartment door and I spin around to see his mother standing in the doorway, a layer of shock on her face.

"Mother," Ryle says. "Meet Lily. My blasphemous whore."

Oh dear God.

His mother reaches for me and pulls me in for a hug, and her laughter is everything I need to get me through this moment. "Lily!" she says, pushing me out to arm's length so she can get a good look at me. "Sweetie, I don't think you're a blasphemous whore. You're the angel I've been praying would land in Ryle's lap for the last ten years!"

She ushers us into the apartment. Ryle's father is the next to greet me with a hug. "No, definitely not a blasphemous whore," he says. "Not like Marshall here, who sank his teeth into my little girl when she was only seventeen." He glares back at Marshall, who is sitting on the couch.

Marshall laughs. "That's where you're wrong, Dr. Kincaid, because Allysa was the one who sank her teeth into me first. My teeth were in another girl who tasted like Cheetos and . . ."

Marshall doubles over when Allysa elbows him in the side.

And just like that, every single fear I had has vanished. They're perfect. They're normal. They say *whore* and laugh at Marshall's jokes.

I couldn't ask for anything better.

Three hours later, I'm lying on Allysa's bed with her.

Their parents went to bed early, claiming jet lag. Ryle and Marshall are in the living room, watching sports. I have my hand on Allysa's stomach, waiting to feel the baby kick.

"Her feet are right here," she says, moving my hand over a few inches. "Give it a few seconds. She's really active tonight."

We remain quiet while we both wait for her to kick. When it happens, I squeal with laughter. "Oh my God! It's like an alien!"

Allysa holds her hands on her stomach, smiling. "These last two and a half months are going to be hell," she says. "I'm so ready to meet her."

"Me too. I can't wait to be an aunt."

"I can't wait for you and Ryle to have a baby," she says.

I fall onto my back and put my hands behind my bed. "I don't know if he wants any. We've never really talked about it."

"It doesn't matter if he doesn't want any," she says. "He will. He didn't want a relationship before you. He didn't want to get married before you, and I feel a proposal coming on any month now."

I prop my head up on my hand and face her. "We've barely been together six months. Pretty sure he wants to wait a lot longer than that."

I don't push things with Ryle when it comes to speeding things up in our relationship. Our lives are perfect how they are. We're too busy for a wedding anyway, so I don't mind if he wants to wait a lot longer.

"What about you?" Allysa presses. "Would you say yes if he proposed?"

I laugh. "Are you kidding me? Of course. I'd marry him tonight."

Allysa looks over my shoulder at her bedroom door. She purses her lips together and tries to hide her smile.

"He's standing in the doorway, isn't he?"

She nods.

"He heard me say that, didn't he?"

She nods again.

I roll onto my back and look at Ryle, propped up against the doorframe with his arms folded over his chest. I can't tell what he's thinking after hearing that. His expression is tight. His jaw is tight. His eyes are narrowed in my direction.

"Lily," he says with stoic composure. "I would marry the *hell* out of you."

His words make me smile the most embarrassing, widest smile, so I pull a pillow over my face. "Why, thank you, Ryle," I say, my words muffled by the pillow.

"That's really sweet," I hear Allysa say. "My brother is actually sweet."

The pillow is pulled away from me and Ryle is standing over me, holding it at his side. "Let's go."

My heart begins to beat faster. "Right now?"

He nods. "I took the weekend off because my parents are in town. You have people who can run your store for you. Let's go to Vegas and get married."

Allysa sits up on the bed. "You can't do that," she says. "Lily's a girl. She wants a real wedding with flowers and bridesmaids and shit."

Ryle looks back at me. "Do you want a real wedding with flowers and bridesmaids and shit?"

I think about it for a second.

"No."

The three of us are quiet for a moment, and then Allysa starts kicking her legs up and down on the bed, giddy with excitement. "They're getting married!" she yells. She rolls off the bed and rushes toward the living room. "Marshall, pack our bags! We're going to Vegas!"

Ryle reaches down and grabs my hand, pulling me to a stand. He's smiling, but there's no way I'm doing this unless I know for sure he wants it.

"Are you sure about this, Ryle?"

He runs his hands through my hair and pulls my face to his, brushing his lips against mine. "Naked truth," he whispers. "I'm so excited to be your husband, I could piss my damn pants."

Chapter Nineteen

"It's been six weeks Mom, you gotta get over it."

My mother sighs into the phone. "You're my only daughter. I can't help it if I've been dreaming about your wedding your whole life."

She still hasn't forgiven me, even though she was there. We called her right before Allysa booked our flights. We forced her out of bed, we forced Ryle's parents out of bed, and then we forced them all on a midnight flight to Vegas. She didn't try to talk me out of it because I'm sure she could tell that Ryle and I had made up our minds by the time she made it to the airport. But she hasn't let me forget it. She's been dreaming of a huge wedding and dress shopping and cake tasting since the day I was born.

I kick my feet up on the couch. "How about I make it up to you?" I say to her. "What if, whenever we decide to have a baby, I promise to do it the natural way and not buy one in Vegas?"

My mom laughs. Then she sighs. "As long as you give me grandchildren someday, I guess I can get over it."

Ryle and I talked about kids on the flight to Vegas. I wanted to make sure that possibility was open for discussion in our future before I made a commitment to spend the rest of my life with him. He said it was definitely open for discussion. Then we cleared the air about a lot of other things that might cause problems down the road. I told him I wanted separate checking accounts, but since he makes more money than me, he has to buy me lots of presents all the time to keep me happy. He agreed. He made me promise him I'd never become vegan. That was a simple promise. I love cheese too much. I told him we had to start some kind of charity, or at least donate to the ones Marshall and Allysa like. He said he already does, and that made me want to marry him even sooner. He made me promise to vote. He said I was allowed to vote Democratic, Republican, or Independent, as long as I made sure to vote. We shook on it.

By the time we landed in Vegas, we were completely on the same page.

I hear the front door unlocking so I flip onto my back. "Gotta go," I say to my mother. "Ryle just got home." He closes the door behind him and then I grin and say, "Wait. Let me rephrase that, Mom. My *husband* just got home."

My mother laughs and tells me goodbye. I hang up with her and toss my phone aside. I bring my arm up above my head and rest it lazily against the arm of the couch. Then I prop my leg over the back of it, letting my skirt slide down my thighs and pool at my waist. Ryle drags his eyes up my body, grinning as he makes his way over to me. He drops to his knees on the couch and slowly crawls up my body.

"How's my wife?" he whispers, planting kisses all around my mouth. He presses himself between my legs and I let my head fall back as he kisses down my neck.

This is the life.

We both work almost every day. He works twice as many hours as I do and he only gets home before I'm in bed two or three nights a week. But the nights we actually do get to spend together, I tend to want him to spend those nights buried deep inside me.

He doesn't complain.

He finds a spot on my neck and he claims it, kissing it so hard it hurts. "Ouch."

He lowers himself on top of me and mutters into my neck. "I'm giving you a hickey. Don't move."

I laugh, but I let him. My hair is long enough that I can cover it, and I've never had a hickey before.

His lips remain in the same spot, sucking and kissing until I can no longer feel the sting. He's pressed against me, bulging against his scrubs. I move my hands and shove his scrubs down far enough so that he can slide inside of me. He continues kissing my neck as he takes me right there on the couch.

• • •

He took a shower first, and as soon as he got out, I jumped in. I told him we needed to wash the smell of sex off of us before we had dinner with Allysa and Marshall.

Allysa is due in a few weeks, so she's forcing as much couple time on us as she can. She's worried we'll stop coming to visit after the baby is born, which I know is ridiculous. The visits will just grow more frequent. I already love my niece more than any of them, anyway.

Okay, maybe not. But it's close.

I try to avoid getting my hair wet as I rinse off, because we're already running late. I grab my razor and press it under my arm when I hear a crash. I pause.

"Ryle?"

Nothing.

I finish shaving and then wash the soap off. Another crash.

What in the world is he doing?

I turn off the water and grab a towel, running it over myself. "Ryle!"

He still doesn't respond. I pull my jeans on in a hurry and open the door as I'm pulling my shirt over my head. "Ryle?"

The nightstand by our bed is tipped over. I move to the living room and see him sitting on the edge of the couch, his head in one of his hands. He's looking down at something in his other hand.

"What are you doing?"

He looks up at me and I don't recognize his expression. I'm confused by what's happening. I don't know if he just got bad news or . . . *Oh, God. Allysa.*

"Ryle, you're scaring me. What's wrong?"

He holds up my phone and just looks at me like I should know what's happening. When I shake my head in confusion, he holds up a piece of paper. "Funny thing," he says, setting my phone on the coffee table in front of him. "I dropped your phone by accident. Cover pops off. I find this number hidden in the back of it."

Oh, God.

No, no, no.

He crumbles the number in his fist. "I thought, '*Huh. That's weird. Lily doesn't hide things from me.*'" He stands up and picks up my phone. "So I called it." He tightens his fist around the phone. "He's lucky I got his fucking voice mail." He chunks my phone clear across the room and it crashes against the wall, shattering to the floor.

There's a three-second pause where I think this could go one of two ways.

He's going to leave me.

Or he's going to hurt me.

He runs a hand through his hair and walks straight for the door.

He leaves.

"Ryle!" I yell.

Why did I never throw that number away?!

I open the door and run after him. He's taking the stairs two at a time, and I finally reach him when he's at the landing of the second floor. I shove myself in front of him and grab his shirt in my fists. "Ryle, please. Let me explain."

He grabs my wrists and pushes me away from him.

• • •

"Be still."

I feel his hands on me. Gentle. Steady.

Tears are flowing and for some reason, they sting.

"Lily, be still. Please."

His voice is soothing. My head hurts. "Ryle?" I try to open my eyes, but the light is too bright. I can feel a sting at the corner of my eye and I wince. I try to sit up, but I feel his hand press down on my shoulder.

"You have to be still until I'm finished, Lily."

I open my eyes again and look up at the ceiling. It's our

bedroom ceiling. "Finished with what?" My mouth hurts when I speak, so I bring my hand up and cover it.

"You fell down the stairs," he says. "You're hurt."

My eyes meet his. There's concern in them, but also hurt. Anger. He's feeling *everything* right now, and the only thing I feel is confused.

I close my eyes again and try to remember why he's angry. Why he's hurt.

My phone.

Atlas's number.

The stairwell.

I grabbed his shirt.

He pushed me away.

"You fell down the stairs."

But I *didn't* fall.

He pushed me. Again.

That's twice.

You pushed me, Ryle.

I can feel my whole body start to shake with the sobs. I have no idea how bad I'm hurt, but I don't even care. No physical pain could even compare to what my heart is feeling in this moment. I start to slap at his hands, wanting him away from me. I feel him lift off the bed as I curl up into a ball.

I wait for him to try and soothe it out like he did the last time he hurt me, but it never comes. I hear him walking around our bedroom. I don't know what he's doing. I'm still crying when he kneels down in front of me.

"You might have a concussion," he says, matter-of-fact. "You have a small cut on your lip. I just bandaged up the cut on your eye. You don't need stitches."

His voice is cold.

"Does it hurt anywhere else? Your arms? Legs?"

He sounds just like a doctor and nothing like a husband.

"You pushed me," I say through tears. It's all I can think or say or see.

"You fell," he says calmly. "About five minutes ago. Right after I found out what a fucking liar I married." He places something on my pillow next to me. "If you need anything, I'm sure you can call this number."

I look at the crumpled up piece of paper by my head that holds Atlas's phone number.

"Ryle," I sob.

What is happening?

I hear the front door slam.

My whole world comes crashing down around me.

"Ryle," I whisper to no one. I cover my face with my hands and I cry harder than I've ever cried. I am destroyed.

Five minutes.

That's all it takes to completely destroy a person.

• • •

A few minutes pass.

Ten, maybe?

I can't stop crying. I still haven't moved from the bed. I'm scared to look in the mirror. I'm just . . . scared.

I hear the front door open and slam shut again. Ryle appears in the doorway and I have no idea if I'm supposed to hate him.

Or be terrified of him.

Or feel bad for him.

How can I be feeling all three?

He presses his forehead to our bedroom door and I watch as he hits his head against it. Once. Twice. Three times.

He turns and rushes at me, falling to his knees at the side of the bed. He grabs both of my hands and he squeezes them. "Lily," he says, his whole face twisting in pain. "*Please* tell me it's nothing." He brings his hand to the side of my head and I can feel his hands shaking. "I can't take this, I can't." He leans forward and presses his lips hard against my forehead, then rests his forehead against mine. "Please tell me you aren't seeing him. *Please.*"

I'm not even sure I can tell him that because I don't even want to speak.

He stays pressed against me, his hand wrapped tightly in my hair. "It hurts so much, Lily. I love you so much."

I shake my head, wanting the truth out of me so he'll see what a huge mistake he just made. "I forgot his number was even there," I say quietly. "The day after the fight in the restaurant . . . he came to the store. You can ask Allysa. He was only there for five minutes. He took my phone from me and he put his number inside of it, because he didn't believe I was safe with you. I forgot it was there, Ryle. I've never even looked at it."

He breathes out a shaky breath and begins nodding with relief. "You swear, Lily? You swear on our marriage and our lives and on everything that you are that you haven't spoken to him since that day?" He pulls back so he can look me in the eyes.

"I swear, Ryle. You overreacted before giving me the chance to explain," I say to him. "Now get the *fuck* out of my apartment."

My words knock the breath from him. I see it happen. His back meets the wall behind him and he stares at me silently. In shock. "Lily," he whispers. "You fell down the stairs."

I can't tell if he's trying to convince me or himself.

I calmly repeat myself. "Get out of my apartment."

He remains frozen in place. I sit up on the bed. My hand immediately goes to the throbbing in my eye. He pushes himself up off the floor. When he takes a step forward, I scoot back on the bed.

"You're hurt, Lily. I'm not leaving you alone."

I grab one of my pillows and throw it at him, like it could actually do damage. "Get out!" I yell. He catches the pillow. I grab the other one and stand up on the bed and start swinging it at him as I scream, "Get out! Get out! Get out!"

I toss the pillow on the floor after the front door slams shut.

I run to the living room and dead-bolt the door.

I run back to my bedroom and fall onto my bed. The same bed I share with my husband. The same bed he makes love to me on.

The same bed he lays me on when it's time for him to clean up his messes.

Chapter Twenty

I tried salvaging my phone before I fell asleep last night, but it was no use. It was in two completely separate pieces. I set my alarm so I could get up early and stop and get a new one on my way in to work today.

My face doesn't look as bad as I feared it would. Of course, it's not something I could hide from Allysa, but I'm not even going to try and do that. I part my hair to the side to cover up most of the bandage Ryle had placed over my eye. The only thing visible from last night is the cut on my lip.

And the hickey he gave me on my neck.

Fucking irony at its best.

I grab my purse and open the front door. I stop short when I see the lump at my feet.

It moves.

It's several seconds before I realize that lump is actually Ryle. *He slept out here?*

He pulls himself to his feet as soon as he realizes I've opened the door. He's in front of me, pleading eyes, gentle hands on my cheeks. Lips on my mouth. "I'm sorry, I'm sorry, I'm sorry."

I pull back and scroll my eyes over him. *He slept out here?*

I step out of my apartment and pull my door shut. I calmly walk past him and down the stairs. He follows me the entire way to my car, begging me to talk to him.

I don't.

I leave.

• • •

It's an hour later when I have a new phone in my hands. I'm sitting in my car at the cell phone store when I turn it on. I watch the screen as seventeen messages appear. All from Allysa.

I guess it would make sense that Ryle didn't call me all night, since he knew what kind of shape my phone was in.

I start to open a text message when my phone begins ringing. It's Allysa.

"Hello?"

She sighs heavily, and then, "Lily! What in the hell is going on? Oh my God, you can't do this to me, I'm pregnant!"

I start my car and set the phone to Bluetooth while I drive toward the store. Allysa is off today. She's only got a few days left before she gets a jump start on her maternity leave.

"I'm okay," I tell her. "Ryle is okay. We got into a fight. I'm sorry I couldn't call you, he broke my phone."

She's quiet for a moment, and then, "He did? Are you okay? Where are you?"

"I'm fine. Heading to work now."

"Good, I'm almost there myself."

I start to protest, but she hangs up before I have the chance.

By the time I make it to the store, she's already there.

I open the front door, ready to field questions and defend my reasons for kicking her brother out of my apartment. But

I stop short when I see the two of them standing at the counter. Ryle is leaning against it and Allysa has her hands on top of his, saying something to him that I can't hear.

They both turn to face me when they hear the door close behind me.

"Ryle," Allysa whispers. "What did you *do* to her?" She walks around the counter and pulls me in for a hug. "Oh, Lily," she says, running her hand down my back. She pulls back with tears in her eyes, and her reaction confuses me. She obviously knows Ryle is responsible, but if that's the case, it seems she would be attacking him, or at least yelling.

She turns back to Ryle and he's looking up at me apologetically. Longingly. Like he wants to reach out and hug me, but he's scared to death to touch me. He should be.

"You need to tell her," Allysa says to Ryle.

He instantly drops his head in his hands.

"Tell her," Allysa says, her voice angrier now. "She has the right to know, Ryle. She's your wife. If you don't tell her, I will."

Ryle's shoulders roll forward and his head is fully pressed against the counter now. Whatever it is Allysa wants him to tell me has him so agonized, he can't even look at me. I clench my stomach, feeling the angst deeper than my soul.

Allysa spins toward me and puts her hands on my shoulders. "Hear him out," she begs. "I'm not asking you to forgive him, because I have no idea what happened last night. But just please, as my sister-in-law and my best friend, give my brother a chance to talk to you."

• • •

Allysa said she'd watch the store for the next hour until another employee comes in for their shift. I was still so upset with Ryle, I didn't want him in the same car with me. He said he'd send for an Uber and meet me at my apartment.

My entire drive home I agonized over what he could possibly need to tell me that Allysa already knows. So many things went through my head. Is he dying? Has he been cheating on me? Did he lose his job? She didn't seem to know the details of what happened between us last night, so I have no idea how this relates to that.

Ryle finally walks through my front door ten minutes after me. I'm sitting on the couch, nervously picking at my nails.

I stand up and start to pace as he slowly walks to the chair and takes a seat. He leans forward, clasping his hands in front of him.

"Please sit down, Lily."

He says it pleadingly, like he can't take seeing me worry. I return to my seat on the couch, but I scoot to the arm, pull my feet up, and bring my hands to my mouth. "Are you dying?"

His eyes stretch wide and he immediately shakes his head. "No. *No.* It's nothing like that."

"Then what is it?"

I just want him to spit it out. My hands are starting to shake. He sees how much he's freaking me out, so he leans forward and pulls my hands from my face, holding them in his. Part of me doesn't want him touching me after what he did last night, but a piece of me needs the reassurance from him. The anticipation of what I'm about to find out is making me nauseous.

"No one is dying. I'm not cheating on you. What I'm about to tell you isn't going to hurt you, okay? It's all in the past. But Allysa thinks you need to know. And . . . so do I."

I nod and he releases my hands. He's the one up and pacing now, back and forth behind the coffee table. It's as if he's having to work up the courage to find his own words and that's making me even *more* nervous.

He sits in the chair again. "Lily? Do you remember the night we met?"

I nod.

"You remember when I walked out onto the roof? How angry I was?"

I nod again. He was kicking the chair. It was before he knew marine-grade polymer was virtually indestructible.

"Do you remember my naked truth? What I told you about that night and what caused me to be so angry?"

I lean my head down and think back to that night and to all the truths he told me. He said marriage repulsed him. He was only into one-night stands. He never wanted to have kids. He was mad about a patient he'd lost that night.

I start nodding. "The little boy," I said. "That's why you were mad, because a little boy died and it upset you."

He blows out a quick breath of relief. "Yes. That's why I was mad." He stands up again and it's like I see his entire soul crumble. He presses his palms against his eyes and fights back tears. "When I told you about what happened to him, do you remember what you said to me?"

I feel like I'm about to cry and I don't even know why yet. "Yes. I told you I couldn't imagine what something like that will do to that little boy's brother. The one who accidentally shot him." My lips start to tremble. "And that's when you said, *'It'll destroy him for life, that's what it'll do.'* "

Oh, God.

Where is he going with this?

Ryle walks over and drops down to his knees in front of me. "Lily," he says. "I knew it would destroy him. I knew exactly what that little boy was feeling . . . because that's what happened to me. To Allysa's and my older brother . . ."

I can't hold in the tears. I just start crying and he wraps his arms tightly around my waist and lays his head on my lap. "I *shot* him, Lily. My best friend. My big brother. I was only six years old. I didn't even know I was holding a real gun."

His whole body begins to shake and he grips me even tighter. I press a kiss into his hair because it feels like he's on the verge of a breakdown. Just like that night on the roof. And while I'm still so angry at him, I also still love him and it absolutely kills me to find this out about him. About Allysa. We sit quietly for a long time—his head on my lap, his arms around my waist, my lips in his hair.

"She was only five when it happened. Emerson was seven. We were in the garage, so no one heard our screams for a long time. And I just sat there, and . . ."

He pulls away from my lap and stands up, facing the other direction. After a long stretch of silence he sits down on the couch and leans forward. "I was trying to . . ." Ryle's face contorts in pain and he lowers his head, covering it with his hands, shaking it back and forth. "I was trying to put everything back inside his head. I thought I could *fix* him, Lily."

My hand flies up to my mouth. I gasp so loudly, there's no way to hide it.

I have to stand up so I can catch a breath.

It doesn't help.

I still can't breathe.

Ryle walks over to me, taking my hands and pulling me to him. We hug each other for a solid minute when he says, "I would never tell you this because I want it to excuse my behavior." He pulls back and looks me firmly in the eyes. "You have to believe that. Allysa wanted me to tell you all of this because since that happened, there are things I can't control. I get angry. I black out. I've been in therapy since I was six years old. But it is not my excuse. It is my reality."

He wipes away my tears, cradling my head against his shoulder.

"When you ran after me last night, I swear I had no intention of hurting you. I was upset and angry. And sometimes when I feel that much emotion, something inside of me just snaps. I don't remember the moment I pushed you. But I know I did. *I did.* All I was thinking when you were running after me was how I needed to get away from you. I wanted you out of my way. I didn't process that there were stairs around us. I didn't process my strength compared to yours. I fucked up, Lily. I fucked up."

He lowers his mouth to my ear. His voice cracks when he says, "You are my *wife*. I'm supposed to be the one who protects you from the monsters. I'm not supposed to *be* one." He holds me with so much desperation, he begins to shake. I have never, in all my life, felt so much pain radiating from one human.

It breaks me. It rips me apart from the inside out. All my heart wants to do is wrap tightly around his.

But even with everything he just told me, I'm still fighting my own forgiveness. I swore I wouldn't let it happen again. I swore to him and to myself that if he ever hurt me again, I would leave.

I pull away from him, unable to look him in the eye. I walk toward my bedroom to try and take a moment to just catch my breath. I close my bathroom door behind me and grip the sink, but I can't even stand up. I end up sliding to the floor in a heap of tears.

This isn't how this was supposed to be. My whole life, I knew exactly what I'd do if a man ever treated me the way my father treated my mother. It was simple. I would leave and it would never happen again.

But I didn't leave. And now, here I am with bruises and cuts on my body at the hands of the man who is supposed to love me. At the hands of my own husband.

And still, I'm trying to justify what happened.

It was an accident. He thought I was cheating on him. He was hurt and angry and I got in his way.

I bring my hands to my face and I sob, because I feel more pain for that man out there, knowing what he went through as a child, than I feel for myself. And that doesn't make me feel selfless or strong. It makes me feel pathetic and weak. I'm supposed to hate him. I'm supposed to be the woman my mother was never strong enough to be.

But if I'm emulating my mother's behavior, then that would mean Ryle is emulating my father's behavior. But he isn't. I have to stop comparing us to them. We're our own individuals in an entirely different situation. My father never had an excuse for his anger, nor was he immediately apologetic. The way he treated my mother was much worse than what's happened between Ryle and me.

Ryle just opened up to me in a way that he's probably never opened up to anyone. He's struggling to be a better person for me.

Yes, he screwed up last night. But he's here and he's trying to make me understand his past and why he reacted the way he did. Humans aren't perfect and I can't let the only example I've ever witnessed of marriage weigh in on my *own* marriage.

I wipe my eyes and pull myself up. When I look in the mirror, I don't see my mother. I just see me. I see a girl who loves her husband and wants more than anything to be able to help him. I know Ryle and I are strong enough to move past this. Our love is strong enough to get us through this.

I walk out of the bathroom and back into the living room. Ryle stands up and faces me, his face full of fear. He's scared I'm not going to forgive him, and I'm not sure that I *do* forgive him. But an act doesn't have to be forgiven in order to learn from it.

I walk over to him and I grab both of his hands in mine. I speak to him with nothing but naked truth.

"Remember what you said to me on the roof that night? You said, '*There is no such thing as bad people. We're all just people who sometimes do bad things.*'"

He nods and squeezes my hands.

"You aren't a bad person, Ryle. I know that. You can still protect me. When you're upset, just walk away. And I'll walk away. We'll leave the situation until you're calm enough to talk about it, okay? You are *not* a monster, Ryle. You're only human. And as humans, we can't expect to shoulder all of our pain. Sometimes we have to share it with the people who love us so we don't come crashing down from the weight of it all. But I can't help you unless I know you need it. Ask me for help. We'll get through this, I know we can."

He exhales what feels like every breath he's been holding in since last night. He wraps his arms tightly around me and buries his face in my hair. "Help me, Lily," he whispers. "I need you to help me."

He holds me against him and I know deep in my heart that I'm doing the right thing. There is so much more good in him than bad, and I'll do whatever I can to convince him of that until he can see it, too.

Chapter Twenty-One

"I'm heading out. You need me to do anything else?"

I look up from the paperwork and shake my head. "Thank you, Serena. See you tomorrow."

She nods and walks away, leaving the door to my office open.

Allysa's last day was two weeks ago. She's due any day now. I have two other full-time employees, Serena and Lucy.

Yes. *That* Lucy.

She's been married for a couple of months now and came in looking for a job two weeks ago. It's actually worked out pretty well. She keeps herself busy, and if I'm here when she is, I just keep my office door shut so I don't have to listen to her sing.

It's been almost a month since the incident on the stairs. Even with everything Ryle told me about his childhood, the forgiveness was still hard to come by.

I know Ryle has a temper. I saw it the first night we met, before we ever even spoke a word to each other. I saw it that awful night in my kitchen. I saw it when he found the phone number in my phone case.

But I also see the difference between Ryle and my father.

Ryle is compassionate. He does things my father never would have done. He donates to charity, he cares about other people, he puts me before everything. Ryle would never in a million years make me park in the driveway while he took the garage.

I have to remind myself of those things. Sometimes the girl inside of me—the daughter of my father—is really opinionated. She tells me I shouldn't have forgiven him. She tells me I should have left the first time. And sometimes I believe that voice. But then the side of me that knows Ryle understands that marriages aren't perfect. Sometimes there are moments that both parties regret. And I wonder how I'd feel about myself had I just left him after that first incident. He never should have pushed me, but I also did things *I* wasn't proud of. And if I'd have just left, would that not be going against our marriage vows? *For better or for worse.* I refuse to give up on my marriage that easily.

I am a strong woman. I've been around abusive situations my whole life. I will never become my mother. I believe that a hundred percent. And Ryle will never become my father. I think we needed what happened on the stairwell to happen so that I would know his past and we'd be able to work on it together.

Last week we got into another fight.

I was scared. The other two fights we'd gotten into did not end well, and I knew this would be a testament to whether or not our agreement for me to help him through his anger would work.

We were discussing his career. He's finished with his residency now and there's a three-month specialized course in Cambridge, England, he applied for. He'll find out soon if he was approved, but that's not why I was upset. It's a great opportunity and I'd never ask him not to go. Three months is nothing with how busy we are, so that wasn't even what got me so upset. I became upset when he discussed what he wanted to do *after* the Cambridge trip was over.

He was offered a job in Minnesota at the Mayo Clinic and he wants us to move there. He said Mass General is rated the second best neurological hospital in the world. Mayo Clinic is number one.

He said he never intended to stay in Boston forever. I told him that would have been a good subject to bring up when we discussed our futures on the flight to get married in Vegas. I can't leave Boston. My mother lives here. Allysa lives here. He told me it was only a five-hour flight and that we could visit as often as we wanted. I told him it was pretty hard to run a floral business when you live several states away.

The fight continued to escalate and both of us were getting angrier by the second. At one point, he knocked a vase full of flowers off the table and onto the floor. We both just stared at them for a moment. I was scared, wondering if I had made the right decision to stay. To trust that we could work on his anger issues together. He took a deep breath and he said, "I'm going to leave for an hour or two. I think I need to walk away. When I get back, we'll continue this discussion."

He walked out the door and, true to his word, he came back an hour later when he was much calmer. He dropped his keys on the table and then walked straight to where I was standing. He took my face in his hands and he said, "I told you I wanted to be the best in my field, Lily. I told you this the first night we ever met. It was one of my naked truths. But if I have to choose between working at the best hospital in the world and making my wife happy . . . I choose you. You *are* my success. As long as you're happy, I don't care where I work. We'll stay in Boston."

That's when I knew that I had made the right choice. Everyone deserves another chance. Especially the people who mean the most to you.

It's been a week since that fight and he hasn't mentioned moving again. I feel bad, like I thwarted his plans in some way, but marriage is about compromise. It's about doing what's best for the couple as a whole, not individually. And staying in Boston is better for everyone in both of our families.

Speaking of families, I look over at my phone right as a text from Allysa comes through.

Allysa: Are you finished up at work yet? I need your opinion on furniture.

Me: Be there in fifteen minutes.

I don't know if it's the impending delivery or the fact that she's not currently working, but I'm pretty sure I've spent more time at her house this week than I have at my own. I close up the shop and head toward her apartment.

• • •

When I step off the elevator, there's a note taped to her apartment door. I see my name written across it, so I pull it off the door.

Lily,

On the seventh floor. Apartment 749.

—A

She has an apartment here just for extra furniture? I know they're rich, but even that seems a little excessive for them. I get on the elevator and press the button for the seventh floor. When the doors open, I head down the hall toward apartment 749. When I reach it, I have no idea if I should knock or just go inside. For all I know, someone could live here. Probably one of her *people*.

I knock on the door and hear footsteps from the other side.

I'm shocked when the door swings open and Ryle is standing in front of me.

"Hey," I say, confused. "What are you doing here?"

He grins and leans against the doorframe. "I live here. What are *you* doing here?"

I glance at the pewter number plate next to the door and then back at him. "What do you mean you live here? I thought you lived with me. You've had your own apartment this whole time?" I would think an entire apartment would be something a husband would bring up to his wife at some point. It's a little unnerving.

Actually, it's ludicrous and deceptive. I think I might be really angry at him right now.

Ryle laughs and pushes off the doorframe. Now he's filling up the entire doorway as he lifts his hands to the frame over his head and grips it. "I haven't really had a chance to tell you about this apartment, considering I just signed the paperwork on it this morning."

I take a step back. "Wait. What?"

He reaches for my hand and pulls me inside the apartment. "Welcome home, Lily."

I pause in the foyer.

Yes. I said *foyer.* There is a *foyer.*

"You bought an apartment?"

He nods slowly, gauging my reaction.

"You bought an apartment," I repeat.

He's still nodding. "I did. Is that okay? I figured since we live together now we could use the extra room."

I spin in a slow circle. When my eyes land on the kitchen, I pause. It's not as big as Allysa's kitchen, but it's just as white and almost as beautiful. There's a wine cooler and a dishwasher, two things my own apartment doesn't have. I walk into the kitchen and look around, scared to touch anything. *Is this really my kitchen? This can't be my kitchen.*

I look in the living room at the cathedral ceilings and the huge windows overlooking Boston Harbor.

"Lily?" he says from behind me. "You aren't mad, are you?"

I spin and face him, realizing that he's been waiting on me to react for the past several minutes. But I'm completely speechless.

I shake my head and bring my hand up to cover my mouth. "I don't think so," I whisper.

He walks up to me and takes my hands in his, pulling them up between us. "You don't *think* so?" He looks worried and confused. "Please give me a naked truth, because I'm starting to think maybe I shouldn't have done this as a surprise."

I look down at the hardwood floor. It's real hardwood. It's not laminate. "Okay," I say, looking back up at him. "I think it's crazy that you just went and bought an apartment without me. I feel like that's something we should have done together."

He's nodding and it looks like he's about to spit out an apology, but I'm not finished.

"But my naked truth is that . . . it's perfect. I don't even know what to say, Ryle. Everything is so clean. I'm scared to move. I might get something dirty."

He blows out a rush of air and pulls me to him. "You can get it dirty, babe. It's yours. You can get it as dirty as you want." He kisses the side of my head and I don't even say thank you yet. It seems like such a small response to such a huge gesture.

"When do we move in?"

He shrugs. "Tomorrow? I have the day off. It's not like we have a whole lot of stuff. We can spend the next few weeks buying new furniture."

I nod, trying to run through tomorrow's schedule in my head. I already knew Ryle was off tomorrow, so I didn't have anything planned.

I suddenly feel the need to sit down. There aren't any chairs, but luckily, the floor is clean. "I need to sit down."

Ryle helps me to the floor and then he lowers himself in front of me, still holding my hands.

"Does Allysa know?" I ask him.

He smiles and nods his head. "She's so excited, Lily. I've been thinking about getting an apartment here for a while now. After we decided to stay in Boston for good, I just went ahead with it to surprise you. She helped, but I was starting to worry she'd tell you before I had the chance."

I just can't wrap my head around this. I live here? Me and Allysa get to be neighbors now? I don't know why I feel like this should bother me, because I really am excited about it.

He smiles and then says, "I know you need a minute to process everything, but you haven't seen the best part and it's killing me."

"Show me!"

He grins and pulls me to my feet. We make our way through the living room and down a hallway. He opens each door and tells me what the rooms are, but doesn't even give me time to go in any of them. By the time we make it to the master bedroom, I've concluded that we live in a three-bedroom, two-bath apartment. With an office.

I don't even have time to process the beauty of the bedroom as he pulls me across the room. He reaches a wall covered by a curtain and he turns and faces me. "It's not a ground that you can plant a garden in, but with a few pots, it can come close." He pulls the curtain aside and opens a door, revealing a huge balcony. I follow him outside, already daydreaming about all the potted plants I could fit up here.

"It overlooks the same view as the rooftop deck," he says. "We'll always have the same view we had from the night we met."

It took a while to sink in, but it all hits me in this moment and I just start crying. Ryle pulls me to his chest and wraps his arms tightly around me. "Lily," he whispers, running his hand over my hair. "I didn't mean to make you cry."

I laugh between my tears. "I just can't believe I live here." I pull away from his chest and look up at him. "Are we rich? How can you afford this?"

He laughs. "You married a neurosurgeon, Lily. You aren't necessarily strapped for cash."

His comment makes me laugh and then I cry some more.

And then we have our very first visitor because someone begins pounding on the door.

"Allysa," he says. "She's been waiting down the hall."

I run to the front door and swing it open and we both hug and squeal and I might even cry a little more.

We spend the rest of the evening at our new apartment. Ryle orders Chinese takeout and Marshall comes down to eat with us. We have no tables or chairs yet, so the four of us sit in the middle of the living room floor and eat straight out of the containers. We talk about how we'll decorate, we talk about all the neighborly things we'll do together, we talk about Allysa's impending delivery.

It's everything and more.

I can't wait to tell my mother.

Chapter Twenty-Two

Allysa is three days overdue.

We've lived in our new apartment for a week now. We successfully got all of our stuff moved the day Ryle was off, and Allysa and I went furniture shopping the second day we moved in. We were practically settled by the third day. We got our first piece of mail yesterday. It was a utility bill for establishing service, so it finally feels official now.

I'm married. I have a great husband. An awesome house. My best friend just happens to be my sister-in-law and I'm about to be an aunt.

Dare I say it . . . but can my life get any better?

I close my laptop and get ready to leave for the evening. I've been leaving earlier now than I usually do because I'm so excited to get home to my new apartment. Just as I begin to close my office door, Ryle uses his key to open the front door to the store. He lets the door fall shut behind him as he walks in with his hands full.

There's a newspaper tucked under his arm and two coffees in his hands. Despite the frenzied look about him and the urgency in his step, he's smiling. "Lily," he says, walking toward me. He shoves one of the coffees in my hand and then pulls the newspaper out from under his arm. "Three things. One . . . did you see the paper?" He hands it to me. The paper is folded inside-out. He points at the article. "You got it, Lily. You got it!"

I try not to get my hopes up as I look down at the article. He could be talking about something totally different from what I'm thinking. Once I read the headline, I realize he's talking about *exactly* what I was thinking. "I got it?"

I'd been notified that my business was nominated for an award for Best of Boston. It's a people's choice awards the newspaper holds annually, and Lily Bloom's was nominated under the "Best new businesses in Boston" category. The criteria are for businesses that have been open less than two years. I had a suspicion I might have been chosen when a reporter for the paper called me last week and asked me a series of questions.

The title reads *"Best new businesses in Boston. Votes are in for your top ten!"*

I smile and almost spill my coffee when Ryle pulls me in, picks me up, and spins me around.

He said he had three pieces of news, and if he started with that one, I have no idea what the other two could be. "What's the second thing?"

He sets me back down on my feet and says, "I started with the best one. I was too excited." He takes a sip of his coffee and then says, "I got selected for the training at Cambridge."

My face is taken over by a huge smile. "You did?" He nods and then he hugs me and spins me around again. "I'm so proud of you," I say, kissing him. "We're both so successful, it's sickening."

He laughs.

"Number three?" I ask him.

He pulls back. "Oh, yeah. Number three." He casually leans against the counter and takes a slow sip of his coffee.

He gently places his coffee back on the counter. "Allysa is in labor."

"What?!" I yell.

"Yeah." He nods toward our coffees. "That's why I brought you caffeine. We aren't getting any sleep tonight."

I start clapping, jumping up and down, and then panicking as I try to find my purse, my jacket, my keys, my phone, the light switch. Right before we make it to the door, Ryle rushes back to the counter and grabs the newspaper and tucks it under his arm. My hands are shaking with excitement as I lock the door.

"We're gonna be aunts!" I say as I run to my car.

Ryle laughs at my joke and says, "*Uncles*, Lily. We're gonna be *uncles*."

• • •

Marshall calmly steps out into the hallway. Ryle and I both perk up and wait for the news. It's been quiet in there for the past half an hour. We've been waiting to hear Allysa scream in agony—a sign she delivered—but there were no sounds at all. Not even the cries of a newborn. My hands go up to my mouth and seeing the look on Marshall's face has me fearing the worst.

His shoulders just start shaking and tears pour out of his eyes. "I'm a dad." And then he punches the air. "I'm a DAD!"

He hugs Ryle and then me and says, "Give us fifteen minutes and you can come inside to meet her."

When he closes the door, Ryle and I both release huge sighs of relief. We look at each other and smile. "You were thinking the worst, too?" he asks.

I nod and then hug him. "You're an uncle," I say, smiling.

He kisses my head and says, "You too."

Half an hour later, Ryle and I are both standing next to the bed, watching Allysa hold her new baby. She's absolutely perfect. A little too new to tell who she looks like yet, but she's beautiful, regardless.

"You want to hold your niece?" Allysa says to Ryle.

He kind of stiffens up like he's nervous, but then he nods. She leans over and puts the baby in Ryle's arms, showing him how to hold her. He stares down at her nervously and then walks over to the couch and takes a seat. "Have you guys decided on a name yet?" he asks.

"Yes," Allysa says.

Ryle and I both look at Allysa and she smiles, teary eyed. "We wanted to name her after someone Marshall and I both think the world of. So we added an *E* to your name. We're calling her Rylee."

I instantly look back over at Ryle and he blows out a quick breath like he's a little in shock. He looks back down at Rylee and just starts smiling. "Wow," he whispers. "I don't know what to say."

I squeeze Allysa's hand and then walk over and take a seat next to Ryle. I've had a lot of moments when I thought I couldn't love him more than I already do, but once again I'm proven wrong. Seeing the way he looks at his new baby niece makes my heart expand.

Marshall sits down on the bed next to Allysa. "Did you guys hear how quiet Issa was through the whole thing? Not a single peep. She didn't even take drugs." He puts his arm around her and lies down next to her on the bed. "I feel like

I'm in that movie *Hancock* with Will Smith and I'm about to find out I'm married to a superhero."

Ryle laughs. "She's kicked my ass a time or two growing up. I wouldn't be surprised."

"No cussing around Rylee," Marshall says.

"Ass," Ryle whispers to her.

We both laugh and then he asks me if I want to hold her. I make like I have grabby hands because waiting for my turn has been killing me. I pull her into my arms and am shocked by how much love I have for her already.

"When are Mom and Dad coming in?" Ryle asks Allysa.

"They'll be here by lunch tomorrow."

"I should probably get some sleep then. Just got off a long shift." He looks back at me. "You coming with?"

I shake my head. "I want to hang out for a little while longer. Just take my car and I'll catch a cab home."

He kisses me on the side of my head and then rests his head against mine as we both look down at Rylee. "I think we should make one of these," he says.

I glance up at him, not sure if I heard him correctly.

He winks. "If I'm asleep when you get home later, wake me up. We'll start on it tonight." He tells Marshall and Allysa goodbye and Marshall walks him out.

I glance over at Allysa and she's smiling. "I told you he'd want babies with you."

I grin and walk back over to her bed. She scoots over and makes room for me. I hand Rylee back to her and we snuggle together on her bed and watch Rylee sleep, like it's the most magnificent thing we've ever seen.

Chapter Twenty-Three

It's three hours later and after ten o'clock when I make it back home. I stayed with Allysa for another hour after Ryle left and then went back to my office to finish up a few things so that I don't have to go in for the next two days. Whenever Ryle has a day off, I try to coincide my own days off with his.

The lights are off when I walk through the front door, so that means Ryle is already in bed.

The entire drive home I thought about what he'd said. I wasn't expecting this conversation to come up so soon. I'm almost twenty-five, but I had it in my head it would be at least a couple of years before we started trying for a family. I'm still not certain I'm ready for it yet, but knowing it's now something he wants someday has put me in an incredibly happy mood.

I decide to make myself a quick bite to eat before waking him up. I haven't had dinner yet and I'm starving. When I flip on the kitchen light, I scream. My hand goes to my chest and I fall against the counter. "Jesus Christ, Ryle! What are you doing?"

He's leaning with his back against the wall next to the refrigerator. His feet are crossed at the ankles and his eyes are narrowed in my direction. He's flipping something over in his fingers, staring at me.

My eyes fall to the counter to his left and I see an empty

glass that probably recently held scotch. He drinks it on occasion to help him fall asleep.

I look back at him and there's a smirk on his face. My body instantly grows warm at that smile because I know what comes next. This apartment is about to become a frenzy of clothes and kisses. We've christened nearly every room since we moved in here, but the kitchen is one we haven't tackled yet.

I smile back at him, my heart still beating erratically from the shock of finding him here in the dark. His eyes fall to his hand, and I notice he's holding the Boston magnet. I brought it from the old apartment and stuck it on this fridge when we moved in.

He places it back on the fridge and taps it. "Where'd you get this?"

I look at the magnet and then back at him. The last thing I want to do is tell him that magnet came from Atlas on my sixteenth birthday. It would only bring up an already sore subject, and I'm too excited for what's about to come next between us to give him the naked truth right now.

I shrug. "I can't remember. I've had it forever."

He stares at me silently and then straightens up, taking two steps toward me. I back myself against the counter and my breath catches. His hands meet my waist and he slides them between my ass and my jeans and pulls me against him. His mouth claims mine and he kisses me while he begins to lower my jeans.

Okay. So we're doing this right now.

His lips drag down my neck as I kick off my shoes and then he pulls my jeans off the rest of the way.

I guess I can eat later. Christening the kitchen just became my priority.

When his mouth is back on mine, he lifts me and sets me down on the countertop, standing between my knees. I can smell the scotch on his breath, and I kind of like it. I'm already breathing heavily as his warm lips slide across mine. He takes a fistful of my hair and he tugs gently so that I'm looking up at him.

"Naked truth?" he whispers, looking at my mouth like he's about to devour me.

I nod.

His other hand begins to slide slowly up my thigh until there's nowhere left for his hand to go. He slips two warm fingers inside of me, keeping my gaze locked with his. I suck in a rush of air as my legs tighten around his waist. I begin to slowly move against his hand, moaning softly as he stares heatedly at me.

"Where did you get that magnet, Lily?"

What?

My heart feels like it begins beating in reverse.

Why does he keep asking me this?

His fingers are still moving inside of me, his eyes still look like they want me. *But his hand.* The hand that's wrapped in my hair begins to tug harder and I wince.

"Ryle," I whisper, keeping my voice calm, even though I'm beginning to shake. "That hurts."

His fingers stop moving, but his gaze never leaves mine. He slowly pulls his fingers out of me and then brings his hand up around my throat, squeezing gently. His lips meet mine and his tongue dives inside my mouth. I take it, because

I have no idea what's going through his head right now and I pray I'm overreacting.

I can feel him hard against his jeans as he presses into me. But then he pulls back. His hands leave me entirely as he flattens his back against the refrigerator, scraping his eyes over my body like he wants to take me right here in the kitchen. My heart begins to calm down. *I'm overreacting.*

He reaches beside him, next to the stove, and he picks up a newspaper. It's the same newspaper he showed me earlier, with the awards article printed in it. He holds it up, then tosses it toward me. "Did you get a chance to read that yet?"

I blow out a breath of relief. "Not yet," I say, my eyes falling to the article.

"Read it out loud."

I glance up at him. I smile, but my stomach is anxious. There's something about him right now. The way he's acting. I can't put my finger on it.

"You want me to read the article?" I ask. "Right now?"

I feel odd, sitting on my kitchen counter half naked, holding a newspaper. He nods. "I'd like you to take off your shirt first. *Then* read it out loud."

I stare at him, trying to gauge his behavior. Maybe the scotch has made him extra frisky. A lot of times when we make love, it's as simple as making love. But occasionally, our sex is wild. A little dangerous, like the look in his eyes right now.

I set the paper down, pull off my shirt, and then pick the paper back up. I start reading the article out loud, but he takes a step forward and says, "Not the whole thing." He flips the paper over where it starts in the middle of the article and he points to a sentence. "Read the last few paragraphs."

I look down, even more confused this time. But whatever will get us past this and into the bed . . .

"The business with the highest number of votes should come as no surprise. The iconic Bib's on Marketson opened in April of last year, quickly becoming one of the highest rated restaurants in the city, according to TripAdvisor."

I stop reading and look up at Ryle. He has poured himself more scotch and he's swallowing a sip of it. "Keep reading," he says, nudging his head at the paper in my hand.

I swallow heavily, the saliva in my mouth growing thicker by the second. I try to control the trembling of my hands as I continue reading. "The owner, Atlas Corrigan, is a two-time award-winning chef and also a United States Marine. It's no secret what the acronym for his highly successful restaurant, Bib's, stands for: *Better In Boston*."

I gasp.

Everything is better in Boston.

I clench my stomach, trying to keep my emotions under control as I keep reading. "But when interviewed regarding his most recent award, the chef finally revealed the true history of the meaning behind the name. '*It's a long story,*' Chef Corrigan stated. '*It was an homage to someone who had a huge impact on my life. Someone who meant a lot to me. She still means a lot to me.*'"

I put the newspaper on the counter. "I don't want to read anymore." My voice cracks on its way up my throat.

Ryle takes two swift steps forward and grabs the newspaper. He picks up where I left off, his voice loud and angry now. "When asked if the girl was aware he named a restaurant after her, Chef Corrigan smiled knowingly and said, '*Next question.*'"

The anger in Ryle's voice makes me nauseous. "Ryle, stop

it," I say calmly. "You've had too much to drink." I push past him and walk quickly out of the kitchen toward the hallway that leads to our bedroom. There's so much happening right now and I'm not sure I understand any of it.

The article never stated who Atlas was talking about. Atlas knows it was me and *I* know it was me, but how in the hell would Ryle put two and two together?

And the magnet. How would he know that came from Atlas just by reading that article?

He's overreacting.

I can hear him following me as I walk toward the bedroom. I swing open the door and come to a sudden halt.

The bed is littered with things. An empty moving box with the words, "Lily's stuff," written on the side of it. And then all the contents that were inside that box. Letters . . . journals . . . empty shoeboxes. I close my eyes and breathe in slowly.

He read the journal.

No.

He. Read. The. Journal.

His arm comes around my waist from behind. He slides a hand up my stomach and takes a firm hold of one of my breasts. His other hand feathers my shoulder as he moves the hair away from my neck.

I squeeze my eyes shut, just as his fingers begin to trace across my skin, up to my shoulder. He slowly runs his finger over the heart and a shudder runs over my whole body. His lips meet my skin, right over the tattoo, and then he sinks his teeth into me so hard, I scream.

I try to pull away from him, but he has such a tight grip on me he doesn't even budge. The pain from his teeth piercing my collarbone rips through my shoulder and down my arm. I immediately start crying. *Sobbing.*

"Ryle, let me go," I say, my voice pleading. "Please. Walk away." His arms are cutting into mine as he holds me tightly from behind.

He spins me, but my eyes are still closed. I'm too scared to look at him. His hands are digging into my shoulders as he pushes me toward the bed. I start trying to fight him off of me, but it's useless. He's too strong for me. He's angry. He's hurt. *And he's not Ryle.*

My back meets the bed and I frantically scoot back toward the headboard, trying to get away from him. "Why is he still here, Lily?" His voice isn't as composed as it was in the kitchen. He's really angry now. "He's in *everything.* The magnet on the fridge. The journal in the box I found in our closet. The fucking *tattoo* on your body that used to be my favorite goddamn *part of you!*"

He's on the bed now.

"Ryle," I beg. "I can explain." Tears streak down my temples and into my hair. "You're angry. Please don't hurt me, *please.* Walk away, and when you come back, I'll explain."

His hand grips my ankle and he yanks me until I'm beneath him. "I'm not angry, Lily," he says, his voice disturbingly calm now. "I just think I haven't proved to you how much I love you." His body comes down against mine and he takes my wrists with one hand above my head, pressing them against the mattress.

"Ryle, please." I'm sobbing, trying to push him off of me with any part of my body. "Get off me. *Please.*"

No, no, no, no.

"I love you, Lily," he says, his words crashing against my cheek. "More than he *ever* did. Why can't you *see* that?"

My fear folds in on itself, and I become diluted with rage. All I can see when I squeeze my eyes shut is my mother crying on our old living room couch; my father forcing himself on top of her. Hatred rips through me and I start screaming.

Ryle tries to muffle my screams with his mouth.

I bite down on his tongue.

His forehead comes crashing down against mine.

In an instant, all the pain fades as a blanket of darkness rolls over my eyes and consumes me.

• • •

I can feel his breath against my ear as he mutters something inaudible. My heart is racing, my whole body is still shaking, my tears are still somehow falling and I'm gasping for air. His words are crashing against my ear, but the pain is throbbing in my head too hard for me to decipher his words.

I try to open my eyes, but it stings. I can feel something trickling into my right eye and I instantly know it's blood.

My blood.

His words begin to come into focus.

"Sorry, I'm sorry, I'm sorry, I'm . . ."

His hand is still pressing mine into the mattress and he's still on top of me. He's no longer trying to force himself on me.

"Lily, I love you, I'm so sorry."

His words are full of panic. He's kissing me, his lips gentle against my cheek and mouth.

He knows what he's done. He's Ryle again, and he knows what he's just done to me. To us. To our future.

I utilize his panic to my advantage. I shake my head and I whisper, "It's okay, Ryle. It's okay. You were angry, it's okay."

His lips meet mine in a frenzy and the taste of scotch makes me want to puke now. He's still whispering apologies when the room begins to fade out again.

• • •

My eyes are closed. We're still on the bed, but he's no longer fully on top of me. He's on his side, his arm wrapped tightly over my waist. His head is pressed against my chest. I remain stiff as I assess everything around me.

He isn't moving, but I can feel his breaths, heavy with sleep. I don't know if he passed out or if he fell asleep. The last thing I can remember is his mouth on mine, the taste of my own tears.

I lie still for several more minutes. The pain in my head begins to worsen with every minute of consciousness. I close my eyes and try to think.

Where's my purse?

Where are my keys?

Where is my phone?

It takes me a full five minutes to slide out from under him. I'm too scared to move too much at once, so I do it an inch at a time until I'm able to roll onto the floor. When I can no longer feel his hands on me, an unexpected sob breaks from my chest. I slap my hand over my mouth as I pull myself to my feet and run out of the bedroom.

I find my purse and my phone, but I have no idea where he put my keys. I frantically search the living room and kitchen, but I can barely see anything. When he head-butted me, it must have left a gash on my forehead, because there's too much blood in my eyes and everything is blurry.

I slide to the floor near the door, growing dizzy. My fingers are shaking so hard, it takes three tries to get the password right on my phone.

When I have the screen up to dial a number, I pause. My first thought is to call Allysa and Marshall, but I can't. I can't do that to them right now. She just gave birth to a baby a matter of hours ago. I can't do this to them.

I could call the police, but my mind can't even process what all that entails. I don't want to give a statement. I don't know that I want to press charges, knowing what this could do to his career. I don't want Allysa mad at me. I just don't know. I don't completely rule out eventually notifying the police. I just don't have the energy to make that decision right now.

I squeeze the phone and try to think. *My mother.*

I start to dial her number, but when I think of what this would do to her I start to cry again. I can't involve her in this mess. She's been through too much. And Ryle will try to find me. He'll go to her first. Then Allysa and Marshall. Then to everyone else we know.

I wipe the tears from my eyes and then begin dialing Atlas's number.

I hate myself more in this moment than I ever have in my entire life.

I hate myself, because the day Ryle found Atlas's number in my phone, I lied and said I had forgotten it was there.

I hate myself, because the day Atlas placed his number there, I opened it and looked at it.

I hate myself, because deep down inside, I knew there was a chance that I might one day need it. *So I memorized it.*

"Hello?"

His voice is cautious. Inquiring. He doesn't recognize this number. I immediately start crying when he speaks. I cover my mouth and try to quiet myself.

"Lily?" His voice is much louder now. "Lily, where are you?"

I hate myself, because he knows the tears are mine.

"Atlas," I whisper. "I need help."

"Where are you?" he says again. I can hear panic in his voice. I can hear him walking, moving stuff around. I hear a door slam on his end of the phone.

"I'll text you," I whisper, too scared to keep speaking. I don't want Ryle to wake up. I hang up the phone and somehow find the strength to still my hands while I text him my address and the access code for entry. Then I send a second text that says **Text me when you get here. Please don't knock.**

I crawl to the kitchen and find my pants, struggling back into them. I find my shirt on the counter. When I'm dressed, I go to the living room. I debate opening the door and meeting Atlas downstairs, but I'm too scared I won't be able to make it down to the lobby alone. My forehead is still bleeding and I feel too weak to even stand up and wait by the door. I slide to the floor, clenching my phone in my shaky fist and staring at it, waiting for his text.

It's an agonizing twenty-four minutes later when my phone lights up.

Here.

I scramble to my feet and swing open the door. Arms wrap around me and my face is pressed against something soft. I just start crying and crying and shaking and crying.

"Lily," he whispers. I've never heard my name spoken so sadly. He urges me to look up at him. His blue eyes scroll over my face, and I see it happen. I watch the concern vanish as he darts his head up to the apartment door. "Is he still in there?"

Rage.

I can feel the rage come off of him and he starts to step toward the apartment door. I grab his jacket in my fists. "No. *Please*, Atlas. I just want to leave."

I see the pain roll over him as he pauses, struggling to decide whether to listen to me or bust through the door. He eventually turns away from the door and wraps his arms around me. He helps me to the elevator and then through the lobby. By some miracle, we only run into one person and he's on his phone and facing the other direction.

By the time we make it to the parking garage, I start to feel dizzy again. I tell him to slow down, and then I feel his arm wrap under my knees as he picks me up. Then we're in the car. Then the car is moving.

I know I need stitches.

I know he's taking me to the hospital.

But I have no idea why the next words out of my mouth are, "Don't take me to Mass General. Take me somewhere else."

For whatever reason, I don't want to risk the chance of running into any of Ryle's colleagues. I hate him. I hate him in this moment more than I've ever hated my father. But concern for his career still somehow breaks through the hatred.

When I realize this, I hate myself just as much as I hate him.

Chapter Twenty-Four

Atlas is standing on the other side of the room. He hasn't taken his eyes off me the entire time the nurse has been helping me. After taking a blood sample, she immediately returned and began to attend to my cut. She hasn't asked me very many questions yet, but it's obvious my injuries are the result of an attack. I can see the pitying look on her face as she cleans up blood from the bite mark left on my shoulder.

When she's finished, she glances back at Atlas. She steps to the right, blocking his view of me as she turns and faces me again. "I need to ask you some personal questions. I'm going to ask him to leave the room, okay?"

It's in that moment that I realize she thinks Atlas is the one who did these things to me. I immediately start to shake my head. "It wasn't him," I tell her. "Please don't make him leave."

Relief washes over her face. She nods her head and then pulls up a chair. "Are you hurt anywhere else?"

I shake my head, because she can't fix all the parts of me Ryle broke on the inside.

"Lily?" Her voice is gentle. "Were you raped?"

Tears fill my eyes and I see Atlas roll across the wall, pressing his forehead against it.

The nurse waits until I make eye contact with her again

to continue speaking. "We have a certain examination for these situations. It's called a SANE exam. It's optional, of course, but I highly encourage it in your situation."

"I wasn't raped," I say. "He didn't . . ."

"Are you sure, Lily?" the nurse asks.

I nod. "I don't want one."

Atlas faces me again and I can see the pain in his expression as he steps forward. "Lily. You need this." His eyes are pleading.

I shake my head again. "Atlas, I swear . . ." I squeeze my eyes shut and lower my head. "I'm not covering for him this time," I whisper. "He tried, but then he stopped."

"If you choose to press charges, you'll need—"

"I don't want the exam," I say again, my voice firm.

There's a knock on the door and a doctor enters, sparing me from more pleading looks from Atlas. The nurse gives the doctor a brief rundown of my injuries. She then steps aside as he examines my head and shoulder. He flashes a light into both of my eyes. He looks down at the paperwork again and says, "I'd like to rule out a concussion, but given your situation, I don't want to administer a CT. We'd like to keep you for observation, instead."

"Why don't you want to administer a CT?" I ask him.

The doctor stands up. "We don't like to perform X-rays on pregnant women unless it's vital. We'll monitor you for complications and if there are no further concerns, you'll be free to go."

I don't hear anything beyond that.

Nothing.

The pressure begins to build in my head. My heart. My

stomach. I grip the edges of the exam table I'm sitting on and I stare at the floor until they both leave the room.

When the door closes behind them, I sit, suspended in frozen silence. I see Atlas move closer. His feet are almost touching mine. His fingers brush lightly over my back. "Did you know?"

I release a quick breath, and then drag in more air. I start shaking my head, and when his arms come down around me, I cry harder than I knew my body was even capable of. He holds me the entire time I cry. He holds me through my hatred.

I did this to myself.

I allowed this to happen to me.

I am my mother.

"I want to leave," I whisper.

Atlas pulls back. "They want to monitor you, Lily. I think you should stay."

I look up at him and shake my head. "I need to get out of here. *Please.* I want to leave."

He nods and helps me back into my shoes. He pulls off his jacket and wraps it around me, then we walk out of the hospital without anyone noticing.

He says nothing to me as we drive. I stare out the window, too exhausted to cry. Too in shock to speak. I feel submerged.

Just keep swimming.

• • •

Atlas doesn't live in an apartment. He lives in a house. A small suburb outside of Boston called Wellesley, where all the homes are beautiful, sprawling, manicured, and expensive. Before we pull into his driveway, I wonder to myself if he ever married that girl. *Cassie.* I wonder what she'll think of her husband bringing home a girl he once loved who has just been attacked by her own husband.

She'll pity me. She'll wonder why I never left him. She'll wonder how I let myself get to this point. She'll wonder all the same things I used to wonder about my own mother when I saw her in my same situation. People spend so much time wondering why the women don't leave. Where are all the people who wonder why the men are even abusive? Isn't that where the only blame should be placed?

Atlas parks in the garage. There's not another vehicle here. I don't wait for him to help me out of the car. I open the door and get out on my own, and then I follow him into his house. He punches in a code on an alarm and then flips on a few lights. My eyes roam around the kitchen, the dining room, the living room. Everything is made of rich woods and stainless steel, and his kitchen is painted a calming bluish-green. The color of the ocean. If I wasn't hurting so much, I would smile.

Atlas kept swimming, and look at him now. He swam all the way to the fucking Caribbean.

He moves to his refrigerator and pulls out a bottle of water, walking it over to me. He takes the lid off and hands it to me. I take a drink and watch as he turns the living room light on, then the hallway.

"Do you live alone?" I ask.

He nods as he walks back into the kitchen. "Are you hungry?"

I shake my head. Even if I was, I wouldn't be able to eat.

"I'll show you your room," he says. "There's a shower if you need it."

I do. I want to wash the taste of scotch out of my mouth. I want to wash the sterile smell of the hospital off of me. I want to wash away the last four hours of my life.

I follow him down the hallway and to a spare bedroom where he flips on the light. There are two boxes on a bare bed and more stacked up against the walls. There's an oversized chair against one wall, facing the door. He moves to the bed and takes off the boxes, setting them against the wall with the others.

"I just moved in a few months ago. Haven't had much time to decorate yet." He walks to a dresser and pulls open a drawer. "I'll make the bed for you." He takes out sheets and a pillowcase. He begins making the bed as I walk inside the bathroom and close the door.

I remain in the bathroom for thirty minutes. Some of those minutes are spent staring at my reflection in the mirror. Some of those minutes are spent in the shower. The rest are spent over the toilet as I make myself sick with thoughts of the last several hours.

I'm wrapped in a towel when I crack the bathroom door. Atlas is no longer in the bedroom, but there are clothes folded on the freshly made bed. Men's pajama bottoms that are too big for me and a T-shirt that goes past my knees. I pull the drawstring tight, tie it, and then crawl into bed. I turn the lamp off and pull the covers up and over me.

I cry so hard, I don't even make a noise.

Chapter Twenty-Five

I smell toast.

I stretch out on my bed and smile, because Ryle knows toast is my favorite.

My eyes flick open and the clarity smashes down on me with the force of a head-on collision. I squeeze my eyes shut when I realize where I am and why I'm here and that the toast I smell is not at all because my sweet and caring husband is making me breakfast in bed.

I immediately want to cry again, so I force myself off the bed. I focus on the hollowness in my stomach as I use the bathroom, and tell myself I can cry after I eat something. I need to eat before I make myself sick again.

When I walk out of the bathroom and back into the bedroom, I notice the chair has been turned so that it's facing the bed now instead of the door. There's a blanket thrown over it haphazardly, and it's obvious Atlas was in here last night while I slept.

He was probably worried I had a concussion.

When I walk into the kitchen, Atlas is moving back and forth between the fridge, the stove, the counter. For the first time in twelve hours, I feel an inkling of something that isn't agony, because I remember he's a chef. A *good* one. And he's cooking me breakfast.

He glances up at me as I make my way into the kitchen.

"Morning," he says, careful to say it without too much inflection. "I hope you're hungry." He slides a glass and a container of orange juice across the counter toward me, then he turns and faces the stove again.

"I am."

He glances back over his shoulder and gives me a ghost of a smile. I pour myself a glass of orange juice and then walk to the other side of the kitchen where there's a breakfast nook. There's a newspaper on the table and I begin to pick it up. When I see the article about the best businesses in Boston printed across the page, my hands immediately begin to shake and I drop the paper back on the table. I close my eyes and take a slow sip of the orange juice.

A few minutes later, Atlas sets a plate down in front of me, then claims the seat across from me at the table. He pulls his own plate of food in front of him and cuts into a crepe with his fork.

I look down at my plate. Three crepes, drizzled in syrup and garnished with a dab of whipped cream. Orange and strawberry slices line the right side of the plate.

It's almost too pretty to eat, but I'm too hungry to care. I take a bite and close my eyes, trying not to make it obvious that it's the best bite of breakfast I've ever had.

I finally allow myself to admit that his restaurant deserved that award. As much as I tried to talk Ryle and Allysa out of going back, it was the best restaurant I'd ever been to.

"Where did you learn to cook?" I ask him.

He sips from a cup of coffee. "The Marines," he says, placing the cup back down. "I trained for a while during my first stint and then when I reenlisted I came on as a chef." He taps his fork against the side of his plate. "You like it?"

I nod. "It's delicious. But you're wrong. You knew how to cook before you enlisted."

He smiles. "You remember the cookies?"

I nod again. "Best cookies I've ever eaten."

He leans back in his chair. "I taught myself the basics. My mother worked second shift when I was growing up, so if I wanted dinner at night I had to make it. It was either that or starve, so I bought a cookbook at a yard sale and made every single recipe in it over the course of a year. And I was only thirteen."

I smile, shocked that I'm even able to. "The next time someone asks you how you learned to cook, you should tell them *that* story. Not the other one."

He shakes his head. "You're the only person who knows anything about me before the age of nineteen. I'd like to keep it that way."

He begins telling me about working as a chef in the military. How he saved up as much money as he could so that when he got out, he could open his own restaurant. He started with a small café that did really well, then opened Bib's a year and a half ago. "It does okay," he says with modesty.

I glance around his kitchen and then look back at him. "Looks like it does more than just okay."

He shrugs and takes another bite of his food. I don't talk after that as we finish eating, because my mind wanders to his restaurant. The name of it. What he said in the interview. Then, of course, those thoughts lead me back to thoughts of

Ryle and the anger in his voice as he yelled the last line of the interview at me.

I think Atlas can see the change in my demeanor, but he says nothing as he clears the table.

When he takes another seat, he chooses the chair right next to me this time. He places a reassuring hand on top of mine. "I have to go in to work for a few hours," he says. "I don't want you to leave. Stay here as long as you need, Lily. Just . . . please don't go back home today."

I shake my head when I hear the concern in his words. "I won't. I'll stay here," I tell him. "I promise."

"Do you need anything before I go?"

I shake my head. "I'll be fine."

He stands up and grabs his jacket. "I'll make it as quick as I can. I'll be back after lunch and I'll bring you something to eat, okay?"

I force a smile. He opens a drawer and pulls out a pen and paper. He writes something on it before he leaves. When he's gone, I stand up and walk to the counter to read what he wrote. He listed instructions for how to set the alarm. He wrote his cell phone number, even though I have it memorized. He also wrote down his work number, his home address, and his work address.

At the bottom in small print, he wrote, *"Just keep swimming, Lily."*

Dear Ellen,

Hi. It's me. Lily Bloom. Well . . . technically it's Lily Kincaid now.

I know it's been a long time since I've written to you. A really long time. After everything that happened with Atlas, I just couldn't bring myself to open up the journals again. I couldn't even bring myself to watch your show after school, because it hurt to watch it alone. In fact, all thoughts of you kind of depressed me. When I thought of you, I thought of Atlas. And to be honest, I didn't want to think of Atlas, so I had to cut you out of my life, too.

I'm sorry about that. I'm sure you didn't miss me like I missed you, but sometimes the things that matter to you most are also the things that hurt you the most. And in order to get over that hurt, you have to sever all the extensions that keep you tethered to that pain. You were an extension of my pain, so I guess that's what I was doing. I was just trying to save myself a little bit of agony.

I'm sure your show is as great as ever, though. I hear you still dance at the beginning of some episodes, but I've grown to appreciate that. I think that's one of the biggest signs a person has matured—knowing how to appreciate things that matter to others, even if they don't matter very much to you.

I should probably catch you up on my life. My father died. I'm twenty-four now. I got a college degree, worked in marketing for a while, and now I own my own business. A floral shop. Life goals, FTW!

I also have a husband and he isn't Atlas.

And . . . I live in Boston.

I know. Shocker.

The last time I wrote to you, I was sixteen. I was in a really bad place and I was so worried about Atlas. I'm not worried about Atlas anymore, but I am in a really bad place right now. More so than the last time I wrote to you.

I'm sorry I don't seem to need to write to you when I'm in a good place. You tend to only get the shit end of my life, but that's what friends are for, right?

I don't even know where to start. I know you don't know anything about my current life or my husband, Ryle. But there's this thing we do where one of us says "naked truth," and then we're forced to be brutally honest and say what we're really thinking.

So . . . naked truth.

Brace yourself.

I am in love with a man who physically hurts me. Of all people, I have no idea how I let myself get to this point.

There were many times growing up I wondered what was going through my mother's head in the days after my father had hurt her. How she could possibly love a man who had laid his hands on her. A man who repeatedly hit her. Repeatedly promised he would never do it again. Repeatedly hit her again.

I hate that I can empathize with her now.

I've been sitting on Atlas's couch for over four hours, wrestling with my feelings. I can't get a grip on them. I can't understand them. I don't know how to process them. And true to my past, I realized that maybe I need to just get them out on paper. My apologies to you, Ellen. But get ready for a whole lot of word vomit.

If I had to compare this feeling to something, I would compare it to death. Not just the death of anyone. The death of the *one. The person who is closer to you than anyone else in the whole world. The one who, when you simply imagine their death, it makes your eyes tear up.*

That's what this feels like. It feels like Ryle has died.

It's an astronomical amount of grief. An enormous amount of pain. It's a sense that I've lost my best friend, my lover, my husband, my lifeline. But the difference between this feeling and death is the presence of another emotion that doesn't necessarily follow in the event of an actual death.

Hatred.

I am so angry at him, Ellen. Words can't express the amount of hatred I have for him. Yet somehow, in the midst of all my hatred, there are waves of reasoning that flow through me. I start to think things like "But I shouldn't have had the magnet. I should have told him about the tattoo from the beginning. I shouldn't have kept the journals."

The reasoning is the hardest part of this. It eats at me, little by little, wearing down the strength my hatred lends to me. The reasoning forces me to imagine our future together, and how there are things I could do to prevent that type of anger. I'll never betray him again. I'll never keep secrets from him again. I'll never give him reason to react that way again. We'll both just have to work harder from now on.

For better, for worse, right?

I know these are the things that once went through my mother's head. But the difference between the two of us is that she had more to worry about. She didn't have the financial stability that I have. She didn't have the resources to leave and give me what she thought was a decent shelter. She didn't want to take me away from my father when I was used to living with both parents. I have a feeling reasoning really kicked her ass a time or two.

I can't even begin to process the thought that I'm having a child with this man. There is a human being inside of me that we created together. And no matter which option I choose—whether I choose to stay or choose to leave—neither are choices I would wish upon my child. To grow up in a broken home or an abusive one? I've already failed this baby in life, and I've only known about his or her existence for a single day.

Ellen, I wish you could write back to me. I wish that you could say something funny to me right now, because my heart needs it. I have never felt this alone. This broken. This angry. This hurt.

People on the outside of situations like these often wonder why the woman goes back to the abuser. I read somewhere once that 85 percent of women return to abusive situations. That was before I realized I was in one, and when I heard that statistic, I thought it was because the women were stupid. I thought it was because they were weak. I thought these things about my own mother more than once.

But sometimes the reason women go back is simply because they're in love. I love my husband, Ellen. I love so many things about him. I wish cutting my feelings off for the person who hurt me was as easy as I used to think it would be. Preventing your heart from forgiving someone you love is actually a hell of a lot harder than simply forgiving them.

I'm a statistic now. The things I've thought about women like me are now what others would think of me if they knew my current situation.

"How could she love him after what he did to her? How could she contemplate taking him back?"

It's sad that those are the first thoughts that run through our minds when someone is abused. Shouldn't there be more distaste in our mouths for the abusers than for those who continue to love the abusers?

I think of all the people who have been in this situation before me. Everyone who will be in this situation after me. Do we all repeat the same words in our heads in the days after experiencing abuse at the hands of those who love us? "From this day forward, for better, for worse, for richer, for poorer, in sickness and health, until death do us part."

Maybe those vows weren't meant to be taken as literally as some spouses take them.

For better, for worse?

Fuck.

That.

Shit.

—Lily

Chapter Twenty-Six

I'm lying on Atlas's guest bed, staring up at the ceiling. It's a normal bed. Really comfortable, actually. But it feels like I'm on a water bed. Or maybe a raft, adrift at sea. And I scale over these huge waves, each of them carrying something different. Some are waves of sadness. Some are waves of anger. Some are waves of tears. Some are waves of sleep.

Occasionally, I'll place my hands on my stomach and a tiny wave of love will come. I have no idea how I can already love something so much, but I do. I think about whether or not it'll be a boy or a girl and what I'll name it. I wonder if it will look like me or Ryle. And then another wave of anger will come and crash down on that tiny wave of love.

I feel robbed of the joy a mother should have when she finds out she's pregnant. I feel like Ryle took that from me last night and it's just one more thing I have to hate him for.

Hatred is exhausting.

I force myself off the bed and into the shower. I've been in my room most of the day. Atlas returned home several hours ago and I heard him open the door at one point to check on me but I pretended to be asleep.

I feel awkward being here. Atlas is the very reason Ryle was angry at me last night, yet he's the one I ran to when I needed help? Being here fills me with guilt. Maybe even a little bit of shame, as though my calling Atlas lends credibility to Ryle's anger. But there's literally nowhere I can go right now. I need a couple of days to process things and if I go to a hotel, Ryle could track the credit card charge and find me.

He'd be able to find me at my mother's. At Allysa's. At Lucy's. He's even met Devin a couple of times and would more than likely go there, too.

I can't see him tracking down Atlas, though. Yet. I'm sure if I go a week avoiding his calls and texts, he'll look everywhere he can possibly look to find me. But for now, I don't think he would show up here.

Maybe that's why I'm here. I feel safer here than anywhere else I could possibly go. And Atlas has an alarm system, so there's that.

I glance at the nightstand to look at my phone. I skip over all the missed texts from Ryle and open the one from Allysa.

Allysa: Hey, Aunt Lily! They're sending us home tonight. Come see us tomorrow when you get home from work.

She sent a picture of her and Rylee, and it makes me smile. Then cry. Damn these emotions.

I wait until my eyes are dry again before I walk into the living room. Atlas is sitting at his kitchen table, working on his laptop. When he looks up at me, he smiles and closes it.

"Hey."

I force a smile and then look in the kitchen. "Do you have anything to eat?"

Atlas stands up quickly. "Yeah," he says. "Yeah, sit down. I'll get something ready for you."

I take a seat on the couch as he works his way around the kitchen. The television is on, but it's muted. I unmute it and click on the DVR. He has a few shows recorded, but the one that catches my eye is *The Ellen DeGeneres Show.* I smile and click on the most recent unwatched episode and hit Play.

Atlas brings me a bowl of pasta and a glass of ice water. He glances at the TV and then sits down next to me on the couch.

For the next three hours, we watch a full week's worth of episodes. I laugh out loud six times. It feels good, but when I take a bathroom break and come back to the living room, the weight of it all starts to sink in again.

I sit back down on the couch next to Atlas. He's leaning back with his feet propped up on the coffee table. I naturally lean into him and just like he used to do when we were teenagers, he pulls me against his chest and we just sit there in silence. His thumb brushes the outside of my shoulder, and I know it's his unspoken way of saying he's here for me. That he feels bad for me. And for the first time since he picked me up last night, I feel like talking about it. My head is resting against his shoulder and my hands are in my lap. I'm fidgeting with the drawstring on the pants that are way too big for me.

"Atlas?" I say, my voice barely a whisper. "I'm sorry I got so angry at you that night at the restaurant. You were right. Deep down I knew you were right, but I didn't want to believe it." I lift my head and look at him, cracking a pitiful smile. "You can say, '*I told you so*' now."

His eyebrows draw together, like my words somehow hurt him. "Lily, this is not something I wanted to be right about. I prayed every day that I was wrong about him."

I wince. I shouldn't have said that to him. I know better than to think Atlas would ever think something like *I told you so.*

He squeezes my shoulder and leans forward, kissing the top of my head. I close my eyes as I soak up the familiarity of him. His smell, his touch, his comfort. I've never understood how someone can be so rock solid, yet comforting. But that's always how I've viewed him. Like he could withstand anything, but somehow still feels the weight that everyone else carries.

I don't like that I was never fully able to let go of him, no matter how hard I tried. I think about the fight with Ryle over Atlas's phone number. The fight about the magnet, the article, the things he read in my journal, the tattoo. None of that would have happened if I would have just let go of Atlas and thrown it all away. Ryle wouldn't have had anything to be so upset with me about.

I pull my hands up to my face after that thought, upset that there's a part of me trying to blame Ryle's reaction on my lack of closure with Atlas.

There's no excuse. None.

This is just another wave I'm being forced to ride on. A wave of complete and utter confusion.

Atlas can feel the change in my composure. "You okay?"

I'm not.

I'm not okay, because until this moment, I had no idea how hurt I still am that he never came back for me. If he'd have just come back for me like he promised, I would have never even met Ryle. And I would have never been *in* this situation.

Yep. I'm definitely confused. How am I possibly lending blame to Atlas for any of this?

"I think I need to call it a night," I say quietly, pulling away from him. I stand up and Atlas stands up, too.

"I'll be gone most of the day tomorrow," he says. "Will you be here when I get home?"

I cringe at his question. Of course he wants me to get my shit together and find another place to stay. What am I even still doing here? "No. No, I can get a hotel, it's fine." I turn to walk toward the hallway, but he puts a hand on my shoulder.

"Lily," he says, turning me around. "I wasn't asking you to leave. I was just making sure you'd still be here. I want you to stay as long as you need to."

His eyes are sincere, and if I didn't think it would be a little inappropriate, I would throw my arms around him and hug him. Because I'm not ready to leave yet. Just a couple more days before I'm forced to figure out what my next step is.

I nod. "I need to go in to work for a few hours tomorrow," I tell him. "There are some things I need to take care of. But if you really don't mind, I'd like to stay here for a few more days."

"I don't mind, Lily. I'd prefer it."

I force a smile and then head to the guest bedroom. At least he's giving me a buffer before I'm forced to confront everything.

As much as his presence in my life confuses me right now, I've never been more thankful for him.

Chapter Twenty-Seven

My hand is trembling when I reach for the doorknob. I've never once been scared to walk into my own business before, but I've also never been this on edge.

The building is dark when I enter it, so I flip on the lights, holding my breath. I walk slowly to my office, pushing the door open with caution.

He's nowhere, yet he's everywhere.

When I take a seat at my desk, I turn on my phone for the first time since I went to bed last night. I wanted a good night's sleep without having to worry about whether or not Ryle was trying to contact me.

When it powers on, I have twenty-nine missed texts from Ryle. It just so happens to be the same number of doors Ryle knocked on to find my apartment last year.

I don't know whether to laugh or cry at the irony.

I spend the rest of the day like this. Glancing over my shoulder, looking up at the door every time it opens. I wonder if he's ruined me. If the fear of him will ever leave me.

Half a day goes by without a single phone call from him while I catch up on paperwork. Allysa calls me after lunch and I can tell by her voice that she has no idea about the fight Ryle and I had. I let her talk about the baby for a while before I pretend I have a customer and hang up.

I plan on leaving when Lucy returns from her lunch break. She has half an hour left.

Ryle walks through the front door three minutes later.

I'm the only one here.

As soon as I see him, I turn stone cold. I'm standing behind the counter, my hand on the cash register because it's close to the stapler. I'm sure a stapler couldn't do much harm against the arms of a neurosurgeon, but I'll use what I have.

He slowly makes his way to the counter. It's the first time I've seen him since he was on top of me on our bed the other night. My whole body is immediately taken back to that moment, and I'm engulfed in the same level of emotions as I was in that moment. Both fear and anger rush through me when he reaches the counter.

He lifts his hand and places a set of keys on the counter in front of me. My eyes fall to the keys.

"I'm leaving for England tonight," he says. "I'll be gone for three months. I paid all the bills so you won't have to worry about it while I'm gone."

His voice is composed but I can see the veins in his neck as they prove his composure is taking all the effort he has. "You need time." He swallows hard. "And I want to give that to you." He grimaces and pushes the keys to my apartment toward me. "Go back home, Lily. I won't be there. I promise."

He turns and begins walking toward the door. It occurs to me that he didn't even try to apologize. I'm not angry about it. I understand it. He knows that an apology will never take back what he did. He knows that the best thing for us right now is separation.

He knows what a huge mistake he made . . . yet I still feel the need to dig that knife in a little deeper.

"Ryle."

He looks back at me and it's as if he puts a shield up between us. He doesn't turn all the way around and he's stiff as he waits for whatever I'm about to say. He knows my words are going to hurt him.

"You know what the worst part about this whole thing is?" I ask.

He doesn't say anything. He just stares at me, waiting for my answer.

"All you had to do when you found my journal was ask me for a naked truth. I would have been honest with you. But you didn't. You chose to not ask for my help and now we'll both have to suffer the consequences of your actions for the rest of our lives."

He grimaces with every word. "Lily," he says, turning toward me.

I hold up my hand to stop him from saying anything else. "Don't. You can leave now. Have fun in England."

I can see the war waging inside of him. He knows he can't get anywhere with me in this moment, no matter how hard he wants to beg for my forgiveness. He knows the only choice he has is to turn and walk out that door, even though it's the last thing he wants to do.

When he finally forces himself out the door, I run and lock it. I slide down to the floor and hug my knees, burying my face against them. I'm shaking so hard, I can feel my teeth chatter.

I can't believe part of that man is growing inside me. And I can't believe I'll one day have to admit that to him.

Chapter Twenty-Eight

After Ryle left me his keys this afternoon; I debated going back to our new apartment. I even had a cab pull up to the building, but I couldn't force myself out of the car. I knew if I went back there today, I'd probably see Allysa at some point. I'm not ready to explain the stitches on my forehead to her. I'm not ready to see the kitchen where Ryle's harsh words cut through me. I'm not ready to walk into the bedroom where I was completely destroyed.

So instead of returning to my own home, I took the cab back to Atlas's house. It feels like my only safe zone right now. I don't have to confront things when I'm hiding out here.

Atlas has already texted me twice today checking on me, so when I get a text a few minutes before seven o'clock in the evening, I assume it's from him. It's not; it's from Allysa.

Allysa: You home from work yet? Come up and visit us, I'm already bored.

My heart sinks when I read her text. She has no idea what happened between me and Ryle. I wonder if Ryle even told her he left for England today. My thumb types and erases and types some more as I try to come up with a good excuse as to why I'm not there.

Me: I can't. I'm in the emergency room. Hit my head on that shelf in the storage room at work. Getting stitches.

I hate that I lied to her, but it'll save me from having to explain the cut and also why I'm not home right now.

Allysa: Oh no! Are you alone? Marshall can come sit with you since Ryle is gone.

Okay, so she knows Ryle left for England. That's good. And she thinks we're fine. This is good. That means I have at least three months before I have to tell her the truth.

Look at me, sweeping shit under the rug just like my mother.

Me: No, I'm fine. I'll be finished up by the time Marshall could even get here. I'll come by tomorrow after work. Give Rylee a kiss for me.

I lock the screen on my phone and set it on my bed. It's dark outside now, so I immediately see the scroll of the headlights as someone pulls into the driveway. I instantly know that it isn't Atlas, because he uses the driveway to the side of the house and parks in the garage. My heart begins to race as fear rushes through me. Is it Ryle? Did he find out where Atlas lives?

Moments later, there's a loud knock at the front door. More like pounding. The doorbell also rings.

I tiptoe to the window and barely move the curtains over far enough to take a look outside. I can't see who's at the door, but there's a truck in the driveway. It doesn't belong to Ryle.

Could it be Atlas's girlfriend? Cassie?

I grab my phone and make my way down the hallway, toward the living room. The pounding on the door and the chime of the doorbell are still going off simultaneously. Whoever is at the door is being ridiculously impatient. If it is Cassie, I already find her extremely annoying.

"Atlas!" a guy yells. "Open the damn door!"

Another voice—also male—yells, "My balls are freezing up! They're raisins, man, open the door!"

Before I open the door and let them know Atlas isn't home, I text him, hoping he's about to pull in the driveway and deal with this himself.

Me: Where are you? There are two men at your front door and I have no idea if I should let them in.

I wait through more presses of the doorbell and more pounding, but Atlas doesn't immediately text me back. I finally walk to the door and leave the chain bolted, but unlock the deadbolt and open the door a few inches.

One of the guys is tall, about six feet or so. Despite the youthful look to his face, his hair is salt and pepper. Black with a little bit of gray sprinkled in. The other one is shorter by a few inches, with sandy brown hair and a baby face. They both look to be in their late twenties, maybe early thirties. The tall one's face twists into confusion. "Who are you?" he asks, peeking through the door.

"Lily. Who are you?"

The shorter one pushes in front of the taller one. "Is Atlas here?"

I don't want to tell them no, because then they'll know I'm here alone. I don't necessarily hold much trust in the male population this week.

The phone in my hand rings and all three of us jump from the unexpectedness of it. It's Atlas. I swipe the answer button and bring it to my ear.

"Hello?"

"It's fine, Lily, they're just friends of mine. I forgot it was

Friday, we always play poker on Fridays. I'll call them now and tell them to leave."

I look back at the two of them and they're just standing there, watching me. I feel bad that Atlas feels like he has to cancel his plans just because I'm crashing at his house. I shut the door and unlock the deadbolt, then open the door again, motioning them inside.

"It's fine, Atlas. You don't have to cancel your plans. I was about to go to bed anyway."

"No, I'm on my way. I'll have them leave."

I still have the phone pressed to my ear when the two men enter the living room.

"See you soon," I say to Atlas and then end the call. The next few seconds are awkward as the guys assess me and I assess them.

"What are your names?"

"I'm Darin," the tall one says.

"Brad," the shorter one says.

"Lily," I say to them, even though I already told them my name. "Atlas will be here soon." I move to close the door and they seem to relax a little. Darin heads into the kitchen and helps himself to Atlas's refrigerator.

Brad takes off his jacket and hangs it up. "Do you know how to play poker, Lily?"

I shrug. "It's been a few years, but I used to play with friends in college."

Both of them walk toward the dining room table.

"What happened to your head?" Darin asks as he takes a seat. He asks it so casually, like it doesn't even cross his mind that it might be a sensitive subject.

I don't know why I have an urge to give him the naked truth. Maybe I just want to see how someone will react when they find out my own husband did this to me.

"My husband happened. We got into a fight two nights ago and he head-butted me. Atlas took me to the emergency room. They gave me six stitches and told me I was pregnant. Now I'm hiding out here until I figure out what to do."

Poor Darin is frozen, halfway between standing and sitting. He has no idea how to respond to that. Based on the look on his face, I think he's convinced I'm crazy.

Brad pulls out his chair and takes a seat, pointing at me. "You should get some Rodan and Fields. The amp roller works wonders for scarring."

I immediately laugh at his random response. Somehow.

"Jesus, Brad!" Darin says, finally sinking into his seat. "You're worse than your wife with this direct sales shit. You're like a walking infomercial."

Brad raises his hands in defense. "What?" he says innocently. "I'm not trying to sell her anything, I'm being honest. The stuff works. You'd know that if you'd use it on your damn acne."

"Screw you," Darin says.

"It's like you're trying to be a perpetual teenager," Brad mutters. "Acne isn't cool when you're thirty."

Brad pulls out the chair next to him while Darin begins shuffling a deck of cards. "Have a seat, Lily. One of our friends decided to be an idiot and get married last week, and now his wife won't let him come to poker night anymore. You can be his fill-in until he gets a divorce."

I had every intention of hiding out in my room tonight,

but these two make it hard to walk away. I take a seat next to Brad and reach across the table. "Hand me those," I say to Darin. He's shuffling the cards like a one-armed infant.

He raises an eyebrow and pushes the deck of cards across the table. I don't know much about card games, but I can shuffle cards like a pro.

I separate the cards into two piles and scoot them together, pressing my thumbs to the ends, watching as they beautifully intertwine. Darin and Brad are staring at the deck of cards, when there's another knock on the door. This time the door swings open without pause and a guy walks in dressed in what looks like a very expensive tweed jacket. There's a scarf wrapped around his neck, and he begins to unwind it as soon as he slams the door behind him. He nudges his head in my direction as he walks toward the kitchen. "Who are you?"

He's older than the other two, probably in his mid-forties. Atlas definitely has an interesting mix of friends.

"This is Lily," Brad says. "She's married to an asshole and just found out she's pregnant with the asshole's baby. Lily, this is Jimmy. He's pompous and arrogant."

"Pompous and arrogant are the same thing, idiot," Jimmy says. He pulls out the chair next to Darin and nudges his head at the cards in my hands. "Did Atlas plant you here to hustle us? What kind of average person knows how to shuffle cards like that?"

I smile and begin to pass cards out to each of them. "I guess we'll have to play a round to find out."

• • •

We're on our third round of bets when Atlas finally walks in. He closes the door behind him and looks around at the four of us. Brad said something funny right before Atlas opened the door, so I'm in the middle of a fit of laughter when Atlas locks eyes with me. He nods his head toward the kitchen and begins walking in that direction.

"Fold," I say, laying my cards flat on the table as I stand up to follow him. When I get to the kitchen, he's standing where he isn't visible to the guys at the table. I walk over to him and lean against the counter.

"You want me to ask them to leave?"

I shake my head. "No, don't do that. I'm actually enjoying it. It's keeping my mind off things."

He nods and I can't help but notice how he smells like herbs. Rosemary, specifically. It makes me wish I could see him in action at his restaurant.

"You hungry?" he asks.

I shake my head. "Not really. I ate some leftover pasta a couple hours ago."

My hands are pressed into the counter on either side of me. He takes a step closer and puts one of his hands over mine, brushing his thumb across the top of it. I know he doesn't mean for it to be anything more than a comforting gesture, but when he touches me, it feels like a whole lot more. A rush of warmth moves up my chest and I immediately drop my eyes to our hands. Atlas pauses his thumb for a second, like he feels it, too. He pulls his hand away and backs up a step.

"Sorry," he mutters, turning toward the refrigerator, pretending to look for something. It's obvious he's trying to spare me from the awkwardness of what just happened.

I walk back to the table and pick up my cards for the next round. A couple of minutes later, Atlas walks over and takes the seat next to me. Jimmy shuffles out a round of new cards to everyone. "So, Atlas. How do you and Lily know each other?"

Atlas picks up his cards one at a time. "Lily saved my life when we were kids," he says, matter-of-fact. He glances over at me and winks, and I drown in guilt for the way that wink makes me feel. Especially at a time like this. *Why is my heart doing this to me?*

"Aw, that's sweet," Brad says. "Lily saved your life, now you're saving hers."

Atlas lowers his cards and glares at Brad. "Excuse me?"

"Relax," Brad says. "Me and Lily are tight, she knows I'm kidding." Brad looks at me. "Your life might be complete crap right now, Lily, but it'll get better. Trust me, I've been there."

Darin laughs. "You've been beat up and pregnant and hiding out at another man's house?" he says to Brad.

Atlas slaps his cards on the table and pushes back in his chair. "What the hell is wrong with you?" he yells at Darin.

I reach over and squeeze his arm reassuringly. "Relax," I say. "We bonded before you got here. I actually don't mind that they're making light of my situation. It really does make it a little less heavy."

He runs a frustrated hand through his hair, shaking his head. "I'm so confused," he says. "You were alone with them for ten minutes."

I laugh. "You can learn a lot about someone in ten minutes." I try to redirect the conversation. "So how do you all know each other?"

Darin leans forward and points at himself. "I'm the sous chef at Bib's." He points at Brad. "He's the dishwasher."

"For now," Brad interjects. "I'm working my way up."

"What about you?" I say to Jimmy.

He smirks and says, "Take a guess."

Based on the way he dresses and the fact that he's been called arrogant and pompous, I'd have to assume . . . "Maître d'?"

Atlas laughs. "Jimmy actually works in valet."

I glance back at Jimmy and raise an eyebrow. He tosses three poker chips down and says, "It's true. I park cars for tips."

"Don't let him fool you," Atlas says. "He works in valet, but only because he's so rich he gets bored."

I smile. It reminds me of Allysa. "I have an employee like that. Only works because she's bored. She's actually the best employee I have."

"Damn straight," Jimmy mutters.

I take a look at my cards when it's my turn and toss in the three poker chips. Atlas's phone rings and he pulls it out of his pocket. I'm raising the pot with another chip when he excuses himself from the table to take the call.

"Fold," Brad says, slapping his cards on the table.

I'm watching the hallway Atlas just disappeared down in a hurry. It makes me wonder if he's talking to Cassie, or if there's someone else in his life. I know what he does for a living. I know he has at least three friends. I just know nothing about his love life.

Darin lays his cards on the table. Four of a kind. I lay down my straight flush and reach forward for all the poker chips as Darin groans.

"So does Cassie not usually come to poker night?" I ask, fishing for more information on Atlas. Information I'm too scared to ask him myself.

"Cassie?" Brad says.

I stack my winnings up in front of me and nod. "Isn't that his girlfriend's name?"

Darin laughs. "Atlas doesn't have a girlfriend. I've known him for two years and he's never mentioned anyone named Cassie." He begins passing out new cards, but I'm trying to absorb the information he just gave me. I pick up my first two cards when Atlas walks back into the room.

"Hey, Atlas," Jimmy says. "Who the hell is Cassie and how come we've never heard you talk about her?"

Oh, shit.

I'm completely mortified. I tighten my grip around the cards in my hands and try to avoid looking up at Atlas, but the room grows so quiet, it would be more obvious if I *didn't* look at him.

He's staring at Jimmy. Jimmy is staring at him. Brad and Darin are staring at me.

Atlas folds his lips together for a moment and then says, "There is no Cassie." His eyes meet mine, but only for a brief second. But in that brief second, I can see it written all over his face.

There never *was* a Cassie.

He lied to me.

Atlas clears his throat and then says, "Listen, guys. I should have cancelled tonight. This week has been kind of . . ." He rubs his hand over his mouth and Jimmy stands up.

He squeezes Atlas on the shoulder and says, "Next week. My place."

Atlas nods appreciatively. The three of them begin to gather their cards and poker chips. Brad pries my cards from my fingers apologetically because I'm unable to move as I clutch them tightly.

"It was lovely meeting you, Lily," Brad says. I somehow find the strength to smile and stand up. I give them all hugs goodbye and after the front door closes behind them, it's just me and Atlas in the room.

And no Cassie.

Cassie's never even been in this room, because Cassie doesn't exist.

What the hell?

Atlas hasn't moved from his spot near the table. Neither have I. He's standing firm with his arms folded across his chest. His head is slightly tilted down but his eyes are boring into me from across the table.

Why would he lie to me?

Ryle and I weren't even an official couple yet when I ran into Atlas at that restaurant the first time. Hell, if Atlas had given me any reason to believe there was a chance between us that night, I know without a doubt that I would have chosen him over Ryle. I barely even *knew* Ryle at that point.

But Atlas didn't say anything. He lied to me and told me he'd been in a relationship for an entire year. Why? Why would he do that unless he didn't want me to think I had a chance with him?

Maybe I've been wrong all this time. Maybe he never even loved me to begin with and he knew that inventing this Cassie person would keep me away from him for good.

Yet, here I am. Crashing at his house. Interacting with his friends. Eating his food. Using his shower.

I can feel the tears begin to sting my eyes and the last thing I want is to stand in front of him and cry right now. I walk around the table and rush past him. I don't make it far when he grabs my hand. "Wait."

I stop, still facing the other direction.

"Talk to me, Lily."

He's right behind me now, his hand still wrapped around mine. I pull it away from him and walk to the other side of the living room.

I spin and face him just as the first tear rolls down my cheek. "Why did you never come back for me?"

He looked prepared for anything to come out of my mouth other than the words I just spoke to him. He runs a hand through his hair and walks to the couch, taking a seat. After blowing out a calming breath, he carefully looks over at me.

"I did, Lily."

I don't allow air to move in or out of my lungs.

I stand completely still, processing his answer.

He came back for me?

He folds his hands together in front of him. "When I got out of the Marines the first time, I went back to Maine, hoping to find you. I asked around and found out which college you went to. I wasn't sure what to expect when I showed up, because we were two different people by then. It had been four years since we saw each other. I knew a lot about both of us had probably changed in those four years."

My knees feel weak, so I walk to the chair next to him and lower myself. *He came back for me?*

"I walked around your campus the whole day looking for you. Finally, late that afternoon, I saw you. You were sitting in the courtyard with a group of your friends. I watched you for a long time, trying to work up the courage to walk over to you. You were laughing. You looked happy. You were vibrant like I'd never seen you before. I had never felt that kind of happiness for another person like I felt when I saw you that day. Just knowing you were okay . . ."

He pauses for a moment. My hands are clenched around my stomach, because it hurts. It hurts knowing I was so close to him and I didn't even know.

"I began walking toward you when someone came up behind you. A guy. He dropped to his knees next to you and when you saw him, you smiled and threw your arms around him. Then you kissed him."

I close my eyes. *He was just a boy I dated for six months. He never even made me feel a fraction of what I had felt for Atlas.*

He blows out a sharp breath. "I left after that. When I saw that you were happy, it was the worst and best feeling a person could ever have at once. But I believed at that point that my life was still not good enough for you. I had nothing to offer you but love, and to me, you deserved more than that. The next day I signed up for another tour in the Marines. And now . . ." He tosses his hand up lazily in the air, like nothing about his life is impressive.

I bury my head in my hands to take a moment. I quietly grieve what could have been. What is. What wasn't. My fingers move to the tattoo on my shoulder. I begin to wonder if I'll ever be able to fill in that hole now.

It makes me wonder if Atlas ever feels like I felt when I got this tattoo. Like all the air is being let out of his heart.

I still don't understand why he lied to me after running into me at his restaurant. If he really felt the things I felt for him, why would he make something like that up?

"Why did you lie about having a girlfriend?"

He rubs a hand over his face and I can already see the regret before I even hear it in his voice. "I said that because . . . you looked happy that night. When I saw you telling him goodbye, it hurt like hell, but at the same time I was relieved that you seemed to be in a really good place. I didn't want you to worry about me. And I don't know . . . maybe I was a little jealous. I don't know, Lily. I regretted lying to you as soon as I did it."

My hand goes to my mouth. My mind starts to race just as fast as my heart is racing. I instantly start thinking about the what-ifs. *What if he would have been honest with me? Told me how he'd felt? Where would we be now?*

I want to ask him why he did it. Why he didn't fight for me. But I don't have to ask him, because I already know the answer. He thought he was giving me what I wanted, because all he's ever wanted for me was happiness. And for some stupid reason, he's never felt I could get that with him.

Considerate Atlas.

The more I think about it, the more difficult it becomes to breathe. I think about Atlas. Ryle. Tonight. Two nights ago. It's too much.

I stand up and make my way back to the guest bedroom. I pick up my phone and grab my purse and go back to the living room. Atlas hasn't moved.

"Ryle left for England today," I say. "I think I should probably go home now. Can you drive me?"

A sadness enters his eyes and when it does, I know that leaving is the right thing to do. Neither of us has closure. I'm not sure we'll ever get it. I'm beginning to think closure is a myth, and being here right now while I'm still processing everything that's happening to my life is just going to make things worse for me. I have to eliminate as much confusion as possible, and right now, my feelings for Atlas top the list of most confusing.

He presses his lips tightly together for a moment, and then he nods and grabs his keys.

• • •

Neither of us speaks the entire drive to my apartment. He doesn't drop me off. He pulls into the parking lot and gets out of his car. "I'd feel better if you let me walk you up," he says.

I nod and we wade through even more silence as we ride the elevator up to the seventh floor. He follows me all the way to my apartment. I fish around in my purse for the keys and don't even realize my hands are shaking until my third failed attempt to open the door. Atlas calmly takes the keys from me and I step aside as he opens the door for me.

"Do you want me to make sure no one's here?" he asks.

I nod. I know Ryle isn't here because he's on his way to England, but I'm honestly still a little scared to walk into the apartment by myself.

Atlas walks in before me and flips on the lights. He continues walking through the apartment, flipping on all the lights and walking into each of the rooms. When he makes it back to the living room, he slides his hands in his jacket pockets. He takes a deep breath and then says, "I don't know what happens next, Lily."

He does. He knows. He just doesn't want it to happen, because we both know how much it hurts to say goodbye to each other.

I look away from him because seeing the look on his face right now cuts straight to my heart. I fold my arms over my chest and stare at the floor. "I have a lot to work through, Atlas. *A lot*. And I'm scared I won't be able to do it with you in my life." I lift my eyes back to his. "I hope you don't take offense to that, because if anything, it's a compliment."

He regards me silently for a moment, not at all surprised by what I'm saying. But I can see there's so much he wants to say. There's a lot I wish I could say to him, too, but we both know discussing the two of us isn't appropriate at this point. I'm married. I'm pregnant with another man's baby. And he's standing in the living room of an apartment that another man bought for me. I'd say these aren't very good conditions in which to bring up all the things we should have said to each other a long time ago.

He looks at the door momentarily as if he's trying to decide to leave or speak. I can see the twitch in his jaw right before he locks eyes with me. "If you ever need me, I want you to call me," he says. "But only if it's an emergency. I'm not capable of being casual with you, Lily."

I'm taken aback by his words, but only momentarily. As much as I wasn't expecting him to admit it, he's absolutely right. Since the day we met, there has been nothing casual about our relationship. It's either all in or not in at all. That's why he separated ties when he left for the military. He knew that a casual friendship would never work between us. It would have been too painful.

Apparently, that hasn't changed.

"Goodbye, Atlas."

Saying those words again tears me up almost as much as the first time I had to say them. He winces and then turns and walks to the door like he can't leave fast enough. When the door closes behind him, I walk over and lock it, then press my head against it.

Two days ago I was asking myself how my life could possibly get any better. Today I'm asking myself how it could possibly get any worse.

I jump back with the sudden knock at the door. It's only been ten seconds since he walked out, so I know it's Atlas. I unlock it and open it and I'm suddenly pressed against something soft. Atlas's arms wrap tightly around me, desperately, and his lips are pressed against the side of my head.

I squeeze my eyes shut and finally let the tears fall. I've cried so many tears for Ryle over the past two days, I have no idea how I still have any left for Atlas. But I do, because they're falling down my cheeks like rain.

"Lily," he whispers, still holding me tightly. "I know this is the last thing you need to hear right now. But I have to say it because I've walked away from you too many times without saying what I really want to say."

He pulls back to look down at me and when he sees my tears, he brings his hands up to my cheeks. "In the future . . . if by some miracle you ever find yourself in the position to fall in love again . . . fall in love with me." He presses his lips against my forehead. "You're still my favorite person, Lily. Always will be."

He releases me and walks away, not even needing a response.

When I close the door again, I slide to the floor. My heart feels like it wants to give up. I don't blame it. It's suffered through two separate heartaches in the course of two days.

And I have a feeling it's going to be a long time before either of those heartaches can even begin to heal.

Chapter Twenty-Nine

Allysa drops onto the couch beside me and Rylee. "I miss you so much, Lily," she says. "I'm thinking about coming back to work a day or two a week."

I laugh, a little shocked by her comment. "I live downstairs and I visit almost every day. How can you possibly miss me?"

She pouts as she pulls her legs up beneath her. "Fine, it's not you I miss. I miss work. And sometimes I just want out of this house."

It's been six weeks since she had Rylee, so I'm sure she would be cleared to come back to work. But I honestly didn't think she'd even want to come back now that she has Rylee. I bend forward and give Rylee a kiss on her nose. "Would you bring Rylee with you?"

Allysa shakes her head. "No, you keep me too busy for that. Marshall can watch her while I work."

"You mean you don't have *people* for that?"

Marshall is passing through the living room when he hears me say that. "Shush, Lily. Don't speak like a rich girl in front of my daughter. Blasphemy."

I laugh. That's why I come over here a few nights a week, because it's the only time I laugh. It's been six weeks since Ryle left for England, and no one knows what happened between us. Ryle hasn't told anyone, and neither have I. Everyone, my mother included, believes he simply left for the study at Cambridge and that nothing has changed between us.

I also still haven't told anyone about the pregnancy.

I've been to the doctor twice. It turns out I was already twelve weeks along the night I found out I was pregnant, which makes me eighteen weeks along now. I'm still trying to wrap my head around it. I've been on the pill since I was eighteen. Apparently being forgetful a few times caught up with me.

I'm beginning to show, but it's cold out so it's been easy to hide. No one suspects a thing when you have on a baggy sweater and a jacket.

I know I need to tell someone soon, but I feel like Ryle should be the first one I tell, and I don't want to do that over a long-distance phone conversation. He'll be back in six weeks. If I can somehow keep things quiet until then, I'll decide where to go from there.

I look down at Rylee and she's smiling up at me. I make silly faces at her to make her smile more. There have been so many times I've wanted to tell Allysa about the pregnancy, but it makes it hard when the secret I'm keeping is being kept from her own brother. I don't want to put her in that kind of situation, no matter how much it kills me that I can't talk to her about it.

"How are you holding up without Ryle?" Allysa asks. "You ready for him to come home?"

I nod, but I don't say anything. I always try to brush off the subject when she brings him up.

Allysa leans back into the couch and says, "Is he still liking Cambridge?"

"Yes," I say, sticking my tongue out at Rylee. She grins. I wonder if my baby will look like her. I hope so. She's really cute, but I might be a little partial.

"Did he ever figure out the subway system there?" Allysa laughs. "I swear, every time I talk to him, he's lost. He can't figure out whether to take the A-line or the B-line."

"Yeah," I tell her. "He figured it out."

Allysa sits up on the couch. "Marshall!"

Marshall walks into the living room and Allysa pulls Rylee out of my hands. She hands her to Marshall and says, "Will you change her diaper?"

I don't know why she asks him that. I just changed her diaper.

Marshall scrunches up his nose and lifts Rylee out of Allysa's arms. "Are you a stinky girl?"

They're wearing matching onesies.

Allysa grabs my hands and yanks me off the couch so fast, I squeal.

"Where are we going?"

She doesn't answer me. She marches toward her bedroom and then slams the door once we're both inside. She paces back and forth a few times and then she stops and faces me.

"You better tell me what the hell is going on right now, Lily!"

I pull back in shock. *What is she talking about?*

My hands instantly go to my stomach, because I think maybe she's noticed, but she doesn't look at my stomach. She takes a step forward and pokes a finger in my chest. "There *is* no subway system in Cambridge, England, you idiot!"

"What?" I am so confused.

"I made that up!" she says. "Something hasn't been right with you for a long time. You're my best friend, Lily. And I know my brother. I talk to him every week, and he isn't the same. Something happened between you two, and I want to know what it is right now!"

Shit. I guess this is happening sooner rather than later.

I slowly bring my hands up to my mouth, not sure what to tell her. How *much* to tell her. I had no idea until this moment how much it's been killing me that I haven't been able to talk to her about this. I almost feel a little relieved that she reads me so well.

I walk to her bed and take a seat on it. "Allysa," I whisper. "Sit down."

I know this is going to hurt her almost as much as it hurt me. She walks over to her bed and sits down next to me, pulling my hands to hers.

"I don't even know where to start."

She squeezes my hands, but says nothing. For the next fifteen minutes, I tell her everything. I tell her about the fight. I tell her about Atlas picking me up. I tell her about the hospital. I tell her about the pregnancy.

I tell her about how, for the last six weeks, I cry myself to sleep every night because I have never felt so alone and so scared.

When I'm finished telling her everything, we're both crying. She hasn't responded to what I've told her with anything other than the occasional *"Oh, Lily."*

She doesn't have to respond, though. Ryle is her brother. I know she wants me to take his past into consideration just like the last time it happened. I know she'll want me to work things out with him because he's her brother. We're supposed to be one big, happy family. I know exactly what she's thinking.

She's quiet for a long time as she struggles through everything I've told her. She finally lifts her eyes to mine and squeezes my hands. "My brother *loves* you, Lily. He loves you so much. You have changed his entire life and have made him someone that I never thought he could be. As his sister, I wish more than anything that you could find a way to forgive him. But as your best friend, I have to tell you that if you take him back, I will never speak to you again."

It takes a moment for her words to register, but when they do, I start sobbing.

She starts sobbing.

She wraps her arms around me and we cry over the mutual love we have for Ryle. We cry over how much we hate him right now.

After several minutes of us sobbing pathetically on her bed, she releases me and walks over to her dresser to retrieve a box of tissues.

We're both wiping our eyes and sniffling when I say, "You're the best friend I've ever had."

She nods. "I know. And now I'm gonna be the best aunt." She wipes her nose and sniffles again, but she's smiling. "Lily. You're having a *baby*." She says it with excitement, and it's the first moment I've been able to share any sense of joy over my pregnancy. "I hate to say it, but I noticed you put on weight. I thought you were just depressed and eating a lot since Ryle left."

She walks to the back of her closet and starts pulling things out for me. "I have so many maternity clothes to give you."

We start going through clothes and she pulls down a suitcase and opens it. She begins to throw things toward the suitcase until it starts to overflow.

"I could never wear these," I tell her, holding up a shirt that still has the tag on it. "They're all designer. I'll get them dirty."

She laughs and shoves them into the suitcase anyway. "I won't need them back. If I get pregnant again, I'll just have my people buy me more." She pulls a shirt off a hanger and hands it to me. "Here, try this one on."

I take my shirt off and then pull the maternity shirt over my head. When I get it into place, I look in the mirror.

I look . . . pregnant. Like *you-can't-hide-this-shit* pregnant.

She puts a hand on my stomach and stares in the mirror with me. "Have you found out if it's a boy or a girl?"

I shake my head. "I don't really want to know."

"I hope it's a girl," she says. "Our daughters can be besties."

"Lily?"

We both spin around to find Marshall standing in the doorway. His eyes are on my stomach. On Allysa's *hand* still on my stomach. He tilts his head. He points at me.

"You . . ." he says, confused. "Lily, there's a . . . do you realize you're pregnant?"

Allysa calmly walks to the door and puts her hand on the doorknob. "There are some things you are never, ever to repeat if you want to keep me as your wife. This is one of those things. Understood?"

Marshall raises his eyebrows and takes a step back. "Yes. Okay. Got it. Lily is not pregnant." He kisses Allysa on the forehead and looks back at me. "I am not telling you congratulations, Lily. For absolutely nothing." Allysa shoves him all the way out the door and closes it, then turns back to me.

"We need to plan a baby shower," she says.

"No. I need to tell Ryle first."

She waves her hand dismissively. "We don't need him to plan a shower. We'll just keep it between the two of us until then."

She pulls out her laptop, and for the first time since I found out I was pregnant, I feel happy about it.

Chapter Thirty

It's rather convenient only having to take an elevator to get home from Allysa's, as much as I want to move out of my own apartment at times. It's still strange living there. We only lived there a week before we split up and Ryle left for England. It never even had the chance to feel like home and now it feels a little tainted. I haven't even been able to sleep in our bedroom since that night, so I've been sleeping in the guest room on my old bed.

Allysa and Marshall are still the only ones who know about the pregnancy. It's only been two weeks since I told them, which makes me twenty weeks along now. I know I should tell my mother, but Ryle will be back in a few weeks. I feel like I should tell him first before anyone else finds out. If I can just somehow hide my baby bump from her until he gets back to the States.

I should probably just accept the fact that I'm more than likely going to have to call him and tell him long-distance. I haven't seen my mother face-to-face in two weeks. It's the longest we've gone without seeing each other since she moved to Boston, so if something doesn't happen soon she'll show up at my front door when I'm not prepared.

I swear my stomach has doubled in size these last two weeks alone. If someone sees me who knows me well, it'll be impossible to hide. So far, no one at the floral shop has asked about it. I think I'm still on the cusp of *"Is she pregnant? Or just chubby?"*

I start to unlock the door to my apartment, but it begins to open from the other side. Before I can pull the jacket over to hide my stomach from whoever is on the other side of the door, Ryle's eyes land on me. I'm wearing one of the shirts Allysa gave me and it's kind of impossible to hide the fact that I'm wearing a maternity shirt when he's staring right at it.

Ryle.

Ryle is here.

My heart begins to smash against the walls of my chest. My neck begins to itch, so I bring my hand up and rest it there, feeling the pounding of my heart against my palm.

It's pounding because I'm terrified of him.

It's pounding because I hate him.

It's pounding because I've missed him.

His eyes slowly crawl from my stomach to my face. A hurtful expression takes over him, like I've just stabbed him straight through the heart. He takes a step back into my apartment and his hands come up to his mouth.

He begins to shake his head in confusion. I can see the betrayal all over his face when he barely forces out my name. *"Lily?"*

I stand frozen, one hand on my stomach in protection, the other hand still flat against my chest. I'm too scared to move or say anything. I don't want to react until I know exactly how *he's* going to react.

When he sees the fear in my eyes and the small gasps of breath I'm barely inhaling, he holds up a reassuring palm.

"I'm not going to hurt you, Lily. I'm just here to talk to you." He swings the door open wider and points into the living room. "Look." He steps aside and my eyes fall to someone standing behind him.

Now *I'm* the one who feels betrayed.

"Marshall?"

Marshall immediately holds up his hands in defense. "I had no idea he was coming home early, Lily. Ryle texted and asked for my help. He specifically told me not to say anything to you or Issa. Please don't let her divorce me, I'm simply an innocent bystander."

I shake my head, trying to understand what I'm seeing.

"I asked him to meet me here so you'd feel more comfortable talking to me," Ryle says. "He's here for you, he's not here for me."

I glance back at Marshall and he nods. It gives me enough reassurance to enter the apartment. Ryle is still somewhat in shock, which is understandable. His eyes keep meeting my stomach and then flicking away like it hurts to look at me. He runs two hands through his hair and then points down the hallway while looking at Marshall.

"We'll be in the bedroom. If you hear me get . . . if I start to yell . . ."

Marshall knows what Ryle is asking him. "I'm not going anywhere."

As I follow Ryle into my bedroom, I wonder what that must be like. To have no idea what might set you off or how bad your reaction will be. To have absolutely no control over your own emotions.

For a brief moment, I feel a minuscule amount of sorrow

for him. But when my eyes fall to our bed and I remember that night, my sorrow diminishes completely.

Ryle pushes the door shut, but doesn't close it all the way. He looks like he's aged an entire year in the two months it's been since I've seen him. The bags under his eyes, the furrowed brow, the sunken posture. If regret took human form, it would look identical to Ryle.

His eyes fall to my stomach again and he takes a slow step forward. Then another. He's cautious, as he should be. He reaches out a timid hand, asking for permission to touch me. I nod softly.

He takes one more step forward and then places a steady palm against my stomach.

I can feel the warmth of his hand through my shirt, and my eyes snap shut. Despite the resentment I've built up in my heart toward him, it doesn't mean the emotions aren't still there. Just because someone hurts you doesn't mean you can simply stop loving them. It's not a person's actions that hurt the most. It's the love. If there was no love attached to the action, the pain would be a little easier to bear.

He moves his hand over my stomach and I open my eyes again. He's shaking his head, like he can't process what's happening right now. I watch as he slowly sinks to his knees in front of me.

His arms snake around my waist and he presses his lips against my stomach. He clasps his hands around my lower back and presses his forehead against me.

It's hard to describe what I feel for him in this moment. Like any mother would want for her child, it's a beautiful thing to see the love he already has. It's been hard not sharing this with anyone. It's hard not being able to share this with *him*, no matter how much resentment I hold toward him. My hands go to his hair while he holds me against him. Part of me wants to scream at him and call the police like I should have done that night. Part of me feels for that little boy who held his brother in his arms and watched him die. Part of me wishes I would have never met him. Part of me wishes I could forgive him.

He unwraps his arms from around my waist and presses a hand into the mattress next to us. He pulls himself up and then sits on the bed. His elbows rest on his knees and his hands are drawn up to his mouth.

I sit next to him, knowing we have to have this conversation, but not wanting to. "Naked truths?"

He nods.

I don't know which one of us is supposed to go first. I don't really have much to say to him at this point, so I wait for him to speak first.

"I don't even know where to start, Lily." He rubs his hands down his face.

"How about you start with, *'I'm sorry I attacked you.'*"

His eyes meet mine, wide with certainty. "Lily, you have no idea. I am *so* sorry. You have no idea what I've been through these past two months knowing what I've done to you."

I clench my teeth together. I can feel my fingers as they fist around the blanket beside me.

I have no idea what *he's* been through?

I shake my head, slowly. "*You* have no idea, Ryle."

I stand up, the anger and hatred spilling out of me. I spin, pointing at him. "*You* have no idea! You have *no* idea what it's like to go through what you've put me through! To fear for your life at the hands of the man you love? To get physically sick just thinking about what he's done to you? *You* have no idea, Ryle! *None! Fuck* you! *Fuck* you for doing this to me!"

I suck in a huge breath, shocked at myself. The anger just came like a wave. I swipe at my tears and spin around, unable to look at him.

"Lily," he says. "I don't . . ."

"No!" I yell, spinning around again. "I am not finished! You don't get to say your truth until I've said mine!"

He's grabbing at his jaw, squeezing the stress out of it. He drops his eyes to the floor, unable to look at the rage in mine. I take three steps toward him and drop to my knees. I place my hands on his legs, forcing him to look me straight in the eyes while I speak to him.

"Yes. I kept the magnet Atlas gave me when we were kids. Yes. I kept the journals. No, I didn't tell you about my tattoo. Yes, I probably should have. And yes, I still love him. And I'll love him until I die, because he was a huge part of my life. And yes, I'm sure that hurts you. But none of that gave you the right to do what you did to me. Even if you would have walked into my bedroom and caught us in bed together, you *still* would not have the right to lay a hand on me, you goddamn son of a bitch!"

I push off his knees and stand up again. "*Now* it's your turn!" I yell.

I continue pacing the room. My heart is pounding like it wants out. I wish I could give it a way out. I'd set the motherfucker free right now if I could.

Several minutes pass as I continue to pace. Ryle's silence and my anger eventually just fold together into pain.

My tears have exhausted me. I am so tired of feeling. I fall desperately onto my bed and cry into my pillow. I press my face so hard against my pillow, I can barely breathe.

I feel Ryle lie down next to me. He places a gentle hand on the back of my head, attempting to sooth away the pain he's causing me. My eyes are closed, still pressed into the pillow, but I feel him gently rest his head against mine.

"My truth is that I have absolutely nothing to say," he says quietly. "I'll never be able to take back what I did to you. And you'll never believe me if I promise it won't happen again." He presses a kiss against my head. "You are my world, Lily. *My world*. When I woke up on this bed that night and you were gone, I knew I would never get you back. I came here to tell you how incredibly sorry I am. I came to tell you I was taking that job offer in Minnesota. I came to tell you goodbye. But Lily . . ." His lips press against my head again and he exhales sharply. "Lily, I can't do that now. You have a part of me inside of you. And I already love this baby more than I've ever loved anything in my whole life." His voice cracks and he grips me even harder. "Please don't take this away from me, Lily. *Please*."

The pain in his voice ripples through me, and when I lift my tear-soaked face to look at him, he presses his lips desperately to mine and then pulls back. "Please, Lily. I love you. *Help* me."

His lips briefly meet mine again. When I don't push him away, his mouth comes back a third time.

A fourth.

When his lips meet mine the fifth time, they don't leave.

He wraps his arms around me and pulls me to him. My body is tired and weak, but it remembers him. My body remembers how his body can soothe everything I'm feeling. How his has a gentleness in it that my body has been craving for two months now.

"I love you," he whispers against my mouth. His tongue sweeps softly against mine and it's so wrong and so good and so painful. Before I know it, I'm on my back and he's crawling on top of me. His touch is everything I need and everything I shouldn't.

His hand wraps in my hair and in an instant, I'm transferred back to that night.

I'm in the kitchen, and his hand is tugging my hair so hard it hurts.

He brushes the hair from my face and in an instant, I'm transferred back to that night.

I'm standing in the doorway, and his hand is trailing across my shoulder, right before he bites into me with all the strength in his jaw.

His forehead rests gently against mine and in an instant, I'm transferred back to that night.

I'm on this same bed beneath him when he slams his head against mine so hard I have to get six stitches.

My body becomes unresponsive to his. The anger begins to roll back over me. His mouth stops moving against mine when he feels me freeze.

When he pulls back and looks down on me, I don't even have to say anything. Our eyes, locked together, speak more naked truths than our mouths ever have. My eyes are telling his that I can no longer stand being touched by him. His eyes are telling mine that he already knows.

He begins to nod, slowly.

He backs away from me, crawling down my body until he's at the edge of the bed with his back to me. He's still nodding as he comes to a slow stand, fully aware that he's not getting my forgiveness tonight. He begins heading toward my bedroom door.

"Wait," I say to him.

He half-turns, looking back at me from the doorway.

I lift my chin, looking at him with finality. "I wish this baby wasn't yours, Ryle. With everything that I am, I wish this baby was not a part of you."

If I thought his world couldn't crumble more, I was wrong.

He walks out of my bedroom and I press my face into my pillow. I thought if I could just hurt him like he had hurt me, I would feel avenged.

I don't.

Instead, I feel vindictive and mean.

I feel like I'm my father.

Chapter Thirty-One

Mom: I miss you. When am I going to see you?

I stare at the text. It's been two days since Ryle found out I'm pregnant. I know it's time to tell my mother. I'm not nervous about telling her I'm pregnant. The only thing that scares me is discussing my situation with Ryle with her.

Me: Miss you, too. I'll come over tomorrow afternoon. Can you make lasagna?

As soon as I close out the text to her, I get another incoming text.

Allysa: Come upstairs and eat dinner with us tonight. It's homemade pizza night.

I haven't been to Allysa's in a few days. Since before Ryle came home. I'm not sure where he's staying, but I assume it's with them. The last thing I want right now is to have to be in the same apartment as him.

Me: Who all will be there?

Allysa: Lily . . . I wouldn't do that to you. He's working until 8 tomorrow morning. It'll just be the three of us.

She knows me way too well. I text her back and tell her I'll come over as soon as I finish up with work.

• • •

"What do babies eat at this age?"

We're all seated around the table. Rylee was asleep when I got here, but I woke her up so I could hold her. Allysa didn't mind; she said she doesn't want her wide awake when she's ready to go to bed.

"Breast milk," Marshall says with a mouthful. "But sometimes I stick my finger in my soda and put it in her mouth so she can taste it."

"Marshall!" Allysa yells. "You better be kidding."

"Totally kidding," he says, although I can't tell if he really is.

"But when do they start eating baby food?" I ask. I figure I need to learn this stuff before giving birth.

"Around four months," Allysa says with a yawn. She drops her fork and leans back in her chair, rubbing her eyes.

"You want me to keep her at my place tonight so you guys can get a full night of sleep?"

Allysa says, "No, it's fine," at the same time Marshall says, "That would be awesome."

I laugh. "Really. I live right downstairs. I don't work tomorrow so if I don't get any sleep tonight I can just sleep in tomorrow."

Allysa looks like she's contemplating it for a moment. "I could leave my cell phone on in case you need me."

I look back down at Rylee and grin. "Did you hear that? You get to have a sleepover with Aunt Lily!"

• • •

With everything Allysa is throwing in her diaper bag, it looks like I'm about to take Rylee on a trip across the country.

"She'll let you know when she's hungry. Don't use the microwave to heat the milk, just put it in . . ."

"I know," I interrupt. "I've made her like fifty bottles since she's been alive."

Allysa nods and then walks over to her bed. She drops the diaper bag down beside me. Marshall is in the living room feeding Rylee one last time, so Allysa lies down beside me on the bed while we wait. She props her head up on her hand.

"Do you know what this means?" she asks.

"No. What?"

"I get to have sex tonight. It's been four months."

I crinkle up my nose. "I didn't need to know that."

She laughs and falls down on her pillow, but then sits straight up. "Shit," she says. "I should probably shave my legs. I think it's been four months since I did that, too."

I laugh, but then I gasp. My hands move quickly to my stomach. "Oh my God! I just felt something!"

"Really?" Allysa puts her hand on my stomach and we're both quiet for the next five minutes as we wait for it to happen again. It does, but it's so soft, it's almost unnoticeable. I laugh again as soon as it happens.

"I didn't feel anything," Allysa says, pouting. "I guess it'll be a few more weeks before you can feel it from the outside, though. Is this the first time you felt it move?"

"Yeah. I've been scared I was growing the laziest baby in history." I keep my hands on my stomach, hoping to feel it again. We sit quietly for a few more minutes, and I can't help but wish my circumstances were different. Ryle should be here. He should be the one sitting beside me with his hand on my stomach. Not Allysa.

The thought almost takes away all the joy I'm feeling. Allysa must notice because she puts one of her hands on mine and squeezes. When I look at her, she isn't smiling anymore.

"Lily," she says. "I've been wanting to say something to you."

Oh, God. I don't like the sound of her voice.

"What is it?"

She sighs and then forces a gloomy smile. "I know you're sad that you're going through this without my brother. No matter how involved he is, I just want you to know that this is going to be the best thing you've ever experienced in your life. You're gonna be a great mom, Lily. This baby is *really* lucky."

I'm glad Allysa is the only one in here right now, because her words make me laugh, cry, and snot like a hormonal teenager. I hug her and tell her thank you. It's amazing how hearing those words gives me back the joy I was feeling.

She smiles and then says, "Now go get my baby and take her away from here so I can have some sex with my filthy rich husband."

I roll off the bed and stand up. "You sure know how to bring levity into a situation. I'd say it's your strong point."

She smiles. "That's what I'm here for. Now go away."

Chapter Thirty-Two

Of all the secrets I've held over the last few months, I'm the saddest about keeping everything from my mother. I don't know how she'll take it. I know she'll be excited about the pregnancy, but I don't know how she'll feel about me and Ryle splitting up. She loves Ryle. And based on her history with these types of situations, she'll probably find it very easy to excuse his behavior and try and convince me to take him back. And in all honesty, that's part of the reason I've been stalling this, because I'm scared there's a chance she might be successful.

Most days I'm strong. Most days I'm so mad at him that the thought of ever forgiving him is ludicrous. But some days I miss him so much I can't breathe. I miss the fun I had with him. I miss making love to him. I miss *missing* him. He used to work so many hours that when he would walk in the front door at night I would rush across the room and jump in his arms because I missed him so much. I even miss how much he loved it when I would do that.

It's the not-so-strong days when I wish my mother knew about everything that was going on. I sometimes just want to drive over to her house and curl up on the couch with her while she tucks my hair behind my ear and tells me it'll all be okay. Sometimes even grown women need their mother's comfort so we can just take a break from having to be strong all the time.

I sit in my car, parked in her driveway, for a good five

minutes before I work up the strength to go inside. It sucks that I have to do this because I know that in a way, I'll be breaking her heart, too. I hate it when she's sad and telling her I married a man who might be like my father is going to make her really sad.

When I walk through the front door, she's in the kitchen layering noodles in a pan. I don't remove my coat right away for obvious reasons. I'm not wearing a maternity shirt but my bump is almost impossible to hide without a jacket. Especially from a mother.

"Hey, sweetie!" she says.

I walk into the kitchen and give her a side hug while she layers cheese over the top of the lasagna. Once the lasagna is in the oven, we walk over to the dining room table and take a seat. She leans back in her chair and takes a sip from a glass of tea.

She's smiling. I hate it even more that she looks so happy right now.

"Lily," she says. "There's something I need to tell you."

I don't like this. I was coming over here to talk to *her*. I'm not prepared to *receive* a talk.

"What is it?" I ask hesitantly.

She grips her glass of tea with both hands. "I'm seeing someone."

My mouth drops open.

"Really?" I ask, shaking my head. "That's . . ." I'm about to say *good*, but then I grow instantly worried that she's just put herself in a similar situation she was in with my father. She can see the worry on my face, so she grabs my hands in both of hers.

"He's good, Lily. He's so good. I promise."

Relief washes over me in an instant, because I can see she's telling the truth. I can see the happiness in her eyes. "Wow," I say, not expecting this at all. "I'm happy for you. When can I meet him?"

"Tonight, if you want," she says. "I can invite him over to eat with us."

I shake my head. "No," I whisper. "Now's not a good time."

Her hands squeeze around mine as soon as she realizes I'm here to tell her something important. I start with the better part of the news first.

I stand up and remove my jacket. At first, she doesn't think anything of it. She just assumes I'm making myself comfortable. But then I take one of her hands and I press it against my stomach. "You're gonna be a grandma."

Her eyes widen and for several seconds, she's stunned speechless. But then tears begin to form. She jumps up and pulls me into a hug. "Lily!" she says. "Oh my God!" She pulls back, smiling. "That was so fast. Were you trying? You haven't even been married for very long."

I shake my head. "No. It was a shock. Believe me."

She laughs and after another hug, we both sit down again. I try to keep up my smile, but it's not the smile of an elated expectant mother. She sees that almost immediately. She slides a hand over her mouth. "Sweetie," she whispers. "What's the matter?"

Until this moment, I've fought to remain strong. I've fought to not feel too sorry for myself when I'm around other people. But sitting here with my mother, I crave weakness. I just want to be able to give up for a little while. I want her to take over and hug me and tell me it'll all be okay. And for the next fifteen minutes while I cry in her arms, that's exactly what happens. I just stop fighting for myself because I need someone else to do it for me.

I spare her most of the details of our relationship, but I do tell her the most important things. That he's hurt me on more than one occasion, and I don't know what to do. That I'm scared to have this baby alone. That I'm scared I might make the wrong decision. That I'm scared I'm being too weak and that I should have had him arrested. That I'm scared I'm being too sensitive and I don't know if I'm overreacting. Basically, I tell her everything I haven't even been brave enough to fully admit to myself.

She retrieves some napkins out of the kitchen and comes back to the table. After our eyes are finally dry, she begins to crumple the napkin up between her hands, rolling it over in circles as she stares down at it.

"Do you want to take him back?" she asks.

I don't say yes. But I also don't say no.

This is the first moment since this has happened that I'm being completely honest. I'm honest to her *and* to myself. Maybe because she's the only one I know who has been through this. She's the only one I know who would understand the massive amounts of confusion I've been experiencing.

I shake my head, but I also shrug. "Most of me feels like I'll never be able to trust him again. But a huge part of me grieves what I had with him. We were so good together, Mom. The times I spent with him were some of the best moments of my life. And occasionally I feel like maybe I don't want to give that up."

I wipe the napkin beneath my eye, soaking up more tears. "Sometimes . . . when I'm really missing him . . . I tell myself that maybe it wasn't that bad. Maybe I could put up with him when he's at his worst just so I can have him when he's at his best."

She puts her hand on top of mine and rubs her thumb back and forth. "I know exactly what you mean, Lily. But the last thing you want to do is lose sight of your limit. Please don't allow that to happen."

I have no idea what she means by that. She sees the confusion in my expression, so she squeezes my arm and explains in more detail.

"We all have a limit. What we're willing to put up with before we break. When I married your father, I knew exactly what my limit was. But slowly . . . with every incident . . . my limit was pushed a little more. And a little more. The first time your father hit me, he was immediately sorry. He swore it would never happen again. The second time he hit me, he was even *more* sorry. The third time it happened, it was more than a hit. It was a beating. And every single time, I took him back. But the fourth time, it was only a slap. And when that happened, I felt relieved. I remember thinking, *'At least he didn't beat me this time. This wasn't so bad.'*"

She brings the napkin up to her eyes and says, "Every incident chips away at your limit. Every time you choose to stay, it makes the next time that much harder to leave. Eventually, you lose sight of your limit altogether, because you start to think, *'I've lasted five years now. What's five more?'*"

She grabs my hands and holds them while I cry. "Don't be like me, Lily. I know that you believe he loves you, and

I'm sure he does. But he's not loving you the right way. He doesn't love you the way you deserve to be loved. If Ryle truly loves you, he wouldn't allow you to take him back. He would make the decision to leave you himself so that he knows for a fact he can never hurt you again. That's the kind of love a woman deserves, Lily."

I wish with all my heart that she didn't learn these things from experience. I pull her to me and hug her.

For whatever reason, I thought I would have to defend myself to her when I came over here. Not once did I think I would come over here and learn from her. I should know better. I thought my mother was weak in the past, but she's actually one of the strongest women I know.

"Mom?" I say, pulling back. "I want to be you when I grow up."

She laughs and brushes the hair from my face. I can see in the way she looks at me that she'd trade spots with me in a heartbeat. She's feeling more pain for me in this moment than she ever felt for herself. "I want to tell you something," she says.

She reaches for my hands again.

"The day you gave your father's eulogy? I know you didn't freeze up, Lily. You stood at that podium and refused to say a single good thing about that man. It was the proudest I have ever been of you. You were the only one in my life who ever stood up for me. You were strong when I was scared." A tear falls from her eye when she says, "Be *that* girl, Lily. Brave and bold."

Chapter Thirty-Three

"What am I going to do with three car seats?"

I'm sitting on Allysa's couch, staring at all the stuff. She threw me a baby shower today. My mother came. Ryle's mother even flew in for it, but she's in the guest room sleeping off her jet lag now. The girls from the floral shop came and a few friends from my old job. Even Devin came. It was actually a lot of fun, despite the fact that I've been dreading it for the past several weeks.

"That's why I told you to start a registry, so none of the gifts would be duplicated," Allysa says.

I sigh. "I guess I can have Mom return hers. She's bought me enough stuff as it is."

I stand up and start gathering all the gifts. Marshall already said he'd help me carry them down to my apartment, so Allysa helps me throw everything inside trash bags. I hold them open while she picks everything up from the floor. I'm almost thirty weeks pregnant now, so she doesn't get the easier job of holding open the trash.

We have everything bagged up and Marshall is on his second trip down to my apartment when I open Allysa's front door, prepared to drag a trash bag full of gifts to the elevator. What I'm not prepared for is Ryle, who is standing on the other side of the door looking back at me. We both look equally as shocked to see each other, considering we haven't spoken since our fight three months ago.

This encounter was bound to happen, though. I can't be best friends with my husband's sister and live in the same building as him without eventually running into him.

I'm sure he knew I was having the shower today since his mother flew in for it, but he still looks a little surprised when he sees all the stuff behind me. It makes me wonder if him showing up just as I'm leaving is a coincidence or a suitable convenience. He looks down at the trash bag I'm holding and he takes it from my hands. "Let me get this."

I let him. He takes that bag and another one down to the apartment while I gather my things. He and Marshall are walking back inside the apartment as I'm preparing to walk out.

Ryle grabs the last bag of stuff and begins to head toward the front door again. I'm following behind him when Marshall gives me a silent look, asking me if I'm okay with Ryle going downstairs with me. I nod. I can't keep avoiding Ryle forever, so now is as good a time as any to discuss where we go from here.

It's only a few floors between their apartment and mine, but the elevator ride down with Ryle feels like the longest it's ever taken. I catch him staring at my stomach a couple of times and it makes me wonder how it must feel, going three months without seeing me pregnant.

My apartment door is unlocked, so I push it open and he follows me inside. He takes the last of the stuff to the nursery and I can hear him moving things around, opening boxes. I stay in the kitchen and clean things that don't even need cleaning. My heart is in my throat, knowing he's in my apartment. I don't feel scared of him in this moment. I just feel nervous. I wanted to be more prepared for this conversation because I absolutely hate confrontation. But I know we need to discuss the baby and our future. I just don't want to. Not yet, anyway.

He walks down the hallway and into the kitchen. I catch him looking at my stomach again. He glances away just as quickly. "Do you want me to assemble the crib while I'm here?"

I should probably say no, but he's half responsible for the child growing inside of me. If he's going to offer physical labor I'm going to take it, no matter how angry I still am at him. "Yeah. That would be a big help."

He points toward the laundry room. "Is my toolbox still in there?"

I nod and he heads toward the laundry room. I open the refrigerator and face it so I don't have to watch him walk back through the kitchen. When he's finally in the nursery again, I close the refrigerator and press my forehead against it as I grip the handle. I breathe in and out as I try to process everything that's happening inside of me right now.

He looks really good. It's been so long since I've seen him, I forgot how beautiful he is. I have an urge to run down the hallway and jump into his arms. I want to feel his mouth on mine. I want to hear him tell me how much he loves me. I want him to lie down next to me and put his hand on my stomach like I've imagined him doing so many times.

It would be so easy. My life would be so much easier right now if I would just forgive him and take him back.

I close my eyes and repeat the words my mother said to me. "*If Ryle truly loves you, he wouldn't allow you to take him back.*"

That reminder is the only thing that prevents me from running down the hallway.

• • •

I keep myself busy in the kitchen for the next hour as he remains in the nursery. I eventually have to walk past it to grab my phone charger from my room. On my way back down the hallway, I pause at the door of the nursery.

The crib is assembled. He even put the bedding on. He's standing over it, gripping the railing, staring inside the empty crib. He's so quiet and still, he looks like a statue. He's lost in thought and doesn't even notice me standing outside the doorway. It makes me wonder where his mind has wandered.

Is he thinking about the baby? The child he won't even be living with when it sleeps in that very crib?

Until this moment, I wasn't sure if he even wanted to be a part of the baby's life. But the look on his face proves to me that he does. I've never seen so much sadness in one expression, and I'm not even facing him straight on. I feel like the sadness he's feeling in this moment has absolutely nothing to do with me and everything to do with thoughts of his child.

He glances up and sees me standing in the doorway. He pushes off the crib and shakes himself out of his trance. "Finished," he says, waving a hand toward the crib. He begins putting his tools back inside the tool case. "Is there anything else you need while I'm here?"

I shake my head as I walk over to the crib and admire it. Since I don't know if it's a boy or a girl, I decided to go with a nature theme. The bedding set is tan and green with pictures of plants and trees all over it. It matches the curtains and will eventually match a mural I plan to paint on the wall at some point. I also plan to fill the nursery with a few live plants from the shop. I can't help but smile, finally seeing it all start to come together. He even put up the mobile. I reach up and turn it on and Brahms's Lullaby begins to play. I stare at it as it makes a full spin and then I glance back at Ryle. He's standing a few feet away, just watching me.

As I stare back at him, I think about how easy it is for humans to make judgments when we're standing on the outside of a situation. I spent years judging my mother's situation.

It's easy when we're on the outside to believe that we would walk away without a second thought if a person mistreated us. It's easy to say we couldn't continue to love someone who mistreats us when we aren't the ones feeling the love of that person.

When you experience it firsthand, it isn't so easy to hate the person who mistreats you when most of the time they're your godsend.

Ryle's eyes gain a little bit of hope, and I hate that he can see that my walls are temporarily lowered. He begins to take a slow step toward me. I know he's about to pull me to him and hug me, so I take a quick step away from him.

And just like that, the wall is back up between us.

Allowing him back inside this apartment was a huge step for me in itself. He needs to realize that.

He hides whatever rejection he's feeling with a stoic expression. He tucks the toolbox under his arm and then grabs the box the crib came in. It's filled with all the trash from everything he opened and put together. "I'll take this to the

Dumpster," he says, walking toward the door. "If you need help with anything else, just let me know, okay?"

I nod and somehow mutter, "Thank you."

When I hear the front door close, I turn back and face the crib. My eyes fill with tears, and not for myself this time. Not for the baby.

I cry for Ryle. Because even though he's responsible for the situation he's in, I know how sad he is about it. And when you love someone, seeing them sad also makes *you* sad.

Neither of us brought up our separation or even a chance at reconciliation. We didn't even talk about what's going to happen when this baby is born in ten weeks.

I'm just not ready for that conversation yet and the least he can do for me right now is show me patience.

The patience he still owes me from all the times he had none.

Chapter Thirty-Four

I finish rinsing the paint out of the brushes and then walk back to the nursery to admire the mural. I spent most of yesterday and all of today painting it.

It's been two weeks since Ryle came over and put the crib together. Now that the mural is finished and I brought in a few plants from the store, I feel like the nursery is finally complete. I look around and feel a little sad that no one is here to admire the room with me. I grab my phone and text Allysa.

Me: Mural is finished! You should come down and look at it.

Allysa: I'm not home. Running errands. I'll come look at it tomorrow, though.

I frown and decide to text my mother. She has to work tomorrow, but I know she'll be just as excited to see it as I was to finish it.

Me: Feel like driving into town tonight? The nursery is finally finished.

Mom: Can't. Recital night at school. I'll be here late. I can't wait to see it! I'll come by tomorrow!

I sit down in the rocking chair and know that I shouldn't do what I'm about to do, but I do it anyway.

Me: The nursery is finished. Do you want to come look at it?

Every nerve in my body springs to life as soon as I hit Send. I stare at my phone until his reply comes through.

Ryle: Of course. On my way down now.

I immediately stand up and begin making last minute touches. I fluff the pillows on the loveseat and straighten one of the wall hangings. I'm barely to the front door when I hear his knock. I open it and *dammit. He's wearing scrubs.*

I step aside as he makes his way in.

"Allysa said you were painting a mural?"

I follow him down the hallway toward the nursery.

"It's taken two days to finish," I tell him. "My body feels like I ran a marathon and all I did was walk up and down a step ladder a few times."

He glances over his shoulder and I can see the concern in his expression. He's worried that I was here doing it all on my own. He shouldn't worry. I've got this.

When we make it to the nursery, he stops in the doorway. On the opposite wall, I painted a garden. It's complete with almost every fruit and vegetable I could think of that grows in a garden. I'm not a painter, but it's amazing what you can do with a projector and transparent paper.

"Wow," Ryle says.

I grin, because I recognize the surprise in his voice and I know it's genuine. He walks into the room and looks around, shaking his head the whole time. "Lily. It's . . . wow."

If he were Allysa, I'd clap and jump up and down. But he's Ryle and with the way things have been between us, that would be a little awkward.

He walks over to the window where I set up a swing. He gives it a little push and it begins moving from side to side.

"It also moves front to back," I tell him. I don't know if he even knows anything about baby swings, but I was pretty impressed by that feature.

He walks over to the changing table and pulls one of the diapers out of the holder. He unfolds it and holds it up in front of him. "It's so tiny," he says. "I don't remember Rylee being this tiny."

Hearing him mention Rylee makes me a little sad. We've been living apart since the night she was born, so I've never been able to see him interact with her.

Ryle folds up the diaper and puts it back in the holder. When he turns to face me, he smiles, lifting his hands to motion around the room. "It's really great, Lily," he says. "All of it. You're really doing . . ." His hands drop to his hips and his smile falters. "You're doing really well."

A thickness seems to form in the air around me. It's suddenly difficult to take in a full breath because for whatever reason, I feel like I need to cry. I just really like this moment and it saddens me that we couldn't spend the entire pregnancy full of moments like these. It feels good sharing this with him, but I'm also scared I might be giving him false hope.

Now that he's here and he saw the nursery, I'm not sure what to do next. It's glaringly obvious that we need to discuss a lot of things, but I have no idea where to start. Or how.

I walk over to the rocking chair and take a seat. "Naked truth?" I say, looking up at him.

He exhales a huge breath and nods, then takes a seat on the sofa. "*Please*. Lily, please tell me you're ready to talk about this."

His reaction eases my nerves a little, knowing he's ready to discuss everything. I wrap my arms around my stomach and lean forward in the rocking chair. "You go first."

He clasps his hands together between his knees. He looks at me with so much sincerity, I have to glance away.

"I don't know what you want from me, Lily. I don't know what role you want me to have. I'm trying to give you all the space you need, but at the same time I want to help more than you possibly know. I want to be in our baby's life. I want to be your husband and I want to be good at it. But I have no idea what's going through your head."

His words fill me with guilt. Despite what has happened between us in the past, he's still this baby's father. He has the legal right to be a father, no matter how I feel about it. And I *want* him to be a father. I want him to be a *good* father. But deep down, I'm still holding on to one of my biggest fears, and I know I need to talk to him about it.

"I would never keep you from your child, Ryle. I'm happy you want to be involved. But . . ."

He leans forward and buries his face in his hands with that last word.

"What kind of mother would I be if a small part of me doesn't have concern in regard to your temper? The way you lose control? How do I know something won't set you off while you're alone with this baby?"

So much agony floods his eyes, I think they might burst like dams. He begins to shake his head adamantly. "Lily, I would never . . ."

"I know, Ryle. You would never intentionally hurt your own child. I don't even believe it was intentional when you hurt me, but you did. And trust me, I want to believe that you would never do something like that. My father was only abusive toward my mother. There are many men—*women* even—who abuse their significant others without ever losing their temper with anyone else. I want to believe your words with all my heart, but you have to understand where my hesitation comes in. I'll never deny you a relationship with your child. But I'm going to need you to be really patient with me while you rebuild all the trust you've broken."

He nods in agreement. He has to know that I'm giving him much more than he deserves. "Absolutely," he says. "This is on your terms. Everything is on your terms, okay?"

Ryle's hands come together again and he begins to chew nervously on his bottom lip. I sense he has more to say, but he's doubting whether or not he should say it.

"Go ahead and say whatever you're thinking while I'm in the mood to talk about it."

He tilts his head back and looks up at the ceiling. Whatever it is, it's hard for him. I don't know if it's because the question is hard to ask or because he's scared of the answer I might give him.

"What about us?" he whispers.

I lean my head back and sigh. I knew this question would come, but it's really difficult to give him an answer I don't have. Divorce or reconciliation are really the only two options we have, but neither is a choice I want to make.

"I don't want to give you false hope, Ryle," I say quietly. "If I had to make a choice today . . . I'd probably choose divorce. But in all honesty, I don't know if I would be making that choice because I'm overloaded with pregnancy hormones or because it's what I really want. I don't think it would be fair to either of us if I made that decision before the birth of this baby."

He blows out a shaky breath and then brings a hand up to the back of his neck, squeezing tightly. Then he stands up and faces me. "Thank you," he says. "For inviting me over. For the conversation. I've been wanting to stop by since I was here a couple of weeks ago, but I didn't know how you'd feel about it."

"I don't know how I would have felt about it, either," I say with complete honesty. I try to push myself out of the rocking chair, but for some reason it's become a lot harder in the past week. Ryle walks over and reaches for my hand to help me up.

I don't know how I'm supposed to last until my due date when I can't even get out of a chair without grunting.

Once I'm standing, he doesn't immediately release my hand. We're just a few inches apart, and I know if I look up at him I'll feel things. I don't want to feel things for him.

He finds my other hand until he's holding both of them down at my sides. He threads his fingers through mine and I feel it all the way to my heart. I press my forehead against his chest and close my eyes. His cheek meets the top of my head and we stand completely still, both of us too scared to move. I'm scared to move because I might be too weak to stop him from kissing me. He's scared to move because he's afraid if he does, I'll pull away.

For what feels like five full minutes, neither of us moves a muscle.

"Ryle," I finally say. "Can you promise me something?"

I feel him nod.

"Until this baby comes, please don't try to talk me into forgiving you. And *please* don't try to kiss me . . ." I pull away from his chest and look up at him. "I want to tackle one huge thing at a time, and right now my only priority is having this baby. I don't want to add any more stress or confusion on top of everything that's already happening."

He squeezes both of my hands reassuringly. "One monumental life-changing thing at a time. Got it."

I smile, relieved that we've finally had this conversation. I know I didn't make a final decision about the two of us, but I still feel like I can breathe easier now that we're on the same page.

He releases my hands. "I'm late for my shift," he says, tossing a thumb over his shoulder. "I should get to work."

I nod and see him out. It isn't until after I've shut the door and am alone in my apartment that I realize I have a smile on my face.

I'm still incredibly angry with him that we're even in this predicament to begin with, so my smile is simply due to making a little headway. Sometimes parents have to work through their differences and bring a level of maturity into a situation in order to do what's best for their child.

That's exactly what we're doing. Learning how to navigate our situation before our child is brought into the fold.

Chapter Thirty-Five

I smell toast.

I stretch out on my bed and smile, because Ryle knows toast is my favorite. I lie here for a while before I even attempt to get up. It feels like it takes the effort of three men to roll me out of bed. I eventually take a deep breath, and then throw my feet over the side, pushing myself up from the mattress.

The first thing I do is pee. It's really all I do now. I'm due in two days and my doctor says it could be another week. I started maternity leave last week, so this is my life right now. I pee and watch TV.

When I make it to the kitchen, Ryle is stirring a pan of scrambled eggs. He spins around when he hears me walk in. "Good morning," he says. "No baby yet?"

I shake my head and put my hand on my stomach. "No, but I peed nine times last night."

Ryle laughs. "That's a new record." He spoons some eggs onto a plate and then tosses bacon and toast on it. He turns around and hands me the plate, pressing a quick kiss to the side of my head. "I gotta go. I'm already late. I'm leaving my phone on all day."

I smile when I look down at my breakfast. *Okay, so I eat, too. Pee, eat, and watch TV.*

"Thank you," I say cheerfully. I take my plate to the

couch and turn on the TV. Ryle rushes around the living room, gathering his stuff.

"I'll come check on you at lunch. I might be working late tonight, but Allysa said she can bring you dinner."

I roll my eyes. "I'm *fine*, Ryle. The doctor said light bed rest, not complete debilitation."

He starts to open the door, but pauses like he forgets something. He runs back toward me and leans down, planting his lips on my stomach. "I'll double your allowance if you decide to come out today," he says to the baby.

He talks to the baby a lot. I finally felt comfortable enough to let him feel the baby kick a couple of weeks ago and since then, he stops by sometimes just to talk to my belly and doesn't even say much to me. I like it, though. I like how excited he is to be a father.

I grab the blanket Ryle slept on the couch with last night and wrap it over me. He's been staying here for a week now, waiting for me to go into labor. I wasn't sure about the arrangement at first, but it's actually been really helpful. I still sleep in the guest bedroom. The third bedroom is now a nursery, which means the master bedroom is available for him to sleep in. But for whatever reason, he chooses to sleep on the couch. I think the memories in that bedroom plague him just as much as they plague me, so neither of us even bothers going in there.

The last several weeks have been really good. Aside from the fact that there's absolutely no physical relationship between us at this point, things feel like they've kind of gone back to how they used to be. He still works a lot, but on the evenings he's off, I've started having dinner upstairs with all of them. We never eat alone as a couple, though. Anything that might feel like a date or a couples thing, I avoid. I'm still trying to focus on one monumental thing at a time, and until this baby is born and my hormones are back to normal, I refuse to make a decision about my marriage. I'm sure I'm just using the pregnancy as an excuse to stall the inevitable, but being pregnant allows a person to be a little selfish.

My phone begins to ring, and I drop my head into the couch and groan. My phone is all the way in the kitchen. That's like fifteen feet from here.

Ugh.

I push myself off the couch, but nothing happens.

I try it again. *Still sitting.*

I grab hold of the arm of my chair and pull myself up. *Third time's the charm.*

When I stand, my glass of water spills all over me. I groan . . . but then I gasp.

I wasn't holding a glass of water.

Holy shit.

I look down and water is trickling down my leg. My phone is still ringing on the kitchen counter. I walk—or waddle—to the kitchen and answer it.

"Hello?"

"Hey, it's Lucy! Quick question. Our order of red roses was damaged in shipment, but we've got the Levenberg funeral today and they specifically wanted red roses for the casket spray. Do we have a backup plan?"

"Yeah, call the florist on Broadway. They owe me a favor."

"Okay, thanks!"

I start to hang up so I can call Ryle and tell him my water broke, but I hear Lucy say, "Wait!"

I pull the phone back to my ear.

"About these invoices. Did you want me to pay them today or wait . . ."

"You can wait, it's fine."

Again, I start to hang up but she yells my name and starts firing off another question.

"Lucy," I say calmly, interrupting her. "I'll have to call you about all this tomorrow. I think my water just broke."

There's a pause. "Oh. OH! GO!"

I hang up right when the first sign of pain shoots through my stomach. I wince and start dialing Ryle's number. He picks up on the first ring.

"Do I need to turn around?"

"Yes."

"Oh, God. Really? It's happening?"

"Yes."

"Lily!" he says, excited. And then the phone goes dead.

I spend the next few minutes gathering everything I'll need. I already have a hospital bag, but I feel kind of gross, so I jump in the shower to rinse off. The second burst of pain comes about ten minutes after the first. I bend forward and clench my stomach, letting the water beat down on my back. Right when I near the end of the contraction, I hear the bathroom door swing open.

"You're in the *shower*?" Ryle says. "Lily, get out of the shower, let's go!"

"Hand me a towel."

Ryle's hand appears around the shower curtain a few

seconds later. I try to fit the towel around me before pulling the shower curtain aside. It's odd, hiding your body from your own husband.

The towel doesn't fit. It covers up my boobs but then opens like an upside-down V over my stomach.

Another contraction hits as I'm stepping out of the shower. Ryle grabs my hand and helps me breathe through it, then walks me into the bedroom. I'm calmly picking out clean clothes to wear to the hospital when I glance over at him.

He's staring at my stomach. There's a look on his face I can't decipher.

His eyes meet mine and I pause what I'm doing.

There's a moment that passes between us where I can't tell if he's about to frown or smile. His face twists into both somehow, and he blows out a quick breath, dropping his eyes back to my stomach. "You're beautiful," he whispers.

A pang shoots through my chest that has nothing to do with the contractions. I realize this is the first time he's seen my bare stomach. It's the first time he's witnessed what I look like with his baby growing inside of me.

I walk over to him and take his hand. I place it on my stomach and hold it there. He smiles at me, brushing his thumb back and forth. It's a beautiful moment. One of our better moments.

"Thank you, Lily."

It's written all over him, the way he's touching my stomach, the way his eyes are looking back at mine. He's not thanking me for this moment, or any moment that came before this one. He's thanking me for all the moments I'm allowing him to have with his child.

I groan, leaning forward. "Fucking hell."

The moment is over.

Ryle grabs my clothes and helps me into them. He picks up all the things I tell him to carry and then we make our way to the elevator. Slowly. I have a contraction when we're halfway there.

"You should call Allysa," I tell him when we pull out of the parking garage.

"I'm driving. I'll call her when we get to the hospital. And your mom."

I nod. I'm sure I could call them right now, but I kind of just want to make sure we make it to the hospital first, because it feels like this baby is being really impatient and wants to make its debut right here in the car.

We make it to the hospital, but my contractions are less than a minute apart when we arrive. By the time the doctor scrubs in and they get me to a bed, I'm dilated to a nine. It's only five minutes later when I'm being told to push. Ryle doesn't even have a chance to call anyone, it all happens so fast.

I squeeze Ryle's hand with every push. At one point, I think about how important the hand I'm squeezing is to his career, but he says nothing. He just allows me to squeeze it as hard as I possibly can, and that's exactly what I do.

"The head is almost out," the doctor says. "Just a few more pushes."

I can't even describe the next few minutes. It's a blur of pain and heavy breathing and anxiety and pure, unequivocal elation. And pressure. Such an enormous pressure, like I'm about to implode, and then, "It's a girl!" Ryle says. "Lily, we have a daughter!"

I open my eyes and the doctor is holding her up. I can only make out the outline of her, because my eyes are full of too many tears. When they lay her on my chest, it's the absolute greatest moment of my life. I immediately touch her red lips and cheeks and fingers. Ryle cuts the umbilical cord, and when they take her from me to clean her up, I feel empty.

A few minutes later she's back on my chest again, swaddled in a blanket.

I can do nothing but stare at her.

Ryle sits on the bed next to me and pulls the blanket down around her chin so we can get a better look at her face. We count her fingers and her toes. She tries to open her eyes and we think it's the funniest thing in the world. She yawns and we both smile and fall even more in love with her.

After the last nurse leaves the room and we're finally alone, Ryle asks if he can hold her. He raises the head of my bed to make it easier for both of us to sit on the bed. After I hand her to him, I lay my head on his shoulder and we just can't stop staring at her.

"Lily," he whispers. "Naked truth?"

I nod.

"She's so much prettier than Marshall and Allysa's baby."

I laugh and elbow him.

"I'm kidding," he whispers.

I know exactly what he means, though. Rylee is a gorgeous baby, but no one will ever hold a candle to our own daughter.

"What should we name her?" he asks. We didn't have the typical relationship during this pregnancy, so the baby's name hasn't been something we've discussed yet.

"I'd like to name her after your sister," I say, glancing at him. "Or maybe your brother?"

I'm not sure what he thinks of that. I personally think naming our daughter after his brother could be somewhat healing for him, but he may not see it that way.

He glances over at me, not expecting that answer. "Emerson?" he says. "That's kind of cute for a girl name. We could call her Emma. Or Emmy." He smiles proudly and looks down at her. "It's perfect, actually." He leans down and kisses Emerson on her forehead.

After a while, I pull away from his shoulder so I can watch him hold her. It's a beautiful thing, seeing him interact with her like this. I can already see how much love he has for her just from the little time he's known her. I can see that he would do anything to protect her. Anything in the world.

It isn't until this moment that I finally make a decision about him.

About us.

About what's best for our family.

Ryle is amazing in so many ways. He's compassionate. He's caring. He's smart. He's charismatic. He's driven.

My father was some of these things, too. He wasn't very compassionate toward others, but there were times we spent together that I knew he loved me. He was smart. He was charismatic. He was driven. But I hated him so much more than I loved him. I was blinded to all the best things about him thanks to all the glimpses I got of him when he was at his worst. Five minutes of witnessing him at his worst couldn't make up for even five years of him at his best.

I look at Emerson and I look at Ryle. And I know that I have to do what's best for her. For the relationship I hope she builds with her father. I don't make this decision for me and I don't make it for Ryle.

I make it for her.

"Ryle?"

When he glances at me, he's smiling. But when he assesses the look on my face, he stops.

"I want a divorce."

He blinks twice. My words hit him like voltage. He winces and looks back down at our daughter, his shoulders hunched forward. "Lily," he says, shaking his head back and forth. "Please don't do this."

His voice is pleading, and I hate that he's been holding on to hope that I would eventually take him back. That's partly my fault, I know, but I don't think I realized what choice I was going to make until I held my daughter for the first time.

"Just one more chance, Lily. *Please.*" His voice cracks with tears when he speaks.

I know I'm hurting him at the worst possible time. I'm breaking his heart when this should be the best moment of his life. But I know if I don't do it in this moment, I might never be able to convince him of why I can't risk taking him back.

I begin to cry because this is hurting me as much as it's hurting him. "Ryle," I say gently. "What would you do? If one of these days, this little girl looked up at you and she said, *'Daddy? My boyfriend hit me.'* What would you say to her, Ryle?"

He pulls Emerson to his chest and buries his face against the top of her blanket. "Stop, Lily," he begs.

I push myself up straighter on the bed. I place my hand on Emerson's back and try to get Ryle to look me in the eyes. "What if she came to you and said, '*Daddy? My husband pushed me down the stairs. He said it was an accident. What should I do?*' "

His shoulders begin to shake, and for the first time since the day I met him, he has tears. Real tears that rush down his cheeks as he holds his daughter tightly against him. I'm crying, too, but I keep going. For *her* sake.

"What if . . ." My voice breaks. "What if she came to you and said, '*My husband tried to rape me, Daddy. He held me down while I begged him to stop. But he swears he'll never do it again. What should I do, Daddy?*' "

He's kissing her forehead, over and over, tears spilling down his face.

"What would you say to her, Ryle? Tell me. I need to know what you would say to our daughter if the man she loves with all her heart ever hurts her."

A sob breaks from his chest. He leans toward me and wraps an arm around me. "I would beg her to leave him," he says through his tears. His lips press desperately against my forehead and I can feel some of his tears as they fall onto my cheeks. He moves his mouth to my ear and cradles both of us against him. "I would tell her that she is worth *so* much more. And I would *beg* her not to go back, no matter how much he loves her. She's worth so much more."

We become a sobbing mess of tears and broken hearts

and shattered dreams. We hold each other. We hold our daughter. And as hard as this choice is, we break the pattern before the pattern breaks us.

He hands her back to me and wipes his eyes. He stands up, still crying. Still trying to catch his breath. In the last fifteen minutes, he lost the love of his life. In the last fifteen minutes, he became a father to a beautiful little girl.

That's what fifteen minutes can do to a person. It can destroy them.

It can save them.

He points toward the hallway, letting me know he needs to go gather himself. He's sadder than I've ever seen him as he walks toward the door. But I know he'll thank me for this one day. I know the day will come when he'll understand that I made the right choice by his daughter.

When the door closes behind him, I look down at her. I know I'm not giving her the life I dreamed for her. A home where she lives with both parents who can love her and raise her together. But I don't want her to live like I lived. I don't want her to see her father at his worst. I don't want her to see him when he loses his temper with me to the point that she no longer recognizes him as her father. Because no matter how many good moments she might share with Ryle throughout her lifetime, I know from experience that it would only be the worst ones that stuck with her.

Cycles exist because they are excruciating to break. It takes an astronomical amount of pain and courage to disrupt a familiar pattern. Sometimes it seems easier to just keep running in the same familiar circles, rather than facing the fear of jumping and possibly not landing on your feet.

My mother went through it.

I went through it.

I'll be damned if I allow my daughter to go through it.

I kiss her on the forehead and make her a promise. "It stops here. With me and you. It ends with us."

Epilogue

I push through the crowds of Boylston Street until I get to the cross street. I pull the stroller to a crawl and then stop at the edge of the curb. I pull the top of it back and look down at Emmy. She's kicking her feet and smiling like usual. She's a very happy baby. She has a calm energy about her and it's addictive.

"How old is she?" a woman asks. She's standing at the crosswalk with us, staring down at Emerson appreciatively.

"Eleven months."

"She's gorgeous," she says. "Looks just like you. Identical mouths."

I smile. "Thank you. But you should see her father. She definitely has his eyes."

The sign flashes to walk, and I try to beat the crowd as we rush across the street. I'm already half an hour late and Ryle has texted me twice. He hasn't experienced the joy of carrots yet, though. He'll find out today just how messy they are, because I packed plenty in her bag.

I moved out of the apartment Ryle bought when Emerson was three months old. I got my own place closer to my work so I'm within walking distance, which is great. Ryle moved back into the apartment he bought, but between visiting Allysa's place and Ryle's days with Emerson, I feel like I'm still at their apartment building almost as much as I'm at mine.

"Almost there, Emmy." We make a right around the corner and I'm in such a rush, a man has to step out of our way and into the wall just to avoid being plowed over. "Sorry," I mutter, ducking my head and making my way around him.

"Lily?"

I stop.

I turn slowly, because I felt that voice all the way to my toes. There are only two voices that have ever done that to me, and Ryle's doesn't reach that far anymore.

When I look back at him, his blue eyes are squinting against the sun. He lifts a hand to shield it and he grins. "Hey."

"Hi," I say, my frenzied brain trying to slow down and allow me to play catch-up.

He glances at the stroller and points at it. "Is that . . . is this your baby?"

I nod and he walks around to the front of the stroller. He kneels down and smiles widely at her. "Wow. She's gorgeous, Lily," he says. "What's her name?"

"Emerson. We call her Emmy sometimes."

He puts his finger in her hand and she starts kicking, shaking his finger back and forth. He stares at her appreciatively for a moment and then stands back up again.

"You look great," he says.

I try not to give him an obvious once-over, but it's hard. He looks as good as ever, but this is the first time seeing him that I'm not trying to deny how gorgeous he turned out to be. A far cry from that homeless boy in my bedroom. Yet . . . somehow still exactly the same.

I can feel the buzz of my text message going off in my pocket again. *Ryle.*

I point down the street. "We're really late," I say. "Ryle has been waiting for half an hour."

When I say Ryle's name, there's a sadness that reaches Atlas's eyes, but he tries to disguise it. He nods and slowly steps aside for us to pass.

"It's his day to have her," I clarify, saying more in those six words than I could in most full conversations.

I see the relief flash in his eyes. He nods and points behind him. "Yeah, I'm running late, too. Opened a new restaurant on Boylston last month."

"Wow. Congratulations. I'll have to take Mom there to check it out soon."

He smiles. "You should. Let me know and I'll make sure and cook for you myself."

There's an awkward pause, and then I point down the street. "We have to . . ."

"Go," he says with a smile.

I nod again and then duck my head and continue walking. I have no idea why I'm reacting this way. Like I don't know how to hold a normal conversation. When I'm several yards away, I glance back over my shoulder. He hasn't moved. He's still watching me as I walk away.

We round the corner and I see Ryle waiting beside his car outside the floral shop. His face lights up when he sees us approaching. "Did you get my email?" He kneels down and begins to unstrap Emerson.

"Yeah, about the playpen recall?"

He nods as he pulls her out of the stroller. "Didn't we buy one of those for her?"

I press the buttons to fold the stroller and then walk it

to the back of his car. "Yeah, but it broke like a month ago. I threw it in the Dumpster."

He pops the trunk, and then touches Emerson's chin with his fingers. "Did you hear that, Emmy? Your mommy saved your life." She smiles up at him and slaps playfully at his hand. He kisses her on the forehead and then picks up her stroller and tosses it in the trunk. I slam the trunk shut and lean over to give her a quick kiss.

"Love you, Emmy. See you tonight."

Ryle opens the back door to put her in the car seat. I tell him goodbye and then I start to head back down the street in a rush.

"Lily!" he yells. "Where are you going?"

I'm sure he expected me to walk to the front door of my store, since I'm already late opening it. I probably should, but the nagging in my gut won't go away. I need to do something about it. I spin around and walk backward. "There's something I forgot to do! I'll see you when I pick her up tonight!"

Ryle lifts Emerson's hand and they wave goodbye to me. As soon as I round the corner, I break out into a sprint. I dodge people, bump into a few and cause one lady to curse at me, but it's all worth it the moment I see the back of his head.

"Atlas!" I yell. He's heading in the other direction, so I keep pushing through the crowd. "Atlas!"

He stops walking but he doesn't turn around. He cocks his head like he doesn't want to fully trust his ears.

"Atlas!" I yell again.

This time when he turns, he turns with purpose. His

eyes meet mine and there's a three-second pause while we both stare at each other. But then we both start walking toward each other, determination in every step. Twenty steps separate us.

Ten.

Five.

One.

Neither of us takes that final step.

I'm out of breath, panting and nervous. "I forgot to tell you Emerson's middle name." I put my hands on my hips and exhale. "It's Dory."

He doesn't immediately react, but then his eyes crinkle a little in the corners. His mouth twitches like he's forcing back a smile. "What a perfect name for her."

I nod, and smile, and then stop.

I'm not sure what to do now. I just needed him to know that, but now that I've told him, I didn't really think of what I'd do or say next.

I nod again, and then glance around me, throwing a thumb over my shoulder. "Well . . . I guess I'll . . ."

Atlas steps forward, grabs me, and pulls me hard against his chest. I immediately close my eyes when he wraps his arms around me. His hand goes up to the back of my head and he holds me still against him as we stand, surrounded by busy streets, blasts of horns, people brushing us as they pass in a hurry. He presses a gentle kiss into my hair, and all of that fades away.

"Lily," he says quietly. "I feel like my life is good enough for you now. So whenever you're ready . . ."

I clench his jacket in my hands and keep my face pressed

tight against his chest. I suddenly feel like I'm fifteen again. My neck and cheeks flush from his words.

But I'm *not* fifteen.

I'm an adult with responsibilities and a child. I can't just allow my teenage feelings to take over. Not without a little reassurance, at least.

I pull back and look up at him. "Do you donate to charity?"

Atlas laughs with confusion. "Several. Why?"

"Do you want kids someday?"

He nods. "Of course I do."

"Do you think you'll ever want to leave Boston?"

He shakes his head. "No. Never. Everything is better here, remember?"

His answers give me the reassurance I need. I smile up at him. "Okay. I'm ready."

He pulls me tight against him and I laugh. With everything that has happened since the day he came into my life, I never expected this outcome. I've hoped for it a lot, but until now I wasn't sure if it would ever happen.

I close my eyes when I feel his lips meet the spot on my collarbone. He presses a gentle kiss there and it feels just like the first time he kissed me there all those years ago. He brings his mouth to my ear, and in a whisper, he says, "You can stop swimming now, Lily. We finally reached the shore."

Note from the Author

It is recommended this section be read after reading the book, as it contains spoilers.

• • •

My earliest memory in life was from the age of two and a half years old. My bedroom didn't have a door and was covered by a sheet nailed to the top of the door frame. I remember hearing my father yelling, so I peeked out from the other side of the sheet just as my father picked up our television and threw it at my mother, knocking her down.

She divorced him before I turned three. Every memory beyond that of my father was a good one. He never once lost his temper with me or my sisters, despite having done so on numerous occasions with my mother.

I knew their marriage was an abusive one, but my mother never talked about it. To discuss it would have meant she was talking ill of my father and that's something she never once did. She wanted the relationship I had with him to be free of any strain that stood between the two of them. Because of this, I have the utmost respect for parents who don't involve their children in the dissolution of their relationships.

I asked my father about the abuse once. He was very candid about their relationship. He was an alcoholic during the years he was married to my mother and he was the first to admit he didn't treat her well. In fact, he told me he had two knuckles replaced in his hand because he had hit her so hard, they broke against her skull.

My father regretted the way he treated my mother his entire life. Mistreating her was the worst mistake he had ever made and he said he would grow old and die still madly in love with her.

I feel that was a very light punishment for what she endured.

When I decided I wanted to write this story, I first asked my mother for permission. I told her I wanted to write it for women like her. I also wanted to write it for all the people who didn't quite understand women like her.

I was one of those people.

The mother I know is not weak. She was not someone I could envision forgiving a man for mistreating her on multiple occasions. But while writing this book and getting into the mind-set of Lily, I quickly realized that it's not as black and white as it seems from the outside.

On more than one occasion while writing this, I wanted to change the plotline. I didn't want Ryle to be who he was going to be because I had fallen in love with him in those first several chapters, just as Lily had fallen in love with him. Just as my mother fell in love with my father.

The first incident between Ryle and Lily in the kitchen is what happened the first time my father ever hit my mother. She was cooking a casserole and he had been drinking. He pulled the casserole out of the oven without using a pot holder. She thought it was funny and she laughed. The next thing she knew, he had hit her so hard she flew across the kitchen floor.

She chose to forgive him for that one incident, because his apology and regret were believable. Or at least believable enough that giving him a second chance hurt less than leaving with a broken heart would have.

Over time, the incidents that followed were similar to the first. My father would repeatedly show remorse and promise to never do it again. It finally got to a point where she knew his promises were empty, but she was a mother of two daughters by then and had no money to leave. And unlike Lily, my mother didn't have a lot of support. There were no local women's shelters. There was very little government support back then. To leave meant risking not having a roof over our heads, but to her it was better than the alternative.

My father passed away several years ago, when I was twenty-five years old. He wasn't the best father. He certainly wasn't the best husband. But thanks to my mother, I was able to have a very close relationship with him because she took the necessary steps to break the pattern before it broke us. And it wasn't easy. She left him right before I turned three and my older sister turned five. We lived off beans and macaroni and cheese for two solid years. She was a single mother without a college education, raising two daughters on her own with virtually no help. But her love for us gave her the strength she needed to take that terrifying step.

By no means do I intend for Ryle and Lily's situation to define domestic abuse. Nor do I intend for Ryle's character to define the characteristics of most abusers. Every situation is different. Every outcome is different. I chose to fashion Lily and Ryle's story after my mother and father's. I fashioned Ryle after my father in many ways. They are handsome, compassionate, funny, and smart—but with moments of unforgivable behavior.

I fashioned Lily after my mother in many ways. They are both caring, intelligent, strong women who simply fell in love with men who didn't deserve to fall in love at all.

Two years after divorcing my father, my mother met my stepfather. He was the epitome of a good husband. The memories I have of them growing up set the bar for the type of marriage I wanted for myself.

When I finally did reach the point of marriage, the hardest thing I ever had to do was tell my biological father that he wouldn't be walking me down the aisle—that I was going to ask my stepfather.

I felt I had to do this for many reasons. My stepfather stepped up as a husband in ways my father never did. My stepfather stepped up financially in ways my father never did. And my stepfather raised us as if we were his own, while never once denying us a relationship with my biological father.

I remember sitting down in my father's living room a month before my wedding. I told him I loved him, but that I was going to be asking my stepfather to walk me down the aisle. I was prepared for his response with every rebuttal I could think of. But the response he gave me was nothing I expected.

He nodded his head and said, "Colleen, he raised you. He deserves to give you away at your wedding. And you shouldn't feel guilty about it, because it's the right thing to do."

I knew my decision absolutely gutted my father. But he was selfless enough as a father to not only respect my decision, but he wanted *me* to respect it, too.

My father sat in the audience at my wedding and watched another man walk me down the aisle. I knew people were wondering why I didn't just have both of them walk me down the aisle, but looking back on it, I realize I made the choice out of respect for my mother.

Who I chose to walk me down the aisle wasn't really about my father and it wasn't even really about my stepfather. It was about her. I wanted the man who treated her how she deserved to be treated to be given the honor of giving away her daughter.

In the past, I've always said I write for entertainment purposes only. I don't write to educate, persuade, or inform.

This book is different. This was not entertainment for me. It was the most grueling thing I have ever written. At times, I wanted to hit the Delete button and take back the way Ryle had treated Lily. I wanted to rewrite the scenes where she forgave him and I wanted to replace those scenes with a more resilient woman—a character who made all the right decisions at all the right times. But those weren't the characters I was writing.

That wasn't the story I was telling.

I wanted to write something realistic to the situation my mother was in—a situation a lot of women find themselves in. I wanted to explore the love between Lily and Ryle so that I would feel what my mother felt when she had to make the decision to leave my father—a man she loved with all her heart.

I sometimes wonder how different my life would have been if my mother had not made the choice she did. She left someone she loved so that her daughters would never think that kind of relationship was okay. She wasn't rescued by another man—a knight in shining armor. She took the initiative to leave my father on her own, knowing she was about to embark on a completely different kind of struggle with added stress as a single mother. It was important to me that Lily's character embody this same empowerment. Lily made the ultimate decision to leave Ryle for the sake of their daughter. Even though there was a slight possibility that Ryle could have eventually changed for the better, some risks are never worth taking. Especially when those risks have failed you in the past.

Before I wrote this book, I had a lot of respect for my mother. Now that I've finished it and was able to explore a tiny fraction of the pain and struggle she went through to get to where she is today, I only have one thing to say to her.

I want to be you when I grow up.

Resources

If you are a victim of domestic violence or know someone who could use assistance in leaving a dangerous situation, please visit: www.thehotline.org.

For a list of resources for homeless individuals, please visit: www.homelessresourcenetwork.org.

To listen to music created specifically for this novel, visit: https://www.colleenhoover.com/portfolio/it-ends-with-us/.

Acknowledgments

There may only be one name listed as the author of this book, but I couldn't have written it without the following people:

My sisters. I would love you both just as much if you weren't my sisters. Sharing a parent with you is just an added bonus.

My children. You are my biggest accomplishment in life. Please never make me regret saying that.

To Weblich, CoHorts, TL Discussion Group, Book Swap, and all the other groups I can turn to online when I need some positive energy. You guys are a huge part of the reason I can do this for a living, so thank you.

The entire team at Dystel & Goderich Literary Management. Thank you for your continued support and encouragement.

Everyone at Atria Books. Thank you for making my release days memorable and some of the best days of my life.

Johanna Castillo, my editor. Thank you for supporting this book. Thank you for supporting me. Thank you for being the biggest supporter of my dream job.

To Ellen DeGeneres, one of only four people I hope I never meet. You are light where there is darkness. Lily and Atlas are grateful for your shine.

Thank you to Marion Archer and Karen Lawson for the valuable feedback. My beta-readers and early supporters of each and every book. Your feedback, support, and constant friendship are more than I deserve. I love you all.

To my niece. I will get to meet you any day now, and I've never been so excited. I'm going to be your favorite aunt.

To Lindy. Thank you for the life lessons and the examples of what it is to be a selfless human. And thank you for one of the most profound quotes that will stick with me forever. "*There is no such thing as bad people. We are all just people who do bad things.*" I'm grateful my baby sister has you for a mother.

To Vance. Thank you for being the husband my mother deserved and the father you didn't have to be.

My husband, Heath. You are good, all the way to your soul. I couldn't have chosen a better person to father my children and spend the rest of my life with. We are all so lucky to have you.

To my mother. You are everything to everyone. That can sometimes be a burden, but you somehow see burdens as blessings. Our entire family thanks you.

And last but not least, to my damned ol' daddy, Eddie. You aren't here to see this book come to life, but I know you would have been its biggest supporter. You taught me many things in life—the greatest being that we don't have to end up the same person we once were. I promise not to remember you based on your worst days. I will remember you based on the best, and there were many. I will remember you as a person who was able to overcome what many cannot. Thank you for becoming one of my closest friends. And thank you for supporting me on my wedding day in a way that many fathers would not have. I love you. I miss you.

About the Author

Colleen Hoover is the #1 *New York Times* bestselling author of more than twenty-three novels, including *It Starts with Us, It Ends with Us, All Your Perfects, Ugly Love,* and *Verity*. Colleen lives in Texas with her husband and their three boys. For more information, please visit ColleenHoover.com.

Don't miss the highly anticipated sequel to the **"riveting"** (*Kirkus Reviews*, starred review) #1 *New York Times* bestselling novel

IT ENDS WITH US

Available **October 2022** wherever books are sold or at SimonandSchuster.com

ATRIA BOOKS

87055